Praise for

WHO NUN IT? THE CONVENT MYSTERIES

Take a delicious sip of *Who Nun It? The Convent Mysteries*, Sue Mattern's delightful cozy mystery, as bubbly as a fizzy drink. Set in a convent, the story features a coterie of nuns who become swept up in diabolical murder when Kristen, a young postulate and her English teacher, Sister Inez, come upon what seems to be the body of a nun in the trunk room at the dead of night.

The two women embark on a sleuthing adventure that lands them in all kinds of trouble with the powers-that-be in the convent.

What makes the book a joy to read is the sparkling personality of the protagonist Kristin, a mix of breezy subversiveness, a mischicvous streak, snappy sarcasm and all-pervasive humor. Kristen's dedication to being a nun is called into question when she finds herself mightily attracted to the detective who comes to investigate thc case.

Now factor in a twisty plot involving a chalice, and you have a very satisfying end to the mystery. The author made it fun for this reader to try and solve the murder before all was revealed. I will confess that the author outwitted me.

This book is a terrific read and I recommend it to all lovers of mysteries.

—ROSELYN TEUKOLSKY, Author of *A Reluctant Spy.*

Who Nun It?

The Convent Mysteries

Susan Mattern

Sibylline
Press

WHO NUN IT? THE CONVENT MYSTERIES
Copyright @ 2025 by Susan Mattern.
All Rights Reserved.

Published in the United States by Sibylline Digital First,
an imprint of All Things Book LLC, California.

Sibylline Press is dedicated to publishing the brilliant work
of women authors ages 50 and older.

www.sibyllinepress.com
Sibylline Press

ISBN paperback: 9781960573834
ISBN ebook: 9781960573568
Library of Congress Control Number: 2025931541

Cover Design: Alicia Feltman
Book Layout: Leo Baquero

Sibylline
Press

To my wonderful family

TABLE OF CONTENTS

#1
THE HOLY GRAIL

May 23, 1967
Motherhouse
St. Louis, Missouri

CHAPTER 1

"How did she ever talk me into this?" I wondered as I slid one hand across the damp plaster walls of the dark convent basement, holding up my long woolen skirts with the other. The feeble light of Sister Inez's flashlight barely penetrated a few feet in front of us.

We had been sitting in her office just a few minutes earlier, when she startled me "Damn, I forgot my notes on T.S. Eliot for my lecture tomorrow. Kristen, be a sweetheart and come down to the basement with me to get them."

Sister Inez was my English professor and didn't usually call anyone sweetheart. She had to be really tired. I was a lowly first-year student studying to become a nun. It was one in the morning, and I had broken dozens of convent rules already by staying up too late. We had been talking about English, vocations, and life.

"But Sister Miriam says we shouldn't go in the basement at night. There might be men down there."

Sister Miriam was the directress of our group of first-years.

Inez laughed out loud. "Men in the basement! Oh my God! And you believed her? That would have to be some desperate man, hiding out all day, waiting for some unsuspecting nun to come down after bedtime. How ridiculous."

Now I just felt silly.

"Come on, let's go." She grabbed my arm and pulled me up. I followed her obediently, as I was trained to do, feeling just a little stupid, almost tripping over my long habit as we walked quickly to the elevator. She pushed the red button, and the elevator clanked its way up, making altogether too much noise for one in the morning. The elevator was usually reserved for the elderly nuns, but it was the only way to access the basement. The iron box gradually wheezed into view and stopped. She pulled open the two rusted grates and we stepped inside. I felt a cool breeze from the elevator shaft, not unwelcome on the warm May night as we descended the four floors, but almost like a ghostly presence reaching up from the basement. Boy, I was tired imagining all sorts of strange things. We were both silent on the slow ride down, not wanting anyone to hear us talking. The thrill of the long talk with Inez faded as we passed each floor.

The elevator thudded to a stop, and we hurried out. The sooner we finished, the faster I would be up in my dorm asleep. Inez turned on a light, but it was only an emergency light at the end of the corridor.

We had to navigate our way through the dark underground catacombs of the huge motherhouse basement to get to the side tunnel, which would lead to the trunk room.

The foundation held up the huge motherhouse, built in the last century, housing over four hundred sisters, a city and a college all in one.

"We're almost there," Inez whispered.

"You don't have to whisper," I whispered.

"I know," she said. I could almost see her smile at my expense.

Inez hesitated at the turn, her hand feeling for a light switch. As I turned into the tunnel, I stumbled over something on the ground. I jumped back quickly.

"Inez, stop! There's something here." It felt like a laundry bag that someone had left in the middle of the corridor, but harder. It scared me. Whatever it was, it didn't belong there.

She moved the light down to the floor, but all we could see were some clothes. She felt again for the light switch. Suddenly the light bulbs above, hanging on a wire, all lit up with a cold bright light. I looked down. The thing I felt was a body. I started to scream. Then I felt a cold hand on my mouth, covering it tightly. Somebody was grabbing my face and stopping me from screaming. I clawed at the hand, desperately pushing it away. Inez whispered, "Shut up. It's me. Stop screaming. Stop it!"

I nodded. Her hand slowly moved away from my mouth, ready to cover it again quickly. I was quiet as I looked down at the body. It was a nun. Her legs were white and bare. Her black habit was scrunched up above her knees, her veil thrown aside. She was face down, but the back of her short blond hair was dark with what looked like blood. Her skull was bashed in, lying in a pool of dark red. She was dressed like me, a postulant in our order, except she was wearing loafers. We didn't wear loafers. I backed away quickly, in shock, but Inez made the sign of the cross, then carefully squeezed next to me and bent over the body. She lifted the nun's wrist.

"What are you doing?" I whispered, horrified.

"Trying to find a pulse."

Inez held the woman's hand, feeling it in different places, and finally put it down gently. Only a few seconds went by, but it seemed like forever. The body, the brown loafers, the blackish blood, her head, the discarded veil, the shadows covering most of her body, all those impressions were seared into my brain. Who she was, why she was there, what had happened to her, who had done this horrible thing? A thousand questions crowded my brain.

I felt a horrible sense of loss. Someone lay there whose life had ended before it had a chance to start. I felt such sorrow for her—her life lost forever. And then another part of me was thinking, *No, this isn't really happening, I'll wake up in a minute, it's a dream.* The sense of normalcy that tries to rush back in to fill up the spaces.

Inez stood up. "She's dead. Let's go."

"What do you mean, let's go?" The words didn't seem to register.

"We have to call the police."

"Oh," I said numbly.

We turned and walked quickly back down the corridor to the elevator. How could the corridor be so long? I didn't think we would ever get to the end of it. What if the murderer was still there, following us? This was no dream. We got to the elevator. It opened quickly and we walked inside. I jabbed at the red button. Why was it taking so long? Inez and I didn't say a word.

We ran back to her office. She grabbed a phone book from her bookshelf, turned to the first few pages, went to the phone on her desk and dialed the police. I stepped outside in the corridor and leaned up against the wall. I couldn't hear. What about Sister Miriam and Sister Alphonse, the head of the order? Why wasn't Inez calling them? My mind felt jumbled. Of course she had to call the police first. The nun, the person, whoever she was, had been murdered.

The nun had been dressed as a postulant—like me. We first-year students had a slightly different habit than the other sisters, and a shorter veil that showed our hair in front. And I hadn't even checked to see who she was. I should have turned her face over. I couldn't. I didn't want to touch her. I shouldn't have touched her. I did the right thing. I think I did. But what if she was one of my classmates? I should have checked. What if I knew her? Oh my God. I started to shake. Why was Inez still talking? Inez walked out to meet me, her face pale in the dim light of the corridor.

"The police will meet us at the front entrance. You have to come with me."

Of course. I knew I did. This wasn't just staying up too late and disobeying a convent rule. Someone was dead. She had to have been murdered.

★ ★ ★

Inez and I headed quickly down the large staircase from her fourth-floor office to the main floor. I didn't know how long it would take the police to get there. We stood inside the main entrance, the ornately carved wooden doors towering above us. The small votive candles from the chapel entrance across the hall cast flickering red shadows, making the walls and ceiling come alive in the darkness. In the motherhouse, which had always seemed like a gentle and welcoming home, it now felt like every doorway or alcove held a dead body or worse, someone wielding a murder weapon. Someone had killed her. I realized again they might still be in the building.

I crossed my arms tightly in front of me, shivering. I had never seen a dead body before. It was horrible. Her life, her only life, had just gone from her. I wondered if we have a soul that leaves the body and goes somewhere else after death. Yes, we did. I hoped we did. But all that was left there on the floor was the shell of a person who had once lived and breathed. I had to stop thinking about it. I started to say the "Lord's Prayer," but I couldn't get past the first line. Too many thoughts were racing through my brain. I wanted to pray but I just couldn't.

I looked out the window to the blackness outside, almost wanting to see the harsh lights of a police car. They could take over. Inez and I didn't say anything. Then finally she said, "Let's at least go into the parlor." It was right next to the front entrance, and we could see out the large window and sit down in the high wing-back chairs while we waited. I had to sit down. My legs felt rubbery. Inez's face was expressionless, but she had a handkerchief that she kept wadding up and moving from one hand to the other, back and forth.

I saw the bright red and blue flashing lights. The car stopped right in front of the large statue of Mary with her arms outstretched in welcome, and two policemen got out of the car. They walked quickly toward the building. Inez and I jumped up, unlocked the two locks, and opened the door.

Two uniformed policemen stood there with badges and guns at their side. One was older and his uniform was tight. His beer belly bulged out slightly and the buttons on his shirt looked strained. The other looked younger and slimmer. He was holding a camera. The older one said, "St. Louis County Police, Ma'am. Sergeant Harper, Officer Jackson. We received a call that a body was found."

"Yes, we're the ones who called," Inez answered quickly.

"We'll need you to take us there."

"Of course. Come with me." Inez turned and started walking towards the elevator. I followed her quickly. The two policemen followed us.

"Is this the only entrance to the basement?" the older officer asked.

"No, there's more on the other side of the building," Inez answered. The older officer, the one called Harper, took out a pair of gloves before he pressed the red button. "Please don't touch anything."

"But we already touched it before and after we found the body," I explained.

"I understand. But this is a crime scene, so we want to keep it as clean as possible."

We got off the elevator and retraced our steps from earlier. It seemed to take forever. The harsh lights were still on. Both officers stopped when they saw the body, taking in the whole scene. They were careful where they stepped. Sergeant Harper knelt down and felt for her pulse, and the other took pictures with his Polaroid camera. They didn't touch anything else.

"Are there any other lights down here?"

Inez said, "No, this is it."

"Can you get a signal?" he asked the other policeman, who was trying to contact someone on his radio.

"No, I'll have to go back upstairs."

Harper told us, "We need to call the coroner to establish a cause and time of death. We're blocking off this whole area. We have to make sure that no evidence is destroyed."

He pulled out a notebook and pen. "Do either of you know who she is?"

"I haven't even seen her face," I said, a lot more bravely than I felt. I could feel my voice shaking.

"Neither have I," said Inez.

The younger policeman told us to follow him carefully as he walked around the side of the body. He shone his flashlight on her face and we leaned over one at a time to look. I had never seen her before. She was young, thin, her face pale and wasted looking. Inez shook her head.

I said, "She's not a postulant here, although she's dressed like one of us. And she's wearing loafers. We don't wear loafers."

"Who's in charge here?" asked Harper.

Inez said quickly, "That would be Mother Alphonse, the head of our order. Do you want me to wake her up?"

"Officer Jackson, would you go with the sister? I'll wait here. And call when you get upstairs."

"Yes sir," the younger policeman answered.

I was alone with Sergeant Harper. He was probably in his late forties. His face looked ashen in the bright lights and was lined in a permanent frown. I could see the gun at his waist and his badge reflected the harsh light. His hair was already grey and he was clean shaven. He told me to come with him out to the main corridor. I was exhausted. All I wanted was to sit down. I could feel my body start to shake from the cold and the exhaustion and the sheer horror of what had happened, but there was nowhere to sit.

He opened a small notebook and started asking me questions.

"What's your name?"

"Kristen Byrne."

"And you're a sister in this order?"

"Not really."

He looked up at me, questioningly.

"I mean, I am, but I'm just a first-year student. I'm not a real sister yet."

"And how did you happen to find the body?"

I thought wildly of all the excuses I could give to keep me out of trouble. I could say that Sister Inez needed someone to go downstairs with her and went up to the dorms and I just happened to have gone to the bathroom and was returning to my dorm. That would work. I almost said it. And then I realized that I had to tell the truth. Even if I got kicked out for disobeying the rules. I knew people who had gotten kicked out for much less. The police had to know where I was and what I had been doing. They needed to know the absolute truth.

"I was in Sister Inez's office really late and we were talking."

"Her office? Where is that?"

"It's on the fourth floor of this building."

"Why were you there?"

"She's my English teacher and I went up to her office around nine and I worked on my term paper and we talked about my vocation—my wanting to be a nun—and I heard the grandfather clock chime one."

"And why did you come down here?"

"Sister Inez remembered that she needed some notes for her

lecture tomorrow—I guess it's today now—and she asked me to go down to her trunk to get them and I didn't really want to come down here, but she said it would only take a few minutes, so we came down and found the body. That was it."

I was talking way too much, but I couldn't help it.

"What do you mean, 'go down to her trunk'?"

"This is where all the trunks belonging to the sisters are stored."

"Where are they?"

"Further along this passageway."

"There's nothing else down this tunnel?"

"No, just the rooms with the trunks."

"Can you get out this way?"

"No, you'd have to go back the way we came."

"You hadn't been down here earlier in the day?"

"No, I hardly ever come down here. Nobody does. We only come down when we need something out of our trunks, maybe once a month or less."

"What do people keep in their trunks?"

"Stuff like extra slips, stockings, or old notes from classes. Stuff that we rarely need."

"Do you think that's why this nun might have been down here, looking for something in her trunk?"

"No, I don't think she even belongs here. I don't think she's a nun. I don't know what she was doing here."

We heard the policeman, Sister Inez, and Mother Alphonse coming down the corridor.

Mother Alphonse didn't even look at me. She strode up to the body, her eyes bloodshot and her veil slightly crooked, but her face with the usual scowl that frightened most of the people she encountered. Sergeant Harper stopped her.

"I'm sorry sister, you can't go beyond this point."

She pulled up shortly, an angry look on her face. She clearly wasn't used to taking directions from anyone. "She's dressed as a postulant. How can that be? I need to see her face."

He led her carefully around the body and shone his flashlight so she could see the woman's face.

Mother Alphonse had no expression on her face, just a blank look. "I don't know her. I've never seen her before. She's not one of us. I don't understand this at all."

Behind them, I realized as I looked up, were three other policemen in the dim light. We were all asked to move as the police let the coroner pass and have access to the body. Other policemen started putting yellow tape around the whole area. There was a new policeman, a younger one, who stood back in the shadows of the corridor. But then he walked toward all of us.

"Officer, can you take them upstairs, and I'll be up in a few minutes?"

"Yes, of course."

"I'm Detective David Kelly. I'll be working on the case. Could you all please go with the sergeant."

Sergeant Harper turned and we followed him.

"Is there a place we could sit and talk, Sister?" the sergeant asked Sister Inez. She looked more in charge than Mother Alphonse at that point, who seemed to be hanging back, lost in thought.

"Yes, we can go to one of the parlors."

We all piled into the ancient elevator. I worried that it wouldn't hold us all, but it struggled up to the first floor. We walked to one of the parlors. I tried to focus on my watch as the bright lights of the parlor practically blinded me. We postulants never got to sit in the parlors. They were for guests only. A few of us got to clean them as part of our cleaning duties. About ten brocaded wing-back chairs were scattered around the room next to tables with fresh flowers on each of them.

It was three in the morning. I looked around me with bleary eyes. Sergeant Harper looked tired. After about fifteen minutes the detective came to the door of the parlor.

He looked wide awake. He was young with black hair and very blue eyes. His hair was longer than I thought it should be for a police officer. I thought they all wore crew cuts. He was very handsome. I was so tired. I couldn't believe I was thinking this. I had just seen a dead body. Someone had been murdered, and I was thinking about how handsome a policeman was. I felt ashamed of myself. I looked down at the floor, which seemed to waver before my eyes.

Detective Kelly pulled up a chair, sat down, took out a notebook, and asked Sister Inez how we had discovered the body. I tried to catch her eye, hoping she wouldn't lie for me. I knew it was something Inez would do, and she had no idea I had already told the other policeman what really had happened.

"Well, I was in my office, and I remembered that I had a lecture tomorrow and that my notes were in my trunk in the basement ..."

She wasn't going to say I was there. I knew it. I couldn't let her go on. I had to be rude and interrupt.

"I was with Sister Inez in her office," I interrupted. "I knew it was late and I was supposed to be in bed, but we were talking and she asked me to go down to the trunk room with her. That's how we both ended up in the basement at one in the morning."

Inez gave me a strange look but went on seamlessly. "We took the elevator and walked down the corridor and Kristen stumbled on the body. I turned on the lights, felt for the woman's pulse, and then we both ran back to my office and called the police."

"Did you see or hear anything else in the basement?"

"No," we both answered quickly.

"How many entrances are there to the basement?"

Mother Alphonse answered that. "You can reach the basement by the elevator on the north side where we came down. There are three sets of stairs behind locked doors from the first floor to the basement. And there are three exits to the outside from the basement."

"It would be relatively easy for someone to get into the basement from the outside?"

"Those entrances are locked at all times."

The detective turned to Harper. "Have the men check all those exits."

He turned back to us. "Is there anyone else who might know the identity of the sister?"

I sat quietly. Sister Inez turned to Mother Alphonse. "We probably should wake Sister Miriam. She's the director."

Detective Kelly questioned, "But you both say the victim is not a … what do you call it?"

"Postulant," I finished the sentence for him.

"Yes, a postulant."

"That's right."

"What is that?"

"Like me. A freshman in college, also the first year of studying to become a sister."

He just nodded. "I don't think we need to wake anyone else up right now if none of you know her. I'll be here tomorrow afternoon to speak with all of you separately. Meanwhile, Sister Alphonse, I want you to know that the body will be removed when the coroner has determined his findings and the police have finished their work, but the entire motherhouse is now a crime scene. The basement and all access to it will be restricted. You need to inform everyone this morning. We'll be gathering evidence and conducting interviews over the next few days, so there will be a large police presence here for a while."

"You just can't roam freely around the motherhouse gathering evidence." Mother Alphonse looked even angrier than usual.

The detective looked up at her. "Yes, we can. This is a homicide investigation, and we'll be collecting evidence."

Mother Alphonse stared at him. "Well then, I trust you will let us have an additional sister in the room when you conduct your interviews. We do have a convent policy that a sister can't be alone in a room with a man."

Detective Kelly stared back at her. "No, sister, that's not going to happen."

"Mother," she corrected him.

"Mother," he said graciously, and continued, "we might try to have another policeman in the interview, perhaps a woman officer if one is available. But every sister here is potentially a suspect in this investigation, so no, we would never have another sister in an interview. This is our investigation, not yours."

Mother Alphonse didn't say a word, and her glare didn't seem to frighten him. I had a feeling he had seen scarier things than Mother Alphonse. He got up, nodded to the three of us, his eyes meeting mine for a little longer than I thought necessary, and left the room.

We all left the parlor quietly, although I knew there was so much left unsaid. And Sister Miriam would have a heart attack the next morning when she found out about the murder. Come to think of it, next morning was just about now. It was four-thirty and I heard the large copper hand bell ringing upstairs to awaken us all for Mass. It was still dark outside, but I could see the sky beginning to lighten in the east. I just couldn't do it. I walked up the steps past the other postulants coming down the steps to Mass, not looking at anyone, slipped into my dorm, and fell onto my bed with all my clothes on. I didn't remember another thing.

CHAPTER 2

May 24, late morning

I opened my eyes. The sun was bright on the wall of the dorm and my friend Pam was standing over me, shaking my arm. I had that one second where the world was fine and the sun was shining. I knew where I was. And then I remembered.

"You've got to get up, Kristen. The whole place is in an uproar. You'll never believe what happened. Someone was killed in the basement last night."

I just let out a groan and turned over. "What time is it?"

"It's one in the afternoon. Didn't you hear me? Someone was killed in the basement last night! Everybody's worried about you, but I checked on you earlier, and for some weird reason Miriam said to let you sleep. I told everybody you were okay!"

Five o'clock to one o'clock. I couldn't believe I'd slept for seven or eight hours.

Pam was bursting with information. "Oh my God, Kristen, it was a postulant! Well, she wasn't. I mean, the woman was dressed like us. And the police think somebody killed her. And Mother Alphonse came around after breakfast and told us all about it and then she said that you were okay even though you weren't there this morning, and that we weren't supposed to wake you up. It was the weirdest thing. Why weren't you there? Miriam didn't even know what that was about. And there are police cars all around and policemen and you have to get up.

Miriam told me to get you up cause some policeman wants to talk to you."

"What? When?" I sat up and put my legs over the side of the bed. I felt dirty and disgusting.

"She said at two o'clock. What the hell is going on?"

I looked at my watch. It was one-ten.

"I've got to get up and take a shower and get dressed. I'll tell you as soon as I can."

Pam reluctantly turned away and left the dorm. I practically ran to the shower, washed my hair and got dressed in my clean habit. I wanted to at least look good for the detective. Like that was even possible in this ugly habit. The heavy black serge material covered me like a sack of potatoes.

The whole night was a jumble of odd memories and snatches of dreams. Funny, the strangest thing was that Miriam let me sleep all day. I couldn't imagine her doing that, even for a murder.

I figured this was probably my last day in the order. I was in so much trouble for being in Sister Inez's office so late at night and admitting it. I had to talk to Inez today.

I ran downstairs. The study hall was empty. I checked my watch again. Everyone was in class. Sister Miriam saw me walk by her office and called my name.

"Kristen, a policeman wants to meet with you in the front parlor at two o'clock. Don't be late."

That was it. No reprimand. No yelling at me for breaking the rules. I guessed that would come later. I knew it would come later. I sat at my desk. It was one-fifty. I picked up a book but read the same sentence four times. When I looked down again it was one-fifty-seven. I got up and walked down to the parlor. The murder seemed unreal, like I had dreamt it.

Detective Kelly was standing outside the parlor, looking tall and serious and, well, just handsome.

"Sister?" he motioned to the room.

"Just Kristen," I said as I walked past him. "I'm not a sister yet."

"Oh, okay. I don't know anything about nuns."

I sat down in an upholstered wing-back chair and he pulled up a chair right across from mine, way too close to me. The first thing he said was, "Did you get some sleep?"

I smiled. "Yes, I did. How about you?"

I realized how stupid that sounded the minute I said it—that was his job—but I couldn't take it back. I looked down at the floor.

"I'm fine. I'm good at sleeping whenever I can get some. Comes with the job."

I looked up at him, noticing every detail: the curly black hair, the blue eyes. He was over six feet tall, trim, not movie-star good looking, but nice looking. Intelligent eyes. My grandfather had kind eyes like his. He must be Irish, with a name like Kelly. I was completely Irish; my father had been born in Ireland and my mother's relatives were all Irish. I had the red hair and freckles to go with my name. He was saying something.

"I'm sorry. What did you say?"

"I asked you if there was anything else you noticed last night."

"Well, I knew right away that she wasn't a nun because she was wearing loafers."

"You don't wear those?"

"No."

"What do you wear?"

"We have these regulation black shoes that we have to wear."

"What do you mean?"

Oh God, I was going to have to show him. I hated my old lady black shoes with a passion. My legs looked pretty good, but he wasn't going to see much of them, just the horrible shoes. I lifted my skirt up a little. "Like these. That's all we can wear."

I lowered my skirt and felt my face flaming. It probably matched my red hair. He didn't notice or was too polite to say anything. I felt completely humiliated. I really didn't want to be a nun right then. I wanted to call my parents. They could pick me up. They would be thrilled. I could get dressed in normal clothes—something casual, but nice, maybe that red skirt I used to have and a peasant blouse. It didn't really go with my red hair ... Oh my God—concentrate!

"You're sure about the shoes?"

"Well, you asked me what I noticed, and that was the first thing. Well, besides that she was dead," I said stupidly.

He took out a pad of paper and started scribbling on it. He looked up. "Anything else? Do you have any ideas about how this murder could have happened?"

"Well, somebody, one of the four hundred of us, had to have given her the postulant's habit. There's nowhere else she could have gotten it."

He asked, "How easy would it be to get?"

"The sewing room is right down the hall from here. Anyone could walk by, go in, and pick one up. Any nun, that is."

"And somehow give it to her."

"I guess."

He stared at me. "So you're saying that someone in this convent killed her."

I shook my head. "Of course not!" But then I realized that was exactly what I was saying.

I desperately tried to think of another explanation. "Just because someone gave her the habit doesn't mean they killed her," I said quickly.

He looked at me. "Well, it isn't much of a motive, is it? But there must have been a reason they gave her the habit. Can you think of anything else?"

I was thinking all sorts of things, but I didn't want to say another word. He was pretty sharp and had already jumped to the conclusion that some nun had probably killed her. I felt like in a minute I'd be confessing to the murder if I said much more.

"No, not really."

"Here's my card with my private office number if you think of anything else. Give me a call anytime."

"What happens next?" I asked.

"We'll find out who she is. Unfortunately, she had no identification on her, nothing at all, so we have to rely on fingerprints, which might take a while. We'll be interviewing a few more sisters and completing our search of the crime scene. I'll be talking to you again."

I looked beyond him out the window. The trees out on the front lawn were just beginning to turn green with new leaves. I figured I'd better tell him.

"I probably won't be here."

"What do you mean?"

"I broke a lot of rules last night, and people have been kicked out for a lot less. I figure I'll be gone by tomorrow."

He frowned. "You'd get kicked out for staying up too late?"

"Yes, absolutely."

"How do you put up with rules like that?"

I sure didn't feel like explaining that to him, so I didn't say a word.

And then he said, "Don't worry, I don't think that's going to happen. Can I ask you something?"

"Sure." I couldn't imagine what else he needed to ask. I already told him everything I knew about last night.

"Why do you want to become a nun?"

That question couldn't have come at a worse time. I was still tired, feeling guilty about being attracted to him, about to be kicked out, a witness to a dead body less than twenty-four hours ago, and wondering if I even had a vocation.

But I needed to convince him that I knew what I was doing. I didn't want him to think I was completely clueless about the direction of my life. I was only eighteen, but I was serious about my choice. Just because he was older by a few years didn't mean he knew any more.

I was so close to him I could smell his cologne and soap, and I stumbled for an answer. I knew why I wanted to become a nun.

"Well, I want to teach and help people, and I figured this was a good way to accomplish that."

"But you have to give up so much, like a family, and your freedom to do what you want."

"By not having a family, we can dedicate our lives to doing what God asks of us."

I was reciting platitudes, ones that I had heard for years and believed. But when I said them out loud, they didn't even convince me.

He looked puzzled. "Well, my parents were Methodist, not that I am anymore, and our ministers get married, and so do rabbis, and that's never prevented them from helping people."

Why didn't I have a good answer?

"The Catholic Church has always thought it was better to have people who could dedicate their whole lives to others."

"It just doesn't make any sense to me. How can you understand what it's like to be married, or to love a child, if you've never experienced those things?"

I was getting defensive and angry. Not at him. At me. I knew why I wanted to become a nun, but it was hard to put into words. Or maybe I didn't really know.

I tried to sound very sure of myself. "Well, I don't think I need to experience all those things in order to understand them.

Each person only has their own experiences, but you try to relate it to others."

Oh, God, that sounded so stupid. And I wanted to sound eloquent. I was glad Sister Miriam wasn't there to hear my horrible answers.

"Hey, I'm sorry," he put me out of my misery. "It's really none of my business."

I smiled an insincere smile. "I'm always glad to explain it to people."

"I just don't understand it. Maybe if I was Catholic ... Well, I'll be talking to you again. Thank you," he said politely as he shook my hand and held it for what seemed a little too long. I'm sure I turned red again as he turned and walked out the door, leaving me standing on the old wooden floor, feeling things I couldn't quite describe.

Why couldn't I explain why I wanted this life? I was angry at him for asking, but I should have been angry at myself for not explaining it correctly. I knew why I wanted to be a nun. I did want to help people, and I didn't mind giving up marriage and a family.

I had gone to an all-girls high school and didn't have much experience with boys. All right, none at all. But they were so immature. I went to the prom with a boy who seemed about thirteen and couldn't even manage a simple conversation. That was about it. But this policeman, David Kelly, was a grown man, and he seemed intelligent and was good looking and ... I needed to stop thinking about him. He wasn't going to help me decide if I really wanted to be in religious life. And he wasn't interested in me. That was just my imagination working overtime. He wanted to solve the murder. That was all.

But I was having problems with religious life. I had entered with great hope and optimism about the future. The Second Vatican Council in the early sixties had made sweeping reforms.

When the pope died, he was replaced with a more conservative pope and the reforms had stalled or were going backwards. And our convent was a relic of the nineteenth century. Nothing had changed in a hundred years, and the nuns didn't seem eager to adopt any reforms at all. I loved God, but I wondered if this life was worth it.

My parents hadn't wanted me to enter, so I was even more determined to give it my best. I wasn't ready to accept defeat. Not yet.

* * *

I headed slowly back to the study hall and sat at my desk. Sister Miriam opened her door, looked directly at me, making sure I had gotten back safely, and then retreated to her office. I couldn't understand why she hadn't yelled at me about last night. It would be coming very soon, I knew.

I had missed my class with Inez as well as all of my other classes. I had lost the whole day. Everyone sat quietly in study hall, studying for our usual hour before prayer and dinner. I noticed people looking at me, but I didn't return their glances. I wouldn't even have a chance to talk to Inez at all. I didn't dare go up to her office.

Dinner was silent as usual, while we listened to Sister Miriam read from her favorite book *The Lives of the Saints*. Those virgins and martyrs were supposed to give us hope for the future, I guessed. After dinner we played volleyball in the high school gym so I didn't even have a chance to talk to anyone. I felt I was in some strange world where reality circled around me but never quite reached me.

I could feel that Sylvia and Pam and Charlene wanted to say something to me, to ask a few questions, but as usual, there was no time. We studied quietly. The Great Silence started at nine and we weren't supposed to talk till morning. I took my time putting my books away and was the last one to leave the study hall. I slowly walked upstairs but couldn't stand it for another minute. I was going to get kicked out anyway and would only stay in Inez's office for two minutes. At the fourth floor, I veered off the stairs, ran down the corridor to her office, and knocked. She answered with a polite, "Yes?"

"Can I come in?"

"Get in here fast. Oh my God, are you okay?"

"Yeah, how about you?"

"I'm good. Did you talk to the detective?"

"Yes. I couldn't tell him much though."

"Me neither. But you're going to be in real trouble if Miriam finds you in here."

"So what? I'm going to get kicked out anyway. I don't know why it hasn't happened yet."

"I know why."

"You do?"

"Yeah. Alphonse was ready to kick you out when you woke up, but the detective said no."

"What?"

"He said no. He said you were a witness to a murder and part of the police investigation and he didn't want her interfering because of some two-bit stupid convent rule."

"He said that? To Alphonse?"

"Yeah. You should have seen her face. It got all red. I don't think anybody's ever talked to her like that. So you won't get kicked out ... yet. But don't push it!"

I sat quietly for a second, savoring that image of her red face.

"Okay, okay, I'm leaving right now."

"Hold on. We do have to talk though. After class tomorrow?"

"Okay."

"Good. Now go. Get out of here. I'll check the hall first."

She got up, went to the door and looked out. She gave me the all-clear sign and I hurried up the stairs to my dorm.

CHAPTER 3

May 25

I slept well again, although I wasn't sure why. The next day seemed almost normal. Sister Miriam looked at me like she was afraid of me, not the other way around. She didn't say a word.

The police were still a presence, but if they had discovered anything about the murder, we would be the last to know. We couldn't go into the basement, and all the entrances and exits had wide yellow tape across them. Our superiors were not very forthcoming about information, even when it related to us.

We got one copy of the *St. Louis Post-Dispatch* every morning in the study hall, but it was carefully censored, most articles cut out before it was folded up and put on the front desk. Who knows what was cut out of it? Probably anything related to sex. The Catholic Church was very careful about our virginity, and I guess even reading about sex could do irreparable harm, although I doubted if we could get pregnant from the newspaper. There was nothing in it about the murder.

The only way I was going to find out more was to talk to my senior friends, and they would be over in the music department where I would see them every few days. I wasn't supposed to talk to them either. We postulants weren't supposed to speak with anyone outside of our class, but I had been talking to them for the last eight months and wasn't going to stop now.

That's another thing I was having trouble with. I was having a hard time making friends with the members of my class. Pam was a good friend, and Charlene and Sylvia, but that was it. I belonged to a study group for my English class with Linda, but I much preferred to talk to my older friends—the ones I wasn't even supposed to be friends with!

They were exchange students from our northern province in Mankato, Minnesota, studying here for the semester. They would return after they graduated to teach up north.

I headed over there in the morning. Sister Joan and Sister Maribeth were sitting in the music library, studying. Joan said, "Hey, where have you been? We've missed you! Lots of stuff going on! Have they been keeping you up to date on the murder?"

She pushed a newspaper over to me, a real one that hadn't been cut.

"Body discovered in Notre Dame convent in Lemay." That was the headline in the local section. I quickly read the article. There wasn't much that I didn't already know.

I pushed the paper back.

"Did Sister Alphonse tell you guys all about it?" Joan asked.

"Yeah, but I was there," I answered simply.

"What? What do you mean, you were there? Of course you were there when she told you." She stared at me, puzzled.

"Sister Inez and I were the ones who discovered the body."

"You what? Oh my God, what happened?" Joan whispered.

Maribeth looked shocked. "What were you doing in the basement?"

I briefly told them the story.

"That must have been awful for you," said Joan.

"Yeah, it was awful."

"Who was it? Did you know her?" Joan looked concerned.

"No, because she wasn't a postulant."

"What? It says here that she *was* a postulant."

"It says she was dressed like a postulant. But she's not in my class."

"You're sure?" asked Maribeth.

I glanced at Maribeth. "Of course I'm sure. I'd never seen her before in my whole life. She looked thin and sick, like she was on drugs or something. And hard, like she had had a tough life."

"She was dressed like a postulant?" Joan kept asking questions.

"Yeah, exactly. Except for one thing. Her shoes."

"What do you mean?"

"She was wearing loafers."

"Loafers?" Joan grinned. "Then she wasn't a postulant. I would've killed my grandmother to wear loafers. I still would."

I stared at her. "This is serious."

"I'm just kidding. Good grief."

"But why was she dressed like that?"

We heard someone coming down the corridor. I flipped open a book and we sat quietly, studying. The nun walked by, not even glancing in our direction. Most of them didn't care if we talked, but I didn't want to get in any more trouble unnecessarily.

"How did she get in the basement? How did you get there?" Joan kept asking.

"I have no idea how she got there. I told you Inez and I were going to the trunk room to get some notes. We just found the body. Nobody knows who she is or what happened. I guess that's up to the police to figure out."

"You said she was young?" Joan asked.

"She wasn't much older than us."

"What a horrible thing. To lose your life when it was just starting." Joan looked so sad.

"Maybe it was her fault." Maribeth said quietly.

"What do you mean?" I was surprised she had said that.

"Well, if she was on drugs, and was sneaking in here, dressed up like a nun, she wasn't up to any good, that's for sure."

"Well, she didn't deserve to die," Joan said, "no matter what she might have done."

Maribeth just shrugged her shoulders.

Joan looked at Maribeth. "I'm sure you don't mean that."

Maribeth looked up, "No, I don't think she should have died. Of course not. But what was she doing here? It sounds pretty suspicious. I hope the police can figure it out before anyone else gets hurt."

Joan and I both nodded.

I closed my book. "Hey, let me know if you read anything else in the paper. Miriam cuts everything out."

"After you take vows, they let you read the whole newspaper, even the sexy parts," Joan laughed.

I reminded her, "You were a postulant just three years ago. Remember?"

"Yeah, I know. Don't remind me. It does get better. Look at me now. I can do anything I want."

"Right." I could be sarcastic too.

"Well, when we get out on mission we'll be free." Joan was the optimist.

I laughed at that one. Going out and teaching would certainly be better. The nuns at my high school could pretty much go where they wanted and had a lot more freedom than any of us. It didn't compare to the real world, though.

Maribeth looked tired and was unusually quiet. I remembered our last conversation a few days earlier.

"Hey, how's your mom?"

"She's doing ok. The doctors want to operate, but Mom isn't sure whether she wants the operation."

"What do you think they should do?"

"I think she should have it, but we can't force her to."

"I'm really sorry. I hope everything works out."

"Yeah." Maribeth sat quietly for a minute.

"Hey, I've got class." Joan grabbed her books. "See you tomorrow." Maribeth left with her.

CHAPTER 4

May 26

Inez looked tired during class the next morning. I couldn't concentrate, knowing we'd be talking about the murder right after class. I stayed in my seat after she dismissed us.

She walked back to me. "Let's go to my office. It's more private there."

We walked down the long corridor to her office. I tried not to notice the stares of the other postulants in the hall. After she closed the door she said, "You okay?"

"I'm fine. How about you?" I was no longer the student. We had become equals in a sense two nights ago.

She nodded, and I wondered how much we had to say now that we were together again.

She sat back in her chair. "Well, I don't think the police have a clue."

I nodded in agreement. "I don't think anybody does. Do you think they've found anything?"

"Who knows? They won't be telling us! Do you want a drink?"

"Sure."

She pulled open a small ice chest next to her desk, took out two Coke cans, and handed one to me. I hadn't had a Coke since last summer. I flipped the top and took a drink. It tasted sickly sweet, not like I remembered. But I drank it eagerly; it wasn't that bad after a few sips.

"That detective told me that she had been killed by repeated blows to the head, which we already knew, although they're going to have to do an autopsy to determine the actual cause of death."

I nodded. "That's more than he told me."

"I think that you and I are going to solve this murder," Inez said.

I swallowed the mouthful of soda too quickly and started coughing. After I got my breath back, I spit out, "How are we going to do that?"

"We'll wait a while, but the police won't get anywhere. The woman was dressed as a postulant to get in here and take something. We just have to figure out what's missing."

"What? What are you talking about?" I started thinking that she might be delusional as well as tired.

"Well, there's only one reason that anyone would dress up like one of us. Think about it. So she could sneak in and take something."

I was in shock. I blurted out, "Okay, let's say that you're right. First of all, there's nothing here. I didn't bring anything from home, even underwear. What could possibly be valuable in this place? The elevator?"

She smiled her insincere professor smile. "You're not thinking creatively enough. There has to be something that she stole, because she was murdered for it."

There was a dark ugly painting of some pope in the music corridor. I doubted if it was a Rembrandt. A tall, antique grandfather clock stood at the end of the corridor that I cleaned every day. That would be hard to steal. Besides, I had just cleaned it this morning. The stained-glass windows in the chapel were just like those of a thousand other churches, old but not very beautiful. There were some passports and journals of Mother Genevieve's, our founder, in a display case, but I couldn't think of a thing anyone would want.

"That's a great idea, but there's nothing of value in the motherhouse, well, at least the part that I've been in. What's in the forbidden part that's so valuable? Any statues by Michelangelo?"

There were plaster of Paris statues in the alcoves along all the corridors.

She laughed. "Well, I agree, not our statues. They're hideous. But why else would she be killed?"

"I have no idea."

"Listen, Kristen," she put her hand on my arm, "I just have a feeling that it's going to be someone on the inside who solves this crime. I think it's going to be us. Are you willing to help me?"

How could I say no? I really did like her and she would be my teacher for three more long years. That was a lot of grades in my future, especially since I was majoring in English.

I looked down at the shiny Coke can and mumbled, "Okay, I guess."

"Well, that was quite a commitment." She was rolling her eyes as I looked up.

"I mean, what can I do? I'm a postulant."

"You can keep your eyes open. Someone in this motherhouse gave her that habit and knows why she was murdered. Or is the actual murderer. Our job is to find out who it is."

"I'd better be getting to bed," I said quickly, anxious to get out of her office.

"Go, go. You need your sleep. Me too. Come and see me anytime. We'll talk more about this."

I got up awkwardly and walked out the office door and down the corridor. My thoughts were racing. I really admired Inez. She was a brilliant teacher, and it seemed she was a very kind and caring person, but this was too crazy.

I couldn't believe she was so naive that she thought *we* were going to solve this murder. That's what police and detectives were for. It wasn't our job to solve the murder. Why she even thought that was beyond my comprehension. Maybe she had read too many murder mysteries. I thought she only read great English literature. When I walked into her office, I expected that we would talk a little about the murder and how awful it was, and we might have that camaraderie that you get when you go through something traumatic together.

I didn't know that she was totally crazy.

In my dorm, I quietly pulled the white curtains around my bed, undressed, put on my white cotton nightgown, and crawled into bed. What a disappointment. I would have liked to have been her friend.

CHAPTER 5

Class, homework, and prayers occupied my time for the next few days. And Sister Miriam cut all the murder articles out of the paper. It was as if it had never happened. I got all my news from the papers that my two friends slipped in with my music books.

The next day's headline read, "Convent covering up murder of sister." They accused us of knowing who the victim was and not revealing it to the police.

The next day, "Convent denies victim was a nun."

The letters to the editor were nasty, all accusing our order of some gigantic cover-up.

I'll bet Mother Alphonse was getting lots of angry phone calls. But we all knew that the dead woman was no nun. Well, Sister Inez and I and all the postulants knew that she wasn't a postulant, for sure.

I got a frantic letter from my parents.

"We read about the murder. We're so worried about you. Maybe you should come home. The killer is still on the loose and the convent is covering all this up. He's targeting nuns. We really think you should come home, at least for a while."

I pulled out my prettiest Monet stationery and wrote a soothing letter. Because of convent rules, I couldn't even call them. I told my parents that the murdered girl was *not* a nun and that I wasn't worried in the least.

As I wrote, I realized I wasn't even convincing myself. There was a killer on the loose, able to get into our property, maybe even living inside our property. We had no idea why this woman had been killed, where she had come from, or what the killer's motive was. I was truly worried.

I sat meditating before Mass the next morning and thought about going up to Inez's office. I had seen her in class but we hadn't said a word to each other. Maybe she realized she had been a little weird about us solving the murder. So that evening after Compline, the last prayer of the day, I snuck up to her office door and knocked softly.

"Come in," she said politely.

"It's me."

"Oh, hi. I haven't talked to you in a while. How are you?"

Wow. Did she not have any hard feelings even though I had obviously been avoiding her? Maybe she hadn't even noticed.

"Sit down," she said, taking a stack of papers off the chair and holding them, not quite sure of where to put them. She finally decided on the floor.

"Have you thought more about what I said?" she asked bluntly. She hadn't forgotten.

I guessed she still thought we were going to solve the murder.

"Have you heard anything?" she asked.

"Me? No, of course not. You know I can't even talk to anyone besides my classmates and faculty members."

"I haven't heard anything either. If there's something missing in the motherhouse, no one's missed it yet."

We talked for a few more minutes. Inez didn't seem as crazy that night. She talked about the missing object, whatever it might be, but with less enthusiasm than before. I guess she realized that neither one of us was going to solve this murder.

She seemed distant and distracted. She kept glancing at the stack of papers she needed to read and grade. I left quickly.

CHAPTER 6

May 30

On Monday afternoon I headed over to the music department to get in a few hours of badly needed practice. I heard a knock at the door and Joan slipped in and sat on the chair next to the piano.

"Keep practicing, don't mind me. I just like to listen. But make sure you play that French piece—I like that." Joan was unusually quiet as I played. She stared out the window. She leaned over after I finished playing a Bach piece.

"Where's Maribeth?" I asked. They usually came as a pair.

"Oh, she was kind of a pain today. She gets like that sometimes. You know, we're not all that close. I'll be glad when the year is over and we go out on mission."

"I thought you guys were really good friends?" I was surprised. They did everything together.

"Well, we are. Don't get me wrong. I like her a lot. It's just that sometimes she gets really judgmental, but she's a good person at heart. We're friends because we were sent down here together to study, nothing more. Anyway, I want to tell you something. Guess what happened yesterday morning before Mass?"

Joan was the assistant sacristan in the chapel, although all the junior sisters took turns helping in the sacristy. The sacristy was the room off the chapel where all the vestments for the priests were stored, as well as the chalices needed for Mass. The sacristan kept everything used in the Mass ready for the priests.

She never had to clean or do chores. Her half hour in the sacristy every morning was her "job," besides going to school like the rest of us.

I laughed out loud. "Something happened?" I said sarcastically. I couldn't imagine a more boring job. No, wait, I had a more boring job. I swept the long main corridor every morning. My only excitement was reaching the grandfather clock at the end of the corridor, and knowing I was finished for the day.

"Sorry. I was only kidding," I said.

"Look, I know it's a boring job." She smiled broadly. "Oh, how about your cleaning today? How did it go?" She matched my sarcasm perfectly.

"Okay, okay. Tell me what happened."

"Well, you know Father Raymond. He's been sick for the past week or so and he finally came back yesterday, because it was Pentecost. I was helping out because the other sacristan was sick."

"I'm surprised he even came back."

"Yeah, I know. I keep expecting him to drop dead every morning, I know that's mean, but he shouldn't even be coming here to say Mass. He should have retired a long time ago. He still manages to get here on time and say the Mass. Anyway, yesterday was Pentecost ..."

"I was there, remember?"

"I know. I'm just saying that because he usually uses that special chalice on feast days—the one in the display case out in front of the chapel."

"No, I have no idea, but go on ..."

"Well, it's locked up because that case is full of Mother Genevieve's stuff, her writings and immigration papers and her shawl and that chalice. Anyway, he used to use the chalice on feast days but it's a pain to open it up because it takes a code and a key, so he doesn't bother anymore."

"Okay."

"But he was walking past it on his way to Mass and he glanced in it and got as white as a sheet and practically choked. I thought he was having a heart attack. I said, 'Are you alright, Father?'"

"He said, 'Yes, my dear. It's just that my chalice is missing. I mean, the chalice that was in here. I can't imagine where it is.'"

"I said, 'But the chalice is right there Father.'"

"He said, 'No, no, this one is old, but it's not Mother Genevieve's chalice. I've used it a hundred times. This one isn't the same.'"

I was almost falling asleep.

"Really, this story is not very exciting. I can tell you about cleaning the main corridor."

"No, wait. I know. But I'm getting to the interesting part."

"Is it coming soon?"

She hit me on the arm. "Yeah, right now."

"Evangeline, the older sacristan, went over to the display case after Mass. She stared at the chalice. She looked really sick. I said, 'Are you okay, Sister?' She just stood there and I could see tears in her eyes. I asked her again if she was all right. She leaned over me. Her breath is horrible; I almost gagged. She whispered, in this weird voice, 'That chalice is missing, Sister. It doesn't belong to him. That chalice is old. Older than you can even imagine. And all those jewels in it are real. That chalice belongs to our convent. It was given to Blessed Mother Genevieve, the founder of our order.'"

"And I said, 'That old one that he's talking about?'"

"She kept leaning over me and whispering. 'Yes, that's the one. It's not very pretty. It's been kept like that, Sister, so no one would know how valuable it is.'"

"She looked at me with her watery eyes and said, 'If that

chalice is gone, we've lost everything. Everything. I don't know what to do.' And then she turned and shuffled away. Now, wasn't that kind of weird? Do you think I should tell someone what she said?"

"I wouldn't bother. Both chalices are old. Maybe they both belonged to her. What difference would it make ..." I started to say. And then I stopped mid-sentence. "What did she say about how valuable it was?"

"She said if that chalice is gone, we've lost everything."

Suddenly Inez seemed a lot smarter than she had a few minutes earlier.

"I've got to go now."

"Okay, whatever. See you tomorrow."

I got my music together and flew down the corridor. Damn, it was almost time for Vespers. I'd have to wait till after nine p.m. to tell Inez.

Every minute that evening seemed like an hour. I had never known time to go so slowly. Prayers, dinner, our walk around the building, then study hall, then Compline. I was itching to get to Inez's office.

We filed up the stairs after our last prayers and I snuck down the corridor. Her office door was slightly open and the lights were off. She wasn't there. Where could she be now that I needed her? Tomorrow in class, I'd write her a note.

I volunteered next afternoon to collect our assignments. Inez looked up, smiled, and continued with her lecture. I made sure my paper was on top, with my note paper-clipped to it. I set them on her desk. Inez looked up at the clock. "I'm sorry, I kept all of you a few minutes late. Go, go so you won't be late for your next class."

I walked out with everyone, hoping I could slip back in and talk to her when she saw my note. As the last student walked out the door, Inez followed her, closed the door, and locked it. She hadn't even taken the papers. I had to wait the rest of the day, and I sat that evening in the study hall drawing circles on my paper and wondering about the chalice.

Miriam called my name. Shit. Not again. And I had to stop thinking all these bad words. I wasn't very nun-like yet. I walked into her office. What did I do now? It was always some little stupid thing. "Kristen, Sister Inez wants you in her office right now." She shook a note in front of my face.

"Are you doing as well as you should in American literature? You seem very distracted lately, and that's a very important class since you're majoring in English. You need to concentrate on your studies."

"Yes, sister, I will," I answered contritely.

"And don't waste Sister Inez's time. I'll expect you back here in fifteen minutes."

Fifteen minutes! Shit. By the time I got up to her office, I wouldn't even have time to tell her what Joan had told me.

I ran up the stairs as fast as I could and knocked on Inez's door.

"Kristen?"

"Yes."

"Come in."

Inez cleaned off the chair.

"I just got your note this evening. What is it?"

"Okay." I sat down. I was still breathless. "I'm friends with Sister Joan and Sister Maribeth, the junior sisters from Mankato. Joan helps in the sacristy."

"Oh." She wasn't impressed yet, but she would be. I told her as fast as I could exactly what Sister Joan had told me.

Her eyes opened wider as I got to the end of the story. "Oh my God. Maybe that's it. I knew something had to be missing. This has to be it. Good job!"

"I've got to go." I told her.

"What? You just got here."

"Miriam said not to waste your time and to be back in fifteen minutes."

Inez lifted up the receiver and dialed Sister Miriam.

"This is Sister Inez. Postulant Kristen is helping me grade some papers. That's why I asked her up here. I'm wondering if she can stay longer?"

A pause. "It might be a few hours. Is that okay? I'll make sure she gets to her dorm safely. Yes, I know. Well, that won't happen again. Yes. Thank you."

Inez put down the phone. "She's quite nice, isn't she?"

"Yeah, to you she's nice. To us, it's another story."

Inez smiled absentmindedly at my remark. I could tell she was thinking about the chalice.

I spoke up. "There's just one problem."

"What?"

"The girl didn't have the chalice when she was murdered."

"Well, of course not." Inez went into her lecture mode. "She stole the chalice with an accomplice, and the accomplice killed her and took the chalice for himself, or herself. Of course we're not going to find it yet. But we need to find out exactly how valuable the chalice is. Maybe the sacristan is mistaken and only thinks it's valuable. I've seen it in that display case, but I've never paid any attention to it. And then, if it is valuable, we have to find out who knew its value. That will lead us directly to the murderer."

It seemed a little too easy, that I had stumbled upon the answer to the murder in less than a week.

"It sounds okay," I agreed, "but it could be a lot of other things."

"Like what?" Inez said. "An incredibly expensive chalice goes missing and a girl is murdered. They're connected. They have to be."

"Okay, and why would they have someone dress up like a postulant to steal the chalice when they could do it themselves?"

"You said something about how Father Raymond didn't bother to use it because it was difficult to get it out of the case. Maybe it has some lock on it that's hard to open. I admit it seems kind of strange. But we'll find out."

"Well, what are you going to do next?"

"What are *we* going to do, you mean?"

"I can't do much of anything. I'm just a postulant."

"So?"

"Well, I can't find out about this chalice."

"You just did."

"I know, but that was just an accident. I can't find out anything else."

"Without you listening to your friend we wouldn't have any clues at all. You have to help me."

"Okay, what do we do now?" I asked reluctantly.

Inez sat back in her chair. "We have to talk to the sacristan, Sister Evangeline, and find out everything she knows about it."

"I guess."

"You're going with me, of course. I'll make an appointment with your Sister Joan and the sacristan tomorrow afternoon. Is four good?"

"Yeah, if Sister Miriam lets me and I don't practice or study."

Inez ignored that remark. "Good. Meet me in the chapel."

CHAPTER 7

May 31

The next afternoon we all met in the sacristy with Sister Evangeline and walked out to the display case. We were afraid to stand there for very long since it was directly down the hall from Mother Alphonse's office, and we didn't want to raise any more suspicions.

Sister Evangeline shook her head as she looked in the case. "This is not Mother Genevieve's chalice. Someone has substituted another old one for hers. I have no idea how anyone could have done this. It's just the most horrible thing."

Sister Inez took her arm. "Let's go down the hall to an empty parlor where we can talk."

"Yes, of course." Sister Evangeline seemed close to tears.

We all walked quietly in single file past Mother Alphonse's office just in case she was peering out into the hall—I didn't know what she did all day!

When we were all comfortable in the parlor, Inez asked, "Sister, how could anyone have gotten the chalice out of the display case?"

"I honestly don't know. I have a key, but there are only three others, and there's a box with a code on the opposite side of it, so you need two people to unlock it. It's a little ridiculous, if you ask me. All that trouble, but the last superior, Mother Caroline, had it installed. She was a little paranoid." Sister Evangeline looked down. "I guess she was right. It was stolen. I can't believe any one of us would have taken it."

"Have you looked everywhere in the sacristy?"

"Yes, of course. I've checked every cupboard and every shelf."

"Is there any other place it could be?"

Sister Evangeline thought for a second. "Father Raymond was the only person who ever used it. And he was the one who noticed it was missing. But why would he have taken it?"

Inez asked, "And there are only four keys?"

"Yes, I have one, Mother Alphonse has another, and the two priests. That's all."

"Can you tell us about it?" Inez asked.

She whispered, "The chalice was owned by Mother Genevieve, the founder of our order, as you know." She stared at me, just in case I didn't know. "A very rich patron supposedly gave it to her in 1823.

"How valuable is it?"

"Well, I know nothing about that. If it's been stolen, it would be a great loss to the order. That's all I know."

"Who would know its value?"

"Mother Alphonse."

"Does she know it's missing?"

Sister Evangeline looked down as she fingered the rosary in her lap.

"Pease don't tell Mother Alphonse about this. Let's try to figure out where the chalice might be. I don't think we have to involve Mother Alphonse just yet."

She looked so pathetic. I wasn't the only one who was scared of her. But what could Mother Alphonse do to S. Evangeline? She wasn't going to throw her out of the order! And it wasn't her fault it had been stolen.

"Thank you for talking to us about the chalice. I really appreciate it." Sister Inez sounded very grateful.

"Please find out what happened to it." Sister Evangeline looked up at Inez with sad eyes.

* * *

As we walked down the hall, before I turned toward the study hall, Inez said, "I think we have to tell Mother Alphonse about this."

"Yeah, I think you probably should tell her. You should tell Detective Kelly about it too."

"You need to come with me to Alphonse's office when I tell her."

"Are you crazy?" I stopped quickly.

Inez whispered, "Tomorrow after class? Come with me."

"No way." I shivered at the thought. She had been ready to kick me out a few days earlier.

"What good would I do?" I blurted out. "You know as much as I do about it, and remember, you're not the one who's close to getting kicked out. I am. You told me yourself that it was only because of the detective that I'm even still here."

"Look, we're in this investigation together, aren't we? You were the one who found out about the chalice in the first place. I think you should be with me when I talk to her. Please?" Inez sounded like she really needed me. I had felt pretty useless all year, and I was going to get kicked out anyway after this was all over, so I gave in. Just like that. I gave in.

"Okay, if I have to."

"Thanks. I'll get you out of class or study hall."

"Okay."

CHAPTER 8

The next afternoon Inez and I stood outside of Mother Alphonse's office. *Why was I doing this*, I wondered for the hundredth time.

"Are you ready?" She looked at me.

"No," I said honestly. I think I felt as nervous as I had when I saw the dead body. I tried to think of her face when Detective Kelly had confronted her about kicking me out. I had replayed the scene every night before I fell asleep. I could just imagine how satisfying it would have been to be there. That helped with the nervousness. Inez knocked softly on the door.

"Come in."

Damn, she had a nice setup. Two large parlor rooms, one with an expensive desk and office furniture, the other attached room was the actual parlor, with at least ten chairs in various spots around the room. The Oriental rugs were beautiful. There were at least four of them.

"Have a seat, Sister." Mother Alphonse looked up at Inez.

Inez sat at the desk.

"You may sit there." She waved her hand dismissively at me.

There was a small upholstered green chair next to the desk, and when I sat down I practically disappeared into the cushions. I tried to sit up straight and look dignified. Not a chance.

"Yes, Sister, what did you want to see me about?" She addressed Inez, not me. "I assume it's to apologize for being up so late and being in the basement the other evening."

"No, Mother, actually we were wondering if you've heard that Mother Genevieve's chalice is missing?"

Mother Alphonse grabbed the sides of her wooden chair so hard I thought she might break it.

"No, what are you talking about?" She smiled thinly.

"I spoke to Sister Evangeline, the sacristan, and the chalice in the display case has been replaced with another one. We think the missing chalice might have a direct connection to the murdered girl."

Mother Alphonse's straight-lined mouth dipped sharply at the ends. She unclenched her hands from the chair and put them on the desk, clasped tightly together.

The sagging frown lines hoisted up to the thin straight line again. She said quietly, "If what you're saying is even true, this information belongs with me and I'll take care of it. I suggest you go back to teaching English."

She glared at me. "And you should go back to your studies. I don't even understand why you're here?"

Inez answered, "She's helping me with some ideas about the murder, since she was there with me that night." I willed Inez to get up and leave. She had said enough. But she wouldn't stop talking. "Mother, if the chalice was stolen by that girl, she could have been murdered for it. How valuable is it?"

"That is none of your business, Sister."

"But Mother, if others know of its value, it could be a motive for the crime."

"Don't be ridiculous. The chalice is a private matter that only concerns our order. You are not to tell the police anything about it. I'll speak to the sacristan and if we feel it's important information, which I doubt, we will give it to the police. You may leave now."

Mother Alphonse suddenly stood up.

Inez did the same. I hoisted myself up out of the chair as quickly as I could and stumbled to my feet.

"Thank you, Mother," Inez said politely.

"Thank you, Mother," I mimicked.

She stared at me. "What is your name again?"

"Kristen."

"You have no idea how close I came to insisting that you leave the morning of the murder, ignoring the rules as brazenly as you did. It was only after praying about it that God helped me realize you should be given one more chance. But one more chance is all you will get. The rule of obedience is one of our vows for a reason. I would suggest that you keep to your studies and keep out of affairs that you know nothing about. That goes for you, too, Sister Inez. I would have expected more from you. This conversation never took place. Do you understand?"

"Yes, Mother," we both said.

"Good. You may both leave."

We couldn't have left any faster if she had pushed us out the door. Inez grabbed the doorknob and pulled it gently closed behind us.

We walked down the corridor silently, till we got a safe distance away.

"Go back to your class. And don't say anything to anybody, including Joan, until we talk."

"Okay." I walked slowly down the corridor back to math class. Wow. I couldn't believe what had just happened. The chalice must be really expensive. Of course, we knew it had to be valuable because it was kept under two locks and only four people had the keys. And she somehow knew that I wanted desperately to call the detective. Now I couldn't do that either. And she said God was the reason I was still here, when I knew it was the detective. Wow. I'd have bet he didn't know he was more powerful than God. I smiled as I walked down the hall. I was sure the chalice was the key to the murder. But what was next?

★ ★ ★

I needed to get more studying done instead of this murder thing. I was forgetting my homework, going late to classes, not paying attention, and not sleeping. The sleepless nights had finally caught up with me. I decided to forget Inez for a while. And now I was in even more trouble with Mother Alphonse, thanks to Inez. If I wasn't careful, I could use up my last chance in a second. Inez was having fun with this, but she was already a nun. They wouldn't kick her out of the order. I heard that she was being considered for the president of the college. They, however, would be happy to get rid of me. I decided to lay low.

Inez caught me a few days later outside of her American Literature class.

"You haven't come up to my office. Are you okay?"

"Yeah, I'm fine. I just figure being in any more trouble with Mother Alphonse is not the best thing for me right now."

"We're getting so close. And you want to just give up?" She looked at me with her innocent brown eyes, like it was my fault.

"So close to what? We don't have a clue except that a chalice is missing. We have no idea who murdered that woman. And no, I don't want to give up. But I don't want to get kicked out either. I have to get to class."

"Okay, listen. I'm going up to the infirmary this afternoon. I want to talk to one of the old sacristans. She might know more about the chalice. Come with me. Miriam will think you're being wonderful, visiting the sick."

"I've only been to the infirmary once because we had to go. I'm sure she'll think I'm up to something."

"I trust you to think of a reason. Meet me up there at three-thirty."

"Okay, I'll try. But don't count on it."

Inez was going to be the reason I left the convent and worked at McDonald's for the rest of my life instead of becoming a teacher. In fact, that sounded pretty good right now. Free hamburgers, fries, milk shakes, no sleepless nights, a nice bed to sleep in, no ugly habit or old lady shoes to wear ...

After class, I knocked on Miriam's office door.

"Yes?"

"Sister, I was wondering if I could go up to the infirmary to visit one of the sisters?"

"Why do you need to go today?" Her untrusting eyes bored into me.

I pretended to be excited. "Well, one of the sisters in the infirmary, Sister Anastasia, is the great-granddaughter of Franz Gruber, the man who wrote 'Silent Night.' I was hoping to do a paper on her for my History of Music term paper."

"Yes, I've heard she's there for a while. An amazing story."

"Yes, sister, I met her when we went up to the infirmary in December."

That was actually true, and I did want to talk to her again. She was eighty-six years old and had such an interesting life. I had always wanted to go back, but I was partly lying, because I didn't have any paper to do—and I wasn't even going to see her.

Miriam fell for it. "Yes, Kristen, you may go. But don't be late for Vespers."

"Oh no, I won't. Thank you, Sister."

It was three-thirty. I saw Inez in the hall outside of the infirmary. We asked one of the nurses which room the old sacristan was in.

"Sister Gertrude? She's in room twenty-four, at the end of the hall."

We walked down the halls of the infirmary. The smell was old and musty. I glanced in the rooms as we passed. Old nuns lay in their beds, frail and useless. I didn't ever want to get old. No wonder none of us visited the infirmary. It was so depressing. We found room twenty-four and knocked gently on the door.

No one answered, so Inez pushed the door open gently and walked in.

Sister Gertrude was lying on her bed, her arms neatly at her sides, and a white blanket pulled up to her chin. She opened her eyes and said, "Hello," very faintly.

"Sister, how are you?" Inez asked.

"Do I know you?"

"No, Sister, I'm one of the English teachers at the college, and I wanted to ask you a question."

"That's fine, dear." Sister Gertrude looked at both of us.

"Here, dear, help me sit up so I can talk to you." She motioned to Inez, and we gently helped her sit up and plumped up a pillow behind her until she said she was comfortable.

"We were wondering if you knew anything about that very old chalice in front of the chapel. The one with the rubies?"

"Oh, Sister, how I would love to see that chalice again." She closed her eyes, and for a minute I thought she was finished talking. Then she spoke with a surprisingly strong voice.

"I haven't thought about it for years. We used to call it the 'Holy Grail.' We weren't being irreverent, I hope." Her black eyes sparkled for a second. I liked her. "But it is very old, probably from the Middle Ages. Chalices were quite the thing back then," she laughed.

Inez encouraged her. "Can you tell us how our convent got the chalice?"

She smiled and opened her eyes even wider. "Yes, of course. Mother Genevieve received it as a gift. Normally a nun would never have gotten or kept anything like a chalice. They belonged to the priests, but Mother, when she was a young sister, had saved the life of a Prussian nobleman in a field hospital. He gave her this as a thank you. It meant nothing to him. He had more money and jewels than he knew what to do with, and he was Protestant, so the chalice wasn't as meaningful to him as it was to us Catholics. Some people thought it might have been made in the Middle Ages. It certainly looks like a medieval chalice."

"How valuable is it?" Inez asked.

"I don't know, Sister. All the jewels in it are real, and there are diamonds and rubies and sapphires. In the Middle Ages, a chalice wasn't some cheap silver cup like the priests use nowadays. They were works of art, worthy to hold the blood of Christ. Sister Genevieve kept the chalice. Never locked it up, like it should have been. She always said God would preserve it from harm. You've seen it of course? It's beautiful. I hope I can get back up and walk again soon. Then I'll be able to go down to the chapel for Mass again."

Sister Gertrude paused and closed her eyes, I supposed imagining what the chalice looked like.

Inez said, "Yes, it is beautiful. It sounds like it's worth a lot of money."

"Oh, I wouldn't know about that. I imagine that it would be. But worth isn't always in money, Sister."

Inez nodded. "That's true. Well, thank you very much for telling us about it."

Sister Gertrude reached out with her hand with its paper-thin skin. "You come again to visit. I enjoy talking to you. What was your name?"

"Sister Inez. I teach English literature at the college."

"Oh, that's good. I used to love to read. I don't do too much of that anymore." She lay back on the pillows. "I think I'll rest now. You come back and see me again."

But Inez had one more question.

"Sister, does everyone know the story about that chalice?"

"Know about it? Why, everyone knew about it when I was the sacristan. Everybody knew how Mother had received it. Don't they tell you that story anymore?"

"Wasn't anyone worried about it being stolen?" Inez asked. I hoped she wouldn't say that it was missing.

"Stolen? It was perfectly safe in the sacristy. And it's locked up now. Mother Caroline saw to that years ago. She was always worried about someone breaking in and stealing things. But we were all nuns. Why would anyone steal it? We wanted to use it and appreciate its beauty. No, I can't imagine anyone stealing it."

"Thank you, Sister. It's been so nice talking to you."

Sister Gertrude turned her head to the side. "You come back, now."

She looked at me. "And you, too, dear."

"We will, Sister." Inez and I turned and left the room.

As we walked down the hall, I told Inez that I wanted to talk to her for a few minutes, so we got past the infirmary doors and opened the door to an empty classroom and sat down in two desks at the back of the room.

"I only have a few minutes before my next class. What is it?"

"I just can't figure out why you don't want to tell the detective about our talk with Mother Alphonse. I mean, she was so adamant about *not* wanting us to tell him. I just thought maybe we should tell him. I think it's important."

Inez looked out of the window. "I don't know what to do, honestly."

I had never seen her ambivalent about anything.

She went on. "I just don't think Alphonse had anything to do with the murder. She has a key, and I don't see why she would steal the chalice. I mean, she practically owns it."

"No, she doesn't own it. It belongs to the order. Maybe she wants to leave and needs the money."

Inez shook her head. "Nuns her age don't leave the order. Where would she go? Besides, she's the head of the whole province. She's in a position of power. She can do pretty much anything she wants. What kind of life would she trade it for?" Inez was quiet for a few minutes. "I know I should call him. It's just that I don't know if I'm right about this whole thing."

"You seemed pretty sure a few days ago when you got me into a lot of trouble." I knew I sounded angry.

"Hey, I thought the chalice was the answer. But now I'm not so sure. I'm starting to agree with you now. I think maybe we should just wait it out and see what happens—if anything happens. I don't want to get you in any more trouble. I've got class. I've got to go. Let's talk later, okay?"

She walked out of the classroom and I sat there for a few minutes, thinking. Getting me in trouble had never stopped her in the past. Maybe she was starting to realize that we really didn't know anything about the murder, that we didn't have any clues, and that we should let the police do their own investigating. I sure hoped so.

★ ★ ★

The next afternoon I sat in the music library listening to a Mozart piano concerto, hoping that Joan or Maribeth would stop by. After about half an hour they walked in the door. I kept my book open and they opened theirs, even though we all knew that our studying was over for at least an hour.

Joan asked right away, "Hey, why did you run off the other day when I told you about the chalice? You just got up and said you had to go. I know it was a boring story, but it wasn't that bad."

"Well, Sister Inez and I were talking about the murder ..."

Joan interrupted, "Just like everyone else in the motherhouse."

"Well, even more, I think, since we found the body, and Inez thought that the girl was dressed up like us to get in here and steal something valuable. We couldn't think of anything and then when you told us about the chalice, I knew I had to tell her. So that's why I left so fast."

"What did she think?" asked Joan.

"She thought that might be the thing that the girl stole—and got killed for."

Maribeth shook her head. "I don't think so."

"Why not?"

"That chalice was probably gone a long time before Father Raymond noticed it on Pentecost. Nobody ever looks in that display case. It could have been gone for months and nobody would have noticed. I think you're crazy thinking it's connected to the murder."

"Well, do you have any better ideas?"

"Me? No, why should I? I have no idea. But I think the police can probably figure it out. She wasn't even a nun, so it really doesn't have anything to do with anything in the motherhouse."

"Well, Inez still thinks it's somehow connected to the chalice."

Joan said sadly, "Well, I just hope they find it somewhere."

Maribeth nodded her head. "Yeah, I never really noticed it, but I hope they find it."

I practiced a little and went back to study hall and did some math problems. I was so far behind I didn't know how I could ever catch up. I was completely engrossed in a calculus problem when I heard my name.

Sister Miriam was standing outside her office and looking directly at me.

"Postulant Kristen, would you come into my office?"

Not again. What was it this time?

I walked into her office as she sat down at her desk. I had to stand.

"A postulant came to me a little while ago, Kristen, and told me something about you which I find very disturbing." Miriam glared at me.

Let's see, I wonder who ratted on me. My mind raced to all the illegal things I had done recently. I talked to Maribeth and Joan regularly, I stopped by Inez's office after lights out at night, I went to the infirmary today under false pretenses, I had a meeting with Mother Alphonse that was a disaster, I had talked to the sacristan with Inez and we sure weren't talking about American Literature. The list was long. I wasn't about to offer any information to Miriam, though. Let's see what she had on me.

"The postulant informs me that you have been coming to bed late in the evening for many nights, not just the evening of the murder."

Damn. It was probably Kathy Hines, that self-righteous postulant that slept in my dorm with the other four of us. I'll bet she even waited up till I got back from Inez's office and counted the number of nights I was late.

Do I deny it or admit my sins? Shit. I tried to think ahead quickly to the consequences of each option. If I denied it, she'd have too much evidence against me. Holy Kathy never told lies. I'll admit it and swear it will never happen again. Besides, Inez would have to help me just a little, getting me out of trouble, especially if she wanted help on this murder investigation.

"Sister Miriam, I have gone to Sister Inez's office in the evening, but I've been helping her grade papers. That's all I've ever done. That's what I was doing the night of the murder. I'm really sorry. It won't happen again."

Miriam's eyes bored into me. She looked ready with more proof—and now she didn't need it. I could feel her switching gears to deal with my confession and wondering how to get angry with me and not with Inez, who had obviously been partially responsible for my misdeeds.

"I don't know why Sister Inez let this happen, but I assure you, just because she is a faculty member doesn't mean she has authority over my postulants. I will speak to her about this. You, however, know the rules, even though Sister Inez may not, and you have thrown them aside willfully. You are not a sister yet. You have no idea of the importance of these rules. We haven't even discussed the evening of the murder. And now to find out there have been other evenings and other meetings that I knew nothing about. I don't know what we're going to do about this. You seem to have no regard for the rules."

She was right about that. I didn't think much of stupid rules.

Miriam went on and on. "They are tried and true over the last century, for your education and formation, and you do not know more than the nuns who have founded and sustained this order. Do you think you know more than they do?"

"No, Sister."

"I will personally come to your dorm every evening to make sure you are there. I no longer trust you, and I will not have a postulant here whom I don't trust. Even Mother Alphonse was ready to ask you to leave the order. But after praying about it, she told me she realized that God wanted you to have a second chance. I agreed. You are on probation for the next two months, Kristin, and I hope that you will think long and hard about your commitment to this order. Do you understand?"

"Yes, I do. It won't happen again."

Sister Miriam picked up a pen and started writing.

I turned and walked out the office door. No one looked at me. Everyone in the room had heard the whole exchange since the door had been wide open. That was one of Miriam's more endearing qualities, that she would yell and scream for the whole world to hear.

I sat down at my desk. Half an hour to go before Compline and bed. I wasn't going anywhere tonight, or any other night.

I stared at Kathy Hines two rows ahead of me. Her back was to me, but I was sure she had a smile on her face.

The next afternoon I stayed in the classroom to talk to Inez. "I've got to talk to you for just a second," I blurted out. "I'm in terrible trouble. I can't come to your office anymore or even talk to you. Miriam knows I've been coming to bed late and she really yelled at me last night."

"Damn these stupid rules. I'll talk to her." Inez continued to pick her books and papers off the desk.

I grabbed Inez by the arm. "No, don't. I'm in so much trouble already. That'll just make things worse."

"You don't know how good I am. Trust me."

"Seriously, this is easy for you. You're not going to get in any trouble, but I am so close to getting kicked out. She told me as much. That she didn't trust me anymore, and I certainly don't think she trusts you."

"Don't worry. I'll take care of it."

CHAPTER 9

June 4

Three days went by and I really concentrated on studying and practicing—and praying. I was in trouble with the two most important people in the order, Mother Alphonse and Sister Miriam, and it was all Inez's fault. I wasn't in any mood to talk to her.

The chalice didn't interest me anymore, although sometimes in the morning, during meditation, I thought about it. I wondered what it looked like, and how valuable it might be, and how the woman had gotten the postulant clothes and broken into the convent and stolen the chalice, and who inside the convent walls knew and killed her.

And I thought about David Kelly, and how nice he looked, and how he had looked at me, and I wondered if I should really be a nun, and why he was the first man to really interest me. I went over the conversations, all two of them, that we had.

He wasn't the slightest bit interested in me, just curious about why "a pretty girl like me would become a nun." Even though he hadn't said it like that, that's what people always asked. I had tried to answer that question so many times before I entered. People just didn't understand, even most Catholics. Why hadn't I been able to give him a good answer? I went over a thousand answers in my head, but they didn't satisfy me. He was right about ministers and rabbis. They were all married and had families, and it had never stopped them from serving God and their churches. Why was I better than a woman who was married and had three children? And the church did put nuns and priests higher than lay people. We had a special calling to serve God. Or so they told us.

And then I thought about the chalice again—and again. Okay. It did interest me. I was obsessed. I made mental lists of all the people who might have known about it, but none of those people had any motive to commit murder.

Father Raymond had the most knowledge about and interest in the chalice, but he could have just taken it. He didn't have to kill anyone. Mother Alphonse was acting very strange, but she had no need to steal the chalice. Inez was right: it was hers, as representative of the order. She could have asked Sister Evangeline for the code and used her key, taken it, and no one would have thought anything about it. Or if they did, what could they have done about it? I wondered about the younger priest, Father Steven, but he had never used the chalice, and was more interested in finishing the Mass and getting out of the motherhouse than in the chalice.

No one who had a key had any reason to steal the chalice. And no one who didn't have a key had the ability to steal it. I would come out of my daydreams to find that the Mass was over, a class had ended, or a lecture was over. I couldn't concentrate on anything.

CHAPTER 10

June 5

I walked into the study hall the next morning before class and sat down. I folded my hands on the thick wooden desk that lifted up to hold all our books. Sister Miriam started our hour-long instructions.

"Postulants, we have some very important news this morning. The murdered girl was *not* a postulant, as you all know, and her boyfriend has just been arrested for her murder. So now that has been settled, and we can concentrate on our studies. I'd like to read and talk about Corinthians today. Could you open your Bibles?"

What? She wasn't going to tell us anything else? I couldn't believe it. I wanted to run up and grab the paper from her desk. Who was the murdered girl? How had she gotten into our convent? And who was this boyfriend? Did he know about the chalice? Did he have the chalice?

I had so many questions whirling through my head, I didn't hear a word Miriam said for the whole hour.

I had to talk to Inez. Were we finished with the investigation? Was the murder really solved? Was that all it was, a lover's spat gone wrong? I couldn't believe that.

I practically ran to the music department. I had to see Joan or Maribeth. Neither one of them were there. I pulled my music books off the practice shelf and picked a practice room. I was practicing Beethoven's Third piano concerto. I had barely gotten to the solo part when the door opened and Joan squeezed in.

"Where have you been?" she practically yelled.

"I got in trouble."

"Here. Look at this." She set the paper on top of my music.

I scanned the article.

"Convent murderer arrested. 'The bizarre case of a Roman Catholic postulant murdered on May 23 in the basement of the Notre Dame motherhouse has been solved,' St. Louis County police chief states.

"The man, Julius Hunter, a boyfriend of the murdered girl, has been arrested at his parent's home in Lemay. The girl, identified as Jane Mueller, who has been in and out of rehab for alcohol abuse, had been seeing Hunter at the time of the murder. He is being held without bail in the St. Louis County jail.

"'When asked about the bizarre circumstances connecting the murder to the St. Louis convent,' Chief Warren states, 'We don't understand all the details right now, but we're confident we have the murderer in custody.'"

"So it didn't have anything to do with the chalice," Joan blurted out. "Father Raymond probably just took it out of there and misplaced it. I'm sure we'll find it. I'm so glad it didn't have anything to do with the murder."

She looked at me like I was the one who insisted on it being the reason. Wow. I put down the paper. The newspaper had gotten the details wrong, yet again, saying that the victim was a postulant—and his girlfriend. But she and the boyfriend had argued and he had killed her. That was pretty obvious, I guessed. But what had they been arguing about, and why was she in the convent basement, and why was she dressed like a postulant, and why was a chalice missing?

But I just nodded and said, "Yeah, I'm sure glad they caught somebody."

Joan stood up. "I've gotta go. I just wanted to show you the paper because I knew Miriam would cut it to pieces. See you soon."

I wanted to know more, to find out why he had killed the woman. Did he have the chalice, was he going to sell it and make a fortune, or was the chalice a stupid, stupid idea from two amateur detective nuns who didn't know anything? Right then I would have guessed the stupid idea. Inez and I were way out of our league. I wanted to call detective Kelly so much. But I would get kicked out for sure, since Mother Alphonse had practically forbidden us to tell the police about the chalice. And what would I say? The murder had been solved. But did the detective think the murder had really been solved? He was a smart man. He had to have a lot of questions. I wondered if he'd come again to talk to me. I wanted him to.

I needed to concentrate on my school and being a nun. I had only a few months to decide if this was the life for me.

I was beginning to think that it wasn't. No, that's not true. I had started to think that eight months ago, when the tall front doors of the convent had shut behind me, blocking out all the sunlight. I wanted to discover the person God wanted me to be. I didn't know quite how to do that, but it wasn't happening here in this convent. I was quite sure that the creator of the entire universe didn't care whether we stayed up too late, or missed a few prayers, or talked to someone who wasn't in our class.

But I still had some hope. There were people like Inez and Maribeth and Joan. There were some young nuns who were doing great things, teaching people, trying to change the world. These were the people and the hope that I clung to.

Forget the chalice. Forget this murder and the stupid compulsion to solve it. I needed to solve myself.

Sister Miriam let us read the newspaper article about the murder in the next day's paper. The only thing I had missed was that his mother said he was a kind boy who loved animals, but everybody's mother said that.

CHAPTER 11

June 6

The next morning Sister Miriam asked to see me in her office.

"I had a long talk with Sister Inez. She assured me that she had no idea she was interfering in your training as a postulant. She was very apologetic and hoped that we could work something out. I asked her why she needed you as an assistant—why she didn't ask one of the junior sisters—and she said that she's always been concerned that the junior sisters are so busy with their last two years of school. That's why she asked you. She also said you were her best student in years."

Miriam smiled like she had been personally responsible for my grades.

"I've decided that you can help her grade papers this semester, and in summer school, as long as you both realize the importance of your being back in the postulancy at a reasonable time. And that means no later than ten o'clock. No more one o'clock sessions. You may go up to her office now and make out a schedule. I will expect a copy of it."

"Thank you, Sister," I said, meekly and gratefully.

I ran up to Inez's office.

"How did you do that? Miriam was furious the other night when she yelled at me."

Inez smiled. "I was very diplomatic. You know there are no papers to grade."

"I figured that. But there's no murder to solve either. So what exactly am I doing here?"

"No murder to solve?" Inez looked at me like I had just told her I was an atheist. "Are you crazy? You don't honestly believe that it was her boyfriend who killed her?"

"Yes, I do," I blurted out. "The police know a whole lot more than we do. I think the whole chalice idea was stupid, now that I think about it. I'm sorry I ever told you about it."

"But you're not sorry that you talked to him?" She took out two cans of Coke from her ever-stocked cooler and handed me one.

"What do you mean by that?" I pulled open the tab and took a drink.

"It's obvious that you like that detective. And listen, that's okay. We all go through that. You just have to decide what's important to you, especially now that you're so close to deciding your future."

"Actually, other people are really close to deciding my future."

Inez ignored that. "Don't throw your vocation away thinking about someone you know nothing about."

"I don't like him. I really don't. You don't understand."

"You know, it's okay to feel that way about him. You just have to decide what's more important to you. We all go through this."

"No, you really don't understand. I thought he might have liked me a little, but he just can't figure out why I want to be a nun. He asked me about it."

"Well, were you able to tell him?"

My face felt red. I was embarrassed, and angry that she was so perceptive. It was like she had stolen him from me right then and made him just a common mistake that I had to get over.

"No, not really. I did a terrible job. I don't want to talk about that. Let's talk about the murder."

"Okay." Inez switched gears quickly. "The boyfriend theory doesn't explain why the woman was dressed as a postulant."

"No," I had to admit. "But I'm sure the police are investigating that part, too, especially since I told the detective about that. And the boyfriend is more than a theory. He's in jail right now."

"I don't believe for a minute that the boyfriend killed her. I'll bet he's going to be released. They're desperate. And besides, the detective was here yesterday talking to all the junior sisters."

"He was?" I couldn't help feel a twinge of—what was it? jealousy maybe—that he hadn't stopped by to talk to me. Oh God, I was acting like he was my boyfriend or something. He was a detective trying to solve a murder!

"Why was he here?" I asked as neutrally as I could.

"The police found out the identity of the victim, as we know. Her name was Jane Mueller and she was homeless. She had been in and out of homeless shelters in the cities. It turns out that she was in the Regina homeless shelter for a while, and our sisters go there to help every weekend, so he was trying to find out if there was a connection there."

"Did he find someone who knew her?"

"As far as I know, he didn't. But the murderer isn't going to admit that they knew her, are they?"

We talked for a little while longer. Then I left and went to bed. Inez was right about the postulant dress. I could admit that. But I think we were wrong about the chalice and all its implications. I fell asleep thinking about the murder instead of what I should be thinking about: whether this was the life for me. I had to decide soon.

CHAPTER 12

June 7

The letter came the next day. I was busy studying calculus at my desk for the test the next afternoon. Laura, one of my least favorite classmates, handed out the mail every day. She walked by and threw a letter on my calculus study guide.

Funny. It had no return address, but a floral postage stamp. It was addressed to Postulant Kristen. No last name. Then the address and city. I opened it up. A three-by-five lined note card was all that was inside. I pulled it out. The letters were cut out carefully from a magazine and pasted on the note card.

"Stop asking questions. You will be sorry."

I dropped the card on my desk. The words didn't really register at first. It was a joke. It had to be a joke. And then, slowly, the meaning of those cut-out black letters, in different shapes and fonts, pieced together and glued, finally penetrated my brain. I started shaking, grabbed my calculus papers and the card, and ran out of the study hall. I flew up the two flights of stairs and down the corridor to Inez's office.

As I reached her door, I could hear her talking to someone. I didn't care. I knocked anyway. The talking stopped. Inez appeared at the door. "Hi Kristen. Could you come back in about twenty minutes?"

"No, I have to see you right now."

It must have been the way I looked, shaking a little, white

as a sheet, that made Inez turn back inside her office. "Sister Jo Ann, would you come back later this evening? I'm so sorry. Something's come up rather suddenly."

"Of course, Sister." I heard the polite reply. Then a junior sister walked out briskly with a thick notebook. She stared at me with a nasty expression, like she was getting kicked out for *me*? I could hear her shoes stomping down the hall as she walked away.

"Come in." Inez called. I walked in and set the note card on her desk in front of her.

"I just got this in the mail. I had to show you."

She stared at the card.

"Pick it up by the edges and put it in the envelope carefully," was the first thing she said.

"There might be fingerprints. Let me get a Kleenex to hold it with."

I carefully put the card back in the envelope.

She sat back in her chair. "We have to call that detective. This is a direct threat from the murderer. I'll call him right now."

I just sat there quietly.

She kept talking. "You do realize what this means?"

"Well, it means that I'm pretty worried, to say the least."

"Well, yes, of course, but it means that the boyfriend isn't the murderer. And the police need to know everything that we know, and that includes the information about the chalice."

"Should we show this to Miriam?" I asked.

"Miriam? Of course not. Don't breathe a word to anyone until we talk to him."

I handed Inez the detective's card, and I heard her call and say she needed to speak with Detective Kelly. I only heard her side of the conversation, which consisted of "ohs" and "yeses" and her phone number, but Inez hung up the phone and told me.

"He's in Quincy tonight but coming back tomorrow and the officer said he'd have him call first thing in the morning. He asked if we needed to speak with anyone else but I said no."

"I guess we'll just have to wait," I said.

"Do you want to leave the envelope with me?" she asked.

"No, I'll keep it."

"But don't handle it. And you know what else it means?" she added.

"No."

"They put this in the mail before the boyfriend was arrested. If they had just waited a few more days, everyone, including us, would have thought the boyfriend was guilty. Now we know he isn't."

I put the envelope in my calculus book.

"Keep it safe," she said as I ran out the door to my class.

"See you in the morning."

"Will you let Miriam know the detective is coming after he calls?"

"Yes, I'll take care of it."

I walked around in a fog the rest of the day, getting more and more worried as night approached. I took a quick shower and went to bed, lying sleepless in the dark. I thought about seeing him again in the morning. I wondered if he would be worried about me.

Then I wondered if the murderer knew where I slept. If she was a nun in the convent, why had she mailed the envelope? Nothing made any sense.

The night felt chilly suddenly. It would be easy for someone to walk into the dorm, find my bed, and put the pillow over my head. They obviously knew the motherhouse. I sat up quickly and wrapped a thin blanket around myself. If I were awake, at least I could scream. This was a real threat from a real murderer. Before it had seemed like a game I was playing with Inez. Well, not a game. I had seen a dead body. But I had nothing to do with it except that Inez and I had found the body. It was exciting and intriguing to think about the chalice as a possible reason for a murder.

But now I knew that we had gotten someone's attention, someone knew that we were asking questions, and the implications of it kept me sitting up in bed all night, waiting for a dark figure to slink up to the side of my bed. Who would even know we were working on the murder investigation? It had to be someone in the convent. No, the letter was sent to the convent from the outside. But who knew except a few people? I could hardly wait till morning. I checked my watch in the dim light from the square outside. Three a.m. Only two hours to go. It was the first time I had looked forward to getting up.

CHAPTER 13

I fidgeted all through Mass and prayers the next morning. Pam even put her hand on my arm and whispered, "What's wrong with you?"

"Nothing." I tried to sit still after that and concentrate on the sermon, which was impossibly boring. I looked at my watch ten times during breakfast and did my chores quickly. Then I went down the hall again. I hoped that he had called Inez.

I sat down in the study hall. Sister Miriam called my name and I jumped up and went to her office.

"Kristen, that detective wants to speak with you again in the parlor at ten o'clock. Please come back here afterwards."

I grabbed my calculus book, hoping I could absorb some of the math just by holding it, and headed down the hall. I knew Inez had class till ten.

Detective Kelly stood up as I entered. I realized again how handsome he was. I felt my face turning red. I willed it not to.

"Why, Kristen, it's good to see you again. What can I help you with? You know we've arrested someone in the murder case. And where is Sister Inez? She was the one who called yesterday."

"She'll be here as soon as her class is over, I guess."

"Why did you call?"

He was all business. Of course he was. I almost wanted him to ask me some personal questions again, just not why I wanted to be a nun. But he wasn't interested in me. He was interested in solving the murder.

I took the envelope from my calculus book and held it out to him. "You might want to be careful touching it," I said. I felt stupid saying that to him. He was the detective, but he didn't know what the note said.

He smiled—somewhat condescendingly, I thought—but opened the envelope carefully, just touching the edges. He read it quickly and looked up at me.

"I don't understand this. When did you receive this and what are they talking about?"

"I got it in the mail yesterday. It scared me. And it's because Sister Inez and I have been trying to find out more about the murder."

Detective Kelly wasn't smiling anymore. "First of all, that's not a very good idea, under any circumstances. And if you did find out anything, you should have called me and let me know. I hought I made that clear in our last interview."

My face started to turn red, but luckily Sister Inez walked in the door. Kelly stood up, they shook hands, and both sat down.

"Kristen was showing me this note and was telling me that you may have some information about the investigation. It sounds like you should have let us know about it earlier."

He took a look at the note in his hand and frowned.

Inez spoke quickly. "Well, it's pure speculation at this point. We figured that the person was dressed like a postulant and was in here because she wanted to steal something. We couldn't think of anything that anyone would want to steal because we all take a vow of poverty."

Inez continued. She could charm anyone and seemed oblivious to Kelly's judgment. "But then Kristen, quite by accident, heard that an old chalice was missing, and we started asking people about the chalice, where it might be, how much it was worth, and questions like that. Then we heard that you made an arrest for the murder, so we figured our ideas weren't very important. Until Kristen got this in the mail yesterday."

Wow, Inez was good at weaseling out of things. I was learning a lot more than English from her.

David looked at both of us. "I can give you this information because it's already been released to the public. The person arrested for her murder has been released. It turns out he had an alibi for the entire evening. Tell me what you found out about this chalice. What's so important about a chalice anyway?"

Inez asked, "You're not Catholic, correct?"

"That's right. I'm not anything at all. My parents were Methodist, but you'll have to explain everything Catholic to me."

She started explaining in full professor mode. "Well, the chalice is just another name for a cup used at Mass, to hold the wine that we believe is turned into the blood of Christ during Mass. It's not just an ordinary cup. It's very special, and there was a chalice that was given to the founder of our order in the last century. We think the chalice is even older than that, possibly made in the Middle Ages, and it's been missing for the past week, possibly since around the time of the murder."

"Where was it?"

"It was in a display case outside of the main chapel with many other items that belonged to our founder."

"Was it broken into? Was it stolen? Who discovered it was missing?"

"Well, that's the strange thing. Nobody knows exactly when it went missing because it was replaced with another old chalice and it wasn't even noticed until last week. The priest who uses it for feast days went to get it out for Mass. He realized it was the wrong chalice and, of course, got really upset."

"You're confusing me. Nobody even knew it was gone?"

I took over the explanation. "There's this display case and it has lots of items in it. The chalice was in the back. I had never even noticed it. The display case was locked and, I didn't know this at all, apparently very difficult to get into. There was a code and a lock that only four people had keys for, so it would have been difficult to break into it."

"Who has the keys?"

Inez said, "Mother Alphonse, Sister Evangeline—she's the sacristan—and the two priests who say Mass here. That's it."

"Go on."

I finished up quickly. "Someone must have gotten not only the code but also the key and gotten into the case, taken the chalice, replaced it with the other one, and all without anyone noticing, maybe even the night she was killed. But we still can't figure out why she was killed or what connection she has to the chalice."

Detective Kelly asked, "How much money are we talking about here?"

Inez spoke up. "Kristen and I went and talked to Mother Alphonse about that a few days ago and she told us to mind our own business and stay out of it. She was pretty angry about the questions we were asking. But another sister told us how important the chalice was. She didn't know how much money it was worth, though."

"Well, the two of you have been busy. I can see why you got the note from the murderer. And that also means the murderer has to be here in the motherhouse. What precautions are you taking for your safety?" He looked at me.

"Uh, nothing," I blurted out. "I don't know what I can do. I haven't told anyone about this yet … except Sister Inez."

"And you say that Mother Alphonse didn't want you to talk about the chalice?"

"She was adamant," Inez told him.

"She doesn't know about this visit today?"

"No, absolutely not."

He sat forward in the chair. "And she shouldn't. You know she has to be on our short list of suspects, especially because she has one of the keys."

I spoke up then. "We really need to find out the value of the chalice before we can use it as a motive for the crime. But we have no pictures or any information that we can find, so I think that will have to wait."

David nodded his head. "If we had the chalice we could get it to an appraiser and determine its value. I don't think this is the right time to ask Mother Alphonse about it. I'm sure you agree. But the important thing is that the two of you are safe, especially you, Kristen, since you received the note." He kept looking at me. "Is there a place you can go till we find out more? A place that would be safer?"

Inez spoke up. "I think we can be careful enough in the motherhouse. My door locks and I'll make sure that Kristen is somewhere safe."

"I don't understand how you can be safe in a dormitory." He looked straight at me. "And you know the murderer is most likely in the motherhouse. I really think you should go home for a few days or go somewhere that's safer than here."

"I don't know how I can do that without just announcing to everyone that I received a threatening note. I'll try to be careful. I'll try to sleep somewhere else. In another empty dormitory or somewhere else."

"But won't you get in trouble like you did before?"

I was quiet. I really didn't know what I was going to do. I kept waiting for Inez to come up with a solution, but she was quiet.

She finally said, "We'll think of something. Don't worry," patting my arm reassuringly.

I was kind of thrilled that he was so concerned about my safety, but then I remembered why he was interested in me. I was a curiosity to him. He didn't *like* me. He just couldn't figure me out. I was a puzzle to him, nothing more.

He looked right at me. "And please be careful. Don't do anything else right now. Let us handle this next step. You know, it's kind of interesting. I was here a few days ago because the victim had stayed at the homeless shelter in downtown St. Louis. I found out that your order regularly visits there. I came down to see if anyone remembered her from the woman's shelter. No one did, or no one said they did. But it did establish a possible connection between the motherhouse and the victim."

"Are there any records of the visits that our sisters make there?" Inez asked.

"No, that's the problem. Your student sisters go to one of three places every Saturday: your home for the elderly, the homeless shelter, or your infirmary. No one keeps a permanent record of where anyone goes. It's impossible to know who might have been in touch with the victim since she wasn't at the shelter that often either."

We stood up and shook hands with him. I liked him. I didn't want him to leave. He seemed to care. He looked at us and said again, "I really don't like the thought of Kristen being in the dormitory without any protection. Sister Inez, will you make sure she's safe?"

Inez looked him straight in the eye and said, "Yes, of course."

He walked down the long corridor with Inez, and I headed back to the postulant wing.

I told Sister Miriam the interview was over and got my broom from the closet. I swept the hall in record time and hoped no one would notice that I hadn't dusted. I ran back to the study hall and got to my first class.

I thought of nothing else but the interview. What David Kelly had said, how he said it, what he implied, how worried I should be, how good it felt to be treated like a human being worthy of respect. I was reading too much into it, like I usually did. I tried to concentrate on my math, but it was hopeless. I worried about the coming night, and I worried about how worried I should be.

"So how are you going to keep me safe?" I asked Inez after my miserable calculus test that afternoon.

"I have no idea, but I'm thinking about it. Give me till tonight. Come up to the office before you go up to your dorm."

I worried through dinner, recreation, and our two-hour study time. I headed up to her office at nine and knocked on the door.

"I don't know what to do to make you less worried," Inez said as I sat down at her desk.

"Have you thought of anything?"

"I tried, but I couldn't think of a single place you could go that would be safer. So here's what I did."

She looked around carefully, even though I was the only one in her office, and pulled opened her second drawer. She took out a kitchen towel and unwrapped it to reveal a large kitchen carving knife with a serrated blade.

"Here, this should help." She actually looked a little proud. "I got it from the kitchen tonight after dinner."

"A knife? What good is this going to do? I was hoping for a locked door! This isn't going to keep me safe!"

"Well, I thought it would help ..." Inez seemed disappointed that I wasn't more excited about the knife.

"You promised that you would think of something."

"I did. I thought this might help you feel safer."

"I thought you would find a room with a lock on it. Wouldn't you be worried?"

"I know I promised, but I really can't think of a single place that you could go to be safer than in your dorm surrounded by the other postulants. And yes, I would be worried, but I don't know how to fix it. I can lock my door, and I know you can't. But having two or three other people in the dorm—and this knife—should make a difference, provide a certain layer of protection. I'm really sorry. I know I promised, but I just don't know what else to do."

I didn't even know what to say. She really had let me down. She had promised the detective—and me—that she would come up with an idea to make me feel and be safer. And yet she had come up with nothing but a kitchen knife. There had to be empty rooms with locks on them in the main part of the building, where the real nuns slept, where I could sleep for a few nights. But there wasn't much I could do about it now that it was already nine-thirty. She didn't seem to be too concerned about it. I grabbed the towel and the knife, said goodnight abruptly, and walked out of her office. If only I had a room to lock, like the detective had said. The postulants in my dorm wouldn't offer much protection.

CHAPTER 14

I crawled into bed and pulled the thin covers over myself. I waited until the dark shadow of Miriam peered by the side of my curtains to make sure I was there. I put the knife under my bed, grabbed my pillow and a blanket, and went down the hall to an empty dorm with a dozen beds. The postulancy didn't fill up like it had in years past, so there were plenty of empty beds and dorms. I walked over to a bed by a corner window and laid down. I covered myself with the blanket and plumped up the pillow under my head.

I listened to the emptiness of the dorm for a long time. I heard the grandfather clock chime one, then two o'clock far below. I heard the wind outside, and the scraping of the branches on the window. It was worse in here than in my dorm. I couldn't fall asleep. But if the murderer knew who I was, then he or she could find out where I slept. He or she would never find me in here, I kept telling myself. I was safe. But the wind blew the branches all night and by four a.m. I was shaking with fear and exhaustion. I grabbed my pillow and blanket and slipped back into my dorm. I laid down on the cool sheets and waited for morning to come.

The next morning's newspaper was being carefully passed around the study hall when I got there after breakfast. It was surprisingly intact. Maybe Sister Miriam didn't have the time to cut it to pieces. One of the postulants started reading it to us.

"It says that the boyfriend of the murdered girl has been released. His alibi held up with multiple witnesses and so he's out of jail. That's terrible," she concluded.

I knew it was going to happen.

Inez pulled me aside after class. "When can we talk?"

"I don't have class right now."

She practically pulled me back inside the classroom and shut the door.

"Sit down," she said abruptly.

"What is it?"

"I had to go to Sister Anne's office last night after you left to pick up a book. She said if she wasn't there to just get the book from her desk."

Sister Anne taught English Literature and had her Ph.D. in medieval literature. She was a great teacher. Everyone loved her. In her sixties, she had the steady grace of someone who knew her field and loved it.

"I went in," Inez continued, "and underneath the book I saw this article that Anne had Xeroxed from an English newspaper. Look."

She practically threw it at me.

"Medieval chalice found in tiny church in Bristol, England, sells for 8 million pounds."

"Don't you think that's a little more than a coincidence?" Inez looked sick.

"Sister Anne wouldn't murder anyone." I was incredulous.

"Well, what's she doing with this article, then?"

"That's her field, medieval stuff, and it's only natural she would be interested in that article."

"I think we have to tell the police," Inez whispered.

"No, wait a minute. You can't really believe it was Sister Anne?" I tried to be reasonable.

"I don't know what to believe anymore. Ever since your note

I've realized that the murderer could be anyone. I mean anyone, all the way up to Mother Alphonse. There are very few people who know the chalice was stolen. Just a handful."

"Did Sister Anne know anything about it? Did you tell her?"

"No, not a word. She and I are in the same department, but we're not friends. I haven't even talked to her since the murder. This is all on her own, which makes it really scary."

"Well, it could just be a coincidence."

Inez rolled her eyes. "A coincidence? That's convenient."

"It is kind of strange."

"I'm going to go talk to her tomorrow."

"What? I don't think that's a good idea." I wasn't going to go with her, that's for sure.

Inez had it all figured out. "I'll go by myself and just ask her about the article and see how she reacts. I'll tell her I'm sorry, but I noticed the article when I picked up the book. It was out there in plain sight."

"Which makes it more unlikely that she was trying to hide anything."

"Oh and come by this evening before you go to bed. I have a plan to make you a lot safer. It's better than any knife. Were you okay last night?"

I loved how I was an afterthought to the whole chalice saga.

"No, I slept in an empty dorm and was awake the whole night."

"Hey, I'm sorry. It'll be better tonight. I promise. Come up at nine."

I snuck up to her office after prayers. She was waiting for me. "Here's a key to an empty room on the third floor. The trouble is that it's in the cloistered part of the building, so you'll have to make sure nobody sees you go in, but once you're in there it should be okay. Set your alarm clock early, though, so you can sneak back to your dorm before the bell. It's room 348, really close to the doors leading inside."

I felt a lot better about this idea, even though I had no business in that part of the building reserved for the nuns who had already taken their vows. If I could sneak into the room, no one would find me all night. I would be able to sleep.

"Okay, thanks. I really appreciate this."

"I hope it works out okay. You better start out in your dorm so Miriam won't have a fit, though."

I got ready for bed and laid down in my bed until Miriam came by an hour later. I didn't think she would ever stop by, but I couldn't chance leaving without her checking up on me.

I waited ten long minutes even after Miriam, then took the key and snuck up the large staircase to the third floor and down the long corridor. All I had to do was go through the swinging doors, find the room and slip in, and I would be safe for the night. The corridor was empty. I started to turn the key in the lock. I have no idea where she came from, but I heard a voice whisper behind me, "What are you doing?"

"I'm using this room tonight." I tried to sound sure of myself.

"You don't belong here. What's your name?" She sounded angry.

"Joan. Joan MacIntyre. That was the first name that I could think of.

"Are you a postulant?"

I was caught. There was no way out of it. At least she didn't know my real name.

"I'm going now." I turned quickly and walked down the hall. I was afraid she would yell at me or follow me, but she was too old and large to do that. She would report me to Sister Miriam tomorrow but I would have been safely in my dorm. Miriam had already checked. I ran back as quickly as I could. I grabbed my pillow and blanket and snuck to the empty dorm once again. At least I felt safe there. And Inez at least had tried.

I went with Inez to see Sister Anne the next day. We both knew I would, and she didn't have to try very hard to convince me. I wanted to hear what Sister Anne had to say, and I knew that her first response would be telling. I didn't want to miss that.

"Sister Anne?" Inez knocked politely on the office door.

"Come in." All the books were stacked neatly on book-shelves. Even though I had Sister Anne for English Literature that first semester, I had never been in her office.

"Sister, when I was picking up that book yesterday, I happened to notice this article about a chalice."

Anne's face brightened. "Isn't it amazing. That chalice is worth over eight million pounds. Those people had it in their parish for hundreds of years without knowing anything about its value."

She smiled as Inez handed her back the article. "Would you like me to make a copy for you?"

"Oh, no, that's okay. I just didn't know that you were interested in that sort of thing."

Sister Anne looked down at her desk. "Well, honestly, I'm not, but Mother Alphonse asked me a few days ago to find out all I could about medieval chalices, and I was at the St. Louis University library and found this article."

"Why would Mother Alphonse want you to research that?"

"Do you know the chalice that's in the display case outside of the chapel?"

We both nodded.

"Well, apparently it's very old, and she was interested in just how old it might be, and how valuable it might be, too, I suppose. I don't think it's worth eight million dollars, but who knows?" She laughed her little embarrassed laugh that I had heard all the time in class. She was an endearing person.

"Have you told Mother Alphonse about that?"

"Oh no. I just started my research. I imagine there's no rush.

That chalice has been around for a long time. It's a good thing the case is locked, though."

"Well, thanks. I hope you can find out some good information on it. Good luck."

Anne didn't want us to leave. "If you want any of the articles I find, I'll be glad to Xerox them for you. I didn't know you were interested."

"That would be great," Inez acknowledged. "I'd appreciate it. Thanks." We walked out the door.

We were quiet till we got back to Inez's office. "Well, that's not what I was expecting. I don't think she's the murderer."

"No, of course not. But it also means that Mother Alphonse really wants to know the value—and doesn't."

We sat in silence. I finally asked Inez if she had any more Cokes. She pulled out two, and gave them both to me.

"You need them more than I do. I can get them anytime. Oh, and how did last night work out? Did you finally get some sleep?"

"No, I got caught, and had to run back to my dorm. At least I gave the nun a fake name so I won't get thrown out for that!"

"Shit. I'm really sorry. I don't know what else to do." Inez at least looked genuinely worried. And I felt a little better knowing that she had at least tried.

I realized that even though we knew the murderer was monitoring our little investigation, we really had no other leads. Every road—and there were so few of them—led to another dead end. I shuddered at the words. Not a good metaphor right now. I still had the night to worry about.

Inez was deep in thought. I sat drinking the Coke.

"Okay." She startled me. "I have an idea. Your friend Joan works in the sacristy, doesn't she? Let's have her ask Father Steven something, or give him some information about the chalice, and we'll see what his reaction is. Does Maribeth ever work in the sacristy?"

I sighed. "I don't know. That's not her job. But all the junior sisters help in the sacristy at one time or another. They all have to so that when they go to parishes they can work in the sacristy."

"Have Joan say something like, 'The police found the chalice.' Then, if he has it hidden anywhere in the motherhouse, maybe he'll go and search for it."

"That's just plain stupid." I was so frustrated. "Joan isn't going to walk up to him and say that."

"You're probably right. But I want to do something, and I have no idea what to do."

Inez sat chewing on an already worn-down fingernail.

I couldn't sit there silently any longer. "Look, I'm the one who got the note telling me to stop the questions. I'm the one who was threatened. I'm the one who doesn't have a safe place to stay at night. You're the one who promised to help me find a safe place. I know you tried, but I'm done with this investigation. I think the detective is right. We need to leave this up to him and the police. He'll check out the chalice and the junior sisters and the homeless shelter. I'm not doing anything else. I need to stay out of it. Or you can call him up right now and tell him about Sister Anne and Father Steven and your brilliant idea. He can do the questioning. Not me. I'm done."

I couldn't believe I had said all that to her, but I was really finished with it all. I was scared, and she was pushy and wanted me to do everything. She didn't have to worry about the consequences, but I did.

Inez was quiet for a full minute. Then she started talking. "Look, I'm sorry. I can understand why you're angry with me about the protection thing, but I tried to think of something. I really tried. I thought it would work." She tried to look remorseful, but it wasn't working anymore.

She continued, "And as far as the investigation, this thing about having Joan ask Father Steven isn't really something that the police can do. It's just a little something to get his reaction. He probably won't react at all, and why would we even tell Detective Kelly about something as trivial as that? If he does react to it, then we'll talk to Kelly about it. But not now. We can do this on our own. It's simple, and we're not interfering with the investigation at all."

I finished my Coke and we sat in silence. I was so tired of Inez and her interfering, but I guessed she was right. Kelly wouldn't want to hear about something so stupid as a question to one of the priests. It was a dumb idea, but if it could get a reaction out of him, it might just be worth it. I couldn't think of another thing to do, and Inez couldn't either.

I threw the empty Coke can in the trash can across the room and made it.

"Ok, I'll ask her, but only because I can't think of anything else to do. But don't try and make me do anything else, because I won't. This is it. I mean it."

I went up to my empty dorm for another sleepless night. I did fall asleep once but had the most frightening dream about tornados and seeing one come straight at me before I woke up in a cold sweat. I listened to the crickets and the sound of a thousand tiny bugs outside in the sweltering June night and wondered what the future would bring.

CHAPTER 15

Joan and Maribeth sat out in the large assembly room listening to me practice. Afterwards I sat with them and talked for a while. I remembered what Joan had said about Maribeth, but she seemed lots of fun today, laughing and talking about classes and one of their teachers until the three of us were laughing so hard we were almost crying. But often she was moody, almost silent. I was glad it was one of her good days, because she was delightful.

We talked a little about the murder. Joan wondered if the police had gotten any leads, since they had released the boyfriend, and Maribeth thought that the chalice was a stupid idea that wouldn't lead anywhere.

"I'm sure they'll find that old chalice somewhere. I still think that Father Raymond got it out of there and just forgot. He's starting to forget everything. You've heard his sermons. They're mostly the same, week after week."

I nodded. She did have a point. I told them I had to practice more, just in case my music teacher came by, and walked up to the front of the hall. They sat in the back, doing some homework, whispering a little, but mostly listening. I finished the Ravel piece—Joan's favorite one—and then went back to where they were sitting.

"Hey Joan, could you do me a big favor?"

"Sure, what is it?"

"I know this is going to sound silly, but it's important. On Sunday morning, when you're in the sacristy with Father Steven, I need you to say something."

"Yeah, like what?"

Joan was looking skeptical already, and Maribeth was frowning.

"Tell Sister Evangeline, and talk loud enough that Father Steven hears, 'The police have found the chalice.'"

"What? They have? Where was it? You never told us that!" Joan said quickly.

"No, they haven't. I just want you to say that to Evangeline so that Father Steven hears it."

"Are you still on that chalice thing? You've got to let it go. Do you really think that Father Steven murdered that girl? You're being ridiculous." Maribeth looked concerned.

"Look, that's all you have to do, just say that. It's not that big a deal."

"Other than being a complete and total lie," Joan said. "And then what am I supposed to do? Follow him as he goes running from the sacristy?"

I laughed. "I doubt that's going to happen. I'll take care of him. I'll be watching him after Mass."

She stared at me. "You're serious, aren't you? You think he's the murderer? You've got to be kidding. And besides, he could just take the chalice. He wouldn't have to kill anyone!"

"Just do this for me. And check his reaction. And let me know if it's suspicious."

Maribeth shook her head. "You and Inez have gone totally overboard on this thing. Really."

I wanted to tell them about the note card that I got, but I had made a promise to David Kelly.

"Look, if he doesn't react, and if he's not the murderer, then it won't do any harm to say that. Will it? What harm will it do?"

"Well, it's a lie, and he'll think we found the chalice. I don't know. Lies just have the worst way of getting back at you when you tell them. I don't like it." Joan was very honest.

"So the worst is that he won't get the chalice back. Big deal. It's not his anyway. It's the convent's."

"Okay, okay. I'm tired of arguing. I'll say it, I'll say it."

"I think it's really stupid, but I'm not the one doing it," added Maribeth.

"Thanks, I really appreciate this."

CHAPTER 16

June 12

I went up to Inez's office that evening.

"Have you asked Joan about tomorrow?"

"Yeah. She wasn't happy about lying, though."

"Kristen, we have to rule some people out."

"At this rate, with so many nuns in the motherhouse, it's going to take a long time."

"No, it won't. We're only going to rule out the people with direct access to the chalice. I think we're getting closer."

She smiled. I had pretty much decided that her smiles meant nothing. A few weeks ago I thought she was quite brilliant, an inspiration to me. Now I didn't know what to think. We were in this together, this ill-fated investigation. The murderer didn't have anything to worry about from us. I just wish he or she knew that we were as far as possible from solving anything.

Inez was a good person. I had seen Inez at her best and at her worst. She was a brilliant, young, liberal teacher whom I had admired greatly. She was also an interfering, overbearing, pushy person and I was getting tired of it all. I hated to realize that she was just an ordinary human being. What did I expect from her? That every day would bring a new insight into a piece of literature or a new challenge to my way of thinking? Life wasn't like that.

And I was still struggling with whether I wanted to go on in religious life. Every day I wavered. I hated the rules and regulations, the mundane and the tedious, but I did have hope that I would be doing some good for others by teaching. And then there was David Kelly. Most of the boys I had known in high school were so immature, I wasn't the slightest bit interested in them. But he was different. I liked the way he looked at me. I was sure it didn't mean anything. He was just concerned that I wouldn't be murdered. That was all. But every time I thought about him, I wanted to get rid of this horrible habit and ugly shoes, and at least have a chance to look pretty. I wasn't very good nun material if I was thinking that. Maybe I shouldn't go on. Maybe I should just quit right now. But I would never see him again or ever find out who had murdered the girl. I had only a few more months to decide.

★ ★ ★

Inez looked out the window at the dark lawns below. "The murderer is still in this convent. Remember that. It's going to be a person whom we don't suspect. They're not going to walk up and announce they've killed someone. I know you don't like asking Joan to do this, but I think it will help."

"She sure isn't happy about lying to a priest."

"Well, I'm not happy knowing there's someone in this motherhouse who killed someone and is threatening to kill you."

I didn't answer because I didn't want to say what I was really thinking. What good would it do? She wasn't happy someone was threatening to kill me, but she wasn't worried enough to actually do something about it. I still felt let down by her. This lying to Father Steven was going to be the end of the investigation for me. But did the murderer know that? And how could I ever let them know that I was done with the investigation—done with Sister Inez's crazy ideas? Would I have to worry every night for the next few years or months until the murder was solved— if it ever was?

I thought a lot that sleepless night in the empty dorm—I was getting used to it by now—about how the people who had the most access to the chalice probably didn't steal it. It had to be someone else. It could be any junior sister who worked in the sacristy and saw Sister Evangeline use the code to get the chalice out on a feast day, or had access to Father Raymond's keys when he set them down in the sacristy to say Mass. But that would have taken some elaborate planning. And how did they know the victim? They might have met her at the shelter, but how could they persuade her to dress up like a nun and steal a chalice? None of this made sense.

CHAPTER 17

June 13

The next morning I got dressed quickly and got to the chapel early. I sat through the Mass as Father Steven droned on and on. His Sunday sermon was on the Gospel reading about the Prodigal Son. How someone could take a perfectly good story with lots of meaning and turn it into utter and complete boredom was a miracle. My mind wandered the entire hour, and only came back to the present when he muttered, "Thanks be to God." I always felt the "Thanks be to God" referred to how thankful we were that the Mass was over.

I wandered over to the sacristy door and heard someone say, "I heard that the police found the chalice."

I could hear the clinking of metal on metal as someone washed something in the sink.

I waited by the chapel door. It wasn't Joan who came out, but Maribeth. She took me by the arm and propelled me to the side of the corridor. She looked pale.

"I said that to Father Steven. Joan was sick this morning, so I'm here instead. He got really red and I could tell he was upset. He stormed out of the sacristy—the other door."

"Where did he go?"

"Well, he headed down the corridor to the postulancy. Maybe he's going down to the basement … Don't you go down there!

I have to finish up in here and then we can talk." She turned and walked back into the sacristy.

I stood with my back to the cool wall, waiting for Maribeth. I wasn't going down to the basement alone. The minutes clicked by. How long was she going to take?

I walked out of the chapel and slowly down the hall. If Father Steven was going to the basement, I had to stop him from getting the chalice. This might be my only chance. I couldn't wait for Maribeth. I walked quickly to the elevator and stopped.

The elevator was moving down to the basement, only one floor down. It had to be him on the elevator. I pressed the well-worn red button. My hand was shaking. The elevator gradually slid back up and came to a pained stop in front of me.

Should I run back and get Maribeth? I shouldn't go down there alone. But by that time, he'd be long gone, and Inez and I would wonder all the rest of our lives what had happened—and what had happened to the chalice. I couldn't be down there alone with him, but everyone was eating breakfast in the main dining room.

I pulled open the rusted grate, then the second one, and stepped on the sagging elevator. I pulled the grate closed and pushed the button for the basement.

The elevator settled with a thump the last few inches. My heart was beating quickly as I got out. I peered down the dark, empty corridor. *I'll go to the right, down the narrow corridor to the trunk room.* That was all there was down here, besides endless winding corridors and dead ends.

Dead ends. I cringed at the word. Damn these stupid shoes. They clicked on the concrete floor with every step. I tiptoed as quietly as I could down the corridor till I reached the catacombs. A few of the bare lights were on, illuminating the shadows and white walls.

I started to shake. Uncontrollably. I stopped walking. I had always been afraid of these walls closing in, and the weight of the entire building above me. It didn't bother me when I was upstairs, but here it was so closed in and dark, I felt claustrophobic. And I hadn't been down here since the night of the murder. When I passed the spot where we had found the body, I felt like I was going to pass out. But I couldn't. I had to keep going.

I walked slowly through an area of piled up trunks, probably belonging to sisters who had died. The dust was thick on all of them.

Then I heard a sound. I stopped. The clicking of my shoes stopped.

"What are you doing here, Sister?" a voice came from behind me.

I screamed a tiny squeak and turned. Father Steven stared at me, his face dark in the dim light.

"I'm sorry I startled you," he said kindly, and for a minute I thought everything would be fine. He was okay. I was just being ridiculous.

"Are you following me?" he said softly. Oh my God, he knew. He knew I had deliberately followed him. Then he smiled broadly and laughed. He was joking.

I stuttered, "I'm sorry, Father. I didn't know you were here. I'm getting some things out of my trunk."

He started looking at more trunks. "Sister Evangeline asked me to get some items for her. She can't get down here anymore."

I thought of Sister Evangeline and how hard it was for her to walk. But she would have asked another nun, never a priest.

"Did you find her trunk?" I tried to keep my voice steady.

"No, maybe you can help me. I think it's back there." He pointed to the furthest alcove, a dead end.

Oh hell! Should I go with him? Was I walking into a trap, or was he really trying to help her out? Shit, I didn't know. Father Steven was okay. He had always seemed nice, and I felt sorry for him, stuck saying Mass in this old motherhouse for the old nuns.

But he had been so upset about the chalice. Why was that? Was he the murderer? If I was right, I could be killed.

"You go ahead," I told him.

He squeezed by a few trunks. "Do you always come down here alone, Sister?" His voice was caring. He always seemed like a kind person. He didn't seem angry right now. I was just being paranoid.

Think quick. "Well, I'm not really alone. Sister Maribeth is coming to help me."

He looked confused. Then he smiled like he knew something I didn't know. Maybe he knew that Maribeth had no intention of coming down here. Oh God, he knew something that I didn't.

I was all alone. He brushed the dust off the top of the trunk where the names were written as he walked ahead of me. Was he trying to show me that I would never find the chalice he had hidden?

We got to the last trunk. "I guess I got the directions wrong. Oh well, she'll have to have someone else help her. You go ahead, Sister."

He wanted me to go out first. Was I completely paranoid? No, I had to go first. He couldn't have squeezed by me if he had wanted.

I had to do something. I had to say something.

"Do you know where that old chalice is? Did you take it?"

Father Steven looked at me sharply. "What are you talking about?"

"You know. The chalice that Father Raymond uses. The one you took from that girl when you killed her."

There. I said it. Oh my God. Why did I do that? He's going to kill me.

"I have no idea what you're talking about. Are you sure you're okay?"

"We know what happened. You were with that girl when you both stole the chalice and then you murdered her right here in the basement."

Father Steven stared at me. His eyes were confused—and angry.

"How dare you accuse me of that. I don't know anything about a chalice, and I had nothing to do with the death of that girl. I'm getting out of here. Let me by."

I backed up to the trunk—practically sitting on top of it—as he squeezed by me. I couldn't let him just leave. But I didn't know what to do. He didn't have the chalice. I had no proof.

He took one last look at me.

"I have no idea what's wrong with you, Sister, but if you're serious about this, you should tell the police. Then you'll know for sure that you're being completely ridiculous."

He stomped through the rest of the trunks and down the corridor.

I was so angry with myself. I had confronted the man who had killed someone, and I was powerless to prove it. I felt weak. He could have killed me, too. Why didn't he? I sat down on the nearest trunk. What had I just done? I was lucky to be alive.

I heard someone call my name.

It was Maribeth. Thank God. "Back here."

She ran up to me. "Are you okay?"

"Yeah."

"I told you I'd come with you. You're crazy coming down here by yourself. I saw him going down the corridor. Boy, was he angry."

"I told him that we thought he had the chalice and that he had killed that girl."

"You what? You said that to him?"

"Yeah, but what good did it do? I don't have the chalice. I don't have proof. And now he's going to go and tell everyone that I accused him. I thought for sure that he was getting the chalice."

"Let's get out of here. Wait, you look terrible. Sit down here for a minute. I need something out of my trunk. I'll be back in a second. It's down in the next section. Just sit. We'll think of something. Don't worry."

I sat on the trunk. I was shaking. Maribeth would think of something. If she didn't, I would be out by morning. I had just accused a priest of murder. And I had no proof. She was right. I should have never come down here alone. I put my head in my hands. I was feeling faint.

I heard Maribeth coming back. She'd help me get out of this mess I had put myself in. I felt a surge of appreciation for her wonderful friendship. I turned my head slightly. Then I felt a searing pain, the worst I had ever felt in my life. I saw Maribeth standing over me, ready to hit me again with the metal chalice. The gems looked ragged and sharp. I put my hands up. Then everything was black.

CHAPTER 18

"Wake up. Can you hear me? Can you open your eyes?" I looked up into the fleshy face of Father Steven. His face was inches from mine.

"Can you stand up?" he asked.

I mumbled something. I don't know what.

He pulled me up to a standing position. Then I didn't remember anything else for a while.

I heard the elevator clanking. He pulled open the grate, dragged me out and leaned me up against a wall in the familiar corridor that I cleaned.

"Help! Somebody, help!" he yelled. "We need an ambulance. Somebody get an ambulance!"

I heard voices—a lot of them. I opened my eyes and saw Steven's face over mine. Worried. I said one word, "Maribeth … "

And then blackness again.

CHAPTER 19

I opened one eye. I could see the slits of sunlight on the ceiling. I didn't know where I was. Then I saw the intravenous drip and the metal rails of a hospital bed. My parents sat across the room with their eyes closed. I lifted my arm to my head. I felt bandages.

"She's awake." My dad stood up. My mom stood up quickly and came to the side of the bed.

"How do you feel, honey?"

"I guess okay. What happened?"

"You're pretty lucky. You had an operation to repair a skull fracture and over 70 stitches. You're lucky that priest found you before you lost too much blood."

"I have to talk to the police."

"No, no, you should just rest."

"No, I have to talk to Detective Kelly."

My mom looked at my dad.

"He was that policeman who was in here this morning. He said to call him at the station when you woke up."

"Let me get a nurse." My dad walked out of the room.

Soon the room was bustling with people. Nurses came in and out. My parents sat quietly across the room.

"He said he was on his way—that policeman."

"Good." I closed my eyes.

The next time I opened my eyes my parents were gone. David Kelly was sitting next to the bed. He smiled at me.

I had to tell him about Maribeth but I started coughing. He poured a small glass of water and helped me sit up and drink.

"It was Maribeth, another nun. She was the one who hit me with the chalice. It wasn't Father Steven."

I closed my eyes. My head hurt.

"Don't talk anymore. I just needed to hear you say that it was Sister Maribeth who attacked you."

"Yes. Not Father Steven."

"Just rest. I'll be back later."

I must have slept a long time, because when I woke up the room was dark, lit only by the faint lights out in the hall. I felt better—and wide awake now that everyone was gone. I clicked on the light behind the bed and glanced at the clock on the green wall. Three in the morning.

I wondered if Inez had been to see me. I guess she knew by now what had happened. We had been right about the chalice, but wrong about the murderer. I couldn't believe I had been so wrong. I had never even suspected Maribeth. She was my friend. Now that I thought back, I should have realized that she needed the money. Maybe her mother didn't have the money for her operation and that was the only thing Maribeth could think of. But why did she kill someone? Nothing made sense.

How could I have overlooked that? Because she was my friend, and I thought I was a pretty good judge of character. I wondered how many other people I was wrong about. Inez and I thought we could solve this murder. Now I realized how stupid I had been.

When I woke up again the sun was streaming across the bed.

"Come in," I called as I heard a knock.

Detective Kelly walked in the door with a small vase of wild-flowers in his hand.

"Hello. Where should I put these?"

He pulled the tray over at the side of the bed and set the vase in front of me.

"Thank you," I blushed.

"How are you?" He pulled up a chair.

"I'm fine," I said automatically.

"No, really, how are you?" he said again.

"Well, my head hurts a little, but it's my ego that hurts the most. Inez and I did a really bad job solving the murder. I had no idea it was Maribeth. She was my friend."

"But you did solve the murder—sort of. Even though you almost got killed doing it."

"Where's Maribeth?"

"She's in jail right now waiting arraignment on one murder charge, and your attempted murder."

"My attempted murder? She hit me on the head, but that was all."

"You would have bled to death if Father Steven hadn't gone back and found you."

"Father Steven. Oh yeah." I hadn't even thought about him. "Why did he come back?"

"He was very upset, seeing as how you had accused him of murder, and went back to talk to you. When he got there he saw you lying on the floor, bleeding. He got you to the elevator and got an ambulance. You lost a lot of blood."

"But how would killing me help Maribeth?"

"No one knew that she had been down in the basement, and a number of people had heard that Father Steven was going down there to help Sister Evangeline. So she saw the perfect opportunity to pin your murder on him."

"I can't believe how wrong I was about everything. I accused Father Steven, and he came back and saved my life."

"Not everything. You knew the chalice was the key to the murder, and you and Sister Inez were right about that."

"I should have suspected Maribeth. I guess she needed the money for her mom's operation."

He looked at me oddly. "What operation?"

"Maribeth's mother needed surgery for cancer."

"Maribeth doesn't have a mother or father. She was raised in an orphanage run by your sisters in Minnesota. She was planning on leaving the convent and was going to sell the chalice and use the money for her new life."

I sat silently. The whole friendship was a lie.

David interrupted my thoughts.

"You're looking much better than you did yesterday."

My hand went to the bandages on my head.

"Not that. I mean, your hair is very pretty. I didn't know it was so red, without that ..."

"Veil?"

"Yeah, that." He looked down at the floor. "You know, the district attorney is going to have to take your deposition."

"I know."

"But it'll wait till you're out of the hospital."

I nodded. "I'll probably get out in a few days."

He was quiet for a few seconds.

"I think it'll be longer than a few days. Where are you going when you get out?"

"What do you mean?"

"Your parents really want you to come home. They told me that yesterday afternoon."

I wasn't ready to argue with him about being a nun.

"I'm not going home," I blurted out.

"They were hoping you would."

"They never did approve of the convent," I explained.

"I agree with them," he said quickly.

"What do you mean by that?" I said it a little nastier than I meant. My defenses went up.

"Hey, I don't mean anything. I just wish you weren't going to be a nun. I'd like to get to know you better."

My head hurt. I didn't want to get to know him better. Yes, I did, but I wasn't going back home. That would mean everyone else was right and I was wrong. I was old enough to make choices about my own life. I knew what I wanted to do, even if I couldn't explain it.

"I don't want to talk about it right now."

"I understand. And I shouldn't stay any longer. You should get your rest. I'll see you tomorrow."

I managed a smile as he left. "Thanks for coming to see me."

"I'll be back."

After he left, I closed my eyes, but the room seemed strangely empty. I wondered if Inez had come to visit. The day stretched out long before me. A nurse came in. She handed me a couple of pain pills.

"Time to take some medicine."

She filled up my water bottle and moved the wildflowers closer.

"That policeman sure likes you."

I smiled. "No, he doesn't. He's the detective assigned to the case."

"Well, honey, that doesn't explain why he's been here for the last three days, just sitting and waiting for you to wake up."

I blushed.

"Really?"

"He's been here more than anybody else."

"I didn't realize that."

"Well, I know you didn't. That's why I'm telling you." She walked out smiling.

CHAPTER 20

Another doctor, a neurosurgeon, came in the room, talked with me for a few minutes, and told me it would be at least a few more days till I could be released. When he left the room, I reached over to the phone to call the motherhouse but stopped. I laid back on the pillows. The window was open and the oak trees shimmered in the morning light. The sunlight lay quietly in strips on the tile floor. I had the room all to myself, the first time in a year I wasn't in a dorm. My head hurt a little but my mind was surprisingly clear.

My decision was already made. I had made a commitment, and I was going to stick to it, at least for another year. My pride wouldn't let me admit that I had made a mistake. I felt sure, not of being in the convent and becoming a nun, but sure that I had to try. The future stretched out in front of me. I could do whatever I wanted. I had helped solve a murder.

The Kristen that had entered the convent months ago had disappeared. I had been frightened by all the rules, by the towering history of the order and the church, of all those who had known so much before me. Now I had seen the flaws of the priests, the Mother Superior, and most of the rules. Not that I was any better, I reminded myself quickly. But equal, yes. I would never again give in to tradition and authority if I knew that I was right.

David Kelly's questions had just made my decision a lot easier. I couldn't explain it to myself or to him, but I had to try to make the best of this life I had chosen. The room seemed empty now that he had left. I almost wished he would come back and we could talk about the murder, or what he was thinking, or just about anything.

My parents spent most of the day in my room, and Inez stopped by. She talked a lot about how right we had been, and how lucky I was, and how happy she was that I was alive. She didn't say much about how wrong we had been. She gave me some of the gossip about Maribeth, but she didn't really know very much.

I heard a quiet knock on the door the next morning. It was Joan. She gave me a hug and started crying right away.

"I'm so sorry. I had no idea that Maribeth had done anything wrong. I can't even believe that she was capable of murder, and to try to murder you, her friend. It's just unbelievable."

She kept on crying. "I'm so, so sorry."

"Joan, there's nothing to be sorry about. She deceived us both."

"But I should have known. I've known her for a lot longer. I should have seen what she was really like. I'm so sorry."

I asked Joan to tell me how Maribeth had planned the murder, because I was curious, but also so she wouldn't keep crying and telling me how sorry she was.

Joan had gone to see Maribeth in jail and had a long talk with her. Maribeth didn't seem to care who knew the story, now that she had been caught. She told Joan that she had met the girl at the homeless shelter in the city. They had a lot in common. Maribeth didn't have a family and the girl wasn't speaking to hers. Maribeth told the girl that if they stole that chalice and sold it, they could split the money. Maribeth had gotten the code months before when she watched Sister Evangeline get into the display case. She got the black habit out of the sewing room, gave it to the girl, and left the sacristy door open so the girl could get in the building. She came on the bus, so there was no car to trace.

Maribeth just took Father Steven's key off his key ring one morning during Mass, knowing he would never miss it. Maribeth met the homeless girl in the chapel late that night, the night that Inez and I were in the office talking. They took the chalice, replaced it with another old one from the sacristy, and went to the basement. But then the girl said she was keeping the chalice. Maribeth killed her and hid the chalice in her trunk.

Her friendship with me—with all of us—had been a lie. She was only in the convent to get a degree and whatever she could steal, then get out and start her real life.

"Were you really sick that morning when you were supposed to ask Father Steven about the chalice?"

Joan looked out the window. "No, I just couldn't lie to him. I asked Maribeth to be the sacristan that morning; I told her I didn't feel good. I knew she'd never ask him about the chalice. She thought it was a stupid idea anyway. I had no idea it would fit into her plans perfectly. I'm so sorry. I was going to tell you later that I just couldn't lie to him, but by then it was too late."

After Joan cried some more, and we talked about how we both had been deceived by Maribeth, she left but promised to come back often to check on me. I slept fitfully, dreaming of that moment when I had turned and saw the chalice above me. I replayed the moment every time I closed my eyes. I woke up often from strange and frightening dreams.

As soon as visiting hours began the next morning, David came. We talked a little about Maribeth and Father Steven, and how the police had sent the chalice away for an appraisal. He showed me a picture of it. It had been cleaned, and it was a work of art. The jewels in it were so large I didn't see how they could possibly be real. He told me he couldn't tell me much about the investigation itself, but I had heard most all of it from Inez and Joan anyway.

I closed my eyes for a second. My head was hurting again.

When I opened them, David had put the folder down and was looking at me.

"You don't really like me coming by here, do you? I keep asking you questions about your life, and you seem very offended by that."

I didn't say anything for a second.

"I do like you, really," I tried to explain. "I just don't like the way you're always attacking my lifestyle, and what I want to do with my life. It makes me very uncomfortable. And it's my life. I don't question what you've done with your life, why you became a policeman or detective. Why is my choice any better or worse than yours?"

"My job is being a detective. It's not my life. I can go home at night and do what I want, someday getting married if I want and having a family. But you can't ever do that. Being a nun is your entire life."

I didn't say anything. I didn't have the energy to argue. He kept going. "I know. I just don't understand your choice at all. I'm just curious about it. But you just seem to be annoyed whenever I'm ask about it."

"No, not annoyed with you. More annoyed with myself, because I can't explain what I'm thinking. And I don't have to explain anything to you. It's just something that I know is right for me."

"Maybe I should just wait and see you when you get out of the hospital and are feeling better. Okay?"

"That's probably a good idea," I said without thinking.

He stood up quickly, touched my hand, and said goodbye. I mumbled goodbye.

After he left, the aide came in with my hot breakfast, but it was tasteless. The day stretched out in front of me. I tried to read a book but got a headache after a few pages and put it down. I stared out the window at the blue sky dotted with white clouds. A clear June day.

Why did I say those things to him? I wished he were here. The thought of not seeing him for the rest of the day—and the rest of my hospital stay—made me unexpectedly sad. And when would I see him again? There would be a deposition and trial, but I'd only have a small part in that. There might not even be a trial. Maribeth had confessed to the murder. Why did I feel so angry with myself?

The day seemed empty. The wildflowers looked wilted. I wondered where he had gotten them. All of a sudden there were so many things I wanted to say to him. What had I done?

CHAPTER 21

The neurosurgeon came in early three days later. "Good news. I think we can discharge you today. Are you ready to go?"

"Oh yes."

I was so tired of hospitals. No sleep, hospital food, being awakened every hour by a nurse to take my blood pressure, or blood. Oh yes, I was ready.

After the doctor left the room, I pulled over the phone and dialed the motherhouse. No one answered in Sister Miriam's office. They were probably having instructions. I'd wait.

I got out of bed and got dressed in the habit I found hanging in the closet. It still had the bloodstains all over it. I couldn't believe that no one had thought to clean it in the whole week I was in the hospital. I packed my little plastic bag and tried calling again. This time Sister Miriam answered. "You're coming back?" she said in a surprised tone. "Oh, of course. Do you need us to get someone to pick you up?"

"That would be great!" I answered more enthusiastically than she sounded.

"Well, I'll see what I can do. Give me your number at the hospital and I'll call back."

"Okay, thank you." I hung up the phone.

She sounded less than happy to hear from me. I sat in the

uncomfortable chair by the window. I could see the roof of the hospital with its air conditioning ducts and vents, and it wasn't a pretty view. In the distance were some houses and the highway.

I finished signing all the paperwork, which took about forty-five minutes, and still no one had called. I couldn't call my parents. How embarrassing to tell them I couldn't get a ride back to the motherhouse. I read a book for another half an hour. Another nurse came in and asked if I needed to fill out the lunch menu. I said no.

David. I could call David. We had parted badly, but I really wanted to see him again and he was the detective working on the case. I grabbed my purse and found his number.

"Could I speak to detective David Kelly?"

"Who may I tell him is calling?"

I gave my name.

"Hold on, please. I'll put you through to his office."

"Detective Kelly speaking."

"Uh, hi, this is Kristen … from the convent." I said lamely.

"Kristen, how are you? Are you out of the hospital?"

"Well, that's actually why I'm calling."

I was feeling stupider by the second. He was busy. Why would he, of all people, be able to pick me up? I should have called my mom and dad.

"I'm being discharged today. Right now, actually, and the convent cars are all being used. They don't have many of them. (I was too embarrassed to say they hadn't bothered to call back.)

"Is there any way you could bring me back to the motherhouse?"

Oh God, I should have never called him. What was I thinking?

"Of course. You're not going home? You're going back to the motherhouse right away?"

"Yes."

"Hold on a second." I could hear muffled voices for a minute. Then he came back on the line.

"I can pick you up in fifteen minutes. Where will you be?"

"In my room."

"Okay, see you there."

"Thank you."

I had to leave the hospital in a wheelchair. Hospital policy. The nurse wheeled me down the long, busy corridor with David by my side. I felt ridiculous, dressed as a nun, with this tall, handsome man next to me. We got in the elevator to a few stares which I tried to ignore. David walked outside quickly to get his car.

The nurse helped me from the wheelchair. I would have gotten up by myself, but she insisted. I hated when people made a fuss over me. I should have just waited for someone at the convent to come.

"I'm sorry, I shouldn't have asked you to pick me up."

"Don't be silly. I'm glad to do it." He paid the money at the gate, drove onto the main road, and reached over and took my hand.

I didn't pull my hand away. I wasn't sure what to do. If I pulled my hand away, it would be insulting to him. I knew he shouldn't be holding my hand, but it felt good. The only other boy who had ever held my hand was Rick Schroeder in eleventh grade in a movie theater. It was all sweaty, and I pulled my hand away quickly. This was different. David had a strong, steady hand. I liked that he liked me. I had too many thoughts going through my head—plus a headache. He kept up the conversation, asking about my recovery time and how could I rest at the motherhouse, all the while holding my hand and playing with my fingers. I turned my hand over and held his. He jerked his hand away suddenly as a car pulled in front of us but put it back immediately over mine.

I felt so comfortable talking with him. I told him the truth. That I couldn't get hold of anyone at the motherhouse that seemed interested in getting me. He just shook his head slightly, but didn't say anything. The ride was long, about forty minutes, but we talked the whole way.

"Where do I turn? I always miss the street."

"It's the next block. The light."

He turned on the avenue leading to the motherhouse. It went by factories and a used car dealership. He pulled over in the next block and stopped.

"This isn't it."

"I know." He put the car in park and leaned over and kissed me. It was a real kiss, on the lips. It caught me by surprise, but I didn't pull away. For a few seconds I felt our lips together. It was wonderful. I could hardly breathe. And then again, even longer. And I couldn't pull away. I wanted more. Then he turned back to the steering wheel, put the car in drive, and continued.

"I'm sorry. I shouldn't have done that. But I don't know if I'll ever see you alone again—and I just had to show you what you mean to me."

I didn't say anything for a minute. We pulled up to the front drive of the motherhouse.

"Let me help you with your things."

He carried my little suitcase up the stairs with me as I rang the bell.

I looked down. "Please don't be sorry. I'd like … I'd like to see you again. I really hope I do," I said lamely as the front door opened and a nun I didn't know looked at me oddly.

"I'm going to the postulate …"

"Come in," she motioned to both of us.

I turned to David. "Thank you so much for bringing me home … and for everything else. I know I'll see you again."

"Sure," he said, but without much meaning in it. "And I hope you keep feeling better and better. Take care. Call me if you have any more questions about the investigation."

I wanted to hug him but I didn't dare. I felt like there were a thousand eyes on me from all the windows of the motherhouse.

He turned and walked to his car.

I walked down the corridor to the empty study hall. Sister Miriam saw me walking by her office and came out.

"How did you get home?" she asked accusingly.

"I called the detective, and he picked me up," I said simply.

"Well, that was unnecessary. We would have gotten you."

"But when? I never heard back from anyone and I couldn't wait any longer at the hospital."

"It was foolish to call that policeman. It makes us look like we wouldn't bother to pick you up."

Which is exactly what happened, I thought to myself. I decided not to say it, though. I didn't have the energy for any more arguments, and my head hurt.

I was right back home, that's for sure. Rules, rules, always doing the wrong thing, and more rules. I was so tired of it, tired of everything.

I just looked at Miriam and said, "I'm going upstairs to sleep. That's what the doctor told me to do."

She just stared at me as I turned and walked slowly down the long corridor and started up the flight of stairs. I had to take it slow. I couldn't believe how tired I was. She hadn't even asked how I was.

And all I could think about was the kiss. No one had ever kissed me before. I had gotten a few pecks on the cheek but never a kiss like that. As I trudged slowly up each step, all that kept me going was the thought of him. I could still feel his lips on mine.

I had to see him again. But how could I see him and get more kisses and still live this life? It wasn't going to work.

I finally reached my dorm. I peeled off all my filthy, blood-stained clothes, put on my nightgown, and laid down on my bed. That's the last thing I remember.

When I woke up it was completely dark. I looked at my watch. It was twelve-thirty in the morning. I had slept almost twelve hours. And I hadn't even called my parents. Well, I couldn't call them now. I'd call them first thing in the morning.

CHAPTER 22

I woke up again that morning and came down in time for breakfast and study hall. It felt strange to be back in the motherhouse. I felt out of place, like I had been gone a long time. The hospital room had seemed friendlier, with all the people coming to visit, and the flowers. And being able to talk to people freely. The motherhouse seemed cold and sterile. Pam was really glad to see me. So was Sylvia and a few other friends, but most of the postulants looked at me strangely, like I was the one who had killed someone. Well, I had accused a priest of murder.

I muddled through the day, going to classes but not really being there except in body. We had lunch and then dinner. I was back, but it would take a while to get back into this life. And the memory of that kiss kept haunting me every few minutes of the day. I remember the evening clearly. One of those rare summer evenings that cooled down after a sudden thunderstorm. The bugs chirped and buzzed in the evening air.

We walked into the study hall and pulled out our books as usual, even though I felt the opposite of usual. I needed to go back upstairs and sleep. Sister Miriam walked up to my desk.

"Come to my office," she whispered.

I felt more than a little special. She always yelled out our names if she wanted to see us.

I walked behind her and sat down in the chair across from her desk. She turned around and closed the door to her office.

I was expecting a question about how I was feeling, and then the appreciation for solving the murder, which we had never talked about. Not flattery—not from Miriam—but at least a few words of concern and appreciation.

"Kristen, after you went to the hospital, and I talked with Sister Inez, I began to realize the extent of your involvement in this murder investigation. You have broken every rule in this convent. I wasn't aware that you and Sister Inez were actually pursuing this investigation and not grading papers. I was not aware that you had met with Mother Alphonse and that she told you to stay out of the investigation. She was, and is, by the way, perfectly capable of handling this with the police.

"I had no idea you had talked to the old sacristan in the infirmary, but believe me, all this has now come to light. And now the slander involving Father Steven's name and the unfounded allegations of murder against him!"

"I'm sorry about that, but Sister Inez and I did solve the murder."

"The real problem is your absolute disregard of authority."

I sat quietly. Let her rant. I didn't have the energy to argue with her.

"Mother Alphonse and I have discussed this at length, and we feel it is not in anyone's interest to have you continue as a member of this order. She only feels bad that she let you stay so long and let that detective persuade her to let you remain in the order after the murder of that girl. You should have been thrown out immediately."

My head hurt. I didn't say anything.

"Tomorrow morning you will call your parents. You will not join us for Mass or breakfast. You will remain in your dormitory to pack and dress in the clothes your parents will bring. You will tell no one about this. Do you understand? By tomorrow at noon you will be gone. I don't want to hear any excuses. Mother Alphonse has made this decision and it's final. Do you have any questions?"

"No."

"You'll be given fifty dollars to help start your new life. You may go now."

Fifty dollars! Wow. That would get me a few meals at a restaurant for a week. I guess if I went to McDonald's I could stretch it out for two. But what did I expect?

I stood up, my head pounding. I really hadn't thought this would happen so quickly. I remember walking to the door, opening it, and walking out to the study hall. I had to tell Inez. But I couldn't get upstairs.

I sat at my desk, idly flipping my pen over and over, as my eyes filled with tears. This life was over. I had tried, and would have tried harder, but it was over. I would say my final prayers and go and see Inez. I had broken every rule anyway, what was one more? The grandfather clock chimed nine times. It echoed up and down the long corridor. I would never hear it again. For some reason that made me feel sad. It was like leaving a friend. I left my books and pulled down the wooden top one last time.

Maybe I could get into Washington University for the fall semester. I couldn't think right now. I could still get a degree and do whatever I wanted.

I walked slowly up to Inez's office. My head was pounding. Her door was closed and the office dark. She would have no idea I was leaving. I turned and slowly walked up the steps to the dorm. As I took off each piece of clothing for almost the last time, I threw them over the chair. I sat up in my bed for a long time watching the grey chapel windows, the bell tower, the lights gradually turning off one by one, as another quick thunderstorm passed overhead.

I couldn't think about getting thrown out. Well, so much for my choice. It had been made for me. I watched the city lights flicker in the distance, disappearing where the Mississippi met the land. I could see the moving light of a tugboat churning up the river.

I shed a few tears, but not many. I was smart and young and I could do anything.

I thought about how glad my parents would be. And David. He would be thrilled. What would happen? Would I call him and tell him? No, too much was happening. I just couldn't keep up with it all.

I wasn't angry with Miriam and Alphonse. I should have been, but I wasn't. They were doing what I would have expected. They couldn't act any other way. The rules had so taken over their thinking that they couldn't see anything else.

The next morning went by in a blur. I got dressed in the habit for the last time and waited up in my dorm for Sister Miriam. Going to the trunk room one last time with Miriam while everyone was at Mass was horrible. I felt physically sick to be down there. I remembered every detail of the night of the murder and of my own attack like it was happening again in real time. I kept looking over my shoulder. I got a few books and some extra notebooks from my trunk. I would ask Inez to get my music books and send them to me at home.

I felt relief wash over me as we got back up to the study hall and I got my textbooks from my desk. Miriam had nothing to say, no word of thanks, or "it was good to know you." Just a curt goodbye when my parents came. I took the clothes they brought, went back upstairs to my dorm, and dressed carefully in a skirt and silk blouse. I still had bandages over one section of my head. My hair was short, but red and curly. It would grow out soon.

My parents, kind and smiling, were careful not to show how thrilled they were. I walked out the front entrance, got into their car, and the brick fortress disappeared forever in the side mirror. A silent trip in the car, past the river and arch and walking into my tiny house that seemed to have shrunk in the past year. The whole house was about the size of one of the large parlors on the first floor of the motherhouse. It was so strange and sudden to be back home. I couldn't quite make sense of it. It had happened too fast.

CHAPTER 23

The next day, the bewildered and angry call came from Inez. She seethed about the stupidity of the rules for a long time, about the unfairness of it all. But there was nothing she could do. We turned to what I would do in the future, and what recommendations she could write for me. She had gone to St. Louis University, but I was tired of Catholic things, and thought I might try to get into Washington University. I could enter as a sophomore. As I hung up, I realized that we wouldn't be friends any more. Too much of the friendship was built on the investigation and the convent, which were now closed doors.

I went into my old tiny room and laid down on my twin bed with the green quilt. I heard the phone ring. I closed my eyes. My head hurt.

"Yes, she's here," my dad said in his Irish accent.

"I think it's that detective," he said as he knocked on my door and pulled up the phone, cord and all, to give to me.

"Was that your father?" David asked.

"Yes, it was."

"Are you at home? I didn't recognize this number."

"Yes."

"Really? Are you there for a visit?"

"No, I'm not in the convent anymore. I left."

"You left? But I just took you back there yesterday! You were so determined to stay. What happened?"

"I got kicked out."

"Kicked out? Well, I'm not surprised."

"Yeah, I guess not. I know you were the one who helped me stay after the murder."

David sounded surprised. "You weren't supposed to know about that. Who told you?"

"I think Inez told me the next day, in great detail. That's when I really started to appreciate you."

"And you did help solve a murder."

"And I broke a lot of rules doing it."

"Can't they see what's important? That solving a murder is worth breaking a few rules?"

"They don't see it that way." I stopped for a second. "David, do you remember what I said the other day in the hospital? About being annoyed with you?"

"Yeah, I remember. I stayed away after that ... until you called."

"Well, I'm really sorry I said that to you. You were right all along. About everything."

"Listen, I don't want to be right. I just want you to be happy."

"After you left, I missed you so much. I wished I hadn't said that about you. And I can't stop thinking about the ride home from the hospital."

"I've thought about it a lot, too."

He didn't say anything for a few seconds.

"Where do you live?"

"In North St. Louis, off Highway 70 and Kingshighway."

"Can I stop by and see you? I promise I won't talk to you about your life choices. Or breaking rules. Or murders."

"Well ..."

"I have a better idea. If you feel okay, I'll pick you up and we can go out to dinner, instead of the convent. And maybe a ride afterwards."

I thought anxiously, a knot in my stomach, of all the rules I'd be breaking to do that. Then the knot untied slowly, and I realized there were no more rules.

"I'd love that." I smiled.

#2
SILENT NIGHT

CHAPTER 1

November 1967

Sister Anastasia, Catholic nun, 87 years old, woke up suddenly in the middle of the night. Where was she? She reached over and turned on her bedside lamp. Now she remembered. She was in her small room at the convent in Franklin, Missouri, where she had lived for a lifetime.

She pushed off the heavy quilt and sat up. The moonlight shone through her open window onto her desk. That's where it was. She really needed to hide it. She was afraid they would steal it from her. Her mother and father would be so upset.

Sister Anastasia sat on the side of the narrow bed and put her wrinkled feet on the cold hardwood floor. She reached out to her walker and pushed it ahead of her as she padded barefoot across the floor. She opened her desk drawer and took it out. Where to hide it where no one would find it? She walked to the cupboard and opened a large cardboard box of old essays from her English students. Some of her own journal writing was there, too, long forgotten. She hid it underneath the essays and pushed the box to the back. There were so many boxes in the cupboard. She would have to go through them in the morning.

She walked unsteadily back to her bed, took a long drink of water, lay down, and fell asleep quickly.

In the morning, she told Sister Hilda she was feeling a little fuzzy. She had forgotten all about the box. She would never remember it again.

CHAPTER 2

March 31, 1968

I was watching Ed Sullivan with my parents when the phone rang. I jumped up to get it, hoping it might be David, even though I had just seen him yesterday, on Saturday. We usually went out on the weekend to Cunetto's, a little Italian restaurant in South St. Louis.

We had been dating for about seven months, ever since I left the convent. He had already asked me to marry him twice, but I had been out of the convent less than a year, and he was my one and only boyfriend so far. I wasn't ready to get married.

My classes had started at Washington University last fall, but I hadn't even decided on a major, much less marriage.

"Hello," I answered.

"Kristen, it's Sister Inez." It had been a few months since I had heard from her, but we were still friends, I suppose. She and I had investigated the last murder at the motherhouse, if you could even call it an investigation. I had gotten kicked out because of it, but she had been promoted to president of the college.

"Hey, congratulations on your new job," I told her sincerely. She was a forward-thinking, liberal educator who would be really good for the college as it was connected to our very traditional order of nuns.

"How are you liking being president?"

"Oh, it's fine," she shrugged it off. "That's not why I'm calling. Have you heard about Sister Anastasia?"

"She was the granddaughter of Franz Gruber. Right?"

"Yes, the one who was in the infirmary for a while when you were here."

"Yes, I got to meet her a few times. She was wonderful. What about her?"

"She died last week."

"Oh no. She was such a sweet person. And so interesting."

"Yeah, but that's not the worst thing."

"What do you mean?"

"The police say she was murdered."

"Murdered! What do you mean?"

"Well, nobody is saying much, but it happened out in Franklin, Missouri, where she lived in our convent there, Our Lady Queen of Angels. And it happened at night. Somebody apparently murdered her in her sleep. I don't know, poison or something, they didn't say, but the paramedics and coroner were sure about it. Has your friend David said anything about it?"

"No, not a word. He's probably not even working on it, or he would have mentioned it."

"Well, I don't know how the police are going to figure it out. It's going to have to be somebody on the inside who figures out who killed her."

"Yeah, right. I've heard that before. Which leaves out you and me."

"Not necessarily."

"Oh, Inez, be serious. I'm not a nun anymore. We can't just go gallivanting out there to investigate a murder. I have nothing to do with the police besides the fact that I'm dating a policeman. Besides, I'm no good at investigations. And neither are you, remember?"

"Okay, here's the thing. I found out that you *do* know someone in the convent there: Sister Elaine Wells."

"Elaine? She's Pam's sister."

Pam had been one of my best friends in the convent, besides Joan and Maribeth. Elaine, a few years older, had been my "big sister" in high school. When we entered as freshmen, the school paired us up with a senior to help us make friends and learn about the school. Elaine and I became friends. That's how I had gotten to know her real sister, Pam, who was in my class. Pam and I later joined the convent together with a few other girls from our senior class.

She had just left the convent in December, a few months after I had gotten kicked out, and I had talked to her just a few weeks ago.

Inez went on. "I know you're on spring break after next week, and I thought maybe you two could visit Elaine and check things out."

"What? Are you crazy? David would have a fit. Oh, and thanks for planning my life!"

"Why? You would just be visiting a friend. He's probably not even working on the case. They have a little retreat house behind the convent for visitors. I've seen it. It's for when people come for retreats or for out-of-town guests. You could go and spend a few days there visiting Elaine."

"No way. There's no way I'm going to do that."

"You know the police are never going to solve it."

"Yes, they are. Remember, that's what they do. They solve crimes and murders. And what if it was Elaine who killed her? I've been wrong before about my friends, remember?"

"No, it wasn't Elaine. She was at a conference all last week when Sister Anastasia was killed. It had to be one of the other sisters there."

"Inez, I'm not going to do this."

"If Pam went to visit her sister, I'll bet the three of you could have a great time together and investigate the murder on the side."

"Inez, stay out of this. I'm not going to do this. How many times do I have to say it? Goodbye."

I hung up the phone. Yes, I know it was rude, but I had to end the conversation.

I was still angry at Inez from the last "investigation." She had promised to protect me when I had been threatened by the murderer—but didn't. She had gotten me into trouble unnecessarily for weeks; she was an interfering busybody. I had come to terms with who she was, and we maintained a Christmas-card kind of friendship, but nothing more. I was finished with the convent—and all convent-related things, including her. I couldn't believe she had the nerve to call me and ask me to investigate this murder.

The *Ed Sullivan Show* was over when I came back in the living room. Mom mentioned quietly, "I hope that wasn't David?" She could hear at least part of the conversation. I didn't want to talk about it, so I just said, "No," and left it at that.

As I lay in bed that night, trying to get to sleep, I remembered I had spoken to Inez one other time last September, a few months after I had gotten kicked out. I needed to know how to contact Father Steven, so Inez gave me his telephone number where he lived at Holy Angels Parish about twenty minutes south of the motherhouse.

I had accused him of murder, and it was time I apologized to him.

I made an appointment to see him with the parish secretary one Friday afternoon in late September. The parish office where the priests worked was set far back from the church and I found it only by asking. It was a poor building, sorely in need of repairs. It looked like it had been built in the late forties and needed a paint job and new siding. I walked in the door, apprehensive about what I was going to do.

"I'm here for my appointment with Father Steven," I told the secretary. She led me to his door and knocked. He opened it, ready for his appointment, but clearly surprised to see me. I was sure he hadn't even looked at my name or recognized it if he had.

"I'm here for my appointment." I could see the sudden recognition on his face. He backed up quickly.

"Can I please talk to you for a few minutes?" I took a step towards him.

"Okay," he said, sounding unsure.

He invited me into his office. I had rehearsed my lines. I took a deep breath.

"I came here today to apologize for what I said to you a few months ago. I had no business accusing you of murdering that girl, and I regret it and ask your forgiveness. And I want to thank you for coming back and saving my life. I'm really sorry for what I said and I hope you'll forgive me."

I was expecting him to be angry, to not accept my apology, or to at least give me a lecture on the impropriety of it all, but what I wasn't expecting was that he laughed. A lot. A delightful laugh.

"Of course I'll accept your apology," he said happily after he stopped laughing. "I've never been accused of murder before, and although I hope I'm never accused again, I have to admit it was quite a unique experience, one that I'll never forget. I'm so very glad I came back and was able to find you before you bled to death. I think God was looking out for you that day, and I'm so pleased he used me to save you. I've thanked him many times for that opportunity."

"You're surprised, aren't you?" He must have noticed my open mouth and stunned expression.

"Well, yes, honestly I am. I wasn't expecting that."

"I've become quite popular in my priestly circles and beyond, telling the story of being accused of murder. I can't tell you how many people have asked me to retell it. And since I'm the one doing the telling, I'm afraid I've come out of it quite the saintly and courageous character. I hope you don't mind that."

By that time I was laughing, too. I could see him at the center of a large group of people, delighting them with his fictionalized version.

He kept going. "Yes, of course you're forgiven, and I'm glad you came down here to talk to me. Sit down. Sit down." He motioned to the chair to my right and I sat.

"Have you completely recovered? That was quite a blow to your head."

"Yes, I had a lot of stitches, but no lasting injuries, thank God. I had a lot of injuries to my ego, accusing you of murder, getting kicked out, and not realizing my friend was a murderer."

"Oh well, that's how we learn, isn't it?" He smiled. "It takes a long time to learn everything. I personally have a long way to go. What are you doing now?"

"Well, I got kicked out of the convent after I recovered, as you probably know, and I started school last semester at Washington University. I'm hoping to get my degree in English and still plan on teaching, just not as a nun. And I'm going out with the detective who investigated the murder case."

"No kidding," he chuckled. "You didn't waste any time, did you? I think that's great—not that you got kicked out, but that you seem to have picked up right away and are going back to school and everything."

"And how are you?" I asked. "Are you still going up to the convent three days a week to say Mass?"

"Yeah, it's not the most interesting job in the world. Actually, the murder there was the most exciting thing that's happened in years. I sort of felt bad when it was all over. I was very sorry that you got injured and I'm happy to see you fully recovered, but it really is boring going up there three days a week. I have enough to do here at my own parish. Hopefully they'll find someone else to go next year."

We talked a little longer about reforms in the church and the fate of Sister Maribeth, how she had deceived everyone, how I had gotten involved, and by the end of our meeting, I felt as if I were leaving an old friend. We promised to stay in touch, but I knew how those things usually worked out. There was too much distance and difference in our lives for anything to be sustained, but he certainly was more delightful than I had ever imagined. I was so glad I had come. That was the last I had heard of anyone connected to the convent or the murder until this call from Inez.

CHAPTER 3

April 1, 1968

I got home from class the next afternoon and had the house to myself. Mom was teaching and Dad was still at work. The phone rang. Oh God, I hoped it wasn't Inez. I wasn't going to go through that again, even though I did feel terrible about Sister Anastasia's murder.

It was Pam. I was so glad. We talked a little bit about how she was doing. She had just found a nice apartment and was going to start a new job in a few weeks.

"Hey, Kristen, I have a great idea."

Oh no. I already knew what it was and who had suggested it.

"I think I'm going to see Elaine next week. I was talking to Sister Inez and she said you were free all week for spring break. You wanna come with me?"

"Were you going to see Elaine before you talked to Inez?"

"Well, no, but she said you might be interested in coming with me, and we could have fun, the three of us."

"I don't know, Pam."

"Think about it. I'd love for you to come. I'm definitely going to go for a few days— maybe a week. Elaine would love to see you. And you and I could do stuff during the day when she teaches. She'll be off most of the week. Otherwise it'll be kind of lonely for me. Please?"

"I'll think about it and call you back, okay?"

"Call me back soon though. I'd want to make plans for next week."

I hung up the phone. Inez was president of the college, for God's sake. She didn't have time for this. That's why she wanted me to go out there and do the work. Well, I might just go out there and do absolutely nothing except relax and have a good time with Pam and Elaine. There wasn't anything wrong with that. I would take Inez's suggestion and throw it right back at her. I wouldn't do a thing except have fun. In fact, the more I thought about it, the better it sounded. Maybe it would teach her a badly needed lesson. Even if it didn't, I could still have fun all week with my two friends, especially Pam. Elaine would be teaching for the first few days, but Pam and I could catch up and talk and shop all week. I wouldn't do one single thing about the murder, no matter how much Inez hoped I would.

I did feel bad about Sister Anastasia, but I didn't know anything about Franklin, Missouri, and I wasn't going to figure anything out in a week, much less a murder.

I didn't breathe a word about it to David when we went out to dinner on Saturday night. It was so much fun to spend the weekends with him. We usually had dinner at my place on Sunday afternoon. My parents loved him. He was Irish, which fulfilled their wildest dreams. He was kind and thoughtful, had never been married, was a policeman—and even more than that—a detective! They wanted me to marry him and couldn't quite understand why I had turned him down twice.

He in turn loved my parents. His parents had been divorced when he was five years old. His mom had moved to Spain and remarried. His dad had been around, but didn't pay much attention to him, and he was mostly raised by his dad's parents in St. Louis. His dad had died about ten years earlier, and his grandparents were gone, so knowing my parents was a wonderful experience of a real family, and he loved it—and them.

I mentioned that I was going to spend most of the week with some friends, which was the truth. He would know soon enough. He mentioned that he was working on another convent murder, so I knew it was Sister Anastasia's. I was prepared to act surprised to hear about it. He would have a fit when he realized that I would be there.

In our seven months of dating, that was the only thing we had ever disagreed about. He felt that Inez had overstepped her boundaries and had gotten too involved in trying to solve the murder in the motherhouse. She had dragged me into the investigation too and I was the one who almost got killed. I agreed with David that we should have let the police do the investigating, but the murder would never have been solved if it hadn't been for Inez and me. Luckily there weren't going to be any more murders so the topic would never come up again. Until now. I wondered what he was going to say.

CHAPTER 4

April 8, 1968

I picked Pam up Monday morning in my new Plymouth Duster, courtesy of my parents, and we drove out west to Franklin, Missouri. It was a beautiful drive, only about twenty minutes from the center of St. Louis, but still in St. Louis County, David's jurisdiction. The sun was shining bright and the leaves were just beginning to turn the trees a soft lime green. The two-lane highway wound through rich farmlands, already plowed and ready for planting.

We drove up from the Missouri River road and used the old church with its tall steeple to find the convent across the street. I parked out in front and we walked up the concrete steps to the front door.

I noticed the peeling paint on the handrail and the door of the convent. The building was old and brick, at least a hundred years old. The second story had a lot of windows. Heavy drapes covered all of them, their pale undersides looking out on the street below. We knocked on the old wooden door.

We rang the doorbell a few times, and then knocked again.

"I wonder if they even remember we're coming."

Just then the door opened a crack and a hefty old nun peered out.

"You must be Sister Elaine's sister, Pam," she said energetically.

That was obvious. Pam and Elaine were the only two Black sisters in the province, or had been, until Pam left last month. Now Elaine was the only one.

I reached out for her hand.

"I'm Kristen, Pam and Sister Elaine's friend. Nice to meet you."

"I'm Sister Hilda. Come on in." She smiled warmly at us both. We walked down a dark corridor into an even gloomier formal sitting room. I'd seen funeral homes that looked friendlier; I hoped the retreat area was more welcoming. Brocaded material covered the six armchairs in the room. An Oriental rug, threadbare in spots, covered the entire floor. The drapes were heavy and green with cream tassels up and down their edges. Retro 1800s?

"Sit down, dears. Would you like some tea?'

We sat, just like we had been trained to do. I could have used a Coke or Dr. Pepper but didn't dare ask for that. I was sure there was a drugstore in town where we could get one later.

Sister Hilda returned in a few minutes with three cups of hot tea and a bowl of sugar and spoons. We sipped our tea as she talked.

"You do know what happened here a few weeks ago, don't you?" she started, sounding properly sad but eager to share the gossip.

"Yes, we heard about it from my sister," Pam answered.

"Oh, of course, she was such a dear. And now they're telling us she was murdered. Well, I simply don't believe it. That investigator is coming back today to interview a few more of us."

"When is he coming?" I tried to ask innocently. "We don't want to get in the way."

"Oh, don't you worry. He's coming after school gets out. You know, they didn't even tell us how she died. And to think she had her very last meal in our kitchen with all of us. Nobody got poisoned from that meal, I can tell you. It was my chicken marsala recipe. I'm sure I'd like to know what happened."

Pam was polite. "What can you tell us about her?"

I would tell David that I hadn't even asked about her—it was Pam!

"Oh, she was a dear. She had dementia, or old timers', or whatever they call it these days. She was a great-granddaughter of Franz Gruber. That was her name: Anastasia Gruber."

"Franz Gruber? Wasn't he the composer?" I acted surprised, even though I knew the story.

"Oh yes, he composed 'Silent Night.' When she was younger, it was an interesting story to hear her tell it, but in the past few years that was all she talked about."

"How could she talk about it so much? She couldn't have known him." Pam asked.

"Of course not, but she knew her grandfather, his son. And he had so many stories about his father that he had heard from him. Poor soul, she got so paranoid these last few years. That's what dementia will do. Always accusing people of stealing things. She'd cry, and say someone stole "it," and nobody knew what she was talking about. Whatever "it" was, I'm sure her niece and nephew got it after she died. They came and took everything. Just this last week."

I reminded myself that I was not investigating a murder. I was here to enjoy myself with Pam and Elaine. But I wasn't going to be rude and stop Sister Hilda from talking. And it was interesting to hear her talk.

"What did she have that they could have wanted?" I found myself asking. I was glad David wasn't around.

Nuns in our order took a vow of poverty, chastity, and obedience. We didn't have any worldly possessions, so I couldn't imagine what she had that was valuable, although my ears perked up at the thought. "Anything of value" might be a good motive to murder her.

"Oh dear, her walls and closets were full of beautiful artwork. She had gotten it from her parents and grandparents. I mean, the real thing, not posters like the rest of us have."

Pam asked, "So the artwork was the thing she was talking about?"

"I don't think so. I think there was something else. Well, I guess we'll never know now, will we? Those relatives came for her funeral and took all the paintings. They had a will that they showed to Sister Janine and then when we were at the reception after the funeral, they came back here and took all the artwork and left."

Sister Hilda paused. "Sister Janine was furious, but she didn't know anything more than their names. She had their phone number, but when she called, it was out of service. We haven't seen them again."

My mind was racing. But her niece and nephew couldn't have murdered her because they weren't even here when she died. I wondered how valuable all those paintings were. And no, I wasn't going to think about it. This was David's investigation. I wasn't even supposed to be here.

Sister Hilda stood up. "Would you girls like to see where you'll be staying?"

"Oh yes, we'd love to," I answered quickly.

She chatted all the way down the corridor, through the kitchen, out the back door, and just a few feet to a ranch style retreat house that had a kitchen, small chapel, and four bedrooms with a common bath. It looked like it had been built only a few years ago. It was so much lighter and more modern than the convent. I breathed a sigh of relief. I wasn't sure if I could have taken a whole week in that gloomy brick, mortuary-style convent.

"Do you use this a lot?" I asked.

"Yes, we do. I wondered why Sister Janine wanted to build it, but we've used it for many small retreats, Bible studies, prayer groups, and then for visitors and families and out of town guests. Just last week Sister Anastasia's relatives stayed here for her funeral. It's used almost every week."

Pam couldn't stop talking about the artwork. "Did Sister Janine call the police when all that artwork was stolen?"

"I don't even know," said Sister Hilda. "She doesn't tell us much. I just know she was plenty angry. I told that detective all about it when he interviewed me. He just nodded. I couldn't tell if he knew about it already."

Pam and I unpacked a few things from our bags in our separate rooms, which were right next to each other. My room had a window that looked out to a park-like area with lots of huge oak trees just beginning to show feathery shades of green. It was beautiful. I thought I might have a really nice, relaxing time here. Especially if I didn't run into David. Maybe he would never even know I had been here. I would make sure Pam and I were far away from the convent when he was around.

Wait! Why was I hiding from him? The best thing would be to see him and say hello. It was none of his business why I was here. I wasn't doing anything that would interfere with the murder investigation. I wasn't doing anything wrong. It just seemed like it.

School must have just gotten out because I could see Elaine rushing down the corridor and into my room. She gave me a big hug. "Kristen, it's so good to see you. Where's Pam?"

"She's in the next room."

Pam heard her, came running out, and they hugged.

"Hey sis, I'm so glad you guys came out here. We're going to have some fun. As much as we can in Franklin!"

Pam, Elaine, and I went back to the main kitchen where we poured some glasses of cold milk and had a few chocolate chip cookies.

"I made them for the detective," Sister Hilda whispered loudly. "But I'm sure he won't mind. He only had one the last time he was here."

I just smiled. I'd have to remember to make him some home-made cookies. I didn't even know he liked them.

Elaine, Pam, and I walked down Cedar Street, past the old, abandoned tire factory, and found her favorite café right across from the train station.

I finally was able to get my Dr. Pepper, Pam got her Coke, and Elaine had a glass of water.

"This is your chance, Elaine. You don't get those at the convent," Pam said.

"That's okay. I'm not used to all that sugar anymore."

I guiltily drank my Dr. Pepper, but still enjoyed every sip of it. It was delightful to catch up with the two of them. This seemed like it would be a really nice week. By the time we got back to the convent it was after three. I cringed as I saw David's dark blue Thunderbird parked in front, right behind my Duster. I hoped he hadn't noticed. I'm sure he had. He was a detective.

He was probably in an interview. I would just sneak in, go down the corridor, and stay in the retreat area till dinner.

I walked in the door with Elaine and Pam. David was standing at the entrance to the parlor with Sister Janine and a woman police officer. His eyes opened wide when he saw me, then he turned back to Sister Janine.

She graciously turned to us. "Detective Kelly, this is Sister Elaine. She's one of our sisters, but she was at a conference last week when Sister Anastasia died. And this is Pamela, her sister, and their friend, Kristen. They're visiting for a few days."

David recovered quickly and smiled. "Nice to meet you all. This is Sergeant Miller." He turned back to Sister Janine.

"We're ready for the next interview, Sister."

I walked to the kitchen with Elaine and Pam. Oh, I would

hear about this. I just didn't know when. He couldn't call me here at the convent. There were only two phones, as far as I knew, probably one in Sister Janine's office, and I had seen one in the corridor by the kitchen. But I knew he'd be talking to me, soon.

I grabbed a chocolate chip cookie on the way through the kitchen and escaped to my room. I took out my Jane Austen book, walked outside, and found a chair on the porch. The March sun was a comfortable seventy degrees and I tried to concentrate on the book, but it was difficult.

It was even more difficult a few minutes later when a pudgy tuxedo cat wandered up to the chair and jumped into my lap.

"Well, hi kitty. Who are you?" It, or he, had a name tag which said JC. He made himself comfortable in my lap and started purring. That was the end of my reading for the moment. He was a beautiful, overly friendly cat. I wondered if he belonged to the sisters. He belonged to someone. There was a telephone number on his tag, but I couldn't remember if it was the convent's.

Elaine and Pam found me a few minutes later. They were in the middle of a discussion about Sister Anastasia. I hadn't even started it.

"I hate to interrupt your discussion, but is this your cat?" I finally got to ask.

"Oh yeah, that's JC. He wandered in one day, and stayed, and nobody knew what to call him, and Hilda said, 'He's just a cat,' so we started calling him Just a Cat, and it got shortened to JC. And it's appropriate for our religious beliefs, maybe slightly blasphemous. Isn't he a beauty? He usually comes in at night and sleeps in the laundry room or my room or wherever he wants. Sister Hilda feeds him twice a day, although it looks like more. He's a lover."

"He's wonderful," I agreed, petting him as he purred loudly.

"Yeah, I sure can't imagine who could have killed her." Elaine went back to the murder.

Pam answered, "Well, it had to be somebody here. Did they say how she was killed?"

"No, they didn't. But it happened overnight, so it had to be somebody who came into her room and killed her."

She whispered to Pam, "I think there were a lot of reasons why someone would kill her."

Pam looked surprised. "You really think that?"

I just listened. I could hardly not listen. They were right next to me. Sorry, David.

JC jumped down from my lap. I hated to see him go. As soon as I had enough money, whenever that day would come, I would get an apartment and a cat. I could hardly wait.

I listened to the conversation.

"Yeah, I do," Elaine continued. "Okay, there's Sister Hilda. I know she's a sweet person, but Sister Anastasia had been so sick and had dementia and Sister Janine refused to put her in a home, so Sister Hilda was the one who had to take care of her. I mean, the rest of us tried to help, but we have to teach, and Sister Hilda ended up doing all the work. And she's seventy-five at least. She just can't do it all anymore. It's too much for her. I know that's a terrible thing to say, but Sister Hilda might not have seen any other way out of a bad situation."

Pam said, "Who else would want to kill her?"

"Well, you know all those stories about her grandfather, and how there was something that Sister Anastasia was paranoid about? I think there really was something she had, and someone might have killed her for it."

I couldn't help it. "But why didn't they just take it? Sister Anastasia wouldn't have even known. Or why didn't they just wait until she died? It wouldn't have been that long."

"Hey, I don't know. I'm just guessing. And all that artwork? That stuff was expensive."

I couldn't help but comment, "It looks like somebody got that anyway. Maybe that was the reason for the murder."

Elaine looked down. "You know, I'm probably the only person here who didn't like Sister Anastasia. Well, not the only one, but I wasn't even here when she was killed. She was a horrible racist, and we didn't really have much to say to each other. But she got pretty confused in the past six months or so, and she was a lot nicer after she got dementia. Do you know what she said when she first saw me here?"

"No, what?" Pam said.

"I walked into the parlor when I first got here in September, and everyone said hello, and she looked at me and said, 'When did they start letting darkies in the order?'"

"Oh my God, she really said that?" I couldn't believe it.

Elaine said, "She was old. She came from a generation that thought like that. I wasn't going to change her, so I just ignored her. I'm glad I wasn't here last week. They would have blamed her murder on me, for sure."

Pam looked at her sister. "No they wouldn't. You would have never done anything like that."

"Of course I wouldn't. I try hard not to hurt anyone. But someone around here did something pretty awful and I'd sure like to know who it was."

JC returned and jumped in my lap again. I felt like the chosen one. He had a felt mouse toy in his mouth. Elaine commented, "JC loves to get things from around the house and carry them. He's kind of like a golden retriever we used to have when we were growing up. It's kind of cute. He likes his mice, but he'll grab string and shiny things, too."

As I sat there petting JC, I couldn't help but wonder what

David would think of all this talk. I hoped he was discovering as much as I was. And I wasn't even supposed to be finding anything out!

We had a very nice dinner that evening of roast, vegetables and potatoes, and I was introduced to the rest of the sisters. There was Sister Hilda, whom I had already met. She looked so tired that I couldn't help but feel sorry for her. Sister Janine was severe looking with big bushy eyebrows and a persistent frown. She was the superior of the convent and the principal of the high school. No wonder she looked so grumpy. Those were two difficult jobs.

Sister Patrice taught art and was tall and thin. She looked like the stereotypical artist, thinking about something else all the time, something more important than gossip. I met Sister Caroline, who taught biology and chemistry. She was in her twenties, seemed very shy at first, very tall and beautiful. Her complexion was perfect without any makeup, white with a hint of peach, the kind that would be on the cover of some fashion magazine. I wondered how David liked interviewing her. Sister Susan was the principal of the grade school. She was in her forties and seemed very serious and harsh. Then there was Sister Martha, who taught music and band. She was in her thirties, a little overweight, and for some reason had kept the old traditional habit, like Sister Janine and Sister Hilda, and seemed pleasant enough at dinner. I tried to keep them all straight, but I wouldn't be interacting with them except at breakfast and dinner, so there wasn't too much point in remembering their names. And I didn't care about any of them. I was here to have fun with Pam and Elaine.

We could have gone out to eat every night, but neither one of us had any money, so we were glad to eat at the convent, even though we did have to listen to convent-related subjects for the entire meal.

The phone rang during dinner. Sister Martha got up to answer it.

"Kristen, it's your father."

"Thanks." I got up and grabbed the phone, a little worried. It wasn't my dad, it was David.

"Kristen, you need to call me first thing tomorrow. Go down to a public phone in town and call me at the office. We need to talk."

"What time is good, Dad?" I asked cheerfully.

"Call me at nine. Okay?"

"Ok, thanks. Love you, Dad, bye." I hung up and walked back to the table where everyone had heard the conversation.

I didn't say a word but sat back down as the conversation resumed. No one said anything about Sister Anastasia. I guess that topic was off limits, except in private. A few sisters helped serve the dessert, a homemade apple pie with vanilla ice cream. No wonder Sister Hilda looked tired. I couldn't imagine doing all the cooking, most of the cleaning, and taking care of Sister Anastasia full time. But she sure didn't seem like the kind of person who would kill anybody.

After dinner all the nuns sat around in the parlor and watched TV. I had quite enough of sitting around with nuns when I was in the convent, of course without the TV, and was glad to escape to the backyard of the retreat house where I met my date for the evening, the beautiful black-and-white kitty. We had a nice conversation, even though he didn't have a word to say about who had killed poor Sister Anastasia. Not that I thought I was going to find the killer anyway, by idle conversation with the cat or anyone in the convent. Yes, David, you are correct. I'm staying out of this one for sure. We did have a nice talk about David and what I was going to say to him in the morning, although JC had no particular advice for that. I was on my own.

I wasn't looking forward to that conversation, and as I brushed my teeth that night, I kept reminding myself that I was doing absolutely nothing wrong. Nothing at all. I had nothing to do with the investigation. If Pam and Elaine wanted to talk about it and speculate about it, that was their concern, not mine. And I wasn't about to tell David anything I found out. Let him figure it out on his own.

CHAPTER 5

April 9, 1968

The next day everyone was off school because of Holy Week, so breakfast was a little later in the morning. I told Pam that I was going to walk down past the train tracks to look at the river. She didn't even express any interest in going with me. I told her I'd be back in a half hour or so.

I asked Elaine about a market and walked down the three blocks to Spencer's supermarket on the corner. I didn't know the town, but I knew how to get down to the Missouri River and back. I hoped there would be a phone booth outside the market, and luckily there was. I walked inside the tiny booth, smelling the mustiness and the faint scent of urine. I left the door partly open, put a dime in the top compartment, and dialed David's number. He answered right away.

"Hi David."

"Kristen, what the hell are you doing in Franklin?"

"Visiting a friend, Sister Elaine, for a few days, maybe a week. It's spring break, cause Easter is Sunday."

"You never said anything about it."

"I don't tell you everything, you know. I told you I was visiting someone this week."

"Is this some half-baked idea of yours and Sister Inez's?"

I was quiet.

"Are you two thinking that you can solve this murder?"

"Look David, I'll be completely honest with you. This did start out as Inez's idea. Elaine is Pam's sister, which you could probably tell. She called me and she called Pam, separately, and I told Inez that I had absolutely no interest in coming out here to investigate anything. I even hung up on her. I really did! But then Pam decided to visit her sister, and she called me back and asked me to come. It actually sounded like a fun week for all three of us, and I decided to come. Not to investigate anything. In fact, that's the last thing I want to do. I'm just going to have a good time with Pam and Elaine. I don't want to hear anything about Sister Anastasia. Nothing at all."

"I wish I could believe you. You need to stay out of this investigation. I know you think that somehow you're going to find out who the murderer is, or find something important related to it …"

"No, I know I'm not going to find the murderer. I'm not even going to try!"

"I know you, Kristen. You're hoping that you'll find out who killed Sister Anastasia. But let us do our work. It's none of your business."

"I'm staying completely out of the way."

"You can't be a part of this investigation. You have to be a member of the police department to be involved in the investigation."

"I know that; I'm not stupid. I know I can't have anything to do with it. That's not why I'm here."

"I can't make you leave, but I sure wish I could."

"You're right about that. Because I'm not doing anything wrong. I'll stay in this little retreat house minding my own business, having fun with Pam and Elaine, and that's it. Nobody is even talking about the murder at meals. The only people I talk to are Elaine and Pam. And they have nothing to do with the murder. It's a subject that's completely avoided. And I'm not interested at all."

"I wish I could believe you."

"Oh, David, I really mean it. You don't seem to realize that Pam is one of my closest friends, and I haven't really talked to her in a long time. And Elaine was my big sister in high school. Yes, I'm curious about who killed Anastasia, but I'm staying out of it. I learned my lesson from the last investigation. And I refuse to get involved with this on any level. I promise you that."

"Okay, do I have your word?"

"Yes, you have my word."

"On the Bible?"

"Oh, don't be so melodramatic."

"Seriously, on a Bible."

"Okay, fine. On a Bible."

"Alright. Have fun this week." He still sounded skeptical and angry. I could hear it oozing out of his every word. He added, "I'll talk to you soon. And I'll probably see you around. But remember, we don't know each other. Does Pam know we're going out?"

"I'm not sure. If she does, I'll tell her to keep quiet about it, though."

"Hey, I love you. I hope we're still on for dinner next week."

I smiled. "Of course we are." Obviously he wasn't too upset. "I love you, too."

We hung up and I got out of the phone booth as quickly as I could. I stopped in Spencer's market and picked up a six-pack of Dr. Pepper for later and walked back to the convent. The conversation had gone a lot better than I had thought. I just had to stay out of any discussion about the murder. It was hard to do. Elaine seemed obsessed with it. I understood completely. She lived there, knew everyone, and wanted to know who had killed Sister Anastasia. And she had to talk to someone. Pam and I were the only ones she could talk to safely, since she knew one of her fellow sisters had killed Anastasia.

I noticed that Sister Patrice, the artist, came down to lunch wearing a smock with paint spattered all over it. After lunch, I asked her what kind of art she was interested in and what she was painting. She invited me to her room to see her latest work. She seemed like a delightful person. She was working on a beautiful portrait of a young woman sitting in a garden. She was eager to talk about how much she loved art and she showed me all her paintings in her room, piled up against the wall.

"You should really display these somewhere. They're just beautiful," I told her. I couldn't believe how talented she was. "You must have worked on these for years. It's a shame that no one can see and enjoy them."

"Oh, these are nothing. You should have seen the artwork that Sister Anastasia had in her collection."

"What were they like?" I was kind of curious to hear about them from an artist's point of view.

"She had artwork from the eighteenth and nineteenth centuries that her grandparents had given her. They had acquired a lot of pieces and she was the sole descendant, so she inherited them all."

"Wow, I'll bet they were worth a lot."

"She had one by Friedrich. He was a nineteenth century German artist. I don't know how much that one was worth. A lot. And one by Albrecht Dürer. That was really old too. All of them had to be worth hundreds of thousands of dollars."

"Were they insured?"

"I have no idea. They should have been. And now they're all gone. Probably sold to some private collector by now."

"If she was the only descendant, then why did those relatives show up and take the whole collection? It should have gone to the convent."

Nuns and priests didn't have any material possessions.

I didn't think they had wills, because everything they owned, which wasn't supposed to be anything, belonged to their order.

"Well, I couldn't believe it. These two people in their fifties, supposedly her niece and nephew, showed up for the funeral with a copy of her will, and then took everything while we were at the reception after the funeral. Sister Janine was furious."

"How could they have a will? I didn't think nuns had wills?" I didn't want to mention that I had been a nun last year. We had never gotten around to discussing wills in our daily instructions.

"Well, I certainly don't have one," she said firmly. "I don't have anything except a few paintbrushes and painting supplies. The convent probably should have gotten the paintings, since she was a member of our order."

Sister Patrice and I talked for a while longer, but then I left her to meet Pam and Elaine. We were going to visit some of the antique shops in the downtown area. It promised to be a fun afternoon.

We spent the afternoon wandering in and out of different shops down by the Missouri River. There wasn't much that any of us were interested in. We were quite literally poor candidates for buying antiques. Elaine was a nun. Pam had just left and had no money at all. I was still living with my parents, without a job, but it was fun to rummage through all the knick-knacks and old items that had different levels of dust on them, depending on how long they had been on display. If there was anything of value, none of us would have even known it. Pam needed some new clothes, though, and we found a few blouses and skirts in a consignment shop on Main Street and finished up our afternoon at the corner drugstore. I told them about my conversation with David.

Pam said, "I sure thought he was the same policeman that came last year to interview us, but you didn't act like you knew each other, so I figured I had to be wrong. I'm glad I wasn't going crazy."

Elaine said, "Well, I won't say anything else about the murder, not that I know anything anyway."

I answered quickly, "No, I don't want you to feel like that. I'm awfully curious about it too, and I don't need to tell David a word about what we talk about in private. We can talk all we want about it. If we solve it, though, I can't tell him! We'll just have to keep it between ourselves."

We all laughed.

"Yeah, like that's going to happen," Elaine said sadly. "I wish it could, though."

She looked scared for a second, like she had just remembered something important. I wondered if it was about the murder. "Oh my gosh, I forgot about something."

Pam and I looked at her with excitement.

"Oh, don't worry, it's not the least bit exciting. Really. I promised Sister Janine that I would clean out the sewing room by this weekend. You guys want to help me go through some old boxes?"

Pam groaned and I sighed. "Wow, just what we came here for. I thought it was for fun and relaxation?"

Elaine explained, "It won't take long at all. It's mostly some boxes up on the shelves. I don't even know who they belong to. They've been there for ages. I think its old material for habits and stuff. It'll take an hour at most—even less if you guys help me. Please?"

"Okay, but you have to promise that we'll find some antique diamond jewelry hidden away by some old nun—and that we get to keep it!" I said.

"I promise," Elaine said as solemnly as she could manage before we all started laughing again.

We walked back to the convent and promised we'd meet Elaine in the sewing room in half an hour. I gravitated to the kitchen for another chocolate chip cookie and glass of milk.

Sister Hilda was there talking to Sister Martha. They stopped talking as soon as I walked in.

"Oh, I'm sorry to interrupt. I was just wondering if you had any more of your delicious chocolate chip cookies, Sister?"

"Yes, of course, dear. Take as many as you like. I'm going to make some more tomorrow, since that detective is coming back then."

I grabbed two cookies and left the room so they could continue talking undisturbed. I met Pam and Elaine in the sewing room. Elaine had already gone through some of the boxes. Most of them had wool material, yarn, buttons, thread, and everything you might expect in a sewing room. She had marked all the contents with magic markers.

They were dragging down the last six large boxes from the shelves on the walls above the sewing tables. Some of them were really heavy. Elaine opened one.

"These are old papers, not material. I guess that's why they weigh so much. I wonder what they're even doing in here." She picked up a few papers on top. "Essays on *Hamlet*, essays on *Huckleberry Finn*, all for a Sister Norma Marie's class. I don't even know who Sister Norma Marie is! Oh my God, the date is 1957. I think we can get rid of all these."

I opened another box. More papers. Notebooks from students—maybe a creative writing class—dated 1962. I was sure we could get rid of those too.

"You know, I don't want to sit here all afternoon and go through these," I said as I sat at the edge of the uncomfortable wooden chair. The upholstered chair in my room was much nicer.

"Why don't we take them back to our rooms and go through them in the next few days. The trash is out in back and we can get rid of the stuff and you will have fulfilled your cleaning duty, Elaine."

"Sounds good to me, if you guys don't mind." Elaine sounded relieved.

"I'm good with that," said Pam.

"Me too," I added. "Give me another box. I don't mind."

We helped each other carry the boxes to our rooms and finished up in the sewing room. The only reason it looked so much cleaner so quickly was because we had moved all the junk to our rooms, but that would be taken care of soon, and Sister Janine wouldn't even know. I would go through both of mine whenever I got bored during the week.

After dinner I heard piano music coming from the front parlor. The door was slightly open, and I slipped into where Sister Martha was practicing. The piano was a little out of tune. I hoped she had a better instrument over in the high school. She played very well, but stopped when I came in.

"No, go on. It's beautiful. A Chopin nocturne?"

"Yes, you must know your music."

"I play, too. And I love classical music."

Anyone else might have said at that point, "Oh, you play too? What do you like to play?"

But Martha ignored me and kept on playing. I didn't see any music books. She must have had them all at the high school. I listened for a while longer, then left the room quietly.

I walked outside where Pam and Elaine were sitting and talking.

"Can I join you?"

"Of course," Pam said. "You can probably guess what we're talking about."

"You guys solve it. I don't want to have anything to do with it."

"I wish we could," said Elaine.

"Hey Elaine, you know Sister Martha pretty well. Do you like her?"

"Wow, Martha's a strange one. No, I don't like her at all. She thinks she's way better than the rest of us. She's not racist or anything—she just thinks she's something special, with all her musical talent. She was really good friends with Sister Anastasia, at least she acted like she was. She listened to all her stories and complimented her all the time. I just never thought she was very sincere. And she and Sister Hilda are always talking together. I guess they're talking about family stuff."

"Family stuff? What do you mean?"

"Martha is Hilda's niece. It's weird how they ended up in the same convent. That's why Martha joined, because of Sister Hilda, so they're always together talking. Like you and I." She looked at Pam. "I guess Sister Hilda is all that's left of Martha's family, since her mom and dad are both gone, and Hilda is the only relative left. But Martha doesn't really want to be here. I've heard her say before how her talent is wasted on high school students and teaching band and chorus. Well, she's probably right, but that's what she signed up for. I don't know how she can change that, unless she leaves and goes into something else."

"But she liked Sister Anastasia?" I asked.

"Yeah, she spent a lot of time with her. And a lot of time recently, which was kind of strange, because nobody else did except Hilda. And Hilda had to, because she was Anastasia's caretaker."

Pam broke in. "Why didn't Sister Janine put Sister Anastasia in St. Mary's Home?"

"She should have, a long time ago. I don't know why she didn't. They could have taken so much better care of her at our senior center. They have nurses there, and dementia care. It was so hard on Sister Hilda, taking care of her all the time. And Sister Hilda is old, too. She was too old to be doing that full time, as well as all the cooking and housekeeping."

Elaine kept talking. "And I wonder about Caroline. I kind

of like her, but she's pretty insincere. I don't think she likes me much either. She can say a beautiful prayer, but I don't know if she means any of it. I hate people like that."

Pam shook her head. "Elaine honey, you sound like you don't really like anybody here. Why are you still here? You should get out and we could rent a place together and get teaching jobs."

Elaine was quiet for a long time. Then I saw a few tears. I didn't know whether to get up and leave or to stay. I decided to stay.

"I don't know. You're right. It hasn't been easy. I just hate to quit. It's only my first year on mission. I keep thinking it's going to get better."

Pam nodded her head. "I thought that too, for the longest time … well, not all that long. Just a year and a half. But I tried. I really did. And it didn't get any better. It's nothing to be ashamed of, sis."

I couldn't help adding, "I felt the same way, Elaine. I really wanted to prove to everybody that I could do it. I really wanted to stay. But they kicked me out anyway, and I'm sure glad they did. It was hard at first, but I think it was the best thing that ever happened to me."

Elaine wiped away a tear with the back of her hand. "I don't know what to do. There's just not enough people here to be friends with. It's not like when I was at home—or even at the motherhouse. There were so many people there I could talk to."

"Aw, sis. I'll do whatever I can to help you. We all will. You just take your time. I know it's not an easy decision to make."

I felt it was time to leave. "Hey, I'm going to go back to my room and get started reading all those essays from the 1950s. I can hardly wait."

They both smiled. Elaine said, "Hey, I really appreciate it. You know. Listening and everything."

I got ready for bed and decided to go through one box. I sat on the floor next to the box and started in. Who had kept all these papers? And why? I couldn't imagine. Probably some sister who had gotten transferred years ago and had just left them there, forgotten. Well, it was time for them to go. I looked through the first few inches of essays and was about ready to dump the whole box, but David's voice was there in my mind.

"You never know what you might find that's important."

"Okay, fine, David," I answered his imaginary voice. "Even though this is all trash and you don't want me to find anything anyway and neither do I, I'll still be extra careful—for you."

I glanced at each paper, not reading them. That would have been a penance that even Sister Miriam or Mother Alphonse would never have been mean enough to give.

The pile of trash kept growing larger and larger. At last I reached the bottom of the box. I could see a few scraps of old brown paper and a paper clip, possibly the first one ever made. I had done my duty.

"You would be so proud of me, David."

I piled all the papers into the box again, ready for the dumpster. Only one more box to go. Time for that tomorrow—or the next day. I climbed into bed and turned off the light. There was a streetlight far down the block and I watched the light play with the shadows of the leaves until I fell asleep.

CHAPTER 6

April 10

The only reason I knew David was coming on Wednesday afternoon was that Sister Hilda had mentioned that she was baking the chocolate chip cookies for the detective. I knew Mass was in the large church, Our Lady Queen of Angels, at seven a.m., and that all the nuns would be attending. I didn't go, but slept in. Breakfast wouldn't be till after Mass, so I got up at seven, went to the empty kitchen, and fixed myself a cup of coffee, then headed back to my room. I looked at the second box of papers. Better get it done now. I wanted the rest of the day to myself and to have some fun time with Pam and Elaine.

I sat on the chair and leaned over the box. The papers on top were some creative writing papers on a favorite person the student knew in their life. They were all from the 1950s. I'm sure some of them might have been interesting, but not to me. I threw them in the trash pile. A few inches down I saw that there were some essays from Sister Anastasia's classes. Now that could be interesting. I didn't even know she had taught English. But they were just as boring as all the rest. Essays on *The Taming of the Shrew*. Those went in the trash pile. Sorry, all you hard-working students. A little further down was an envelope with a name of a lawyer's office on the return address. That was strange. I opened it up. The cover letter was addressed to Sister Anastasia and the date on the letter was 1957. I read it quickly. It was her will. Nuns didn't have wills! But here it was.

"I Sister Anastasia Gruber, SND, Sister of Notre Dame, will my entire art collection to the St. Louis Art Museum. Whoever comes into possession of the manuscript of 'Silent Night' at my death may benefit from its proceeds in auction, but I would like it to eventually be sold to the Salzburg Museum, Germany to be displayed and enjoyed by the public. My grandparents and parents were Lutheran and would not want these items given to the Catholic Church, even though I am a member of one of its religious orders. This will is signed by my own hand on this 10th day of July, 1957, in St. Louis, Missouri." It was signed by two other lawyers and notarized.

Oh my God. My first thought was … I don't know. I had so many thoughts I couldn't get them all straight. I was now completely involved in the murder, even though I had tried my best to stay out of it. The will that gave everything to her out-of-town relatives couldn't have been the real one. This looked like the real one.

David was right. I was a busybody and had no business being here at all. Now I'd gotten myself into a mess of my own making. Secondly, she had a will that left nothing to the order. Third, all the artwork had been stolen anyway. Wait a minute! There was a manuscript of "Silent Night." That must be the thing that she had been so paranoid about. The missing item that someone had tried so hard to find. It certainly wasn't the artwork. All that art was out in plain sight, ready to be stolen as soon as she was dead.

But a manuscript of "Silent Night"? I wondered how old it might have been. Maybe it was one of the first editions that had been printed. That would be amazing. And to think that it might have survived all these years. I thought I remembered reading that the song became popular right away and was published and reprinted many times over the years. But my knowledge was really limited. I didn't even know when it had been written, except that Sister Anastasia's great-grandfather had written it, whenever that was. Sometime in the last century.

I had to tell David about this. But first I had to finish going through the rest of the box. I had half of it to go. I was pretty sure I had found the most important thing I would ever find. What was it doing in a box of old essays? And what good was her will anyway, when the artwork was gone and no one knew where the old manuscript was—or if it even existed anymore.

I picked up a few more essays. There was a notebook further down. It was Sister Anastasia's. I eagerly thumbed through it. I was sure it had to be interesting, but it wasn't. It was more like a to-do list. "Take clothes to dry cleaners. Pick up notebooks from office supply company. Dr. Blakely Monday 10:30 a.m." I was careful to go through each page, but there was nothing that was vaguely interesting, except to the person who had written the notes so many years ago.

I hated to throw it on the trash pile, but that's where it went. Another old notebook was underneath it. I opened it up, and there was a plastic cover with brown cardboard inside. I pulled it out carefully. Inside the cardboard were two manuscript pages.

I lifted the cardboard carefully, not wanting to tear what was underneath. The page said "Stille Nacht, Heilige Nacht" in difficult-to-read script, and underneath it a hastily scrawled musical staff, treble and bass, notes, guitar chords, and the words to "Silent Night" in German. The signature at the bottom read Franz Gruber with the date of December 24, 1818. Another name was on the manuscript, Joseph Mohr. I lifted the page carefully. The second page listed what I guessed were the words to the remaining verses in small cursive.

I put the cardboard back on the pages and slid them carefully back into the plastic covering. Was this the night that it had first been performed? Was this the original manuscript? It couldn't be. It had to be a copy, maybe one of the earliest copies.

How could I find out? I had to find out right away. Everyone who had keys to the high school, and the high school library, was still at church. I had no idea if the convent had any encyclopedias or music books. My mom! I could call her. I put the manuscript on the small desk in the room under my books, walked in the back door of the convent, and grabbed the phone in the hall. I called my parents' number.

"Mom, hi."

"Hi, hon. How are you? How's your visit going with Pam?"

"It's great. We're having a good time, even if it is in a convent. Listen, I have a big favor to ask you."

"Sure, if I can do it."

"You know our World Book Encyclopedias?"

"Yes?"

"Can you look up Franz Gruber or "Silent Night" and find out when exactly when it was written?"

"Okay, I guess," she said, clearly confused at my request.

"I really need to know right away."

"Okay. I'll go into the living room and look it up. Give me a minute."

If that was the date it was written and first performed, it would be worth its weight in gold. It didn't weigh very much, I thought to myself. I hoped it was worth more than that! It probably was just a copy. I hoped Mom could find out the information. I had a sick feeling in my stomach that it was probably the wrong date.

She finally picked up the phone as I held my breath.

"Kristen, it says here, 'The piece, lyrics written by Father Mohr and melody by Franz Gruber, was written on December 24, 1818, and performed that Christmas Eve night at their small chapel in …'"

"Okay, thanks Mom."

"There's more here. Don't you want me to read it? I thought you needed the information."

"No, that's enough, I just needed the date."

"What's this all about?"

"Oh, I'll tell you later. Just something I needed to know. Thanks Mom. I really appreciate it. I'll talk to you maybe tomorrow, okay? Say hi to dad. Love you both."

I hung up the phone and walked back slowly to my room. I sat at my desk, looking at my unopened book and thinking about the manuscript that was underneath it.

Elaine and Pam walked by my open door, returning from church.

"Hey lazy, come and get breakfast with us. How come you didn't go to Mass?"

I shrugged. "Elaine gave me so much work to do going through those boxes, I had to finish them this morning."

"Oh, yeah, did you find any diamond jewelry?" Elaine asked.

"No, and you promised I would." I tried to sound upset.

We had a lovely breakfast but I wasn't really there mentally. I was thinking about how I could get ahold of David and talk to him privately about what I had found. I figured I would just wait by the front door and literally grab him as he came in. There was no other way I could be sure of talking to him.

I asked Sister Hilda when he was coming, presumably so I could know when to be out of the way, and she told me he was coming after lunch, so I went back to the retreat house and out on the porch to do some reading. I wasn't about to tell anyone about my discovery, except David.

Pam and Elaine were already there, talking.

"She was so angry about it. I thought she was going to yell at me." I caught the tail end of what Elaine was saying.

Pam filled me in. "Caroline saw Elaine taking out one of those boxes to the trash this morning and asked her what it was. Elaine told her it was from the sewing room and I guess she told Martha and Martha just about had a fit."

Elaine finished the story. "Yeah, she said, 'What are you doing with those? What if some of those belonged to Sister Anastasia? What if you threw out something valuable?'"

"I told her that the three of us had gone through all the boxes and they all had student essays in them from years ago that nobody wanted. They were all still in the trash if she wanted to go through them herself. Both of them were really angry.

"I told her, 'Hey, if I had known you wanted them, I would have had you clean them out yourself. It's not a big deal. I don't know what you're so upset about.'"

I couldn't help but say, "She's upset because she thinks the thing Sister Anastasia was always talking about might have been in one of those boxes, I guess."

Pam said, "Well, that would have made it a lot more interesting, wouldn't it?"

I didn't say a word.

"Do you think she's going to go through the trash?" I asked Elaine.

"I wouldn't put it past her. I kind of wish she would. She'll be awfully disappointed."

We sat and read for a while on the porch.

Pam put her book down. She was always the fidgety one who could never concentrate for more than ten minutes. She turned to Elaine. "So what do you think about our murder mystery today, sis? Any brilliant ideas?"

Elaine put her book down on the wooden table next to her chair. JC jumped up on her lap and she started petting him. I could hear the purr from ten feet away. "I wish I had some more ideas, but they're all about the same as yesterday. No new insights."

I put my book down, too. I didn't think there would be any more reading for me this morning. I sat back and listened to them.

Pam said, "Okay, be perfectly honest, like you're investigating the murder. Who do you think did it?"

Elaine sat quietly for a minute. "Okay, I'll speculate, but you have to promise that you guys won't say anything to anybody."

We both nodded.

"Of course not," I said out loud.

"Well, Sister Hilda had the most reason, since it was so hard for her to take care of Sister Anastasia, but Sister Hilda is really sweet and I can't see her hurting anyone ever."

Pam asked, "But what if Sister Anastasia really wanted to die, and Sister Hilda felt like she was doing the right thing by killing her—the merciful thing?"

"I don't know. Sister Anastasia certainly didn't have much of a life anymore, but you know it's a mortal sin to take a life. That's God's decision, not ours, and I think Sister Hilda would never do that—take a person's life into her own hands."

Elaine went on. "I don't like Caroline, but aside from being insincere, I don't see any reason she would have to kill Anastasia. I mean, there was nothing in it for her. She likes it here, liked Anastasia, although she didn't have much to do with her, but she didn't have to take care of her, either, so there was no motivation on her part. She could have wanted the artwork, though, like anyone else. And I don't get why she was so upset about those boxes."

I suggested, "Maybe she thought that thing of Anastasia's was in them."

Elaine laughed, "Yeah, in an old sewing box from 1957? I don't think so."

"Okay," Pam said. "Who's next?"

"Well, there's Patrice. She's an artist, and she knew the value of all those paintings more than anyone else. She could have arranged with someone to come in and steal the paintings and then they're going to sell them later on and split the money or something."

"Wow, Elaine," I said. "You sure have a devious mind. Patrice seems really nice."

"Well, somebody killed Anastasia!" she answered quickly.

"What about Sister Janine?" I asked, since we were speculating about everyone.

"I don't know. I can't see any reason for her to be the murderer. But anyone could have wanted the paintings or the mysterious object that Anastasia always talked about."

"If it even exists," I mentioned.

"Yeah, that's true." Elaine said. "No one even knew what it was or where it was. It might have just been something that Anastasia's grandfather or great-grandfather had at one time and she never even had it in her possession. And Sister Janine was under a lot of pressure to put Anastasia in our senior home."

Pam said, "But that's no reason to kill her. She could have just put her there so easily. I don't understand why she didn't."

I still didn't understand one thing. "Why didn't the murderer just wait until Sister Anastasia died a natural death? Or they could have found the mysterious thing, taken it, and Sister Anastasia would have never even known. They didn't have to kill her for it!"

Elaine shook her head. "I don't get that either. I don't get any of it, truthfully."

"What about Susan?

"Well, she's kind of interesting. There was something a long time ago about the artwork, actually. Sister Susan thought that it should go to the motherhouse because it was the property of the order, and she talked to Mother Alphonse about it years ago. She was pretty upset that it was out here in Anastasia's room just 'rotting away,' as she said. Anyway, Anastasia was really upset about it and wanted to keep it and said that it belonged to her and her parents and grandparents. In the end, Mother Alphonse decided that it should stay here with Sister Anastasia for the rest of her life. That was a long time ago, but they've hated each other ever since. I don't think they've spoken in ten years at least."

"That's awful," I said. "There's a lot of hatred going on out here." I thought about the will that left the artwork to the St. Louis Art Museum and the manuscript to a museum in Salzburg. Nothing to the convent. What a disappointment to the order. Maybe that argument with Sister Susan had convinced Sister Anastasia to write her will. The timing would have been right.

"What about Martha?"

"Martha didn't have any reason. She liked Anastasia, at least she acted like she did. But like I said before, she spent a lot of time with her lately, not really helping out, just being with her, in her room."

"She was helping out by spending time with her," Pam commented.

"Unless she was looking for something," I mentioned.

Elaine said, "How hard could this mysterious thing have been to find? Somebody would have found it a long time ago. Our rooms are tiny, and Anastasia wouldn't have ever left it out of her sight, much less her room. I'm sure whoever was looking for it would have found it easily. It probably doesn't even exist."

Pam was getting tired, "So where does that leave you? Nowhere. I think you should leave it to the police. I hope they have a better idea of what's going on."

Elaine sighed. "I hope so, too. I'd be terrible at figuring out who murdered her. And I live with all these people! And there's not that many of them. And we know it has to be one of them!"

It was time for lunch, so we all went back for the meal. I just had to be there when David showed up, plan a time to talk with him, and then go for a walk in the afternoon till he was finished with whatever he was doing.

I sat with Caroline, Martha, and Sister Hilda. No one said much, except Sister Hilda talked about the sermon from the morning, which I acted interested in, but wasn't. I had lost a lot of interest in the Catholic church since I left the convent. I still went to Mass occasionally, but not regularly. I figured I had a lot of Masses in my personal bank and didn't need to deposit any more for a while. I'd probably go to the Easter service with my parents at the end of the week, but that would be it.

I deposited myself in the front parlor with a book, waiting for David to show up. At one-thirty the doorbell rang. I was the closest to the front door, so I opened the door and David tried not to look at me directly.

"I'm here to do a few more interviews. Could you let Sister Janine know that I'm here?"

"Yes, of course." I looked around and saw Sister Janine coming down the hall.

I whispered, "I have to talk to you after the interview. It's really important."

He gave me a strange look that I couldn't interpret. Annoyed, frustrated, please-don't-get-involved-in-this, all rolled into one look. But he just said, "Okay, where can I find you?"

"I'll be in the kitchen."

"It'll take about an hour, probably."

I went to my room for twenty minutes, looked out the window, picked up the envelope with the will, and the manila folder with the manuscript, put them in a notebook, and walked into the kitchen. Sister Hilda was already cooking dinner. I sat quietly on one of the chairs, but of course Sister Hilda started talking right away. She sat down next to me with a cup of coffee and a piece of toast.

"Oh, what do you have there?" she asked.

"Just something I'm working on for school. Nothing important. What are we having for dinner tonight?" I asked quickly, hoping to get her attention off the notebook in front of me. I moved it over to my side, just in case her coffee spilled accidentally.

"Oh, you don't have to hide it, dear, whatever it is," she laughed. "I'm fixing a pork roast. I hope you'll like it." I nodded, hoping I wouldn't be here for dinner, that I would be with David somewhere so we could talk.

I did miss him. I was having a nice time catching up with Pam and Elaine, but I was ready to go back home and be done with all this. I had a feeling that it was just starting, though.

David walked in the kitchen. Sister Hilda stood up right away. "Oh, Detective, would you like some cookies?"

"Why, thank you, Sister Hilda. You know how much I love your homemade cookies." He took two. She pressed a small sandwich bag with a few more into his hand.

He looked at me. "Can you come with me for a few minutes, Kristen? Thank you."

I got up, taking the notebook with me, avoiding Sister Hilda's questioning glance, and followed him into the corridor.

"I've got the rest of the afternoon. Where do you want to go?"

"I know a little place downtown. That's actually the farthest I've been in town, but we can get a bite to eat there and talk."

"Okay, sounds good. Do you want to walk there?"

"Sure," I answered. It was a beautiful day, and I went back to my room to get my purse.

David and I started to walk downtown.

"Do you have something to show me?"

"I'll show you when we sit down."

"Are you having a good time with your friends?"

"Yes, it's been really nice to catch up with both of them. Too bad it had to be in a convent. The retreat house is nice though. And Pam and I haven't spent too much time there anyway."

"What is this place?" he asked as he stopped and stared at the abandoned factory on the next block.

"It's an old tire factory. I guess it was Franklin's claim to fame at one time. That and its zither factory. I don't know where that was located. I just heard about it. Pretty impressive, don't you think?"

He laughed. "Now I can see why you wanted to come out here to visit! I had no idea you were proficient on the zither! And I thought it was some other silly reason, like a murder."

"Don't make fun of zithers," I joked. "They were banned by our order. We couldn't play them in the convent."

"You're kidding."

"No, I'm not. It was in the rule book. One of many ridiculous rules. I think it was too secular of an instrument. I guess the organ was more God-like."

We reached the little restaurant and walked inside. I asked for a quiet table, which was easy since we were the only ones there. We sat by the window in front, with a great view of the empty Main Street. A tired-looking waitress took our orders. A cheeseburger for David. I got the BLT and fries, plus my Dr. Pepper.

"Okay." I took a deep breath. "I have something important to show you, and it's about the murder investigation. But before you say a word let me tell you how it all happened."

David was quiet, but smiling, as I told him about Elaine and the sewing room, the boxes, the stacks of essays, the piles of trash, and how we had divided the boxes up to help her go through them.

"I thought of you the whole time I was going through the boxes. How you would say to be careful and never overlook anything because it might be important. So I felt you were right there with me. I know it sounds stupid, but that's the way I felt.

When I got about halfway down in the second box, I found this envelope."

I opened my notebook and pushed the envelope with the will across the table to him.

He frowned, picked it up, and opened it. He read it slowly and then put it carefully back in the envelope.

"Wow, I can't believe you found this. And I know that you weren't looking for it. I believe you. So there really was a manuscript. She was right about being paranoid. Wonder what ever happened to it? It might be why she was murdered. But we checked her room thoroughly. And I imagine the murderer did too, many times before we got there."

I took the manila envelope out of my notebook and handed it to him. "This was a little further down in the same box. Be careful with it."

He opened it like it was a piece of fragile glass and pulled the cardboard gently off of the manuscript. He looked at it carefully.

"When was this piece first performed? Do you have any idea?"

"December 24, 1818."

"That's this date." He looked up at me.

"Yeah, I know."

"That means this could be the original manuscript."

"Yes, it could be."

"Do you realize what that means?"

"Yes, I do."

"Wow."

David never said "Wow." And I had just heard him said it twice in one minute. But I felt the same way.

"Look," I told him, just talking so he wouldn't have a chance to say anything. "I know you didn't want me getting involved, and I really didn't mean to. In fact, I tried to stay out of it. I just listened to Elaine talk about it a little, but I honestly didn't care, because I'm only here to have a nice visit with Pam and Elaine, no matter what Inez's agenda was for me. I really had no intention of getting involved, and I still don't. But I knew you had to see these and have them. So here they are. They belong to you now. Or the police department. I guess they're evidence in the crime. Whatever it takes to solve the murder."

He put the manuscript back in the manila envelope.

"I wonder how much this is worth? It must be a tremendous amount, if it's the original."

"I don't know when you can do this, but at some point you, the police department, whoever, should take this to Dr. Charles Hanson at Washington University. He's a music historian and he could probably tell you if it was the original and maybe even get estimates about how much it was worth."

"Well, we'll need that information at some point, but now, it's just good that we have this as evidence. The murderer knew that there was something important. Sister Anastasia must have told her or someone close to her that this existed."

David handed back the envelopes for me to put back in the notebook. I carefully placed it on the seat behind my purse. We sure didn't want to spill anything on them. The waitress brought our food.

David stared at me. And then he smiled. He had the most wonderful smile. That was one of the first things I had noticed about him. His smile. It lit up his whole face.

"You really are something. You just can't help yourself, can you? I mean, even when you want to stay out of an investigation, you get right in the middle of it. Although I have to say, coming to the scene of the crime was a pretty stupid idea."

I took a drink of Dr. Pepper and smiled.

"Without me, you wouldn't have those two very important items to help solve your murder, Mr. Kelly."

He sighed. "You know I can't talk to you about the investigation."

"I know that. You don't have to explain."

"We have a long way to go. I can say that at least."

"Well, I hope these two things help a little, or I'll have to stay here longer and do even more investigating." I tried to look as serious as I could.

He laughed. "Sometimes I wish you could help us. Whatever fate it was that got you to find those boxes, I know it'll help in the investigation, and that's what we need right now. Someday I'll be able to talk to you about it. Just not now."

We finished our lunch and walked back to the convent. As we were standing outside and got to his car, I took the two envelopes out of my notebook and handed them to David. I saw a motion in the drapes in the front parlor—or thought I did.

"David, please be careful with these."

"Are you kidding? I'm going to guard them with my life. Here, hold them for a minute while I get my car keys." He handed the envelopes back to me as he opened the car door, took out his briefcase, and put them carefully inside. We said goodbye, shaking hands, no kisses of course, and he promised to be back soon for a few more interviews. I walked inside and glanced in the front parlor. I had the feeling that someone had been in there a few minutes ago and had seen us walking up the street together and talking. I wondered what they'd think of that, even though we hadn't done anything wrong. I didn't much care. No one knew I had found the manuscript except David, and he was the only person who would ever know. I didn't trust anyone at the convent except Elaine and Pam, and I wasn't about to tell even them.

From now on I was staying out of the investigation completely. There was nothing else to find anyway.

★ ★ ★

After dinner, Pam and I sat out back in the warm spring night till we could see the fireflies come out. JC joined us and we fed him some leftover salmon from the refrigerator. He played with some string that he found on the ground and rolled over and over with it, having lots of fun.

Elaine wasn't outside with us, which was strange, but we figured she might just be tired. Pam worried about finding a job so late in the year, although she was pretty sure she had gotten one in the St. Louis school district for the following year. Elaine finally joined us and sat down quietly. She was pretty angry.

"You'll never believe what just happened."

"What?" said Pam.

"Caroline, Susan, and Martha asked me to come into the front parlor with them and I had no idea what they wanted. You know what it was? I thought it was going to be about the boxes again, but it wasn't. It was about you, Kristen, and that detective. Caroline accused you of knowing him and plotting something with him. I told her she was being ridiculous. What was there to plot? I told her that yes, you had met him briefly from another investigation, but that you were out here to see Pam and me. Susan said someone told her she saw him giving you something, a manila envelope, outside the convent this afternoon, and I said, 'So what? She knows him. I already told you that.'

"She seemed really angry about it. I have no idea what's going on in her head. Caroline was like that with the boxes, too. She acted like we're hiding something. Maybe we're hiding 'it,' that thing that Sister Anastasia always talked about."

I had to think fast. "I did meet the detective before, when he came to the motherhouse last year for that other murder investigation. He interviewed everyone in the postulancy because they thought the victim was a postulant. But she wasn't. So that's how I met him. That's it."

I didn't say a word about the manila envelope I had given David. I hoped that no one would notice the omission. I kept talking. "I sure hope somebody finds out what 'it' is pretty soon. You'd think someone would have found it by now!"

Everybody laughed, but I was getting a little concerned about Caroline and Martha. And Susan hated Anastasia. Only two more nights here, and then we would head home. I wondered how David really was doing with the investigation. I hoped it would be solved soon—and I hoped someone could find that artwork. David had interviewed Sister Janine earlier that day. She seemed to be in a very bad mood the rest of the day. I wondered what had happened in the interview. I kept reminding myself not to care.

CHAPTER 7

April 11

The next morning I slept in. It was Holy Thursday, and there wasn't any Mass, only a service later that evening. In the Catholic liturgy, it's the one day in the year where there isn't a Mass celebrated.

I didn't care about breakfast. We could get some cereal and hot chocolate later. I would go exploring a little more of the town. If Pam wanted to go with me, that would be fun. I was thinking of driving to one of the wineries by the Missouri River. I thought they'd be beautiful that time of year. Or we could go shopping. The day was ours. I didn't know if I wanted to go to the service at the church later.

I had taken David to a Christmas service a few months ago which he hadn't really enjoyed. He had been raised Methodist, but his parents had rarely taken him to church, or anywhere, and he didn't believe in anything supernatural. He felt being a good, honest person who cared about other people was the most important thing in life, and he had more "Christian" values than most Christians I knew.

He loved the music at the Christmas service, but the prayers and the constant getting up and down were confusing and distracting to him. I wasn't going to invite him to the Easter services when we got back home. Maybe I wouldn't even go myself, even though I was sure that my parents would invite me to our own church. Was I a bad Catholic? Probably. I was just tired of the whole religion thing. The hypocrisy, the meaningless rules, everything. I needed to take a break.

I was in the kitchen fixing my hot chocolate and thinking about religion when Sister Patrice came in the front door. She practically ran into the kitchen. "Have you seen Sister Janine?"

"No." I couldn't figure out why she was so upset.

"Where's Sister Hilda?"

"I don't know."

Patrice went running upstairs, and in a minute they both came down the stairs.

"You check the office, Hilda. I'll check her room."

I sat down at the table, wondering what in the world was happening.

Patrice came back in the kitchen as Sister Hilda walked in. "Her office is pretty empty."

"So is her room. All her clothes and most of her books are gone."

Sister Hilda said, "Well, she said she was taking the car, but I thought it was just for an errand, not that she was leaving permanently. She did look really upset!"

I began to realize what had happened. Sister Janine had left. She must have killed Sister Anastasia. Maybe David was getting a little too close to the truth in his last interview. I had no idea, but that seemed a possibility.

Sister Patrice went into the office and called the police and David. The local police got there quickly. They took down the license plate of the car and the information about Sister Janine. It was about twenty minutes before David arrived. Pam had come in and was sitting at the table with me, wondering what was happening. I didn't want to get in the way, but I didn't want to leave and miss all the excitement. Besides, I wasn't quite sure where to go.

Sister Patrice and Sister Hilda came into the kitchen. David met with the local police officer at the front door and then came back to talk to us.

"They're looking for the car now. They have a bulletin out with the license plate and hopefully they'll spot it before she gets too far. How long would you say she's been gone, Sister?"

He addressed Sister Hilda, who just shook her head and said, "A few hours by now, sir."

"We'll find her, don't worry."

Suddenly the front door opened, and in a few seconds Sister Janine appeared at the entrance to the kitchen. She was pale, almost ashen, as she stood there looking at all of us.

"I just couldn't do it," she said quietly.

"Couldn't do what?" David asked her.

"Let you think that I had killed Anastasia. I have something to tell all of you," she said very quietly.

Before David had a chance to say anything, she blurted out, "It was my niece and nephew, not Anastasia's, who came last week. They came because I told them to get the artwork. They took it all and are in the process of selling it. I was trying to leave and join them in Kansas City. I took as much as I could, but I just ..."

She stopped suddenly.

"You just what, Sister?"

"I knew that if I left suddenly, you would think that I had killed Anastasia, but I didn't. That's why I had to come back. We took the artwork, but she was already dead. It wasn't going to do her any good. And what was the convent going to do with it? Put it in some corridor in the motherhouse? No one would ever see it again. I knew it would do a lot more good for my family. My niece and nephew need the money, and I could start a whole new life away from here. But as I drove out Highway 44, I knew you'd be looking for me, and just had to come back. But I didn't kill her, I swear I didn't!"

"You know that stealing the artwork is a felony?"

"Why is it a felony? I didn't kill her."

"You stole hundreds of thousands of dollars of artwork. That is a felony."

"Are you going to arrest me?"

"Yes, I will. But before I do, do you know who killed Sister Anastasia?"

"No, I swear I don't. But after she was dead, I knew it was my opportunity to get the artwork. Please believe me."

"No, sister, you lied to us, and I don't have to believe anything you say. But it was smart of you to come back and turn yourself in."

He turned to the two police officers. "You can inform her of her rights and take her down to your station now. I'll come out front with you."

David left the room. Sister Patrice followed, and just Sister Hilda, Pam, and I were left. We sat quietly. No one said a word. A few minutes later David came back in the kitchen. I started talking to him. I didn't care anymore that Sister Hilda was there.

"Pam and I are leaving tomorrow. I guess I'll see you back at home. I'm sure glad this week is over. Do you think it was Sister Janine who killed her?"

"I can't really talk about that, but we might be adding that to her list of felonies."

"Okay, I'll be talking to you soon."

He put his hand on my arm, and looked like he might kiss me, but thought better of it and just turned and left. Boy, I'll bet he was tired of driving out here every other day.

Elaine came in from the church a few minutes later.

"You missed all the excitement." Pam could hardly wait to tell her.

"I heard about it. A lot of people practicing for the church service tonight saw Janine being taken away in a police car.

You've got to give me all the details. Were you here when it all happened?"

"Sitting right in the kitchen," Pam answered.

After Pam gave Elaine all the details, Elaine asked the question that we had been asking all day. "Do you really think Janine killed Sister Anastasia?"

Pam wasn't sure. "It just didn't sound like she did. And she did come back and confess to stealing all the artwork."

I was a little more skeptical. "She knew she'd be caught, taking the car like that. The police would have found her and arrested her. She was smart to come back, but it doesn't mean she didn't kill Anastasia."

Pam and Elaine and I had a wonderful day together, our last fun day for a while, although most of what we talked about was the stealing of the artwork and Sister Janine's arrest.

We all took one last walk down to the river before dinner. I could never get tired of looking at the power of the Missouri River, so different from the Mississippi. The Missouri was wilder, with debris and logs swirling in the fast-moving currents. No swimming in that river.

We talked about how nice it was to all be together and talked even more about the possibility of Elaine leaving the order. It wasn't my place to push her, and I did understand her desire to continue, helping people and teaching. I probably would still be in the convent if I hadn't gotten kicked out, although I was certainly thrilled I had been forced to leave. I always tried to explain to David why I had been so stubborn about staying, and now I looked back and wondered the same thing about Elaine. I hoped she wasn't staying just to prove that a Black girl could make it in the order. Not that I would know anything about that, but Pam had talked often about how she felt that everything she did had to be done better, because she was Black.

Dinner was awkward, with the superior not only gone, but in jail. Nobody really knew quite what to say, and although our being there as guests didn't help the stilted conversation, I'm not sure anyone would have said much anyway. Caroline, Martha, and Susan looked through me like I wasn't even there. I guess I was guilty of going through those boxes—and talking to the detective. If only they knew the truth.

At least Sister Hilda was polite and thanked us for coming for the week, telling us we were wonderful guests, and then everyone went upstairs to get ready for the Holy Thursday services that evening.

Pam headed to Elaine's room, where she was going to spend the night, and I walked to my room. The door was open. That was strange. I was almost sure I had closed it when I'd left earlier. I walked inside. JC was inside, curled up on my bed. I smiled at him and sat down and petted him. Maybe he had pushed open the door.

My purse was on the desk where I had left it, but it was on its side, not upright. And my books were piled up neatly next to my purse. I wasn't a neat person and I didn't remember arranging them so meticulously on the dresser. But I could have done all those things without thinking. It just wasn't something I would normally do.

I went to the parlor and read my book for an hour or so and then decided I would go to bed early. I gently pushed JC off my lap, of course, and went out to the retreat house and got ready for bed. As I brushed my teeth, I wondered if someone had been in my room, snooping around. I didn't really have any reason to call David. If he were here right now, I would mention it to him, but I certainly wasn't going to call him and have him drive out here for an open door, a neat pile of books, and a purse that had probably fallen over on my desk. I climbed into bed.

My keys! They had been on the dresser. I got up out of bed and looked for them but couldn't find them. I looked under the purse, in the purse, under the pile of books, behind the dresser. I know they had been there. Someone had taken my keys. I was sure of that. My car keys but also the key to the bedroom door.

I lay quietly, thinking about everything I could to take my mind off this place. I was being totally paranoid. I could have left the keys anywhere. But the only things I could think about involved murder. For an hour I listened to every tiny sound magnified through the empty retreat house, the only night I was there alone, without Pam in the next room. It had started raining, and the wind made even stranger sounds as it blew branches against the windows. I had locked my door, but if someone had the key, my locked door wouldn't stop them.

I tried to think of why anyone would think I had found anything, and all I could think of was the person who had been in that front parlor. She had seen David and I hand the manila envelope back and forth when he got his car keys; no wonder she thought I had something important. It had to have been Martha, or Caroline, or Susan. No, they said someone had told them about David handing me the envelope. It could have been anyone in that front parlor, pulling the drapes aside ever so slightly.

I had to rely on Elaine's opinion of the nuns in the convent, and she thought that just about everyone had a possible motive to kill Anastasia. Money was always a motive. And Anastasia, although living a life of poverty herself, had tremendous wealth in the artwork and now the manuscript. That manuscript alone had to be worth hundreds of thousands of dollars, at least. And although no one claimed to know what she possessed, someone had to know after all those years and all the stories she had told. Someone was lying. David would have said, "Of course someone is lying. The murderer is lying about everything."

I had tried so hard to stay out of this investigation, and here I was in the middle of it. I admit it was the height of stupidity to come out here a week after the murder. Why had I let myself get talked into it?

I could have been home in my bed, enjoying my week off from classes, spending some time with my mom and dad and friends from high school. Instead, I lay shivering in the dark, worried yet again that someone would come in the dark room and try to kill me for a manuscript that I didn't even have. But someone thought that I had it.

By one a.m., I knew that everyone had returned from the services a long time earlier and had gone to sleep. I didn't know where to go. I wasn't going to spend the night here alone. Yes, I was a coward, and I didn't care at the moment. I got the blanket and tiptoed inside to the kitchen. JC would be fine. I left my door open. But where to go now? I didn't want to bother Elaine and Pam and admit that I was a coward.

The only place I knew well was the sewing room. It had all those boxes of material and it was clean, and no one would think of looking for me there. I padded up the steps and walked by Patrice's and Elaine's doors, where I could hear Pam and Elaine still talking quietly. I snuck into the empty sewing room and closed the door. I found a box of heavy wool material and a couch pillow, and made myself a makeshift bed in one of the corners of the room, almost under one of the sewing tables. I covered myself with the blanket and lay there for a long time listening to the rain and the wind that had come up in the night. One of those spring storms that would rain and thunder all night.

CHAPTER 8

April 12

The sun was beginning to shine in the windows when I woke up. I guiltily grabbed my blanket and walked out into the corridor. It was still early, and I heard the sisters praying in their chapel as I passed through the kitchen to my room.

The room was a complete mess. The bed was torn apart. The contents of the dresser had been thrown all over the floor. My books had been scattered everywhere. Papers had been strewn across the floor. I thanked God that I had stayed in the sewing room.

I found my clothes, got dressed quickly and headed to the phone in the corridor to call David on his home phone. He answered on the second ring, almost as if he had been waiting.

"My room was broken into last night."

"What? Are you okay?"

"I'm fine. I think someone saw me give you that manila folder outside the convent yesterday afternoon. Maybe they thought it was something important."

"I'll be there as soon as I can. Is everyone there today?"

"Yes."

"Leave things the way they are. I want to get pictures. See you soon."

I hung up and went into the kitchen where Pam was having breakfast.

"Come with me. I want to show you something."

★ ★ ★

Pam and I were sitting in the parlor close to the front door when David arrived about an hour later and Sister Hilda let him in.

"Why Detective, you're here early today. I didn't think we'd be seeing you again." She looked very confused and apprehensive. "Sister Janine is still in jail, isn't she?"

"Yes, but I need to talk to Kristen."

"I think she's still in her room. I'll get her."

Pam and I stood up quickly and surprised them both in the hall.

"Let me see your room," he said directly to me.

I turned and led David down the hall, right past Hilda, and out the back door to the retreat house.

David walked ahead of me into the room and looked around carefully.

"Wow, they really made a mess of everything, didn't they? And why did they think you had anything related to the murder?"

I had already told him about the boxes, but not about the reactions of the nuns.

"Remember how I told you that Elaine, Pam and I went through those old boxes. Well, apparently, a few people were pretty upset that we had found them and went through them and threw stuff out. I guess they thought something valuable might have been in them."

"Who was upset?"

"Caroline and Martha and Susan, but someone else had told them about the boxes, so it wasn't just them, and I don't know who saw you hand the notebook back to me in front of the convent yesterday. I thought I saw someone in the front parlor."

"So it could have been anyone?"

"I guess."

"I'm going to look through the room to see what I can find. I'll need your help, though, to tell me if anything's not yours."

Pam asked if we needed any help. David told her no, and she went to her room to pack.

He took a few pictures, and then asked me a question about some papers. I told him about my missing keys and how I had spent the night in the sewing room.

JC jumped on my lap as I sat there on the chair. I petted him absentmindedly. I guess I wasn't doing a good enough job, because he jumped down after a few minutes and went to investigate my messy room. I could see him wandering through the room, getting petted a few times by David, and then pawing at a few blankets and sheets, trying to burrow under them.

"Do you want me to get JC out of here?" I asked.

"No, he's no problem at all."

JC went under and then came out from under the bed holding a shiny beaded rosary—meowing loudly—and carried it proudly to me, tripping over it as he dragged it on the floor.

"David," I called out to him, "look at what JC found. This rosary isn't mine. I wonder if the person who was in here dropped it."

David reached down, petted JC, and carefully pried the rosary from his mouth.

"It's not yours?"

"Nope, I left mine at the convent when I left. Never missed it. Besides, mine was regulation black."

This one was a cheap blue crystal one, but obviously attractive to JC. Now we had to figure out whom it belonged to. David finished up going through the room but didn't find anything else.

We walked back into the kitchen.

David asked Hilda, "Sister, do you know whose rosary this is?"

She turned around from the sink quickly and looked over her glasses at it. "Oh, that's Sister Martha's. Where did you find it?"

"Are you sure?"

"Here, let me see."

David handed it to her.

"Yes, one of the beads is missing. I was going to get her a new one."

"Do you know where she is right now?"

"I think she's at the church getting ready for the Good Friday services." Sister Hilda looked confused.

"Thank you, Sister," David said politely. He turned to me.

"I'll be back in a minute. Wait here."

Sister Hilda questioned me, "I wonder what the detective is doing here again?"

"Well, the murder hasn't been solved yet. I guess that's why."

She sat down on one of the chairs by the center island. "It seems pretty obvious that it was Sister Janine. I mean, she stole all the artwork and arranged that with her family. She must have killed poor Sister Anastasia."

I just sat there quietly. I didn't have anything to say.

David and Sister Martha walked into the kitchen. Martha looked furious.

Sister Hilda started to say, "Would you like a cup of tea?" but stopped when she saw Martha's face. "What are you doing here? I thought you were helping in the church."

"I was, until he brought me back here."

David said, "Let's go into one of the parlors so we can talk privately."

Martha just stood there with her arms crossed.

"No, whatever you have to say, you can say it in front of them. I have some questions I want to ask her anyway." She glanced over at me angrily.

"Alright, Sister." David pulled out the rosary from his pocket. "Did you happen to lose this somewhere last night?"

"That's not mine," she answered too quickly. "There's lots

of rosaries that look just like that. Who said it was mine?"

Sister Hilda looked down at the floor. "I told them. I didn't know why I shouldn't."

"Where did you find it?" Sister Martha asked defiantly.

"I think you can tell us that, Sister," David answered simply. "Where were you last night? That's where we found it."

"I was in my room sleeping. Where else would I be?"

"We found this rosary in Kristen's room, which had been ransacked by someone. You must have dropped your rosary when you were in there. How else can you explain it being there?"

I watched the defiant look on Martha's face melt away. It was replaced by an almost childlike sadness as she stood there helplessly.

"I must have dropped it," she said quietly.

"You don't have to answer their questions," Hilda broke in quickly, edging closer to Martha.

Martha uncrossed her arms and held up her hand to stop Hilda from coming closer.

"I'm tired. I'm tired of hiding everything and running away from it. They're going to find out anyway. I killed Anastasia and I wanted to find that manuscript, but I didn't. I looked everywhere but it was gone. She promised me that I could have it. She wanted me to have it. And she got so she didn't even want to live anymore. Hilda will tell you that. She wanted to die. I was only doing what she wanted, in the end."

Martha stood quietly. It was as if she had run out of words.

David said quietly, "Sister Martha, I'm arresting you for the murder of Sister Anastasia. These are your rights."

David recited her rights: to a lawyer, to remain silent, that anything she said could be used against her in a court of law.

Sister Hilda was crying. "I told you not to do anything, that I could take care of myself. I told you not to do it."

She turned to David. "I know she did it for me. Martha

knew taking care of Anastasia was getting too hard for me. I complained about it all the time. This is all my fault."

David turned to her. "Sister, we'll talk to you later about this. For now, I have to take Sister Martha with me."

He took Martha with him into Sister Janine's office. The police arrived quickly, only about ten minutes later.

I sat in the kitchen with Sister Hilda. She was so upset I didn't think she should be alone. I didn't want to say anything to her, but she wouldn't shut up.

"I didn't know she was going to kill her. If I had known, I would have stopped her, but I didn't know till afterwards, and by then it was too late. And I couldn't tell anyone, could I? She's my only remaining relative. My sister would just have been so ashamed, and my mother, too, if they knew she had killed someone. I knew it was wrong, but Anastasia was so old and she really did want to die, and I'm not excusing her or anything, I mean, it was horrible what she did, but Anastasia didn't even know who she was anymore and it wasn't any kind of life and maybe it was the kindest thing to do." She trailed off.

"You knew she had killed her? All this time?" I couldn't believe what I was hearing.

Hilda started crying. "I didn't know what to do. Sister Anastasia showed us the manuscript years ago and told us that she wanted Martha to have it since she was a musician but then she forgot all about it and couldn't remember where she had put it. Martha kept asking her about it all the time and poor Anastasia really couldn't remember anything at that point. I told Martha to stop being so mean but she just kept on and on about it. But I never thought she'd kill her. Martha told me not to say a word about it to anyone. I was scared of her by then. She's my only relative, but she's not a good person. I couldn't say anything. I didn't know what she'd do to me."

I sat quietly while Hilda cried. What could I say? But

I would certainly tell David. They both knew about the manuscript all this time. And Hilda had known all along that Martha had killed Anastasia.

David came back in the kitchen. I stood up.

"Let's get your things from your room and you can go anytime you're ready."

He and I walked back to my room.

"Do you need any help?" he asked.

"No, I'm fine. This won't take long. Pam can help me. You probably should get back to the station to talk to Martha."

"Yeah, I wasn't expecting that, for sure. And JC solved the murder. He's a pretty amazing cat."

"Maybe you should teach him some more techniques and use him as an officer at the station."

"I think everyone would love him."

David stood quietly for a second. "Call me when you get home. We've got lots to talk about. Maybe dinner tonight?"

"I have to tell you some things that Sister Hilda just told me."

"Can they wait until tonight?"

"I think so, but you'll have to talk to Hilda at some point about it."

"I have to talk to Sister Hilda about a lot of things," he answered.

He gave me a kiss, and turned and left quickly, while I turned and started the cleanup of the room and the packing of my bag. Thankfully I didn't have much.

Pam peeked into my room. "Do you need any help?"

"Yeah, that would be great. I don't want Sister Hilda to have to do it. She's pretty upset."

"What about?"

I told Pam what had just happened.

"It was Martha."

"What? Martha killed Anastasia?"

"Yes."

"Does the detective know that for sure or is he just guessing?"

"She confessed to the murder."

Pam stood speechless for a full thirty seconds and then said, "Oh."

"And Sister Hilda knew about it the whole time and didn't say anything."

"What? She knew about it?"

"Not before, I don't think, but afterwards for sure."

"Wow. I'm sure glad we're getting out of here. I wish we could take Elaine with us right now."

"Me too," I answered sincerely. I hated to just leave without telling the rest of the sisters what had happened, but I didn't want to wait any longer. I just wanted to leave as quickly as possible. And it wasn't my job to inform anyone of the arrest. That was David's job. He could call and talk to someone at the convent later on that day.

Pam had already said goodbye to Elaine that morning, so we piled our two bags in my car. Oh my God, I still didn't have my keys! They had to be in Martha's room, or in the trash somewhere.

I ran back into the convent and up the stairs to Martha's room. The room was locked. Damn. I had to go down to the kitchen to see Sister Hilda again.

She was sitting silently at the island, drinking a cup of coffee and staring off into space.

"Oh, you're still here," she said vacantly.

"Sister Martha took my keys from room two nights ago and I think they might be in her room."

Hilda's face showed no expression at all as she stood up wearily and walked in front of me up the stairs. She used her key to open the door to Martha's room. I could see tears streaming down her face.

"Do whatever you need to do," she said.

I walked into Martha's neat room. I didn't see the keys anywhere obvious, so I started opening drawers in her desk. I hated to go through all her things, but I had no choice. I had to get home. If I didn't find my keys there was no way I could leave. David would have to come back and get me and Pam. I sure didn't want that.

I emptied out drawers on her bed, putting all the books, pens, and papers back in them when I was sure my keys weren't there. Then I went to her dresser. When I emptied the second drawer the keys spilled out with her underwear and handkerchiefs onto the bed. I picked them up carefully and just left the rest on the bed. She wouldn't be returning here for a long time. And I didn't care. I just grabbed the keys and ran out of the room. I took the retreat house key off the ring and handed it to Sister Hilda and said a quick goodbye. I couldn't think of anything to say.

I felt sorry for her, but I was angry too. She had known all this time who the murderer was—had known all about the manuscript and hadn't said a word to anyone. I know Martha was her niece, but we were talking about murder. Premeditated murder. I just couldn't find it in my heart to feel sorry for her.

Pam was waiting at the front door for me. Elaine was there, too.

"Wow, what a vacation." Elaine sounded really upset. "I'm so sorry you guys had to go through all of this. I hope next time I see you it'll be under much different circumstances. No murders, no ransacking of your rooms, and, I hope, no convents involved at all."

"Does that mean you're leaving?" I asked.

"I think so. I have to wait till the end of the school year, but

Pam and I are going to room together and see if we can get jobs and make our way in the real world, just like you."

"Well, I'm not doing much yet, but I hope to be soon. And don't feel bad about what happened. We should never have come out here at such a bad time. We should have waited until things got better. I'm sorry about that."

I had one more thing to do before I left. I ran back to the retreat house and found JC lounging on the porch in the sunlight. I picked him up, all sixteen pounds of him, and gave him a big hug. "Love you, sweetie. I hope you have a good life, and that you get enough love." I put him down gently on the porch so he could resume his nap.

I went back inside. Pam gave Elaine a hug and so did I. "See you soon, guys," she waved as we drove off.

"Wow, what a week," Pam sighed. "I'm ready to get home and get back to my normal boring life."

"Me, too. I had been getting tired of sitting around my mom and dad's house. Now I'm looking forward to watching TV in the evenings with them, not trying to figure out a murder. And I'm not even calling Inez, who got us into this mess in the first place."

"Yeah, she did, didn't she?" said Pam. "I wondered why she wanted me to visit my sister so much. She never much cared about me all last year, and then called me up out of the blue and suggested we have this nice little vacation. I should have known."

We drove down Highway 100. The trees looked even greener and more beautiful than they had the previous week. I had managed to make it through the week and still remain on good terms with David. I considered that to be most important. And I had discovered, purely by accident, something very helpful to the investigation. The murder had been solved. Mostly by JC, actually. What an amazing cat. Poor Sister Anastasia. It was so horrible that she had been murdered. And I did feel bad for

Sister Hilda. She worked so hard, and to realize her only relative whom she loved had committed murder. What a sad, strange week. I was glad to be going home.

I wondered what would happen to the "Silent Night" manuscript. All I wanted was that the artwork and manuscript would find their way into museums where they would be enjoyed and appreciated by the public. That was a great reward. I knew David would feel the same way.

"You know, that box I cleaned out did have some interesting things in it," I mentioned to Pam as we were heading into the city.

"Really? You said it was all junk."

"Well, I lied. The manuscript everyone was looking for was in there."

"What!" She turned and grabbed my arm.

"Yeah, I couldn't tell you until now, because it had to be a secret. That's why my room got broken into, because Martha had seen me hand it to David."

"Oh my God, I can't believe you found it. You gave it to David? What's going to happen to it?"

"I guess it'll go to a museum or something, where it belongs. I'm sure glad I got the box that it was in."

"What was it?"

"It was the original copy of 'Silent Night,' the one Franz Gruber wrote the first night it was ever performed."

"Oh wow, that's amazing. Are you guys sure?"

"Pretty sure. David's going to bring it to some music people who know about manuscripts, or the police will, but I think it's the real thing."

"I can't believe you found it. This was sure some week, wasn't it?"

★ ★ ★

All Pam and I talked about all the way home was the murder, and Martha, and Hilda, and by the time I dropped her off at her apartment, I was exhausted from the talking and the speculating and the whole entire week. I drove the last twenty minutes to my parents' house in silence. I didn't even want to listen to any music on the radio.

Settling back into ordinary life was so easy after my week in Franklin.

CHAPTER 9

April 14

David came over for Easter dinner on Sunday evening. He brought over a large Easter basket for me with lots of chocolate bunnies, Peeps, and other treats. I loved it. Chocolate was one of my weaknesses. He didn't say a word about the investigation. I could hardly keep myself from asking, but he obviously didn't want to talk about it in front of my parents. We just had a nice talk about politics and the lovely weather and the first time he even mentioned it was when he left and we stood on the front porch of our house.

"I'm not trying to be difficult, but there just isn't a whole lot to say about the investigation. It's only been three days. You know I'll let you know what I can when I find out more."

"I know. I'm just so anxious to find out about the manuscript and everything."

"I'll know more by next weekend for sure."

He gave me a long, wonderful kiss and I knew we were okay.

CHAPTER 10

The week went by quickly, with school starting back after spring break, and Sunday came faster than I could have imagined.

David and I went to Cunetto's as usual and sat at our regular table in the back.

"I can't tell you about the investigation itself, but I can give you some information about the manuscript. We took it to Professor Hanson. He's convinced it's real. He's in the process of finding out how much it's worth. We're talking hundreds of thousands of dollars."

"Wow, no wonder Martha wanted it so much."

"Well, now it'll be used as evidence against her. She shouldn't have been so greedy."

"And what's going to happen to all that artwork?"

"We're still trying to find most of it. A lot has probably been sold already, but we're tracking it all down, and that will be used as evidence against Sister Janine. We still have a lot of work to do."

I thought about her will. "I hope that the art museum will be able to get some of that artwork, and that the museum in Salzburg can get the manuscript someday."

"Well, you remember her will. I checked with an excellent lawyer downtown and he's looked over it carefully. And I've found out a lot about nuns and wills this past week. In fact, I bet I know more about it than you do, even though you were in the convent."

I smiled. I didn't want to tell him that it wouldn't take much to know more than I did about wills, because I knew absolutely nothing.

I nodded and said, "Tell me what you know. I'm interested."

"Well, did you know there's two kind of nuns? "

"Yeah, I do know that."

"Nuns are locked up—sorry, I don't know the word for it—and they have to be quiet and pray all the time and they never leave the convent, but sisters, like you were, are more outgoing, like helping out in homeless shelters and teaching and things like that. I didn't know that. And nuns can't have wills, because everything they own belongs to their order, but sisters, like you were, can have wills, and they can will their belongings to other people or groups."

"You're right. I didn't know that. So Sister Anastasia did have the right to make a will."

"Yes, and I'm guessing she made it after that altercation with Sister Susan. It would have been around the right time. I suppose she wanted to make sure that the artwork and the manuscript found their way to the right places. I just don't understand why she wasn't more careful about where she kept her will. It would have been lost if it hadn't been for you. And the manuscript too. She should have kept it with the lawyers, at least, just to keep it safe. The lawyer reminded me that she mentioned something about whoever finds it could get some of the proceeds, you read that too. Well, he said that person might be you."

"Me? I don't have anything to do with it. I didn't even know her."

"I know, but she clearly didn't want anyone in the convent to have it, and she mentioned that the person who had the manuscript when she passed away could benefit from the proceeds. It's possible that you could receive some of the money—someday. Right now it belongs to the police and it will be used as evidence in the crime. The next phase of the investigation could take a long time, depending on whether Sister Martha agrees to a plea deal or decides to go to trial, but that's up to her and her lawyer."

"But I don't really want anything. She wanted the manuscript to go to the museum, not a private collector."

"When this is all over, and it might be years, we'll have the lawyer call and you two can discuss this. I'm out of this one."

"And I need to tell you something about Sister Hilda that I found out after you arrested Sister Martha. I was sitting in the kitchen with Hilda and she told me that she knew that Martha killed Anastasia."

"When did she know?"

"I guess very soon after it happened. Martha told her. But she didn't say a word to anyone. She said she was afraid of Martha and what she might do. And she was the last of her family, so I'm sure that was part of her hesitation to tell anyone."

"So she knew all along and didn't say a word to me—or the other police."

"And she knew about the manuscript, too. Martha and Hilda both knew about it and Anastasia had supposedly promised it to Martha years ago. That's why Martha wanted to find it so badly. Well, that and the money."

"I can arrest Hilda because of that. She's an 'accessory after the fact.' She knew about the murder and didn't say a word. I'll have to bring her down to the station and interview her again. I know she's old, but that's no excuse for withholding vital information from the police."

David sat quietly. I could see his frustration with that piece of news about Hilda.

Then he said, " But I do need to talk to you about something else though, Kristen."

"Okay," I answered carefully. He sounded awfully serious. I hoped it wasn't another marriage proposal. Probably not. I knew he was still upset with me going out to Franklin.

"There's so much I want to say to you, but you have this really bad habit, no pun intended, of not listening to anything I say."

I really did try to look serious, but I was still basking in the glow of at least having discovered something important about the murders, something that was very helpful that I never dreamed was possible. And maybe making a little money from it, which I needed badly.

And David sometimes seemed so arrogant. Why did I have to listen to him all the time? I know that he knew lots more than I did about a lot of things, but not everything.

"I know you found the manuscript, but you could have gotten hurt—or killed—and you could have seriously ruined our investigation, just by being out there."

"Come on, David. You know I didn't do anything wrong, and I didn't interfere at all with the investigation. I stayed completely out of it."

"But you should never have come to Franklin when you knew there had been a murder, and that we were investigating it. It was a bad choice of weeks to visit, and you knew that from the beginning. "

"I probably shouldn't have come then. You're right. And I know I was lucky."

I had to admit, I was kind of fascinated by the thought of solving crimes. I so wished I could do that. But I was a woman, and I had no reason to think I would ever be allowed or permitted to help with any investigation. Ever.

I had to tell David what I was thinking. I might as well try to explain myself as best I could.

"David?"

"Yeah?" He gave me his fatherly look in between bites of pasta.

"I really am interested in solving these mysteries, crimes, whatever. I know I'm not very good at it, I realize that, but I really do want to do something, not just sit back and let people go unpunished for what they've done. And there's no way I can help you. It's just not allowed. I can't become a detective like you. Women can't do that kind of work, although it makes me angry that we can't. It was the same in the convent. Not that I wanted to be a priest. But we could never do what the priests did: counseling, administering the sacraments, hearing confessions, saying Mass, all because we were women."

I looked at him. "I promise you I will never do anything like this again. I promise. I really do respect your opinion, not because you're a man, but because I know you're right about this. I way overstepped the boundaries on this one, and I apologize."

We had both stopped eating by this time and the pasta was rapidly cooling on our plates.

"You know, there is a way," he said.

"What do you mean, a way?"

"I think if you are serious, you should major in criminal justice at Washington University, and then go into police work. You haven't declared a major yet. You might consider doing this— at least think about it."

"Won't I run into the same problem that all women have in a mostly men's professions?"

"Yes, you will. But the world is changing, and that will change too. There are so many times that a woman police officer is needed, for domestic violence cases, for abused children, so many times I've wished we had more women on the force."

I had another bite of pasta.

"You really mean it, don't you?" I looked at him.

"I really do. And then we'd never have this conversation again about investigating a case all on your own."

"Well, I don't think there's going to be anymore convent murders anyway. Two of them are enough for a lifetime. Besides, I'll never need to work anyway, if I get rich by selling the manuscript."

"Hold on. You haven't even talked to the lawyer yet. You might still need to get a job."

"Oh, darn."

"Or you could just marry me and live a life of complete luxury."

"Yeah, right." I laughed.

"Well, you should at least think about it. And check out the courses that they offer. See if you might be interested."

CHAPTER 11

May, 1968

I was glad to get back to studying, but I couldn't put David's suggestion about doing police work out of my mind.

If I had discovered one thing about myself in the past year, it was that I was stubborn. I didn't know if it was my Irish heritage or just my own personality. My mom and dad didn't seem particularly stubborn, but I had heard lots of stories about me growing up. My desire to stay in the convent now seemed a pigheaded rebellion against what my parents and everyone else in my life wanted me to do. I was glad now that I had gotten out. I wonder if I would have ever left on my own.

And even though I was very interested in crime and taking classes in criminal justice, just the fact that David had suggested it made me want to do the opposite. I hated for people to tell me what to do.

Did I really want to give up my dream of being an English teacher so I could go into police work, a profession where women were most likely at the bottom of the ladder, unable to climb? It reminded me so much of the convent, where nuns could never be equal to the priests. But what profession wasn't like that? Woman's lib had started to make us more equal, but we still had a long way to go.

And what were the chances of another convent-related

murder? Practically zero. I'd be dreaming of the day when David and I could work together as a team, and that day would never come. Meanwhile, we might have gone our separate ways, and I'd be handing out parking tickets for the rest of my life. I certainly didn't want that.

I decided I might take one class in criminal justice to see if I liked it. But I had too many things I loved. I had English, and teaching, I hoped, and music was always there. I realized that I had to finish the semester, pass my exams, and get a job for the summer before I made any decisions. The week in Franklin faded away like it had never even happened.

CHAPTER 12

June, 1968

David called the next week for our weekly dinner. We decided to rough it at Steak and Shake on Hampton Avenue. He told me about the case.

David mentioned, "A trial date is set for the beginning of October. And I got a call from a lawyer about Sister Anastasia's will."

"Good. What did he say?" I hoped all that artwork and the manuscript would finally get to their rightful homes.

"The artwork will be donated to the Art Museum. They'll be having a special showing at the end of the month and we're invited. Kind of an honor to be included, I think. Get yourself a nice outfit and we can go together, if you want."

"I'd love to."

★ ★ ★

I got a job as a waitress at the St. Louis Airport for the summer, the early shift starting at five a.m. when the cheap restaurant opened in the morning. I mostly served coffee and quick meals to people anxious to catch their flights. No big tips, but it was a job and I needed it desperately. I was off work by early afternoon and had the rest of the day to read and study.

David was so busy I only saw him on weekends, but at least we had that. We were still at an impasse about marriage. I certainly wasn't ready, but I wasn't ready to give him up and see other people either. I wasn't sure how long we could keep going like this. The relationship wasn't going anywhere, but I didn't have a clue about where I wanted it to go. David had been very patient, so far.

David and I got to go for a special viewing of the artwork one Thursday evening at the museum before they were exhibited. I was amazed at their beauty. And to think they had been on her walls in her room, and many of them in her closet. A few had even been in the attic of the convent. I was so glad that they had finally found their rightful place.

I felt sorry for Our Lady Queen of Angels convent. They had lost their principal and superior and a member of their very small community. I knew that Sister Hilda would probably never recover emotionally from the loss of her niece Martha. The whole community would have to start over. I was glad that I wasn't a part of it. And Elaine was gone, too. I couldn't imagine how they were going to build a community out of the ruins.

David had never said anything else about his suggestion about my major, but I thought about it all the time. Fall was quickly approaching, and I decided to take the coward's way out. I signed up for a few English classes and one class in criminal justice, just to see what it would be like. Not that the class had any bearing on the reality of police work. I could get a better idea of that from watching and listening to David describe his long days. Not that mine would be at all like his. He had a ten-year head start on me, and besides he was a man. I would be at the back of the line.

CHAPTER 13

The end of August came quickly and I started my classes at Washington University. I finally felt like I belonged, not like last year, when I had felt like I was somehow there under false pretenses. I felt comfortable, met a few friends, and started hanging out with people at coffee shops at the end of the school day and for study groups. It was wonderful.

I had told my mom and dad all about the murder and the artwork, and the special thing that Sister Martha had murdered for, but I never mentioned that I had found that special thing. I didn't want them to get all excited about something that might never happen.

Pam and I talked often and she asked me about the manuscript each time. I kept telling her that these things with lawyers took months to settle, maybe even years, especially something like this. I had stopped thinking that I might get anything from it. I couldn't imagine that just because I had happened upon the century-old manuscript that I was entitled to anything at all. It could have been anyone who found it. I just happened to be the one who emptied the right box.

Elaine had left the order when school ended, and Pam and Elaine found an apartment together in the city. I hoped it would work out for them. I got a call from Elaine, and after thanking me for my help—I hadn't really done anything—we talked a little about her plans for the future. She had taken JC when she left, but it turned out that Pam was quite allergic to cats, and she was trying to find a home for him, because no one at the convent wanted him back. My heart jumped at the chance. I'd have to ask my parents though. They weren't cat people, but I could keep JC in my room. Would that be fair to him, though? I told Elaine I'd have to think about it, even though my heart told me that JC and I would be a perfect fit. If only I had a place of my own. My mom and dad and I had a very short talk, and it turned out that they were very happy to have a cat, as long as they didn't have to feed him or take care of him. I assured them that JC would be my responsibility and I called Elaine back, thrilled that JC and I would be together.

I had a long talk with Inez, and I told her how annoyed I was about her barging into my life like that. We came to a tentative agreement that I would never again be part of any investigation. Not that there would ever be another one. She was one stubborn lady. Almost as stubborn as I was. Maybe that's why we had become friends in the first place. I told her about the murder, but not about what I had discovered. She would be anxiously looking for something else for me to investigate.

★ ★ ★

David called in early October. He was anxious to tell me the news.

"It's finally over. All of it. Sister Martha was sentenced to fifteen years to life in a plea bargain. No trial."

"But Martha killed her! That's murder!" I didn't know what to think. It seemed like she should have gotten more time for murder.

"It's about right for that kind of case," he replied, not too concerned. "Fifteen years is a long time. It could have gone to trial and you never know what would have happened. The defense would have brought up mercy killing. Martha would have testified that Anastasia thought about dying, but she never asked or consented to Martha killing her, so it could never be argued as mercy killing. She might be paroled after fifteen years, but that's entirely up to the parole board at that time. I think it's reasonable."

After I got talked down and began to see it from a legal viewpoint and not an emotional one, I guess it made more sense.

"What about Sister Hilda?"

"Hers was a difficult case. She pleaded guilty, and got fined a few thousand dollars, which the convent had to pay, but she didn't have to spend any time in jail. She was so afraid of what Martha might do to her, the threats, that she used that as her defense, and that was acceptable to the judge."

"What a mess. I'm sure glad JC was able to solve the crime. I think I'll give him some extra tuna tonight. Not that he needs it …"

David mentioned, "Oh, by the way, I got a call from a lawyer about Sister Anastasia's will."

"Good. What did he say?" I hoped all that artwork and the manuscript would finally get to their rightful homes.

"He wants to spend some more time on the manuscript and finding out how much it might be worth to some dealers and booksellers."

"Why doesn't he just give it that museum in Salzburg like she wanted?"

"I have no idea. You can call him and ask him. I can give you his number."

"No, it's none of my business. I just hope it gets there eventually without too many lawyer fees."

CHAPTER 14

December, 1968

I got a phone call one evening in December from Mr. Jameson, the lawyer, and he asked if I could meet with him and David in the next few days. I drove to his office downtown and met David in the parking lot on a Friday afternoon. I had just seen him a few days before for dinner. He was busy with a new drug case but came over to see me and my parents and JC for a Sunday evening. I loved being with him. I counted the days till the weekend and our dinners. I hoped he did the same. At least he told me that he did.

We walked through the slush on Grand Avenue and wiped our shoes carefully before we went up the elevator to the seventh floor. The waiting room was plush with a beautiful Oriental carpet, no threadbare spots, and wing chairs. Real plants were all over the room, beautiful ones. His blond secretary stood up as we entered, "Mr. Jameson will see you now."

I felt out of place as I walked into his office, the large ornate desk dominating the room. He rose and after exchanging a few pleasantries asked us to sit across from him.

He sat down and placed a piece of paper in front of me.

"I was very pleased with this offer I received on your behalf, Miss Byrne. The Salzburg museum has offered you a sum of $300,000 for the manuscript. They realize that you could get more at auction, but they are hoping that you will abide by Sister Anastasia's wishes that she expressed in her will. This is the museum that has the largest collection of material pertaining to 'Silent Night' in the world."

I just sat for a minute. I had never even dreamed about that kind of money, especially for me, but I didn't want to argue with him about it. After a few seconds—it seemed like hours—I agreed, thanked him for the work he had done on my behalf, and we talked a while about the strange circumstances leading to the recovery of the manuscript. David talked about what had happened since the lawyer had gotten the manuscript, how the person had confessed to the murder, and what would be her punishment. We talked a little about the will and how it was strange that Sister Anastasia didn't want the manuscript to go to the convent. After that, there wasn't much else to say. We left the office politely, after thanking him for his work, but as the elevator doors closed and we went down a few flights, we shouted and hugged and kissed and surprised a lady getting on at the next floor. Neither one of us could believe the amount I would receive.

As we walked out to our cars, David kissed me again and said, "Remember, I asked you to marry me before you got this money."

I laughed. "I remember. We have to tell my parents. Follow me and we can all go out for an early dinner."

On the way home I thought of all the things I could do with the money. I had never even dreamt of having that amount of money in my whole life. I could rent my own apartment, get a decent piano, my own cat. Oh my God, JC and I could have our own beautiful place with a garden for JC. I couldn't think of anything else I really wanted. I would pay my parents for the car and pay my own way through Washington University. I think

I was more excited about JC than anything else. I held David's hand tightly as we walked into the house together. The reality hadn't even started to sink in yet.

Mom was doing the dishes at the kitchen sink and Dad was finishing a cup of coffee at the Formica table with the newspaper in front of him.

"Kristen? David? What a nice surprise." Dad put down his cup. Mom dried her hands on the towel. She looked a little confused that we had stopped by unannounced.

"Mom? Dad? Why don't you both sit down. I have something really amazing to tell you."

#3
ON THE ROOF

Tower Grove Park, St. Louis, Missouri

CHAPTER 1

Tuesday, August 12, 1969 - early evening

I rushed into my apartment and grabbed the phone on its fourth and final ring.

"Kristen, this is Pat. You know, your classmate from the convent. You've got to help me!"

"What do you mean?"

"What's the name of that policeman you're going out with? I need to get ahold of him right away."

"David Kelly? We're not going out anymore, but here's his number." I gave it to her quickly.

"What's wrong? Can I help?"

"I got some letters. Some terrible letters. I've got to go."

The phone went dead.

I stood there, holding the phone and my wet umbrella, with JC, my pudgy tuxedo cat, already curling around my legs and meowing insistently. I whispered to him, "Yes, I know you're hungry."

What a strange call. I was so tempted to call David, my ex-boyfriend, but I figured that Pat would be trying to call him right now. I'd call him later. I hadn't talked to him since we'd broken up almost a year ago. But now I had a good reason to call him. I hoped Pat was all right. What was she so scared about? Letters? What could they have said?

I put my umbrella outside my apartment door. It was still raining, but not as hard as it had been earlier. St. Louis weather was unpredictable. It changed a few times every day. I walked back inside, put my purse on the kitchen counter, walked into the kitchen, and poured myself a glass of Coke. I needed to distract myself. Maybe I'd even call my mom. I loved her, but I hated talking to her lately. We'd talk about school; I was just starting my new semester at Washington University, and she was always anxious to hear about it. That was fine. But we invariably got on the topic of David and how it was such a shame that I had broken up with him. Both my parents loved him, and just couldn't understand why I had been the one to break off the relationship.

I had gotten kicked out of the convent two years ago, and David was the first person I had dated. He had asked me many times to marry him, but I wasn't about to make another vow I couldn't keep. David was Irish like we were, handsome, a policeman, eight years older than me, everything my parents could have dreamed of. I'd make it a short phone call.

My mind jolted back to the convent. Sister Patricia—Pat. We had been acquaintances at best, but of course I remembered her. There had only been thirty-two of us in our freshman class, called postulants. And Pat and I had been in a small English study group with Sister Inez for a semester.

I hadn't heard from or talked to any of my classmates since then, except Pam who had also left soon after I had. I wondered how many were still there. They couldn't write letters or make phone calls—besides, I had been kicked out for accusing a priest of murder, so nobody wanted to talk to me anyway. They were starting their senior year, like me. I was sure I had been long forgotten.

I fed JC his dinner of wet Friskies cat food, and made myself some macaroni and cheese, the Kraft kind. I watched the news, but it was depressing as usual, and I turned it off after the fourth or fifth murder. St. Louis was the murder capital of the U.S. for a few years now, quite a distinction for such a small city.

I'd call Mom tomorrow. I read for a little while but couldn't concentrate on *The Great Gatsby*. I kept thinking about the phone call.

"Time to go to bed," I called to JC, who was already curled up on his little cat bed in the living room. He jumped up and headed into the bedroom with me, where he'd sleep on my bed, usually crowding me to one side. He only weighed about fourteen pounds, but he took up a lot of space in the bed, his long legs curling everywhere.

As I tried to sleep that night, I wondered what Patricia was so worried about. Letters? I wondered what kind of letters she had gotten—and from whom? Terrible? Terrible in what way? I tossed and turned, thinking about her and how maybe I had made a mistake with David and how much I missed him and maybe, somehow, we could get back together.

After my experience with the manuscript of "Silent Night" and the money I received, I was able to get my own apartment, work on my degree, and get my own cat. And I got my old piano from my parents. There wasn't anyone left at home to play it. I toyed with the idea of going into police work, and even took a few classes in law, but my love of English and music won out, and I was studying to get my teaching credential in those two subjects.

I had been in the convent for a year, helped solve two murders, gotten kicked out, and started dated the chief investigator for the cases.

After a few years, my reluctance to make a commitment really began to bother him, and we finally broke up.

★ ★ ★

I remembered that evening so clearly—almost a year earlier. I wore a long paisley skirt and black sweater. My red hair was almost down to my shoulders in the year since I had left.

I had just started my junior year at Washington University, and I heard the knock at the front door. JC ran to the door with his pudgy legs, hoping to escape, but David scooped him up in his arms.

"How's my little detective?" he laughed. I smiled. He always called JC a detective since he had helped solve the last murder investigation.

We arrived at Cunetto's Italian restaurant on the Hill, but I felt sick all through the salad and the shrimp pasta because I knew I had to tell David my decision. It was during the cheesecake that I finally got the courage to say, "David, I have to tell you something."

He looked serious. "What is it?"

Even though I had rehearsed my speech a hundred times, I didn't know what to say.

"I know you've asked me to marry you, but you know I'm just not ready for that kind of commitment."

David's face was impassive. I couldn't tell what he was thinking—at all. And I usually could. Every emotion he had was written on his face. He just couldn't hide the way he was feeling.

He put down his glass of wine. "I know, and I've told you that I'll wait until you're ready."

"But I don't want you to wait," I blurted out. "I mean, I want you to be free. I want to be free, too—to meet other people. You're the first person I've ever gone out with, and I just can't make that kind of decision based on dating just one person."

"You want to break up? Is that what you're saying?"

"No! Well, yes, I guess so, at least for a while. I just need to meet other people.

"I mean, is that okay with you?"

"Really? You're asking *me* if it's okay to break up with me? You must be joking! I know. I understand. But you know that you're doing this for you—not for me. I've been out with a lot of people, and I love you. I really want to be with you. I don't need any more time to decide. But I understand."

The waiter came by to refill our coffee. David put his hand over his cup.

"No thanks. Could we just have the check, please, and some take-out boxes?"

"Of course, sir."

David looked at me. "I'm just going to take this dessert home. I don't feel like eating it right now."

"Okay, me too," I mumbled.

I put my hand on his arm. "Hey, I don't want this to be forever. Just give me a few months, okay?"

He put the desserts in the boxes, the money on the table—with a generous tip, as usual—and we left the restaurant. The ride home was mercifully short—and painfully silent.

"Do you want to come up?" I asked out of habit.

"No, that's okay. Call me sometime—when you're ready." He didn't look at me or give me the usual kiss.

I fumbled with my keys and got out of the car. He waited till I got to the lobby and then drove off.

I knew I had done the right thing, but why did it feel so awful? I cried myself to sleep that night and many nights after that. It was two weeks before I found the courage to tell my parents about the breakup.

They were quiet when I told them. I knew they were trying hard not to tell me what to do, but I could see in Mom's eyes that she thought I had made a terrible choice.

I thought about David constantly, but I forced myself not to call. I had to meet other people. I was only a junior in college. He was eight years older. He knew what he wanted out of life, but I didn't.

CHAPTER 2

Motherhouse, Ripa Avenue, St. Louis
Tuesday, August 12 - evening

"Patricia, wait a minute."

Sister Patricia stopped and turned to face the other nun behind her. They were both standing in the long ground floor corridor of the motherhouse. Everyone else in Sister Patricia's class had already gone into the chapel for evening prayers.

The fall semester was about to begin in a few weeks. Not that anyone had rested much during the summer. The second year in the convent was spent in preparation for taking vows, and much of the year had been taken up with classes in theology and lots of classes about the rules of the order. The junior year was filled with regular classes and this last year, senior year, would be packed with studies for their majors and teaching credentials.

The sister motioned for Patricia to come in the open door of the parlor next to the chapel. She whispered, "Hey, do you want to go up on the roof tonight? There's a meteor shower. I know it rained earlier but I think it'll be clear tonight. I figured we could see it from up there. I know how much you love science and astronomy. I'm going with Sister Rebecca's science class to watch it, but I'll be back around eleven. The view from the roof should be even better because we'll be above the trees."

"Have you been up there before? I never have."

"Oh yeah, lots of times. How could you have gotten through three years here without going up on the roof? It's a little scary, but fun. And the view is amazing."

"Okay, that sounds great. When should I meet you? And where?"

"Meet me in the choir loft at eleven."

"Okay, see you. And thanks. It sounds fun."

★ ★ ★

Even though lights were out at nine p.m., Patricia just laid on her bed with all her clothes on. She set her alarm for ten-forty-five in case she accidentally fell asleep, but she was too excited. After Patricia looked out of her dormitory door at eleven, checking for Sister Karin, their juniorate mistress, she carefully slipped down the empty corridor and sneaked into the choir loft. Darkness covered the chapel, dimly lit by the tiny red votive lights up by the altar, but she could see a shadow in the front pew of the loft. The sister was there waiting for her. They walked purposefully down the fourth-floor corridor, pretending they had a reason for being up so late. The hall was lit only by an emergency light, and they stopped at a small door with no sign.

"Here it is. Hope it's open."

The door pulled open easily and they stepped into a small, dark, dust-filled room.

"Don't turn on the light. Someone might see it. I brought a little flashlight to help us up the stairs." She turned it on, its feeble light making the room look even darker.

A wooden spiral staircase in the center of the room led upwards as far as Patricia could make out in the dim light. The flashlight was almost worthless. The thick bell rope hung down the middle of the staircase next to a long pole.

"Be careful. Don't grab the rope accidentally, because you'll ring the Angelus bell."

The Angelus bell was huge, about six feet wide at the base, and at least six or seven feet tall. It was rung at six in the morning, at noon, and at six in the evening when the sisters said the Angelus prayer. One of the duties of the postulants was to take turns ringing the Angelus bell.

"Okay." Patricia was beginning to think this wasn't the greatest idea. No wonder she had never been up here.

"And I brought two Dr. Peppers and plastic cups for us."

"Where did you get those?" Patricia hadn't had a soft drink in a very long time. She thought back. Probably two years ago.

"I was in Sister Miriam John's office and she gave them to me."

They slowly went up the stairs, Patricia holding on tight to the banister with one hand and clutching her skirt with her free hand. The long habits didn't help. The order had talked for years about changing the habit, and it was happening—but slowly.

The sister opened the trap door at the top and pushed it over all the way with a loud clank, leaving a large opening to the roof.

They cautiously climbed out, both holding their skirts up above their feet and ankles. Patricia finally bunched up her skirt and threw it partly over her shoulder. That was easier. The roof was at about a twenty-degree angle, a little frightening, but not too dangerous.

Patricia sat down carefully on the still-damp tiles. Then she laid back and looked up. "Oh my God, this is beautiful. It's so clear. I'm not going back in till I see a meteor. Or dozens of them!"

"We should see a lot tonight. We saw a few from the front lawn, but Sister Rebecca said that it's better the later it gets. And no moon and no clouds. A perfect night for it. And most of the lights are off now. Just that big one on the side of the building, but there's nothing we can do about that. Here, let me pour you some Dr. Pepper."

"Just hand me the can. That's fine."

"No way. I didn't bring these plastic cups up here for nothing." The sister opened both cans, took out a packet of powder from her pocket and added it to Patricia's drink as she watched the sky.

"There's one!" Patricia practically yelled. "It went all the way across. Did you see it?"

"No, I'll see the next one."

The sister handed her the plastic cup and Patricia sat up and took a long drink. "It tastes weird. Even sweeter than I remember."

"It's been too long since you had a soft drink. Look! Another one!"

The meteor shot across the sky till it disappeared in the trees just above the horizon.

"Hey, Pat, are you doing okay? You seem to be worried about something."

Pat closed her eyes for a second, debating whether to say anything. No, tonight was too beautiful to worry about anything.

"No, I'm fine. Guess I'm just worried about next year. Physics is going to be hard and getting my credential, too."

"Oh, okay, that's tough. But you'll be fine. I'm kind of worried about my schedule too. I've got seventeen units this next semester. I hope I can handle it all."

They lay quietly for a few minutes, waiting for the next meteor.

Patricia put her hand up to her head. She felt dizzy.

"I need to sit up. I don't feel very good. It just hit me."

"We can go back inside if you want." The sister seemed concerned.

"No, I'll be okay. I want to see a few more meteors. I'll feel better in a minute."

The other sister sipped her drink.

"What's that necklace you're wearing? I just noticed it."

Patricia quickly pushed it back under her collar where it must have slipped out when she bunched her habit over her shoulder.

"No, I'd love to see it."

"Okay. I know I shouldn't be wearing it. My grandmother gave it to me last week when we had visiting day. I'm not sure what I'm going to do with it." Patricia unclasped it and handed it to the other nun. The nun took the small flashlight from her skirt pocket and shone it on the necklace.

"It's beautiful." The nun handed it back. "Does anybody else know you have it?"

"No, nobody. I think I'll just give it back to my family next visiting day."

They sat quietly while Patricia finished her drink, wondering about the strange taste, but then she saw another meteor. It streaked across the sky with a red trail. She still felt dizzy. They watched the sky for what seemed a long time.

Suddenly the other sister stood up, "Oh God, I think I see someone on the front lawn. Look!"

She inched closer to the edge, placing her feet carefully. The tiles were still a little slippery from the rain earlier in the day.

"Get up, Pat, look down there."

Patricia tried to get up.

"Here, I'll help you." The other sister pulled Pat to her feet and led her toward the edge.

"See, over there."

"I can't see anything. I'm really dizzy. I'm going back inside."

The sister gave Patricia a hard push, grabbing the necklace from Patricia's hand as she pushed, and Pat screamed as she fell forwards over the edge.

The sister heard a crash like something breaking and then a thud. She emptied the rest of the Dr. Peppers on the tiles, crushed the cans and put them and the plastic cups in her large skirt pocket along with the necklace, and looked over the edge. She didn't see or hear anything. She carefully walked back to the trapdoor, went through it backwards till she felt her foot on a step, closed it, and made sure she latched it.

CHAPTER 3

Kristen's apartment
Wednesday, August 13, 9:00 a.m.

"Hello, Notre Dame Motherhouse. How can I help you?"

"This is Kristen Byrne. Can I speak to Sister Patricia Lawson? She's in the juniorate."

I wasn't sure how they could find her, but if she was there, they could transfer the phone call over to that part of the motherhouse.

"Hold on a second, please."

I held the phone tightly. I hadn't slept much all night, worrying about her strange phone call. I hoped she had been able to reach David.

"How do you know Sister Patricia?"

Wow, I wasn't ready to be interrogated. How ridiculous.

"I'm Kristen Byrne. I really need to talk with Sister Patricia. We were postulants together."

There was silence on the line. What was the problem? Had they gotten even stricter about phone calls after I left?

"Look, I'm returning her call from yesterday. It's important that I talk to her."

Another voice came on the line, older and higher pitched.

"This is Sister Miriam John. Kristen, there's been a terrible accident here this morning. Sister Patricia is dead."

I held the phone tightly. The words were a meaningless jumble.

"What?" I managed to say.

"Sister Patricia's body was found early this morning."

"Found? Found where? Oh my God, what happened?"

"I'm sorry, I'm not able to tell you what happened. We're in quite a state here, as you can imagine."

"I'm so sorry. I understand completely."

"I'm sorry, too. I know you were classmates. I really can't talk right now. The people from the mortuary are here."

The line went silent, then to a busy signal.

I hung up the phone. Patricia was dead. I couldn't believe it. One of my classmates. And had Patricia been able to reach David? I'd have to call him.

I dialed his direct line at the station. There was no answer. I tried his home phone. It had been months since we had spoken, but I remembered the number clearly.

The phone rang four times and I was about to hang up when he answered.

"Yes?"

"David, this is Kristen."

"Kristen, what a surprise," he said cautiously.

"I need your help. Did a Sister Patricia call you last night?"

"No, but I was out till late. Why? What's up?"

He sounded a little disappointed that it wasn't a personal call, or maybe I just hoped he was disappointed.

A surge of jealousy jolted through me at the thought of him being out with someone else, but I said quickly, "A friend of mine, a sister in my class, died last night. She had called me earlier last evening for your number. She was really worried about something."

"And she's dead this morning? Do they know what happened?"

"No, I don't know. At least they wouldn't tell me. I just called down to the motherhouse to talk to her."

"Kristen, what was her name? You should call the station and find out who's on the case."

"I don't think there's a case. The people from some mortuary are there, but they probably think it was an accident. You, or somebody, needs to get down there."

"I'll call them and then get right back to you. Ten minutes."

I hung up the phone and gently pushed JC off my lap. I ran into the bedroom and quickly got dressed. There needed to be a police investigation. Patricia hadn't died a natural death. She had to have been murdered. She had been so afraid. If only she had told me what was wrong.

The phone rang again. It was David. "I'll pick you up in ten minutes, okay?"

"I'll be waiting."

The thought of breakfast made my stomach upset. I checked in the bathroom mirror three times to make sure I looked presentable. I looked terrible. I hadn't slept well, and my hair needed washing. I brushed my hair and put on some pearl earrings. The doorbell rang and I ran to answer it.

David stood there, looking tall and serious. It had been so long since I had seen him. I suddenly wanted to hold him and tell him how utterly stupid I had been and how I really did love him and how I would do anything in the world to get him back, but instead I just said,

"Hi David."

"Are you ready to go?"

"Yes."

"I told the police at my station to get down there, because I think this is going to be a homicide investigation, based on what you told me. We'll talk to them when we get there."

My hands were shaking as I walked down the stairs with him. I wanted him back, but I was sure he had moved on to someone else.

I had gone out on a few dates since we broke up. Francis was a brother of one of my high school classmates. We had gone to a nice restaurant and chatted through the meal. Or rather, he chatted through the meal about his business expertise, his sports prowess, and his love of cars in great detail. By the end of the meal, he knew nothing more about me than my name. That was our first and last date.

Frank Pacelli took me to an expensive Italian restaurant and gave one hint after another about what we could do in bed that night. That was also our first and last date. The only man who seemed promising was named Joseph. He came up to me in the library at Washington University and asked if we could go out for coffee. I really liked him after our first two dates. He gave me a beautiful opal necklace a few weeks after our third date. The next week he told me he had picked it up without paying for it, since he was short on cash. And by the way, could he borrow a few hundred dollars?

I had met someone, though, a few months ago. His name was Paul, and I was seeing him every week. We had gone to school together at Washington University and he had been in my class on criminal justice. He was going into law. We had only seen each other in study groups and that's how he still had my phone number. It had been months since that class, and at first, I didn't know who he was, even when he told me his name.

"Paul, Paul Martinez. Remember, we were in that study group together."

I was embarrassed. "Yes, I'm sorry. I do remember. You have black hair and wear glasses, right?"

"Yep, that's me."

"How are you? How are you doing?" I tried to be friendly and make up for my obvious *faux pas*.

"I'm hoping to go to law school. How about you?"

We talked for quite a while on the phone that evening and

met for dinner at a little restaurant by my apartment. He had been quiet during our study groups but knew how to keep the conversation going during dinner. We talked till the restaurant closed, walked back to my place, where he said goodbye politely. I went to sleep that night feeling for the first time that maybe I could find someone besides David. I just didn't know what to do. I still didn't want to get married—to anyone. Not yet.

Paul was very nice. That was the most exciting word I could think to describe him. After a few more dinners at Acapulco on Kingshighway, he drove me home and at the door, gave me a kiss. I kissed him back, of course, hoping that it would be wonderful. But it wasn't. It was just two people pressing their lips together for a few seconds, and then not. There was no spark, no excitement, no desire. I didn't want more. I just thanked him for the evening, went inside, closed the door and leaned up against it.

Was love just a spark and a desire? No, it was a lot more. It was living together, and caring, and building a life together, maybe a family if we wanted. What difference did it make if the "excitement" wasn't there at first? That would build, I was sure. I just had to give it some time.

I wished I had girlfriends to talk to. Pam wasn't any help. She didn't have a boyfriend yet and wasn't interested in getting one. I had been in a college-bound group in high school. We were proud that we never talked about all that silly gossip about boys. Now I wished I had paid attention to it.

I wandered through a Barnes & Noble bookstore, but it was too high class to find out much about dating advice. I ended up at Kmart and got a few paperback romance novels with pirates and scantily-clad women on the covers. I turned the pages rapidly that evening, shooing away JC so I could keep reading, but I was pretty sure I wasn't learning much about what real love was all about. In fact, I was quite sure I wasn't.

I couldn't ask my mother. She had been the one too embarrassed to have any talk about sex with me at all. I doubted if she wanted to do it now. The all-girls Catholic schools I attended had lots of academic classes, but nothing on reproduction except with chickens in biology.

I kept seeing Paul every week. I liked him. There wasn't that magical feeling I had with David, but I wasn't sure that "magical" feelings were an indication of true, lasting love. After two months, I brought him home to meet my parents for a Sunday dinner. My mom and dad were very polite, but I could tell that they missed David. They had never forgiven me for that.

I came back to the present moment quickly as I looked at David sitting next to me in the car.

We drove quietly for a few blocks until David broke the silence.

"Tell me exactly what Sister Patricia said on the phone."

"She said, 'You've got to help me. Do you have the name of that policeman you're going out with? I need to talk to him.' I told her your name, but said we weren't going out anymore. She asked if I still had your phone number and how to reach you. I gave her your number. She said she got some letters. Some terrible letters. And then she said she had to go. And the line went dead."

"Letters? We'll have to find those."

"She just said she was frightened and then said she had to go and hung up quickly. I have no idea what she was talking about."

"Even though this isn't officially a homicide investigation, we're going to treat it as one, based on what you just told me. I'll get a coroner's report, an autopsy, the whole works. We'll just have to find out what happened."

"I think that's a good idea. I hope I can help—just a little ..." I wasn't sure what to say next. I was looking at him. His black curly hair was even longer, almost to his shoulder, not the usual police look.

"Well, you do know the motherhouse, so I might be asking you a few questions. I already called the chief and talked to him about that and he approved, just in case. How are you, anyway?"

I didn't want to say what I was really feeling so I just answered, "I'm fine. I really like where I am."

"Great. You'll have to help me with these directions. I don't remember where to turn."

"Two more blocks."

"That's right. I remember it now. We'll go to that mother's office first. Is she still the mother or whatever?"

"Mother Alphonse." I smiled. David never did get the superior's names correct. "Yeah, she's still the mother superior, I guess. I haven't really talked to anybody down there until Patricia called yesterday."

"You're not friends with Sister Inez anymore?"

"I sent her a Christmas card—that's about it. Once you leave a place, they don't care as much about you."

David nodded as they pulled up to the front door of the motherhouse. "Yeah, I guess that's true anywhere."

We both walked to the door and David rang the bell.

"This is where we first met, remember? Well, in the basement ..."

"How could I forget that night," I answered smiling, but sad inside.

A tall thin nun answered the door. I had never seen her before, but I was sure there were lots of nuns I had never seen before. The motherhouse was home to about four hundred nuns.

"Police." David showed his badge. "I'd like to speak with the other policemen. Could you take me to them?"

"Follow me, please." The nun led us to a parlor right down the hall where two policemen were sitting with Mother Alphonse.

"Good morning," David said to Mother Alphonse and the two policemen. He nodded to the two policemen and they all walked outside the door together.

I sat opposite Mother Alphonse, who looked ten years older than the last time I had seen her. Her eyebrows were bushy and black hairs stuck out of her chin. She could have at least plucked them. I looked down at the floor. I shouldn't be thinking about things like that right now.

"You're that postulant, aren't you? The one who left. Why are you here?" she said bluntly, staring at me.

I didn't even bother to answer her. I looked out the window at the lawn and trees while I could feel her questioning eyes on me. She didn't scare me anymore.

David walked back into the parlor with the policemen. He turned to Mother Alphonse. "Sister, we need to talk to you about Sister Patricia."

"It's so horrible. We found her body after Mass this morning. One of the sisters saw it on her morning walk and alerted everyone else. She must have accidentally fallen from the roof. We have no idea why she was up there last night."

"Has the body been removed?"

One of the policemen said, "Yes, it's already been taken to Phillips Mortuary."

"I'm requesting an autopsy and opening an investigation into her death. The body will be in police custody for now."

He looked at the two policemen. "I'll be needing your help this morning. This whole area will be a crime scene. We need to check her dormitory and the roof, and I'll be speaking with her classmates."

Mother Alphonse said angrily, "What do you mean? You can't do that! It was a horrible accident."

Then she looked at me. "I still don't understand why she's here. Does this have something to do with *her*?"

"Yes, actually it does," I answered.

David broke in. "She received a disturbing phone call from Sister Patricia yesterday afternoon. She wanted my phone number because she was afraid of someone or something and wanted to talk to the police about it. This is enough evidence for us to open an investigation. We'll be starting the interviews this morning."

"That's ridiculous. You can't just make false accusations against people for an accidental death." She looked at me again. "I remember when you made false accusations against a priest. That's why you were told to leave the order. Isn't it funny that she called you? And no one else. That sounds suspicious to me. And you two are most likely living together in sin! I don't like this at all." She looked at David. "And I will report you to your superiors."

I sat back in shock at her accusations. I never dreamt that I would be accused of making up the whole story. But she was right. I could get proof of a phone call but not what was said during our conversation. I had no proof of the fear in Patricia's voice, being suddenly cut off in the conversation, and the hasty goodbye. All we had was her body.

Her death couldn't have been an accident. Of that I was sure. And David was certainly going to investigate it.

David looked stoic during her tirade and merely replied, "Sister, we'd like to look through her belongings now. I don't need a search warrant. Thank you for getting someone to accompany us to the dormitory."

It was such an obvious dismissal that Mother Alphonse stood and walked out. A few minutes later, a nun meekly walked in. Her eyes were red and she carried a well-worn handkerchief.

"I'm Sister Karin. I just can't believe what happened. We don't understand how she could have fallen."

"Did you know Sister Patricia?"

"Yes, I'm the head of their class. I knew her very well." She started crying.

David said, "I'm very sorry, Sister. Was Patricia upset about anything lately or show any signs of depression?"

"Heavens no. She was such a happy person. She always was there to help everyone." She started sobbing again but quickly got control of herself and wiped her eyes.

"We'd like to speak to some of her closest friends. Can you please arrange that?"

"Yes, of course. I don't really know all of them for sure, but I'll ask some of the sisters. Please wait here."

David stood up. He looked at me. "Maybe you could wait in one of the parlors while we go upstairs."

I walked down the long corridor to the parlor by the main entrance. Thank God I didn't have to wait with Mother Alphonse. The large staircase, climbing up four floors, was off to my left. To my right was the corridor leading to the large chapel with the grandfather clock at the end. I had cleaned this hallway as a postulant—swept it every day, mopped it three times a week. Dusted the balustrades or whatever they were called—the ornately carved posts holding up the railings on the staircase. They were difficult to dust. And Sister Gloria would come by to check to see if I had done a perfect job. She would always find some lingering dust hidden away in a crevice.

I was so glad those days were just memories. What good had all that cleaning done?

I was surprised there wasn't anyone in the corridors. I guess everyone was already in class. I walked into the parlor and sat down on the slippery velveteen chair by the window. In my haste to look good, I had made sure my face and hair looked acceptable but had forgotten to bring a book to read. The parlor wasn't like a doctor's office with plenty of magazines lying around. It was bare. Nothing on the walls either, except for some gloomy pictures of saints. I looked out the window, trying to catch a glimpse of the Mississippi River, but the trees, beautiful in all their varying shades of late summer green, blocked my view.

CHAPTER 4

Wednesday, August 13 - midday

I couldn't just sit for an hour. I'd go see if Inez was in her office on the fourth floor. David didn't say I couldn't go anywhere. I'd leave him a note. No, I'd only be a few minutes, at the most. It would take him a lot longer to complete his investigation. I peeked out the door. No one was there.

I walked up the spiral staircase. It was a lot easier in my short skirt and low heels. I always felt like I was going to trip in the long habit. I'm surprised there weren't a lot more injuries that first year.

Chances were that Inez would be teaching, but then I remembered that she was the president of the college now. She probably had a different office entirely.

But there was her name on her old office door. I knocked softly.

"Yes, come in," a voice called out.

I walked in and peeked around the corner at her desk. Inez had changed her habit to the new, more modern style. She wore a white blouse, blue blazer, blue skirt to her knees, low heels, and a veil that didn't cover all her hair. She looked a lot nicer than she did in that sack-like old habit that we had to wear. I wondered how many had changed. Mother Alphonse and Sister Karin certainly hadn't.

"Kristen?" She smiled. "What are you doing here?"

She took off her glasses, put them on her desk and motioned to the chair next to hers.

"Sit down. It's been a long time."

"I came with David Kelly, the detective, when we heard about Sister Patricia."

"I know, isn't it terrible? But how did you hear about that? I mean, we just found out this morning. It was an accident. She must have fallen off the roof."

"Well, I got a phone call from her last night, and she was upset and wanted David's phone number. That's how we know about it."

"Oh, that's interesting. So how are you? Have you started back to school yet?"

I was stunned at her lack of interest. I had just given her some information that would have fascinated her a few years ago. She would have sat me down and wanted to be part of a murder investigation or at least find out why Patricia had called me and wanted to talk to the police.

I answered carefully, "Oh, I'm fine. I got my own apartment by Tower Grove Park and I'm ready to start my senior year at Washington U."

"Wow, the time sure goes fast. Are you still majoring in English? I hope so."

"Yeah, I took a class in law enforcement, but it wasn't for me. English is really what I want to teach."

"That's great. You know I'm president of the college now?"

"Yes, I heard about that. Congratulations. I guess you're busy."

"I'm teaching one class to seniors, English literature, but the rest of the time is administrative work. I like it, but I like teaching better."

"Well, I should get back to the parlor. I'm waiting there till David finishes his investigation."

I was sure that remark would prompt a few questions.

"Oh well, let's keep in touch," was all she said as she stood up. "Do you have a new phone number? Why don't you give it to me."

I wrote it down on a piece of paper and handed it to her.

"Call me sometime. It was good to see you." She glanced at her watch, a little too obviously.

"Yes, it was good to see you too, Inez. Okay, bye."

And I turned and walked out the door.

This was not the Inez I knew. A few years ago, she would have been all over me, squeezing out every bit of information about Sister Patricia: when she had called, why, what did I think, what had she said? She would have decided that we would solve the murder on our own. She couldn't help herself. That's just who she was.

Only she wasn't anymore. As I walked back to the parlor, I got the strangest feeling that maybe she had something to do with the murder. Maybe she had killed Patricia. No, that was impossible. Maybe she was hiding something she knew. I knew Inez. She would never do anything like that. I knew her well. Or at least I thought I did. I used to know her. I'd been wrong about people before—people who I thought were my best friends.

Why did I have to be so wrong about people? Was I that unaware? That naïve? That gullible? I was beginning to think so.

As I sat back down in the parlor, I debated whether to tell David about my visit with Inez, but before I even thought about it, I heard a knock at the open door.

"Come in," I called out softly. This wasn't my parlor. Anyone could come in. It was Linda, one of my classmates in Patricia's class.

"I was just in the big chapel and was walking down the corridor and I saw you come in here. I need to talk to someone. It's just so terrible about Patricia. You know what happened?"

"Yes, I know."

She started sobbing. "I can't believe it."

I nodded my head.

"What are you doing here?" she managed to get the words out.

Oh, David, I'm so tired of worrying about what you're going to think. I'm going to tell her why I'm here. I'm not part of the investigation. I'm a friend of hers. And you and I aren't even going out anymore, so I don't really care.

"Well, it's the strangest thing. Patricia called me last night. Come to think of it, I don't know how she even got my number since I just moved into my new apartment. But anyway, she called out of the blue and wanted David's number, the detective I've been dating."

"Oh," was all Linda managed to say.

"And then she said something about some letters she had gotten, and she had to hang up, and that was it. I called down here this morning to talk to her and found out she died last night. I called David and we came down together. I'm just waiting for him to finish his preliminary investigation."

"Oh, I'm so glad she called him. She was so worried about the letters."

I interrupted her. "She never got ahold of him. When I talked to him this morning, he said he'd been out late and hadn't gotten any call. What kind of letters were they?"

Linda glanced at the door; I suppose to make sure no one was listening. "They were horrible. They were all about Patricia and me."

"I don't understand." I shook my head.

"We loved each other," she started sobbing again. I just sat there and put my hand on hers. I didn't know what else to do.

I didn't remember that Patricia and Linda were particularly good friends that first year, but a lot can happen in a few years.

Linda tried to go on. "We were going to leave together at the end of our senior year after we graduated and get an apartment together. We could both find teaching jobs in another city and no one would know. We would just be roommates. Well, to everyone else. But we loved each other and wanted to spend the rest of our lives together."

She looked at me carefully as she said this.

"Did anybody here know?" I asked.

"I think a lot of people did. Word got around pretty fast, and some people didn't care, but others were really upset about it. I know it's a terrible sin. But we didn't care."

I sat back in the uncomfortable chair. I had been brought up in the Catholic Church, where homosexuality was a terrible sin, and I was still Catholic, although I was drifting further and further away from the Church. Since I had gotten thrown out of the convent, I had gotten tired of all the rules and prohibitions. I didn't go to Mass very often and I picked and chose what I believed in. I had become a "cafeteria Catholic," that horrible name given to Catholics who were Catholic in name only and picked what beliefs they liked and went to church when they felt like it.

All of that ran through my head when Linda said she had loved Patricia. I wondered what was so bad about that. Love is always better than hate.

"Do you think someone killed her because of that?" I asked carefully.

Linda started crying again. "I don't know. I know she didn't kill herself. She was too happy and had too much to live for. We had wonderful plans for the future. If she was killed because I loved her, I'll never forgive myself."

"You can't think that! If someone killed her, it was because of their hatred, not because of your love!" And I really meant that.

"Do you have the letters?"

"I have them all. Pat didn't want to keep them. She was going to throw them out, but I told her she should keep them. I offered to take them."

"You have to show them to David when he gets here."

Linda shook her head. "I'm too embarrassed. It's one thing to have you know all this, but to have the police know, well, I just can't do that."

I knew we'd have to tell David. Those letters might be the reason Patricia was murdered—if she was actually murdered.

Linda stood up. "I have to go. I just can't sit here anymore. But thanks for listening. I'm going back to the dorm and try to sleep. I can't face anything or anybody else today."

She stood up. I got up and gave her a hug and walked with her to the door. I watched her walk down the corridor and start up the steps to the dorms.

I sat back down. Oh, David, here I was again in the middle of yet another murder investigation. Why had Patricia called me? I couldn't back out of it now.

But this time I didn't care if David was happy or unhappy about it. I was finding my own voice. I could do what I wanted. And right now, I wanted to find out who had killed Patricia. If David and I could work together, that would even be better. If I had to do it on my own, I would still do it. There wasn't any law against it.

I looked at my watch. It was 12:30 and I hadn't heard the Angelus bell. I guessed the roof and bell tower were off limits—probably for the first time in almost a hundred years.

David had been gone about an hour. I watched out the front window, looking at the statue of Mary with her arms outstretched in greeting. I wondered how old the statue was. I wondered what Mary would have thought of Patricia and Linda.

I turned quickly, hearing someone at the door. It was David. I was so glad to see him.

He was apologetic. "It took a long time. I'm sorry you had to wait here with nothing to do."

"Did you find anything?" I asked.

"No, nothing. No blood, no sign of a struggle. The roof tiles were slippery. I could see how someone could be up there and fall accidentally. Except for one thing."

"What was that?"

"The trap door leading to the roof was locked from the inside. So there was someone with her who went back down the stairs afterwards and locked it."

"That was stupid. Why didn't they just leave it open?"

"They weren't thinking? They forgot that someone would know that Patricia hadn't been alone on the roof? Any number of reasons why killers leave their mark. It's rare to see a perfect crime."

"Are you ready to get out of here?" David asked.

"Yes," I answered without hesitation.

"I just have one more thing to do. You can come with me. Sister Karin told me I could talk to your class. She said they'd be at lunch in the dining room."

He walked out the door and went to the right.

"Do you know where you're going?" I asked.

"No, not really. I was hoping you might know."

I took the lead and we turned around. "I know where it is."

David and I walked down the long corridor past the chapel to the dining room. I pushed open the wooden door where everyone was sitting and waiting. A lot of my classmates were crying. Some just looked like they were in shock. They were all wearing the old habits. I guess they hadn't gotten around to giving the students the new ones yet.

Gloria walked up to me. "Oh, it's so good to see you, but isn't it awful about Patricia? Why are you here?" She looked confused.

David turned to Sister Karin.

"I'd like to speak to the class, Sister."

"Of course. Everyone please be silent. This detective would like to say a few words."

I stood off to the side as David went up to the podium. I quickly counted my classmates. We had started with thirty-two in our class. There were only twenty-one left as of this morning.

I could see a few curious stares, but mostly tears and grief.

"Sisters, my name is Detective David Kelly. I want to tell you how very sorry I am about the loss of your classmate and fellow sister. I'm sure she was a good friend to many of you. We'll be investigating her death as a murder investigation, not as an accident."

Many eyes opened wide at that announcement. Heads shook in disbelief. There were some whispers and angry looks.

"We have sufficient evidence to believe that Sister Patricia was murdered last night, and I will be speaking with many of you in the next few days. I'm sorry to be the bearer of even worse news than her death but trust me that we'll find the person or persons responsible and bring them to justice. That's all for now. Thank you, Sister Karin."

He walked back to me, tall and ever the professional. I stood next to him and looked out over this group of sisters who had been my friends and companions but were no longer. It felt so strange to be there. I hadn't seen any of them in over two years, and I felt from a different world and century.

I had left, gotten kicked out actually. I had taken a different road, one that was foreign to them and sometimes myself. I was richer because of the manuscript I had found. I was more independent than any of them, who would be going out on mission wherever they were told. I could do what I wanted. But standing next to David, I wondered if I had given up the one thing that would make me happy: him.

And then my fiercely feminist, independent side screamed, "You don't need a man to make you happy! You need to be happy with yourself first!"

And yes, I knew. I knew all that, as I agreed with myself, but I still felt a loss of something that could have been wonderful, and the tragic feeling that it might be too late. And there was my new friend Paul. Would he turn out to be the one person that I loved more than any other?

I smiled. *If David only knew what I was thinking*, I thought to myself. We walked out, and it wasn't until we were partway down the hall that we could hear the dining room erupt in conversation.

I turned to David. "I'm glad you did that."

"There would be too many rumors if I hadn't. I needed to be clear about why we were here."

We walked in silence out the front door to the already stifling August morning. The trees shimmered in the heat and the car was like an oven.

As we drove down Ripa Avenue, I started the conversation.

CHAPTER 5

August 13 - noon

I had to tell David about the letters. "I need to talk to you about this morning. Do you have time to stop at Steak and Shake for lunch?"

"Does it have to do with the investigation?"

"Oh yes, it definitely does."

"Okay, we can get a quick lunch there."

I noticed that it was only because of the investigation that David had agreed to have lunch. It was a start.

A Steak and Shake was two blocks from my apartment and the air conditioner was already blasting cold air as we walked inside. I grabbed a table and David went up to the counter to order as he called back to me, "Do you want the same as usual?"

"Yes."

We had come so often when we were dating that he knew my order by heart. I watched him at the counter, wondering if he had met someone else. I hoped that he hadn't. What if I had ruined my one chance at happiness? Stop that. I was just tired and emotional. I looked down at the old red-and-white plaid plastic tablecloth, torn in a few places. But then I looked back at him. I couldn't keep my eyes off him. He looked so good.

I turned my head toward the window as he came back with the food and two drinks. After we divided everything, I started to tell him.

"When you were gone this morning, I went up to see Inez."

"Oh no." He wasn't happy to hear that. "Do I have to remind you ..."

"I know. But before you say anything else, she was completely different."

"What do you mean?"

"She knew about Patricia's death, but she completely ignored it. I said I was there because Patricia called me last night and was scared about something—and she just said, 'Oh,' and then asked me if I had started classes yet. That is not Inez!"

"You're right. What else did she say?"

"Just how she was glad I was still majoring in English and then she got my new phone number and said let's stay in touch. And that was it."

"That certainly doesn't sound like the Inez that I remember."

"I think she knows something. A lot more than she's letting on."

David put down his Dr. Pepper.

"Don't. Don't do this. You have nothing, absolutely no reason to think that. Just because she didn't act like *you* thought she should act doesn't mean she was involved in the murder. And I suppose I can't tell you to stay out of this, can I?"

"No, and I'll tell you why. After I was dismissed pretty quickly from Inez's office, I came back to the parlor and Sister Linda knocked on the door and wanted to talk."

"Who's Sister Linda?"

"She's one of my former classmates, and I could hardly tell her to go away," I apologized, hating myself for the apology.

"Of course not." David didn't sound so sure.

"She told me a lot that you should know."

"Go on."

"Well, first of all, she has the letters that Patricia was so worried about. They were hate letters to her and Linda because of their relationship."

"Their relationship? What do you mean?"

"They were in love. They're lesbians, and they were going to leave the order after they graduated, move away, and live together."

I realized it was the first time I had ever used the word "lesbian." Not that it wasn't talked about in the convent, but they were called "particular friendships," and after a few lectures we all figured out what our superiors were warning us about.

"Oh wow." David looked concerned but not shocked or disgusted.

He just said, "I wonder how many people knew about that. We'll have to get the letters. They were most likely sent by the person who killed Patricia."

"I told Linda she should be talking to you, but she felt uncomfortable about it. I guess she was worried about what you might think."

"This is hardly the time to worry about what I might think. We have to find a murderer."

"What do you think, anyway?" I was curious to know. I was still having a difficult time with homosexuality. The Church was so much against it. It wasn't even a topic that was mentioned. Sex education was nonexistent. Probably since we weren't ever going to have any, since nuns took a vow of chastity.

My parents had never spoken to me about sex, and I sure hadn't found anything out in an all-girls high school or the convent. I had a lot to learn.

David and I had kissed a lot, but that was about it. He said he respected me and didn't want to have sex with me until I was ready. Ready to marry him. And I definitely wasn't ready for that, although I was very tempted many times. I'm very sure that he was too.

David took a drink and said, "I had some good friends in theater at the university, and a couple of them were gay. They were great to be around and to be friends with. I guess it never made any difference to me. We even used to joke about it. It didn't think it would happen in the convent, because of the stigma of the Church, but I personally don't care."

"Doesn't it bother you at all? It's taken me a while to realize that it's okay, and that the Church is probably wrong about it being a sin, but I guess I'm just surprised that you feel okay about it."

David was quiet for a few seconds. "My friends got a lot of grief about being gay and I never understood why people were so mean to them, because they were genuinely good people. I guess that's where I got my attitude about it. I never had any church telling me what was right or wrong, since I don't believe in any of that, so it never occurred to me that they were committing a sin. They just loved each other, and it was their own business, not mine. It makes me angry to think there was all that hatred toward Sisters Patricia and Linda. I hope her murder wasn't about that, although it sure seems like it might have been."

We finished breakfast, talking a little more about the nonleads. David wanted to know how my parents were. I knew he wanted to see them, but I couldn't deal with my mother's obvious disapproval of how I had treated him.

"We need to talk to Linda tomorrow," I said. "I mean, you need to. I know I'm not part of this." I looked down at my hamburger that was getting cold and took a bite.

David seemed to choose his words carefully.

"I'm grateful for your help so far. I really mean that. But we can take it from here. That would be the best thing. And from what you just said, Sister Inez won't be interfering either."

My mouth was full of hamburger. I swallowed quickly.

"I know, but you should really talk to her. There's something going on there. I just can't figure out her lack of interest. It's just not her!"

"Okay, we'll talk to as many people as we need to. Don't worry."

David finished the last of his Dr. Pepper.

"Are you liking school and everything?"

"I start this week."

"Oh."

"How's your work going?"

"It's good."

The conversation ground to a halt. That had never happened before. Of course, we had never broken up before. I wanted to ask him if he was dating someone else, if he missed me, if he wanted to get back together, if, if, if, but I didn't know what to say or how to say it.

He broke the silence. "Well, I better get going. I have to get back to work. I'll drop you off at your apartment."

"Okay."

We walked to his car and drove the few blocks to my apartment.

As I got out of the car, I just couldn't stop myself.

"Maybe we could get together for dinner sometime?"

David looked straight ahead, not at me.

"That's probably not a good idea. Let's just keep it professional. It was good to see you, though."

I closed the door and he drove off quickly as I walked to the front door of my old brick building.

Stupid, stupid. Why had I said that? I felt like an idiot.

I was the one who hadn't called him for almost a year. Why would he want to go out now? He was probably seeing someone else. The thought depressed me.

I took the elevator up to the fourth floor and fished in my small purse for my keys. My hands were shaking. Don't be stupid. It's over. And it's all your fault. You had your chance. Now it was time to go and meet some other men and find out what real love was about, not just infatuation.

JC was angry that I had been gone so long, and I scooped

up his chubby body and held him tight. He wriggled out of my grasp and jumped up to the kitchen counter.

"Okay, okay, you don't love me either. I get it. You just want food."

I felt like crying. After I fed JC, I sat down on the couch, and I did cry. For Patricia, for Linda, for me, for everything that was going wrong. For wanting to be part of this investigation and knowing I couldn't be. For losing David forever.

But what could I have done? I wasn't ready to get married. I didn't even know if what I felt for him was love. He was handsome, and I loved being with him, and I loved the way he treated other people. I loved how he treated me! And I loved how I felt when I was with him, but I didn't know if that was love. I did need to meet other people. I knew I had done the right thing. But why did it feel so wrong?

I finally couldn't cry any more. I was just too tired. I didn't feel like doing anything. If I had a hot fudge sundae I would have eaten the whole thing but I didn't have the energy to go get one. Velvet Freeze was in the same shopping center as Steak and Shake, but that seemed miles and miles away.

I walked over to my little upright piano that I had gotten from my parents' home. Someday I would get a beautiful Steinway, but not for a while. And never on a teacher's salary. The money I had gotten from the manuscript was going toward my school tuition and apartment rent. I played a few notes of a Chopin nocturne, but it was too haunting and sad.

I finally called Denise, an acquaintance from last year in school, and we talked about our new schedules and school gossip for a long time. It was just what I needed to get my mind off everything. She had no idea that our mundane and trivial conversation was so important.

CHAPTER 6

Monday, August 18 - morning

By Monday morning I was ready to prepare for my classes and I tried to put the murder behind me. David would take care of it. I probably wouldn't hear from him again. Maybe I could call him in a few weeks to see how the investigation was going. No, I'd wait till he called me, even though it would kill me.

The phone rang as I was listening to the morning news on TV, fixing JC his canned Friskies, still in my pajamas. I put the bowl down in front of JC and picked up the phone in the living room.

"Kristin? It's Linda from the convent. Sorry to bother you."

I cleared my throat. "It's no bother. How are you today?"

"I guess I'm okay. But I know I have to give that detective all those letters today, and I wanted you to see them before I gave them to the police."

"I'm not sure that's a good idea. David, I mean Detective Kelly, will know what to do with them a lot more than I will."

"I know. I understand. And I realize it's an imposition. I just thought if you could come down early—before he got here …"

"Do you know when he's coming?" I asked without really meaning to.

"He told Sister Karin he would be down in the afternoon to get the letters and talk to some people. If you came now, I could show them to you."

"I really don't think you need me, Linda. He's a good detective. And I know he'll understand the situation. He's very open-minded."

"Okay, I understand why you don't want to get involved. You just seemed so understanding yesterday, I really appreciated it." She started to cry.

If she hadn't started to cry, I wouldn't have gone.

"Okay, I can be down there in a half hour. Can I meet you in the library?"

"Yes, yes, and thank you. It's really important to me. It means a lot."

I hung up the phone. No, I didn't want to do this. I'd have to tell Linda that she couldn't tell David that I'd seen the letters. Besides, what good would it do? It's not like they were hidden or anything. And they weren't evidence—yet.

David would have all of them in a few hours anyway. And why did I still care what David thought? Linda was a friend who was asking me to look at the letters. That was all. I could do what I wanted. I wasn't interfering with anything.

I ran back in the bedroom and changed quickly into a nice flowery dress. I wanted to look my best, like I was happy and doing well. And I was, except for David. And that was nobody's fault but my own.

"I'll be back soon." I picked up JC and gave him a squeeze, which he did not like. "Okay, okay. Go do your cat thing, whatever that is."

He squirmed out of my hands onto the floor and ran into the bedroom.

I grabbed my purse and headed back down to the motherhouse. I had a strange feeling that it wouldn't be the last time.

I walked through the large carved wooden door to the motherhouse and across the skyway to the college and library. Damn, we said we'd meet in the library, but it was three stories, and I had no idea where she would be. Luckily, she was sitting by the main entrance with her books and notebooks, looking ready for class. I nodded to her and we walked to a table back in the far corner. Thank God the library was empty. I guess everyone was still doing chores.

She opened a notebook and took out a large manila envelope full of at least twenty letters.

"Here, this is the first one."

I took a Kleenex out of my purse and held the letter with that, trying not to get my fingerprints on it. I knew that much from the other two investigations. It was made up of cut-out taped phrases from newspapers and magazines, carefully glued to make sentences.

> *What you're doing is sin.*
> *You will go to hell.*
> *Disgusting.*
> *Sinner.*
> *Burn in hell.*

I could barely read the crude and horrible letter. Two pages of glued typed words that just repeated over and over.

No wonder Patricia had been scared.

"Are they all like this? And they were addressed to Patricia, not to you?" I managed to say as I handed the first one back to her.

"Yes, all the same, with very few variations. Just over and over. They were coming once, sometimes twice a week, just to Patricia. But this is the strange thing ..."

"What?" I couldn't imagine anything stranger or more disgusting than the letters themselves.

"Every one of them comes from a different city."

"What?"

"Yes, from Austin, Minneapolis, Denver, New York, San Francisco, everywhere. They just crisscross the country."

I stared at the letters. Each one had a bright and interesting stamp from the city or state where it originated.

"So the person who sent them wasn't a sister here."

"No, they couldn't have been."

"Who would have known about you outside the convent? And who would have cared? And who could have gotten in here late at night and killed Patricia? None of this makes any sense."

"I know. That's all I can think about, and I can't figure any of it out."

"But it was somebody who really hated what you were doing."

Linda started to cry again. "I know. We should never have been so obvious. We should have waited till we left and moved away. It's all my fault she got killed."

I took her hand gently.

"No, it's the fault of the person who killed her. It's not your fault. You loved each other and would have never hurt each other—ever."

I still didn't know what good it had done to show me the letters, but I was grateful that she trusted me.

"Please give all of these to the detective. He'll know what to do with them. And he'll be able to figure this all out. It's what he's really good at."

Linda looked right at me. "What happened? Why aren't you guys still going out?"

It was a very personal question and it wasn't any of her business, but I somehow wanted to explain it to her. I didn't exactly know why.

"Well, I really liked him, and he wanted to get married, but he was the only person I'd ever dated. I just wasn't ready to get married and I told him I wanted to meet other people. We haven't gotten back together again."

Linda asked, "Do you want to?"

I blurted out, "Yes, I really do, but I think he's tired of waiting. He's probably found somebody else."

"Do you love him?" she asked.

"I think I do. Yes, I do, I guess. Oh Patricia, you know what it's like. It's awfully confusing. That year inside here with all the talk about sexual prohibitions and everything—well, you of all people know what I mean. How did you and Patricia ever manage to fall in love?"

"It wasn't easy. I mean, the feelings I had for her. I knew they were sins, but I just couldn't stop the feelings. And then when I realized that she felt the same way about me ... well, we both had to come to some decisions about what was right and wrong and what God really wanted for us. It was a difficult year that we went through, with no one to talk to about it. But I don't regret my love for her at all. Not at all, not ever."

I could see the tears streaming down her face.

"If you feel the same way about your friend the detective, don't let anything stand in your way. You'll know if it's love."

I sat there and took her hand. I didn't know what else to do. I couldn't believe I was talking to Linda, a lesbian, about my love life, or lack of it. And that she was sympathetic. And I felt like I could really talk to her about David and that she would understand. It was the strangest experience. I wanted to talk to her longer, but this wasn't the time and I had to get out before David came for the letters.

"Linda," I whispered, "I should probably go. I'm so glad you showed me the letters. I have no idea who could have sent them. Nobody in the order travels around the country like that. It's so strange. But David will figure it out. I know he will."

"Are you coming to the funeral? It's this Saturday at ten. Please come," she practically pleaded.

"I'll try to be there. You know I will. Stay strong."

We both stood and I gave her a hug before I turned and walked through the stacks of books to the entrance of the library.

As I was leaving the library, I saw Sister Rebecca, our science teacher, walking down the hall towards me.

"Kristen, I'm so glad I ran into you. I wanted to talk to you. Do you have a minute?"

"Sure." I couldn't imagine why Sister Rebecca wanted to talk with me. I hadn't had her in class since my freshman year and that was for an introduction to science class. I wasn't the best student either.

"I know this might not be important, but I thought I should tell you. I know you're going out with that detective, and you might want to tell him."

I just let it go. I didn't want to explain our relationship—or lack of it—anymore.

"Anything you can tell us might be important." I figured it would be simpler for me to hear what Rebecca had to say and then tell David.

"Well, my summer school class met over in the science building at about nine last Tuesday night and we went outside on the lawn to watch the meteor shower. Did you know there was a meteor shower last week?"

"No, I completely forgot about it."

"It's called the Perseid shower. It's one of the best in the whole year. Anyway, I invited some sisters from the class who I thought might be interested. I think everyone was back in their dorms by eleven p.m. I had no idea that anyone might go out on the roof afterwards. I probably shouldn't have told them that the meteor shower got better later at night ..."

"Do you think that could be why Sister Patricia was up there?" I asked.

"I have no idea. Someone might have mentioned it to her. I just thought I should say something, because everyone seems to wonder what she was doing on the roof."

"Was she particularly interested in astronomy, Sister?"

"I think so; she was getting a degree in biology, but I know she was interested in a lot of other areas of science. Like I said, I don't know if it means anything, but I thought I should mention it."

"Can I have a list of the people in your group that night?"

"Of course. I'll get it to you tomorrow. I have the members of my class, but there were a few people I didn't even recognize who were there. It wasn't important at the time."

CHAPTER 7

Saturday, August 23

I didn't think I'd hear anything else from David and I was right. Not a word. Why had I been so stupid as to suggest that we could go out for a dinner? That was a thing of the past. But after I talked to Linda, I realized more and more how much I cared for him. Oh damn, I loved him. I couldn't go on denying it. But now I had ruined everything. I tried to think about other things all week. I talked to Mom a lot and practiced the piano and did everything I could to stay busy.

Saturday morning, I dressed carefully to go to the funeral. It was the last place I wanted to be, but I felt a sense of obligation to Patricia—and Linda—to attend. Patricia's mother, father, and younger sister sat in the front pew of the motherhouse chapel, and I sat in the back. I could see David a few rows in front of me, but he didn't notice me. I watched him throughout the service. He stood up when everyone else did, but it was obvious he wasn't quite sure what was going on. That was okay. Most Protestants had no idea of the elaborate rituals that Catholics still followed.

Linda saw me afterwards at the reception and gave me a hug, introducing me to Patricia's parents and sister, and by the time I was able to get away from them and a few other old classmates who wanted to talk about the murder with nothing to say about it, David was gone. But as I walked out to the parking lot, I saw his car was still there. He was sitting in it, doing some paper-work, and called to me as I walked a few aisles over to mine.

"Do you want a quick lunch at Steak and Shake? And then I have to get back to work."

"Okay." I dreamed quickly of this being the chance to get back together with him. I couldn't keep up with this hot and cold relationship. Then I reminded myself—what relationship?

We drove separately to the restaurant on Hampton Avenue. We got our regular orders and got a table by the window look-ing out to the traffic.

"I'm really glad you called me," he said as he squeezed ketchup on his fries. "I know they would've said it was an acci-dent, without your phone message."

"I wish she had gotten to talk to you—or me."

"Well, yeah, I have to admit I'm pretty confused about the whole investigation. Being on the roof that late at night with the murderer, whom she must have trusted."

"Oh, I need to tell you something about that. Sister Rebecca saw me the other day at the motherhouse and told me something interesting."

"When were you at the motherhouse?" he asked.

Damn, he didn't know I was there to look at the letters of Linda's.

"Oh, I don't remember which time it was, but she told me why Patricia might have been on the roof."

I told David what Sister Rebecca told me, and he didn't seem to question why I was there any longer. Thank God. He kept talking. He told me about the letters from all over the country, which I supposedly didn't know anything about.

I answered appropriately. "I don't understand that at all," I said.

"The letters from all over the country? Yeah. Who in your order travels around like that? It wasn't just a person dropping off letters on a road trip. They were from so many different places. And there must be more people who hated that she was a lesbian. And she had quite a few rejected lovers—or "good friends." I'm finding that out from the interviews I've been doing. It could easily have been one of those."

"What are you going to do next?" I asked.

"Keep the interviews going. Maybe I need to ask if anyone knows someone who travels around the country?"

I shook my head. "That could be anyone. Someone's brother, sister, father on business. And it would have to be someone who was in on the murder, who knew what was in the letters."

"Not necessarily," David took a drink of Coke and stared out the window.

I disagreed. "Why would someone agree to mail letters from all over the country? I wouldn't do that. I'd say, 'Mail them yourself.'" I took a last bite of the hamburger.

David was quiet for a few minutes, thinking. Then he said, "When you broke up with me, you wanted to meet new people. I just wondered if you had met anyone these past few months. If you don't mind my asking?"

I couldn't let him know what I was really feeling, so I said, "Yes, I have. His name is Paul. He was in one of my study groups at the university and he's studying law. Are you seeing anybody?"

"Yes, her name's Julie. I met her at a police fundraiser a few months ago."

He smiled. I could tell immediately that he liked her.

"She's really nice."

My heart broke a little when he said that, but I forced myself to ask about her.

"What's she like?"

"She has her degree in political science and is very active in the city campaigns this year. She has a big Italian family, but they've been very welcoming, and I feel part of the family already. Lots of brother and sisters, nieces, nephews. Dinner at their place is chaos. It's great to get back to my apartment with her afterwards for some peace and quiet."

He paused for a few seconds. "She's closer to my age, too. I think maybe that makes a difference. She knows more of what she wants out of life." He took a last drink of soda.

"I'm glad we've both been able to move on with our lives."

David looked like he wasn't sure if he wanted to keep talking, but then he said, "You know, it was really hard for me to lose you. I thought we had something together and then it was over. I kept expecting you to call, but you never did."

I looked out the window at the traffic and willed myself not to cry. "I'm sorry."

"No, it's fine. I would have never met Julie and you would have never met your friend, so it's all worked out for the best."

I didn't dare tell him what I was feeling: that my friendship with Paul was nothing compared to what I felt for him. I had been so stupid, but I thought I was doing the right thing at the time. Now I realized I had done the worst thing possible. There wasn't a chance in the world I'd ever get him back.

We didn't have much more to say after that. We said good-bye politely in the parking lot, like we were just acquaintances, not even friends.

CHAPTER 8

Sunday, August 24

I told myself that it was okay that the relationship was over. I needed to get ready for my semester at Washington University—and the rest of my life. I had nothing to contribute to the investigation except what I had already told David. I was finished with it.

On Sunday evening I was getting all my books ready for the new semester when the phone rang. I'm one of those people who loves when the phone rings. I pushed the books off my lap and ran to the phone, picking it up after four rings.

"Hi," I answered quickly, with just the tiniest hope that it might be David.

"Hi, this is Linda—again. I know I just keep bothering you, but you're the only one I can turn to."

She sounded close to tears again.

"Of course, I understand." I tried to sympathize. I sat down in a dining room chair that I pulled over, knowing this would probably take a while.

"I got another letter."

"Oh no." I was a little surprised. Didn't the murderer know when to stop? What was the need for more letters? The damage had been done.

"Yes, and it was just as horrible as the others."

"Well, give it to David ..."

"I'm worried now that the murderer will come after me."

Oh wow, I hadn't even thought about that. I could see why Linda was worried.

"I know this is a terrible imposition, but ... but I was wondering if I could come and stay at your place for a few days. Classes haven't started yet, so I wouldn't be missing anything in school, and it wouldn't be for long, just till the detective finds out who murdered Patricia. I'm just so worried because someone is still out there who hates me. He or she hated Patricia enough to kill her and they must feel the same about me. I know it's terrible of me to ask this, but I don't know what else to do."

Linda finally stopped long enough to take a breath and I said, "Who was the letter addressed to?"

"It was addressed to Patricia, like all the others."

"That's so strange. Like they didn't even know she was gone."

"Yeah, I know. I don't understand that. If the letters came from the murderer, they would know she was dead."

"You have to tell David right away."

"I already called him and told him about the letter."

"And yes, of course you can stay here as long as you want. At least until David and the police solve the murder. I know how you must feel."

I could hear Linda crying. "Thank you so much. I don't know how I'm going to tell Sister Karin, but I'm just going to tell her that I have to do this. I know she'll understand. I just can't stay here. When can I come?"

"As soon as you can be ready. I can pick you up tomorrow morning if you want."

"Oh, that would be wonderful. I'll have everything ready to go in the morning. I promise I won't be a bother. And I can help you with the cooking and cleaning and everything."

"Linda, you won't be a bother. Don't even think that for a

minute. And tell David where you'll be so he can find you if he needs to contact you."

"Oh, I will. I'll give him a call in the morning before you pick me up. Just come to the main door. I'll make sure Sister Karin knows that you're coming."

After I hung up the phone, I started to straighten up the apartment. It was a good thing I had enough room, and the couch pulled out to a bed in the living room. We could work things out. It was better that Linda felt safe here. I remembered when that "fake postulant" got killed my first year as a nun and I was afraid for my life in the motherhouse. I knew that Linda felt the same way, and it was a terrible feeling. Nowhere to go and not feeling safe anywhere.

Suddenly I wondered what David would think about this little arrangement. He probably would think I was interfering as usual. But I wasn't—Linda had asked me as a friend. And why should I care? We weren't going out anymore and I really didn't care what he thought. But I did.

And why did it thrill me that I might find out more about the murder investigation? It would only help if I did discover something. David should be glad. I was so tired of wondering what David would think. But I still worried.

The next morning, I drove to the motherhouse at ten o'clock. Linda was waiting in the parlor off the main hall.

"Oh, I'm *so* glad to see you. I couldn't sleep at all last night; I was so worried. Thank you so much for having me."

"Did you talk to David?"

"Not yet. I figured I'd call him from your place."

"Okay, I guess we're all set to go."

Linda picked up a little suitcase and a few books and we left the motherhouse. I knew how she felt. I wondered how long she would be staying, though. My apartment wasn't really made for two people. As we turned out of the parking lot I thought about JC. I had forgotten to ask her about cats!

"Linda, do you like cats?" I prayed she wasn't allergic.

"Yeah, I used to have a cat growing up, but he died a long time ago. I miss him."

"Well, I have a cat. I hope you like him."

"What's his name? I'm sure we'll get along just fine."

I felt better already. JC was the friendliest cat I had ever met. He would jump up onto anyone's lap. I was glad Linda wasn't allergic. That would have been a big problem. He and Linda sounded like they might get along, though, which was very important.

After we got home, I heard just a little of what Linda was saying on the phone, I assumed to David, and when she handed the phone to me, I knew that's who she was talking to. I walked in the bedroom, pulling the long cord with me.

"What's this about Linda staying with you?" David asked cautiously.

"She called me and was worried and asked if she could stay with me for a while. That's all."

"Well, okay." There was a long pause. "How are you anyway?"

"I'm fine. Just getting ready for school. It starts next week. How about you?"

"I'm fine. Well, okay, I have to go. I'll keep in touch with Linda about the investigation. Let her know."

"Okay, I will. See ya."

"Bye."

That was the shortest conversation David and I had ever had. Or maybe the second shortest. Who knew. They were all short now. I guess our relationship was really over. Why did I think that it would magically revive itself? I just wish I knew for sure. Don't be an idiot. Of course you know for sure. It's over.

Linda was a great guest. She loved JC and played with him. He loved following his mouse toy around the apartment and pouncing on it unexpectedly. I could tell they both were having a good time. And she was finally able to relax.

After dinner that night—a quick dinner of spaghetti that I picked up from Cunetto's—we sat and talked about a lot of things.

"Everyone's been so kind to me since Patricia died. I know that it wasn't anyone in the convent who sent the letters. But I still can't understand where they came from. They had to come from someone who knew about our relationship, and I can't think of anyone outside who even knew about it."

"I've thought about that a lot, too, and I just can't figure it out. I hope David is able to get more evidence. I feel bad that he can't share anything with us, not that he'd want to share it with me anyway, since we're not even friends anymore."

I talked to Linda about how things turned out so badly with David, and how I wished they could be different.

She told me about how kind people had been since Patricia had died. It was so much more than she had expected, considering their relationship.

"Karen Grady has been wonderful, and Lois, and Geraldine. They've been so sweet. I didn't expect people to be so kind. I kind of felt like everybody was against us, but I'm finding out that a lot of people were okay with our relationship. And Sarah. She always wanted to be friends with me, maybe a little more than I wanted. She's really been there for me. Actually, a little too much. I could use a little space, if you know what I mean. She's constantly asking if I'm okay, which I'm not, but that will just take time. It's not something that will magically get better right away. She's kind of suffocating in a way. That's a terrible thing to say, isn't it? She's such a nice person. But she's another reason why I'll be glad to be here for a while. Have you ever had that happen?"

"Yeah, someone is high school was like that. I finally just told her to leave me alone. I didn't know what else to do. Friendships are weird like that sometimes. It's so hard to find people who like you back in just the same way. I guess it's the same with love."

"I never thought I'd find anyone who loved me until I met Patricia, and then all of a sudden there was someone who liked me just the way I am. I never had *that* happen before. And I felt the same way about her."

I wanted to change the subject quickly. I didn't think she needed to cry again so soon.

"I love the way you play with JC. He loves you. I think he likes you better than he likes me."

"Oh no, he loves you. But he's a cat. He'll play with anybody and have fun. He'll forget all about me when I'm gone."

"Well, I'm sure glad he has another person to play with. He's enjoying it a lot."

I thought that night about what David had said—and implied—the other day when he spoke about Julie. Julie was closer to his age—and knew what she wanted out of life.

It was a nice way of saying that I was immature and had no idea what I wanted in life. The truth of that statement, as kindly put as possible, hit me hard. I *was* immature. I followed what other people wanted me to do. I had joined the convent mostly because of a friend's experience—I followed the rules until I got kicked out. I did whatever Inez told me to do with the investigation. I needed to start growing up.

Breaking up with David was probably the best thing I could have done for him. I was just too immature for him. I wished it had been the best thing for me, though. But maybe it was. Maybe I needed to be on my own for a while before I gave up my freedom and followed someone else again. David could be controlling. And I was easy to control. He needed someone who was independent and sure of themselves though, not a person like me.

I was getting my degree, but the rest of my life seemed to be falling apart. I had lost David, I didn't love Paul, I was immature and didn't know what I wanted, and now I was involved with another murder that I wanted to stay as far away from as possible—with the very person who broke my heart every time I saw him.

CHAPTER 9

Tuesday, August 26

The next day at dinner Linda looked upset and said she wasn't feeling very good.

"What's wrong?" I asked.

"I just found out something today that worries me."

"What are you talking about?"

"Well, after Patricia died and her parents and sisters came for the funeral, they took all her belongings back with them. She didn't have very much, just her books and pictures and some personal things, I guess. But I had given her a necklace last year that she wore every day. It was a diamond and ruby necklace in a very old setting that had belonged to my grandmother. I figured that it had been returned to her parents with all her stuff. I hadn't really thought about it and I didn't want to bring it up at the funeral, but I called them today. They weren't home, so I left a message and asked them about it, hoping that they'll return it to me. It belongs to my family. Anyway, I hope they have it and I hear back from them soon. Just another thing to worry about."

The next few days went by quickly. Linda walked to the market in the next block and did the shopping for the week and decided to fix all our meals. I didn't know what to do with myself, so I practiced the piano a lot and got caught up on my reading for the next semester in school. It was delightful having her there.

I missed David when I practiced the piano. He used to love hearing me play. He would sit on the couch and listen and tell me which pieces he loved and which ones were his favorites. He loved Bach, just like I did, and Chopin. I loved playing for him. The apartment seemed so empty without him listening.

One afternoon the phone rang and I answered it. It was David. He didn't know quite what to say and neither did I.

"Hi, Kristen." He hesitated a second. "Is Linda there?"

"Yes," I said quickly. "I'll get her."

I walked into my bedroom and closed the door so I wouldn't hear the conversation. It was over very quickly.

I walked back out into the living room.

"That was Detective Kelly, as you know. He just wanted to update me on the investigation. There isn't anything new going on. But that was nice of him to call."

I agreed. I just wished he had been able to say a few words to me.

CHAPTER 10

Friday, August 29

David called later in the week, wanting to talk to Linda, of course. She called to me in the kitchen, "Can Detective Kelly come over here tomorrow and ask me a few questions?"

"Of course he can."

"And I asked him if he minded if you were here and he said no. I just feel more comfortable with you here."

"Sure, I'll be here if you want," I said, thinking to myself that David probably wasn't too happy about it.

The next afternoon I dressed carefully in a print dress and made sure my hair looked as best it could. Why I even bothered I don't know, but I guess deep in my heart I hoped there was still a chance, even though I knew there wasn't. I was acting like a teenager, even though I had turned twenty-one on June 30. I never had acted like a teenager when I was one in high school with any boy, so I figured I had the right to do it now. It was so immature, and now I was waiting for him, my heart racing at the thought of seeing him again. I felt myself blushing before he even got to the door. Get over it, I told myself.

The doorbell rang and I answered it, trying to be as cool as possible.

"Hi, how are you?"

"Fine, and you?"

"I'm good."

"Come on in. Linda is waiting for you."

"Where's my little detective?"

JC ran up to David and David picked him up and held him tight. I could hear JC's purr loud and clear.

"He sure loves you," I commented.

"And I feel the same about my little boy." He turned him over and held him like a baby. David was the only person who could get away with that. JC continued to purr.

Linda came in and we all sat at the dining room table. David took out his notepad.

"I wanted to ask you a few questions about some of the sisters that you know in your class and what your impression is of them. It might give me a better idea of who to interview next."

"What is your relationship with Sister Jeanette?"

I could see that Linda didn't feel comfortable at all talking about Jeanette.

"She hated Patricia and me. She had no hesitation telling us what she thought about lesbians. The Catholic Church said it was a sin and so it was a sin. That's what she believed, and she thought we had no business being or staying in the convent. She made that perfectly clear. She hated me."

"Do you think she could have killed Patricia?"

"Killed her? No, absolutely not. Jeanette is a good person. She would never harm anyone. She really felt what she was doing was right, and that we should be saved from sin, whatever that meant. I think she was looking out for our best interests—I guess. She would never hurt anyone."

"What about this Sister Karen?'

"Oh, she used to be my good friend when we were first-year students. I guess you could say we had a relationship. But it didn't last very long, and I think I hurt her a lot when I broke it off. We just didn't have anything in common. And she got over it pretty fast and made other friends, so I didn't feel too bad. I think she really hated me for a while, but she's gotten over it."

"Do you think she could have killed Patricia to get back at you?"

"No, I think she's over it completely and has found other friends and would never kill anyone. She's not the person you're looking for."

"Is there anyone else who we should be talking to?"

"Well, Lois and Geraldine have been so helpful, you certainly don't need to talk with them. Sylvia doesn't really like me, but I don't know if she just dislikes me or if she just didn't like our relationship. There is this one person, but I hate to mention her because she's been so kind to me. Her name is Sarah, and she's really helped me out these past few weeks since Patricia died."

"Then why do you think we should be talking to her?"

"Oh, I don't know. It's just that she's said some things, like she really wants to be better friends with me and is glad that now she has the chance. Kind of like she never had the chance before since I was involved with Patricia. It makes me feel kind of creepy. I know she doesn't mean anything by it though, and she's just being kind, which she is. A little suffocating, though. Have you ever known anyone like that?"

David and I both nodded our heads at the same time. I knew someone in high school who really wanted to be my friend, my best friend, but we didn't even have anything in common and I didn't like her very much. She just hung around and wouldn't leave me alone. I didn't know quite what to do, so I completely understood. I wondered what David's experience had been.

"Do you think she would kill Patricia to be with you?"

"Oh, God no. She's such a sweet person. I don't know why I even mentioned her. It's just that I don't know exactly what to say to her, because I don't want to hurt her feelings.

"And Sylvia has been acting very weird since Patricia's death. She won't even talk to me, and we used to talk a lot. I know that she knew about Patricia and me—at least I thought she knew—but she's been so cold recently. I don't understand it at all. Like she blames me for Patricia's death."

I said quickly, "I'm glad you're staying here for a while. That's one thing you don't have to worry about. The only annoying person around here is JC."

Linda objected. "JC annoying? Of course not! JC is the best for making me feel better. Besides you guys, of course," she added quickly.

"Can you think of anyone else that I might want to interview?" David brought the discussion back to reality.

"No, not really, but it could be anyone. I mean, it doesn't have to be anybody in our class. There's a lot of older sisters especially who really disapproved of our lifestyle, but for someone to murder her is a whole different level of hatred that I can't even imagine anyone possesses."

"I know," said David. "But the fact is that there is someone at the convent who did possess that level of hatred and did kill her, even if we can't imagine it."

I added, "It's horrible to think that we—you and I—lived with a person who was capable of that kind of hatred, and we weren't even aware of it."

David added, "People have depths to their personalities that we can't even imagine. If I've become aware of anything in being a detective, it's that people are way more complex than we know. And for as many good people as there are, there are some very bad ones out there, capable of acts of hatred."

He closed his notebook. "Thanks for your insights. I'll be working on these interviews that you suggested. Hopefully we'll get some leads from them."

"Do you want to stay for lunch or go out and get something," I asked politely since it was almost noon.

"Oh, no thanks," he said quickly, not even looking at me, pretending that the offer had come from Linda. "I've got to get back to the office and get some work done. I'll be talking to you, Linda. Thank you."

I walked out the door after David. I had to tell him something. I ran down the steps and he was just walking out the lobby door as I called to him.

"Could you sit down for a few minutes? I need to talk to you, please."

"Sure." He sat down on the leather couch by the front entrance, and I sat next to him.

I took a deep breath. I had realized that first moment when I saw David again that I loved him and wanted to get back together with him. I didn't even care about marriage anymore. Just to be with him was enough. I really liked Paul, but there was no doubt about who I really loved. I had to do this.

"David, I'm so sorry about these past months. I've learned so much about myself. I realize how important you are to me. I'm hoping we can try again." There. I said it. My heart was beating way too fast. I prayed that he'd give the right answer.

He looked down at the floor for a minute or two. It seemed forever. I felt my face getting red. I had gone too far.

Then he looked right at me and said, "I'm sure you've learned a lot, but here's the thing. I was really hurt when you broke this off. I felt I had found the person I wanted to spend my life with, and I realize you weren't ready yet to make that commitment. I understood. But it still hurt—a lot."

"I'm think I'm ready now to really appreciate the person you are. I know I am."

"I know, but I don't think I am. I don't want to be hurt again when you find someone else. You've already found somebody. And so have I. It wouldn't be fair to either of them for us to get back together. And I just don't think I could do this again. I do miss the time we spent together. I miss your family, your mom and dad, the dinners. I miss all of it. But I just couldn't do it again and end up being miserable. Let's just keep it professional, okay?"

He stood up quickly, turned, and walked out the door to his car. I walked back upstairs to my apartment. I heard JC meowing as I came in the door. I picked him up, but he squirmed out of my hands. He wanted food, not me. I quickly went into my room and closed the door. The last person I wanted to see was Linda. I didn't want to see anyone.

Why was I so stupid to think David would come running back to me when I decided I needed him? It was too late.

Even though Linda fixed a nice meal that evening, it tasted bland, and I couldn't think of much to say to her. I felt bad, but I said I had a headache and went to my bedroom early. She watched TV but I wasn't up to it. I laid awake in bed that night, convincing myself that I had done the right thing. I could understand why David didn't want to go through the same frustration and sadness that I had put him through. We were both right, I realized sadly. The timing was off on what could have been the most wonderful relationship I might ever have.

But I was strong and resilient. I would find someone else, or maybe no one. I had to tell Paul that it wasn't going to work out for us. I couldn't let him think that I loved him when I realized that I didn't. It wasn't fair to him. I could live by myself. I had enough money, my own place. I didn't need a man. I could do it on my own.

I still cried myself to sleep, thinking about what could have been.

Maybe Patricia and Linda were the smart ones. Grab love when you could and hold on to it. What was wrong with loving someone? It was condemned by the Church and society, but it was certainly better than hate. Love was always better than hate. Not that Patricia hadn't made lots of mistakes with her lovers. But I was making lots of mistakes, too.

CHAPTER 11

Sunday, August 30

I finally called Paul Sunday morning. It had been a week since I had heard from him, but he might have tried to call when I was out. He was my boyfriend, after all.

I knew he'd either be sleeping or studying. He picked up the phone quickly.

"Paul, hi, It's Kristen. Sorry I'm calling so early."

"That's fine. I tried calling you a few times this past week, but you weren't home. Everything okay?"

"Yeah, but I just want to let you know some things that have been going on."

"Okay. I'm sorry I haven't called more often. My parents were moving this past weekend and I was helping them. Do you want to go out Tuesday night? And what's been going on?"

"A friend of mine from the convent was murdered and I'm kind of involved in it."

"Murdered? Oh my God, I'm so sorry. What happened? Did you know her well?"

"I lost track of her these past few years, but she called me right before she was murdered and wanted my friend David's number. She didn't reach him before she was killed, so we don't know what happened."

"Oh, that's terrible. Where did it happen? Was she still in the convent?"

"Yes, it happened down at the motherhouse."

"I'm so sorry. Is there anything I can do to help? Do you still want to go out on Tuesday?"

"Yeah, I think it would be good to get my mind off of everything."

"I'll pick you up around five for dinner. Okay?"

"That sounds great. Thanks, Paul."

CHAPTER 12

Tuesday, September 2

Paul picked me up for dinner at our little restaurant on Tuesday night. I was prepared to tell him that I didn't want to see him anymore but had no idea how to start the conversation. We chatted for a while before the waitress took our order. Paul looked at me and said, "I have some exciting news I've been wanting to tell you. I found out last Friday."

"What?" I was happy to put off my conversation for as long as possible.

"I've been accepted at Yale Law School. I'll be going in a week. I wanted to tell you right away."

I didn't know what to say. I didn't have to break up with him. He had just broken up with me, in a very nice, wonderful way. But broken up, nonetheless.

"Paul, that's wonderful. I'm so excited for you." And I really was. That was his dream. And to be accepted at the most prestigious law school in the country was all he could ever want.

He went on. "I'm going to miss you, you know, but it just wasn't going to work out between us anyway. You have your school here, and this is going to take all my time for the next few years, and well, it just would be impossible."

"Oh, Paul, I'll miss you too, but I understand. I really do." I felt a huge sense of relief wash over me. I didn't have to break up with him. I didn't feel too bad about him leaving. And he didn't sound like he felt bad at all about leaving me. He was a wonderful person, but there wasn't that spark, that magic, that I felt with David. I pushed away the thought that even though the magic was there, David wasn't.

As I laid in bed that night, I realized that I had gone from dreams of having two boyfriends and deciding which one to choose, to having none, all in the space of a few days. I felt lonely. JC curled up in bed with me and I petted him behind his ear. He might have to be enough. He was enough. I would be just fine.

CHAPTER 13

Monday, September 8

School started and I was taking a lot of classes. This was my senior year and I was getting a degree in English as well as my teaching certificate. All of a sudden I was busy. Linda was going to start classes the next week at the college and we hadn't decided yet what she was going to do about her living arrangements.

David had a lot of interviews, but he wasn't any closer to finding the murderer than he had been a few weeks before. Linda couldn't stay much longer because she had to start school and she didn't have a car. She had to be at the motherhouse for her classes. I hated to kick her out, but it seemed more and more likely that I was going to have to suggest that she go back to the motherhouse very soon, even if she was terrified. She knew that was going to happen, and I could tell she was getting more worried each day.

I walked into the kitchen to put salmon in the oven for dinner and the phone rang again. I rinsed my hands quickly and picked up the receiver.

"Hello," I said quickly, glad I had gotten it on the final ring.

"Hello, Kristen, this is Sister Karin. Could I speak to Sister Linda, please?"

"Sure, hold on a second."

I handed the phone to Linda, whispering, "It's Sister Karin."

I couldn't help but hear the short conversation.

"Another letter? Okay, I'll come and pick it up, maybe tomorrow. Thanks for letting me know. Bye."

She put the phone down.

"Why would anyone keep on sending Patricia letters? I don't understand it at all. Can you drive me down there sometime to pick it up?"

"Sure, I have class in the morning, but we can go in the afternoon after lunch. Okay?"

"Of course it's okay. I hate to inconvenience you—making you go down to the place you hate."

I thought for a minute before I answered.

"I don't really hate it. If it was up to me, I'd probably still be there. Remember, they were the ones who kicked *me* out, I didn't want to leave."

"Yeah, but I'll bet you're glad you left and started going out and everything."

"Well, I am in a way, but that didn't work out the way I wanted it to, did it?"

"Don't give up yet. I have a feeling that you two will get back together."

I half smiled. "It's going to take a lot more than just a feeling." I hadn't told her about the last conversation I had with David. I knew it was all over.

"I know, but don't give up."

I just smiled, but even that was hard to do.

CHAPTER 14

Tuesday, September 9

The next afternoon I picked up Linda at my apartment after class and we drove down to the motherhouse. I couldn't believe there was another letter. This was getting ridiculous. Why would the person who murdered Patricia keep sending letters from different places all over the country?

Sister Karin was in her office and stood up as Linda knocked on her open door.

"Come in, come in. How are you?"

"I'm okay. Thanks for being so understanding about me staying at Kristen's. I just felt so vulnerable here."

"Oh honey, I understand, with all that's happened. You can stay there as long as you want, at least until we find out who killed Patricia."

She turned to me. "And I hope that's alright with you?"

"Of course. Linda's been wonderful as a roommate. There's just one problem."

They both looked worried.

"I think my cat is starting to love her more than he loves me." I smiled.

Both of them laughed.

"That's not true," said Linda. "He still loves you the most. But he is delightful."

Sister Karin opened her desk drawer, took out a big manila envelope and handed it to Linda.

"I wasn't about to open it—that is, unless you want me too."

"No, I'll open it. I just don't understand why it came now, afterwards … and it's so big!"

Sister Karin handed her a letter opener. "Thanks." She proceeded to open the envelope carefully. There was a smaller envelope inside it with a carefully typed letter on letterhead. That was different.

Linda read over the letter quickly and looked at both of us.

"This is *not* what I expected."

She handed me the letter and the contents of the package.

I braced myself for the same horrible hate mail, but the letter looked very different.

It was from a Vincent Marino, typed neatly on stationery from a law office. It read;

Dear Sister Patricia, you don't know me, but my sister told me you were into stamp collecting. When she asked me to mail all those letters, I hope you enjoyed all the commemorative stamps from the different cities and states. I do a lot of traveling in my job, as you've noticed. A friend was recently giving away his stamp collection, and I thought you might be interested in it. Enjoy!

The manila envelope was filled with stamps. And the man's last name was the same as Sister Jeanette Marino.

I quickly handed it to Sister Karin. She scanned it and just stood there with the letter in her hand, very silent.

I turned to Linda.

"You have to call David right away." I couldn't believe the murder had just been solved, but it seems it had. Sister Jeanette. She seemed so sweet, so incapable of killing anyone. I had been misled before. This wasn't the first time I had misread people's characters. But was I really so bad at it? Apparently, I was.

Sister Karin handed her phone to Linda and Linda turned to me. I gave her the phone number.

"Could I speak to Detective Kelly? This is Sister Linda, calling about a case he's working on. Thank you."

"Detective, this is Sister Linda. Yes. I need you to come down to the motherhouse as soon as possible. I think we know who killed Sister Patricia. When do you think you can come?'

She waited on the line a few seconds.

"Yes, we're sure. Kristen and I will be here for as long as it takes you. We can wait."

I wished I could hear what David was saying but there was no way I could hear from across the room.

"We'll probably be in the main parlor. Just go to Sister Karin's office and she'll know where we are. Okay. Thanks. See you soon."

Linda turned to me. "He says he can be here in about forty-five minutes. Is it okay if we wait for him?"

"Of course. This is important." I turned to Sister Karin. "Where do you want us to wait?"

"Let's see. Just wait in the main parlor, like Sister Linda said. It might be better if nobody knows you're here, especially Sister Jeanette."

Linda and I walked down the main corridor, past the wide wooden steps and the Big Chapel, down the main corridor past the grandfather clock I had cleaned so often as a postulant, and settled down in the main parlor. The slippery velveteen seats were as uncomfortable as I remembered them.

I couldn't believe that Jeanette had killed Patricia. I guess if you came from a famous crime family in St. Louis you were used to that sort of thing, but her brother had apparently gone into a life very different than a life of crime. Judging from the letterhead, he was a successful attorney who traveled all around the country, although doing what I didn't know. Maybe he was a consultant in different cases. I had no idea.

He seemed sincere in not knowing what was in the threatening letters, and seemed to have just put the stamps on them from the various cities and mailed them. Otherwise, he would never have sent that last letter identifying himself.

I suppose that was Jeanette's fatal mistake, not realizing that her brother might think that Linda had a real interest in stamp collecting, a dying hobby.

Linda and I ran out of things to talk about very quickly. After all, we were living together and saw each other at dinner every evening and breakfast every morning. And I think we were both in a state of shock that Sister Jeanette had killed Patricia.

"I know she hated what we were doing, but she's a really good person and I can't believe she would kill anyone deliberately."

"But it had to be deliberate," I said, equally shocked, "because she locked the door to the roof on the way down. She knew what she had done. If Patricia fell off the roof by accident, Jeanette would have run down and told someone what happened. She wouldn't have gone down, locked the door behind her, and gone to sleep."

"I just can't see her doing that, no matter how much she hated what we were doing."

"No, I can't either. But she did. It's frightening, thinking you know someone you live with and as a friend, and then finding out what they're capable of. I found that out when I was a postulant—with Maribeth. Remember, she was the one who tried to kill me."

"Of course I remember. And she was one of your best friends."

"I felt so betrayed—and so stupid that I hadn't realized that she was capable of murder."

CHAPTER 15

Tuesday, September 9

David and Sister Karin appeared at the door of the parlor. He walked right up to Linda.

"What's this about. You sounded pretty sure you know who killed Patricia."

Linda handed him the manila envelope.

"What's this?"

"This letter is completely different."

He quickly scanned the letter.

He turned to Sister Karin. "Can you find Sister Jeanette and bring her here, please?"

"Of course. I'll try to find out which class she's in right now. Just wait here."

David re-read the letter. "He sounds absolutely sincere. And he would never sign his name if he wasn't telling the truth. The Marino family. They're one of the biggest crime families in St. Louis. The Italian mafia controls large parts of the city. It always has."

"I never knew that."

"Well, if you're not in this section of the city and working with businesses and crimes, you wouldn't know anything about the corruption that goes on."

"And Jeanette is part of that family."

"But so is her brother. And he seems to have gone on to be a successful attorney, from the looks of it."

Sister Karin appeared at the door, and Jeanette was behind her. We all got up.

"Sister Jeanette," David said politely, "I have a few questions for you."

David turned to Sister Karin. "Can Sister Jeanette and I go into the parlor next door, please?"

"Of course."

David walked out the door with Jeanette and into the empty parlor. He told her to take a seat and that he would be recording their interview.

"But I already told you everything I know in my other interview."

"I know," said David," but I want you to take a look at this letter. And I have to let you know that anything you say can be used against you ..." He recited her rights to her before she said anything else.

"What are you doing? Arresting me? I haven't done anything wrong."

He held out the manila envelope to her.

She took it and quickly read it. Her face changed from curiosity to fear. She was silent when she handed the letter back to David.

"This is your brother, correct?"

"Yes, it is, but he didn't do anything wrong."

"Sending hate mail from across the country seems the very definition of 'wrong.'"

"I mean, he didn't know what was in the letters. I wrote them and asked him to send them with really interesting stamps from all over the country. I knew it would confuse Patricia. He didn't know what was in them. I had no idea he would ever send this last letter."

"You lied to us, you sent threatening messages to Sister Patricia, and you are now the leading suspect in her death."

Sister Jeanette got even whiter. "I swear I didn't kill her. It wasn't me. I hated what she was doing and I wanted to scare her, but I didn't kill her. I don't even know how to get up on the roof. You have to believe me."

"No, we don't, Sister. And you did threaten her in the letters."

"I said God would punish her. I would never do anything to harm her. God is the only one who can judge her."

"What is your alibi for the night of Sister Patricia's death? If you don't have one, I have to take you down to the station."

"No, you can't. I swear it wasn't me. I was with Sister Rebecca's science group outside the college for hours that night. Sister Rebecca knows I was there."

"But where did you go after the group broke up that night?"

"I went back to the dorm at eleven or so and went to sleep. That's all. It was already late. I went to sleep right away. I didn't kill her!" She burst into tears.

David said to her, "Come with me."

He and Jeanette came back into the room where Linda, Sister Karin, and I were waiting.

"I have to call down to the station."

"Okay," said Sister Karin. "I'll go with you to Mother Alphonse's office where you can call."

As they walked out the door, I wondered if the threatening letters were enough evidence against her. I guessed they would certainly hold up in court, but I wasn't sure if that was enough to convict her of murder. I guessed that she admitted she had sent them. That had to be enough. I wondered why religion had to promote such hatred. I admit, I used to think homosexuality was wrong because the Church always had told me what to think, but now I was starting to wonder. Sister Patricia and Sister

Linda were good, kind people, and one of them was dead and the other's life ruined, and for what? I couldn't see the point in all the hate and judgment. Why couldn't people just love each other?

David went to the front door to wait for the officers and they escorted Sister Jeanette out to the waiting patrol car.

He walked back to the parlor where we were waiting.

"You can both go back home now. I guess we're done here," David commented without any expression.

"Do you really think the letters will be enough to convict her of murder?"

"No, I don't, but I'm going to interview her at the station tomorrow and we'll see what else we can find. We have enough to hold her for seventy-two hours. After that, we'll have to let her go. But I hope we can find more evidence before that happens."

I wanted to mark the end of the investigation with a dinner or at least a cup of coffee, but I didn't have a chance to say anything with Linda by my side.

"Well, you were a huge help, Kristen. And you too, Sister Linda. Thank you both."

Linda turned to me. "If you don't mind, I think I'll stay here at the motherhouse tonight. I feel so much better that Jeanette is in jail now. I don't want to inconvenience you anymore."

"But you have all your things at my apartment?"

"I just have a few things. Most of my stuff is here, up in my dorm. I can pick up my extra clothes some other time, if that's okay with you."

"Okay, if you feel better staying here, that's fine with me."

Linda gave me a hug and said, "Thank you for everything. I'll talk to you tomorrow."

David and I walked down the corridor and out to the parking lot.

I still couldn't believe what had just happened. "I can't believe it ended so quickly and that Jeanette was the one who killed Patricia."

"Well, you know Jeanette a lot better than I do, and I'm sure it comes as a shock when people behave in ways that we can't even imagine."

"Thank you for all the work you did on this case. It seemed really difficult."

"No, thank you. Without your help, I'm not sure if we would have ever found the person responsible for this. I'm so glad we were able to find out who killed her. I felt so sorry about the whole thing. Well, tell your parents hello from me. I'll be in touch."

He opened his car door and got in. Well. It was all over, I guessed. I was glad we had solved the murder, but heartbroken that David and I hadn't solved what was, or at least used to be, between us.

CHAPTER 16

I opened the lobby door with my key and started up the stairs. It was getting dark in the building and as I started to walk upstairs I saw that Mr. Jefferson's door was open on the first floor.

He called out to me. "Hey, Kristen. I've been waiting for you. You might not want to go upstairs. Your door is wide open and JC was meowing at our door, so I brought him inside. I hope that's okay. Do you want me to go upstairs with you and make sure everything is okay?" I looked up and saw that my front door was wide open. I knew I had locked it when I left.

I stood on the steps, not sure what to do. I wanted to call David, but I wasn't sure where he was—if he had gotten home or gone over to Julie's or who knows where.

I was afraid to go inside.

"Are you sure you locked the door when you left?"

"Yes, I'm positive."

Mr. Jefferson was at least six feet, five inches and probably weighed 300 pounds. And it had to be all muscle.

"Don't you worry, Kristen. I'm going up first. You follow me and we'll check everything out."

The door was wide open and as we walked in and turned on the light, the apartment was a complete mess. My tables thrown over, papers everywhere, my beautiful Tiffany-like lamp in pieces on the floor.

No one was there. A note was scotch taped to the oven door. "STOP" was all it said.

He was examining the door. "This lock is broken. It looks like they used a crowbar or something."

I went over to my phone. "I'm going to call the police."

It was then that I saw that the cord had been cut.

"Can I use your phone?"

"Sure, I'll come down with you. Let me try to close this door as best I can."

"No, that's okay. Just leave it all like it is."

I called David's station and Sergeant Harper said he would send someone over right away.

I called David, hoping he was home, instead of out to dinner with someone.

He answered on the second ring,

"Hello?"

"David, it's Kristin. Someone broke into my apartment. I can't stay here tonight."

"Did you call the police?"

"Of course."

★ ★ ★

Two officers arrived at the front lobby. We climbed the steps up to my apartment and walked through it carefully, trying to assess the damage.

I could hear David saying something to Mr. Jefferson. I walked out of the bedroom to meet him.

"Hi, thanks for coming. David, this is Mr. Jefferson, my downstairs neighbor."

David turned to Mr. Jefferson. "And thanks for your offer for Kristen to stay at your place, but I think she'd be better off with me tonight."

"Can I help you anymore—with anything?" Mr. Jefferson asked.

"No, thank you."

"I'll just be downstairs if you need me."

David walked around my apartment, looking carefully at the damage.

"Look at the note taped to the oven."

"That's it? One word?"

"That's all I found. I didn't want to look any further."

"This kind of ties it to our investigation, doesn't it?" David frowned.

"And I hope this was just a one-time thing, now that we've found our killer."

"Let's hope so. You're staying at my place tonight, though. I'll sleep on the couch."

David and I stood at my front door and I wondered how I was going to fix it. I couldn't leave everything open all night. David talked to one of the policemen and then I called a twenty-four-hour locksmith to fix the lock before we left.

It was hours before I got in my car with JC in his cat carrier and followed David to his apartment. He had moved in the last six months but was still only about ten minutes away.

We pulled up to a new apartment complex. He motioned for me to park next to him in the parking garage and we took an elevator up to the sixth floor—the top floor. I carried my little suitcase and he carried the cat carrier with JC making loud complaining noises.

His apartment was more modern than I would have guessed, even with an Oriental rug and a wall of Belgian tapestries. The furniture was sleek and new and the picture window looked out to the city lights and the river beyond.

"Here, put your things in the bedroom. I'll sleep out here."

"No, I don't want you to give up your bed for me. I'm fine here on the couch."

David ignored me and went past me to change the sheets in the other room. I walked in. "Can I help?"

"No, I'm fine. I would feel terrible if you didn't get a good night's sleep."

"Thank you. I really appreciate this."

"And we need to talk about this break-in."

I waited on the couch, my hands folded on my lap. I heard a meow from JC in his cat carrier, and was about ready to let him out, but then I heard another deeper meow from another room.

A large striped ginger cat sauntered into the living room, stopping to look at me and looking around for the source of the strange meow. He cautiously padded over and sniffed and sniffed.

David came out. "I got a cat from the shelter. Isn't he beautiful? His name is Alex."

"Well, let's let them meet. Hope they'll be friends."

JC jumped out of the carrier but froze when he saw Alex. They did some sniffing and one of them hissed, but then Alex walked off to his bed and JC jumped up on my lap.

David sat down on the chair opposite me. "The break-in was obviously to intimidate you and frighten us into stopping the investigation. You do realize what Sister Jeanette's last name is?

"Yeah, it's Marino."

"One of the biggest crime families in the city. Mafia."

"I know. You said that down at the motherhouse." I had no idea, but I had never had any dealings with the Mafia. I was just an English student. David probably had first-hand knowledge of that kind of crime.

"I don't know why they targeted you and not me," he commented. "It doesn't make any sense. But you're the former nun who was going out with me, and Sister Linda is staying with you."

"That's not much of a reason. You're the one who's in charge of the investigation."

"Even though we have Sister Jeanette in custody, you're going to have to be very careful, and you'll definitely be staying with me for a while. You're not safe at your apartment anymore. The problem is, she was terrible to send those letters, but we still don't have any direct evidence linking her to the murder. And no confession. She's insistent that she didn't kill Sister Patricia. We can only hold her for a few days."

"Where do you go from here?" I was tired from the whole day. "And Linda still needs to find out about the necklace—that's the only other clue you might have. And nobody even knows anything about that."

"Except that Patricia didn't have it on her at the time of her death. It's ridiculous to speculate about something like a necklace that probably means nothing."

"Well, you don't have that much to go on besides speculation."

David nodded. "That's for sure." Alex jumped up on the couch, purring loudly as David absentmindedly petted him.

"Let's go to bed," he smiled. "I mean separately, of course."

I smiled back. He had no idea how much I would have loved to go to bed with him. But David hadn't shown the slightest bit of interest in getting back together. And he was with someone else. I had to get over him. It hurt, but I was going to have to accept it and move on.

We both got up. I had grabbed a nightgown, toothbrush, and some clothes in my little case, so I was all set for the night. I carried JC into the bedroom with me. Although they seemed to be getting along just fine, I didn't want to risk any late-night arguments between the cats.

David said, "Good night," closed the door, and I was alone. The view out the bedroom window was the same as in the dining room: beautiful city lights with a large ribbon of black—the river—then more lights and the clear night sky.

I washed my face and slipped on my nightgown. The bathroom had a scent of cologne and Ivory soap. I walked back into the bedroom. I realized that the bed was a king-sized waterbed. I had never slept in one before and I climbed in carefully, moving with each wave. It was an odd feeling at first till the motion calmed down. I tried to lay still and not roll over or even move, and hoped I could sleep.

Part of me wished the night would be like a romantic movie: the knock at the door, David asking if he could come in, telling me how much he still loved me, getting into bed with me. Finally having sex for the first time. Wondering what it would be like. Maybe not in the waterbed, though ...

I woke up in the middle of the night. No, the movie scenario hadn't happened. I went to the bathroom and then sat on the wide wooden frame of the bed looking out the window.

What was he going to do? He had no idea who had killed Sister Patricia. He had to find more evidence, or he'd have to let Sister Jeanette go.

There was something missing from the investigation. He had enough motives, for sure. Hate was one. He had the letters and now knew who had sent them. And the necklace. We didn't even know if that was important. Was it all about money? Or maybe jealousy. People were good at lying. That was one thing I had unfortunately learned those last few years.

I carefully laid back down on the soft moving bed, and the next time I woke up the sun was streaming in the window. I sat up quickly, feeling a little dizzy until I slowed down and got up carefully. It was almost eight o'clock, and I hoped David hadn't left. I knew he wouldn't leave me in the apartment alone with no key. I wasn't looking forward to cleaning my apartment, but it looked like that's what I'd be doing.

I got dressed quickly and used a comb I'd found in the bathroom. I hoped David wouldn't mind. I opened the door and saw him sitting at the table with a cup of coffee, reading the *St. Louis Post-Dispatch*.

I said, "Good morning."

He jumped up quickly. "Hi, you're up. How did you sleep?"

"It was kind of weird. I never slept in a waterbed before."

"Yeah, I'm sorry. I forgot all about that until I was ready for bed. I was going to knock on the door and see if you were okay."

I laughed to myself. The knock on the door wouldn't have meant what I wanted it to.

"No, it was fine. I ended up sleeping really well."

"Once you get used to it, it's great. I love it."

"Eggs? Cereal? Yogurt? Coffee?" he offered.

"I'm fine. I'll just fix some cereal and a cup of coffee, if that's okay?"

"Here, I'll fix it for you. I know how you like it."

We sat at the table for a few minutes in silence.

David spoke first. "I don't want you going back to your apartment yet. I want you to stay here for a few more days, at least. I need to spend some time today researching the Marino family."

I smiled to myself. It was my dream come true. But it was only because he was worried about me. Well, I was fine with that.

"Okay, but I have to go back to get some things this morning—and clean."

"Okay. JC seems to have made himself at home."

He was wandering around the apartment, checking everything out to make sure it hadn't changed since last night. Alex was on the on the leather couch, his head resting on a book.

"I think they'll be fine alone."

I agreed.

We drove to my apartment at the same time—in separate cars. David wanted to make sure nothing else had happened overnight, and I told Mrs. Jefferson that I'd be staying with David for a few days. David went to work and I started to clean up the apartment. He got the Jeffersons' phone number since my phone was gone and I spent a few hours working on the apartment.

I tried to think of it as an opportunity to get rid of items that I didn't really need. That positive attitude got me through about half an hour. Then it just became tedious and depressing.

I heard a knock at the door and froze. "Who is it?" I whispered.

It was Mrs. Jefferson. She invited me down to their apartment, where I had a ham sandwich and a Coke for lunch. They were such wonderful neighbors. I was lucky to have them.

The AT&T repairman came at about one and fixed the phone. By the time David arrived the apartment was looking better than it had in a year.

"I'm pretty sure I can stay here tonight. I even got the phone repaired so I can call you if there's a problem."

David didn't even look at me. "No."

He carried some books out to his car and I followed with a box of clothes.

"Let's stop somewhere for dinner and talk," he said. "I need to tell you a few things."

"Okay."

"How about our old Italian place?"

"That sounds great." But I quickly reminded myself not to get my hopes up, longing for the days when we ate at Cunetto's almost every week. We talked about the investigation all throughout dinner. He had worked on difficult cases before, but this one seemed impossible. Only one real suspect, and although she carefully orchestrated and carried out her hate mail campaign, it just wasn't enough to charge her with murder.

And the only evidence that we had that it was murder was Patricia's frightened call to me, and the fact that the trap door to the roof had been relocked by someone. No fingerprints, no items belonging to the murderer. There was the sedative Patricia had been given, or taken herself. It was in the autopsy report. Also the strange break-in at my apartment.

"We're just being pulled down into this hole of evidence, but none of it points to anyone in particular—except the letters," he thought out loud.

"What are you going to do next?" I looked at David over the vase of fake flowers and the lasagna remains.

"I want you to stay at my place for at least a week, if you can stand the waterbed. We have to discover who broke into your apartment, but we have no fingerprints. I have some pretty good ideas, but that whole crime family pretty much rules south St. Louis and there's no way we're going to get them for a simple break-in."

He sighed. "And we're almost at the end of the interviews. We've interviewed practically everyone."

"It sounds like you're giving up," I said sadly.

"All the better," David replied. "People won't be so guarded. Something is going to come up in the next week or two. It always does. And don't worry, I don't give up. You know that."

I smiled and wished he hadn't given up on me. I had given up on him first though, to be fair.

"How are your parents, Kristen?"

I told him what they had been doing, and then asked about his life.

"That other apartment was too small—and sad. I felt boxed in, so I found my new place, which I really like. I don't ever get tired of that amazing view of the city."

"It is beautiful."

"And I saw what fun you had with JC, and I really liked him, so I got Alex at a shelter off Gravois just a few months ago. I love him. It's fun to have someone who's happy I'm home."

I looked down. Oh David, I would be happy you were home, too.

Would I say yes this time if he asked me to marry him? The thought scared me, but I didn't want to lose him again. I would say yes. Yes, I would.

But we finished the excellent meal without that happening, left the restaurant, and went back to the apartment. The movie scenario wasn't happening.

I sat in the wing-back chair next to the window for a long time later that night, gazing out to the river and the city, thinking about the dead ends of the investigation. I knew David had to move on at his job, and I went to my classes the next day.

I slept better in the waterbed that second night, set my alarm, and woke up in time to have breakfast with him again. He handed me a key. "You can just let yourself in anytime."

I struggled through school all day. But it was less frustrating than thinking about the investigation.

CHAPTER 17

Monday, September 15

I read a lot over the weekend and spent some time with my parents. They were happy to see me. I didn't feel like bothering David all weekend at his apartment, and he wasn't about to let me go back to mine yet. My parents were thrilled that I stayed for dinner on Saturday and Sunday. I didn't want to tell them about the break-in. They would just worry.

I went back to David's apartment after school on Monday. It was strange, letting myself into a place that didn't belong to me. Alex and JC both had a lot tell me about their day, but finally they settled down on my papers.

I was reading the newspaper from the day before and hoping David would be home soon when the phone rang. I didn't know whether to answer it. It rang seven times and then stopped.

I read the next four lines. The phone rang again and kept ringing. It might be David calling me, I realized suddenly. I jumped up and ran into the kitchen and picked up the receiver.

"Hi, this is Kristen Byrne. Can I take a message for David Kelly?"

"Kristen. I'm so glad I got you. This is Linda. I really need to talk to you about something."

"Can you just tell me on the phone?"

"I don't know." She sounded confused. "I guess so. I'd rather talk to you and the detective in person. I don't know if it's important or maybe I'm just being paranoid."

I answered quickly. "You're not being paranoid. After everything that's happened, we want you to let us know about everything. David will be back soon. Can we come down this evening?"

"Yes, I'll just meet you in the Big Chapel. I'll be in the back."

"I don't know when he'll be home, but I'll be there at seven. Okay?"

"Yes, I'll be waiting."

I hung up the phone. I didn't know what she had to tell us, but I wasn't about to make the same mistake I had made with Patricia. I didn't want Linda to get murdered in the night!

Looking out the window, the sky was cloudy and looked like it would rain any second.

I picked up the phone to call David but I heard a key in the door.

"David?"

"Hi. How did your day go? I see our friends are helping." He looked at JC and Alex still spread out on the newspaper.

"We need to go down to the motherhouse. Sister Linda called and wanted to talk to both of us—or me if you can't make it."

"Did she sound upset?"

"Not too much. But she hoped she wasn't being paranoid. I told her that with everything that has happened, she should be careful. I told her we'd meet her at seven."

"Well. It's five-thirty now. Of course, we'll go. We need a break in this case. Guess we can stop somewhere to eat on the way."

I laughed. "All the employees at Steak and Shake know us by now."

"Oh, they've known me for a long time. You're the nice addition. Let me change clothes and relax for five minutes and then we can go."

"Okay."

He disappeared into the bedroom and I opened the refrigerator and found the cat food. JC and Alex were both ready for dinner and I carefully separated their bowls but the food was gone so quickly it didn't really make any difference.

We took my car and pulled into the Steak and Shake parking lot.

"The usual?" David called back to me as I found a place inside. It was very busy. We usually stopped by earlier in the day when it wasn't so crowded.

David came back with our orders.

"I told Sister Linda that we'd be down this evening because I was scared of her ending up dead. I guess I'm the paranoid one."

"No, you're not. Someone was murdered. We have a lot of motives but not much evidence, and your apartment was broken into. You're being sensible and cautious, as you should."

David took a drink of Coke. "The cats are really getting along. I'll feel bad when they're separated."

I swallowed a bite of hamburger. "Go on, go on," I thought to myself. "Ask me to move in. Ask me to marry you. I'm ready. But I'm not ready to ask you myself." I took another bite, not saying a word, hoping he'd go on.

I didn't want to tell him that I had broken up with Paul. Or rather, Paul had just left and I didn't even have to break up with him. I wondered how serious he was about Julie. He hadn't said anything more about her since that one afternoon a few weeks ago.

And he did go on. "I sure hope talking to her this evening helps."

That wasn't what I wanted him to say. The moment had passed, as all of them had recently, and not the way I wanted them to pass. We finished the meal quickly and headed down to the motherhouse.

The door was answered by a short plump nun. David showed his badge and told the nun we were going to meet someone and, yes, we knew the way.

★ ★ ★

We met Linda in the back of the chapel and walked to a small parlor off the main corridor.

Linda got right to the point.

"I finally heard from Patricia's parents. They took their time getting back home after the funeral and stopped by some relatives on the way to see them and, I think, help them take their mind off what had just happened. Anyway, they just got my message about the necklace. They said they never received it. And now I'll never know what happened to it. Whether she lost it or it was stolen or what."

David said, "I think we should go to Mother Alphonse and ask her if anyone has found it in the motherhouse. It could be that Patricia lost it. If no one turned it in, then we have to assume it was stolen, and we have yet another crime to solve."

"Patricia would have told me if she lost it. I know she would have."

"Well, it's Monday now. Maybe we can go down some time next week and see Mother Alphonse and we can ask her together—the three of us. It won't do any harm. How about if we go next Monday when you both get out of classes?"

"I can come down after one," I said.

Linda said, "And my classes are over at three-thirty. Let's meet here in this parlor. Okay?"

David and I drove back home together. It had started to rain and we were both dripping wet by the time we got to the parking lot and in the car.

"Well, what do you think?" David asked me.

"I think you might have a new motive. You already have hatred of lesbians, and now someone could have stolen the necklace for money."

David interrupted my thoughts. "I need to do a few more interviews."

We parked in the underground garage and took the elevator to his apartment. I was getting used to this. But I couldn't get too used to it. I'd be going home soon.

We sat at the table for a few minutes. David poured some wine for both of us.

"I'm glad we talked to her."

"Yeah, at least you have one more lead."

"Another tiny lead," David sighed. "Let's hope this one actually leads somewhere, instead of nowhere. If you don't mind, I'm really tired."

"I feel bad that I'm taking your room and bed."

"It's fine. I've been sleeping great on the couch. It won't be much longer, anyway."

I gathered up my books and purse and headed to the bedroom. I felt bad that he said I wouldn't be there much longer. But did I really want to move in? I wouldn't just move in. I would marry him and then move in. Was I ready for that? Oh my God, just go to bed, I told myself. Stop thinking.

CHAPTER 18

Friday, September 19

I was still at David's all week. He wasn't about to let me go back to my apartment, even though nothing else had happened and my phone was back in order. I actually enjoyed being with him. We stayed very professional, though, and I was frustrated. But he was busy at work and I had school, so I tried not to think about our relationship—or lack of it.

David and I sat at his dining room table.

"I need to go into the station this morning. We'll release Sister Jeanette, but she'll be facing other charges, because of her threats in the mail. I'm glad it's over," he sighed.

"Me too, but I'm worried that it's not over for us. I don't want another break-in at my apartment."

"Don't worry, you're not going back there for a while longer. I wouldn't do that to you. I think that once Sister Jeanette's released, the Marinos won't be bothering you anymore. At least I hope so. But I'm not a hundred percent sure."

"Thanks, I really appreciate your letting me stay at your place."

David hesitated but then spoke. "I was wondering if you could stay at your mom and dad's over the weekend. I have a friend coming in from out of town. And I'm going to see Julie's family this weekend, too."

"Wow, are you kicking me out already? I thought you just said I could stay a little longer," I laughed, but inside I was a little worried.

"No, of course not, but I was hoping you could find another place to stay for those two nights. Have you told your parents about the break-in?"

"No, I didn't want to worry them."

"How have they been able to reach you?"

"Well, they can't, but I've called them almost every day. I'm sure they're wondering why, but they haven't asked."

"Give them my number and tell them to call me if they can't reach you. You have told them you're staying with me, haven't you?"

"No, not at all. They'd just get their hopes up."

"What do you mean?"

"They hope that we'll get back together. They've been bugging me about it ever since we stopped seeing each other."

"Well, just stay with them a couple of nights. It'll help me out."

I called Mom. I told her the management was doing some work in my apartment and wondered if I could stay with them a couple of nights.

She was thrilled. "When will you be over?"

"In a few hours. I hope you don't mind."

"Honey, we always love to see you. You know that. I'll have some dinner ready when you get here."

"That'll be great. Thanks, Mom."

When I got off the phone, David said, "Give me a call at the station on Monday morning and we can meet back here in the afternoon."

"Sure." I packed a few things in my little carry-on suitcase and headed out. I picked up JC and gave him a hug before I left, telling him it would only be a few days. As usual, he didn't appreciate the interruption from his very important nap. I wondered who was coming to see David, but didn't ask. It really wasn't any of my business.

The next morning went by slowly, although it was kind of fun to be back home. I realized how much I had changed. I was no longer the shy child who had entered the convent a few years before. I had met David, had been a part of two murder investigations by accident, gotten my own apartment and my own cat. I had two boyfriends and lost both of them. As I laid in my old twin bed that first night listening to the rain drip from the gutters, I also realized how much I missed David. Just to know he was in the same apartment was comforting.

I hoped that his friend wouldn't stay longer than two days. I did love my apartment and my new independence, but I was almost ready to give it up. Too bad I had ruined my chances. He hadn't said any more about getting back together and neither had I. He was seeing Julie and her family over the weekend. It sounded like he missed her. He had made it very clear that we were no longer together.

CHAPTER 19

Saturday afternoon, September 20

Father George shuffled down the long corridor of the motherhouse. He dreaded coming down here every Saturday afternoon to hear the nuns' confessions for at least two hours. But he couldn't complain. He was eighty-six years old, retired, and his knees were so bad he could hardly walk, much less be of any use in a parish anymore. His doctors told him he was too old for a knee replacement, with his heart condition.

At least in his old parish, St. Francis, the confessions kept him awake. Here he had to struggle not to fall out of his chair. He limped in the confessional box and sat down. The nuns droned on about being late for prayers, being envious of their fellow sisters, taking too much food at mealtimes, and the assorted tiny transgressions that Father George had heard a million times.

"Bless me, Father, I was envious of another sister when she was praised for her good work in one of our classes."

He gave her a few extra Rosaries to say.

"Bless me Father, I took too much food this week at dinner and I committed the sin of gluttony. I'll try not to do it again."

Again, a few Rosaries.

"Bless me Father, for I have sinned. I've been very jealous of someone lately."

"Do you think you can stop being so jealous of her, Sister?" Father George said without too much interest.

"She died a few weeks ago. Now I'm just angry that her friend doesn't pay any attention to me."

Father George was confused. "I don't understand. Who died?"

"The sister who died a few weeks ago. I was jealous of her. I was on the roof with her when she fell, but it was an accident. And now I want to be friends with her lover, and she won't pay any attention to me at all."

Father George knew all about the murder. It was all over the papers and the talk of the whole diocese. And he heard more of the story from the nuns here at the motherhouse. That's what she was talking about! He didn't understand the part about her lover and the jealousy, but she said that the death was an accident. He didn't think the police had found the murderer. He would have read it in the papers or heard something.

"You said she fell off the roof accidentally?"

"Yes. And now the person who was her friend won't even talk to me. I'm so angry about that. I really loved her, but I hate her now. I'm so angry at her."

Father George kept thinking about Sister Patricia's death, but he did hear that last remark.

"And you were there with her on the roof? But the police said it was murder. You need to tell them what really happened, Sister."

"No, I can't do that. They'll blame me. They won't believe me."

"Of course they will, if you explain to them what happened. They need to have that information. Otherwise they'll go on thinking she was murdered. Did you check on her afterwards and report it as an accident?"

"No, I didn't. I just went back to my dorm and went to sleep."

"But she could have still been alive?"

"I doubt it. It was a fall from four stories."

Father George couldn't believe what he was hearing. That she hadn't even checked.

"Why didn't you report it, Sister?"

"Because I was afraid they would blame it on me. I'm not stupid!"

"You need to go to the police, talk to them, and explain what happened." Father George was getting more and more insistent.

And then he remembered what she had said about being so angry. "And what are you going to do about her friend?"

"I don't know. I don't know what I'm going to do. I thought I loved her, but now I hate her. I hate the way she's treating me!"

"You wouldn't hurt her, though, would you?"

"I'm leaving, Father. I thought you'd be a help, but this hasn't helped me at all."

She stood up abruptly, turned and walked out of the confessional. Father George pushed himself up, his bad knee aching, and looked out of the confessional box at the back. He saw her walk down the aisle, black habit, black veil, he couldn't see her face—she was walking away from him. He had no idea who she was. From the back she looked like all the other nuns waiting in line who were now looking at him oddly. He got back in the confessional and sat down.

What had just happened? She said the murder was an accident. She was there on the roof when it happened. Was she the murderer? Were the police wrong? She hadn't checked to see if Sister Patricia was still alive? None of this made any sense.

Father George gave out penances of three Hail Marys and four Our Fathers without really listening for the next half hour. Finally no one else entered the confessional and he was alone. He got up slowly and knelt down in the front pew of the chapel.

He had a suspicion that had just heard the confession of the murderer, whoever she was. He might be old, but he wasn't stupid. Her voice seemed vaguely familiar, but Father George didn't know any of the nuns, only coming once a week to hear confessions and never seeing anyone face to face. And he couldn't tell anyone what he had just heard. He had made a solemn vow never to reveal anything he heard in the confessional. He would automatically be excommunicated from the Catholic Church if he told anyone. Even murder. He wondered how angry she might be that Patricia's lover was rejecting her. That person might be in danger, too. She said she hated that person now—and she didn't answer his question about whether she would hurt her. If she committed one murder, she could certainly hurt another person she hated.

He had been a priest for over fifty years, and he had never heard anyone confess to a murder. Well, she hadn't confessed to a murder. She told him it was an accident. But he didn't believe for one second that what had happened was an accident.

The question of what a priest would do in that situation, although it came up in random discussions, never came up in real life because it never happened in real life.

But it had just happened. And to him, of all people. Sometimes George felt his age. His knees bothered him, but usually he felt quite happy and optimistic about life. He felt younger than his eighty-six years and hoped to be useful for at least a few more. But as he sat there, he felt old. The world had somehow gone past him and left him behind.

For years, he had come to this convent and listened to the same sins over and over, petty and insignificant sins causing guilt that were magnified by the often-meaningless rules of the institution, making sins out of nothing while the real problems of the world beyond its walls remained unsolved and unknown to the nuns inside. It was enough to depress him, and he usually came back to his parish with a renewed sense of helping people who actually needed his help.

But today he felt a despair that he rarely felt.

What could he do? There had to be something. He couldn't go to the police. It wouldn't do any good. He didn't know who she was. He couldn't point her out in a police lineup. He didn't know her name. But she had told him she was on the roof at the same time a person had been murdered and she hadn't even bothered to check on her or report it. He just couldn't let that go. And now he was worried about the other nun and what might happen to her. He had to do something. He got up slowly and walked out of the chapel and down the long corridor to the juniorate.

He knocked on Sister Karin's open office door.

CHAPTER 20

Sister Karin stood up quickly. "Father George! Come in. Sit down."

The priests never came to this section of the building. Ever. They came to the chapel to say Mass every morning and heard confessions once a week and sometimes to the infirmary to see a sick sister, but never to the rest of the building.

"How are you, Sister?"

"I'm fine, Father. I'm just surprised to see you over here in this part of the building. Is anything wrong?"

"No Sister, not at all. You know, I've been reading and hearing a lot about poor Sister Patricia these last few weeks, and I'm wondering if I can speak to her friend. I'm sorry, I forgot her name."

"I think you mean Sister Linda. Yes, of course you can. She's in the study hall right now. I'll get her. And you can talk to her in my office so you don't have to go anywhere else."

"Thank you. I'd appreciate that."

★ ★ ★

Sister Karin walked up to Linda at her desk in the study hall. "Father George wants to speak to you."

"Father George? I don't even know him."

"I'm sure he wants to tell you how sorry he is about Patricia and how he's praying for you. He's waiting in my office."

"Oh, okay." Linda wasn't so sure he wanted to say he was sorry. She could imagine his attitude towards lesbians and it probably wasn't good. She walked into the office, not quite knowing what to expect.

"Hello, Father."

"Hello, Sister. Please sit down. This won't take very long."

"Okay." She sat down and folded her hands on her lap, not knowing what to do with them.

"I'm aware that we don't know each other, but I'm familiar with your situation these past few weeks and I'm very sorry about the loss of your friend. I've been praying for her and for you also."

"Thank you."

"But that's not why I'm here. You need to leave the motherhouse. You're not safe here. Don't ask me how I know this, but you need to go somewhere where no one knows where you are."

"But Father, we found out who killed Patricia and the person is in jail right now. I don't know if you heard that because it just happened. It hasn't even been in the papers yet. So I'm okay now. But thank you for being so concerned. I really appreciate it."

"You're wrong. The person they have in jail didn't kill your friend. I think it was someone else, and you need to leave here today, as soon as you can. I'm not mistaken about this. Everyone thinks I'm old and that I may not know what I'm talking about, but I know for sure that the murderer is still in the motherhouse. I'm going to ask the sisters at my parish if you can stay in their convent for a few days. I mean it. Tell Sister Karin you'll be leaving."

"But Sister Jeanette was the one who sent the horrible threatening letters to Patricia and me. She's the one who killed her."

"I can't tell you any more, except you need to get out of the motherhouse now. This afternoon. Please!"

"Okay, okay, I believe you. And I do have a place I can go where I'll be safe."

"Are you sure?"

"Yes."

"Okay, let me know where you are. And let Sister Karin know so she can tell me. "

Father George got up slowly from the chair.

"Do you need help, Father?"

"No, I'll be fine if I just go slow. But thank you for asking."

"And thank you for letting me know about this."

"I don't want anything to happen to you. I'll be praying for you, my dear."

Father George turned and slowly walked out the door and down the corridor.

Linda picked up the phone and called David's number at his work.

CHAPTER 21

Sunday, August 22

I was eating breakfast with my parents when I got the phone call from David early in the morning. "Hi, Kristen. There's been some more complications."

"Well, that's not a surprise. This case is full of them."

"Linda called me yesterday, right after I got to work, and told me about how this priest told her she couldn't stay in the motherhouse because the murderer was still there."

"What? What are you talking about?"

"Linda said that the priest is really old, but he told her that the person we arrested wasn't the murderer and that Linda needed to leave and go somewhere where she couldn't be found. And she can't stay here with me—at least not this weekend."

"Wow. And it's the one time when she can't stay with me at my apartment. Or at yours. Tell her to call me and she can stay here at my parents' with me at least tonight. Mom and Dad won't mind. They love meeting new people and making new friends. And I can sleep on the couch in the living room."

"Okay, I know she'll be glad to hear that. We can figure out other arrangements tomorrow when we get together."

I picked up Linda at the motherhouse as soon as I could get there and we went to my parents' house together. What we'd do after the weekend, I wasn't sure. David's apartment wasn't meant for three people. He had an extra bedroom, but he just used it as a storage room and there wasn't even a bed in there. And he had that extra person there this weekend—or extra persons. I wasn't sure.

We'd figure something out. I thought she should just leave and go back home to her parents, but they lived out by Wentzville, pretty far north of the city, and I wasn't sure how she'd get to her classes. She wouldn't want to lose a whole semester of her senior year. Better than being killed, though.

Linda told me all about the conversation with Father George. I didn't know him at all. He must have come to say Mass and hear confessions after I left a few years ago. We both wondered if he had heard this in the confessional and that's why he couldn't say anything to anyone.

"But he can tell someone if it's a confession about murder?" I was sure of that.

"No. There are really strict rules for priests and confessions. They can't say a word about anything they hear in confession— even murder. If they tell anyone, they'll be excommunicated and can't ever receive the sacraments anymore."

"I had no idea. So that's why he just told you to get out of the motherhouse and couldn't say anything else—like who the murderer was?"

"I guess so. I'm glad he told me as much as he did. When I saw him, I thought I was going to get a lecture on being a lesbian, which I'm quite sure he didn't approve of, but he didn't say anything at all. In fact, he was very compassionate about it, and told me he was praying for Patricia and me."

CHAPTER 22

Monday, September 22

I called David Monday morning and he asked us to meet him at his apartment in the afternoon around two. I took Linda to the motherhouse for her classes and then I went to my classes at Washington University.

The day went quickly. I loved my English Literature class. The teacher, Dr. Jenkins, was in his fifties I guessed, and made every lecture exciting and worthwhile to listen to. My other class was a creative writing class. I wasn't so sure about that one. I wasn't very good at creative writing and didn't quite know where to start. "Write whatever you want for fifteen minutes," wasn't the kind of assignment I was used to, and I was struggling with it.

I pulled up to David's apartment just as he was just getting out of his car.

"Come with me. I want to show you something. And you need to see JC. He misses you.

How was your visit with your parents?" David asked as we went up the elevator.

"Good. How was your friend?"

"Oh, they were fine."

"Where do you know them from?" I still didn't know if "they" were a man or woman, or if there had been two people.

"From university."

He wasn't very chatty about the friend or friends as we got out on his floor and walked to his apartment. We walked inside and I turned toward the bedroom but David stood in front of me.

"Come and look at this room instead." He led me to the second bedroom, which had been used as a storage room. He opened the door. A new canopy bed was by the window. A beautiful Oriental carpet covered the floor and artwork lined the walls.

"I thought since you were staying here a while, you might like this."

I didn't know what to say. He obviously wanted his room back, but I wouldn't be staying long enough to even use this room.

"It's beautiful, and thank you, but what will you do with it when I leave?"

"It makes a great guest room for my friends, if they ever come back."

"You didn't really have a friend over, did you?"

"Yeah, actually I did. You didn't think I did this all myself? She's very good at decorating, so we worked on this for a few days. I figured you could use a room of your own. For however long you stay here."

"Thank you. It's beautiful." I looked down at the floor. I didn't know what to say.

I wanted to tell him that I wanted to stay forever—maybe not in that room—but with him. But I had already tried once a few weeks ago, and he had made it clear that he didn't want to try again. I just stood there quietly, at an unusual loss for words.

David turned and went back to the kitchen. Oh well, another lost opportunity. There were so many of them. But I wasn't going to beg. I walked over to the window. It was a beautiful view and I would enjoy it for as long as I could, no matter what happened. He had done this for me. I was sure of that. But what exactly did he mean by it? Did he want me to stay? I wasn't sure. I wasn't sure of anything.

I picked Linda up at the motherhouse. This taking her and picking her up was getting old quickly. I hoped she could make other arrangements now that school had started. Mother Alphonse put off our meeting until Tuesday, so we all spent Monday night at David's apartment. We didn't talk about the investigation at all. It was crowded, but David insisted that she would be safer there than at the motherhouse, especially because of what the priest had said. We watched a documentary that evening on animals in Africa and then it was time to go to bed. David went back to his waterbed, and I went to the new room he had prepared. Linda insisted on sleeping on the couch. She kept saying how grateful she was to the both of us for taking care of her. She decided she was going to go home to her parents' in the next few days, even if she had to lose a semester of school. It was worth it to be safe. David was sure that Jeanette would be released in the next day or two.

I thanked him again for fixing the room. It was so special that he had done this for me. Or had he done it for Julie? I just couldn't quite figure out his motivation.

I fell asleep wondering what was going to happen with David and I, and the investigation, which was going nowhere.

CHAPTER 23

Tuesday, September 23

We were going to meet with Mother Alphonse in the afternoon. I was pretty sure that the necklace was long gone. The murderer probably had it and was going to be selling it at some point in the future. I was sure it was hidden away safely.

Linda packed her small suitcase. Her parents were going to pick her up at the motherhouse later that day and she would stay with them until the murder was solved. I drove down to the motherhouse with Linda, David drove separately since he had to go back to work, and the three of us walked down the long corridor to Mother Alphonse's office and knocked on her door.

Linda said, "Why are we meeting with Mother Alphonse and not Sister Karin?"

I answered, even though I wasn't even sure about my reasoning. "We just figured if anyone found the necklace, they'd bring it to Alphonse first."

"Yeah, I guess you're right."

★ ★ ★

"Yes, come in," came Mother Alphonse's shrill voice that still, even years later, had the power to frighten me. I cringed just hearing it.

We walked up to her desk. David said, "Mother Alphonse, we need to find a lost necklace that Sister Patricia wore; we think it may have been stolen."

"A necklace?" Mother Alphonse looked almost pleased. "Can you tell me what it looks like?"

Linda answered. "It's a diamond necklace surrounded by rubies on a gold chain."

Mother Alphonse got up unexpectedly and walked to a file cabinet in the far corner. She opened a drawer and took out a large envelope.

"Look at this." She handed it to David.

He pulled out a gold chain and ruby necklace. The setting looked old. David handed it to Linda.

She nodded. "This is it."

"Where and how did you get this?" David looked puzzled as he turned to Mother Alphonse.

"I don't actually know, Detective. One of the sisters in the kitchen found it on the floor when she was sweeping up, oh, maybe last Friday. Yes, that's when it was. She brought it to me since it looked expensive. Since none of the sisters wear jewelry, they were at a loss to determine where it came from, so they brought it to me."

"Thank you, Sister. It was found last Friday? That's a week after Sister Patricia died."

"Yes, that's when they said they found it."

"Could it have been in the kitchen the whole time and no one noticed?"

Mother Alphonse shook her head. Linda and I did too. Whoever worked in the kitchen had to scour it every night. The different groups took turns. One night it was the postulants, then the novices, then the junior sisters. The counters, the stoves, the floors, everything had to be spotless before we left. I remembered being on kitchen duty. It wasn't any fun. The necklace would have been found the same day it was lost. There was no way it could have been overlooked.

David was looking carefully at it. "The clasp is broken. Maybe that's why it fell off the person who was wearing it."

Mother Alphonse looked confused. "Why are you asking about it? It doesn't have anything to do with you. And what difference does it make when Sister Patricia died? The necklace doesn't even belong to any of you."

"What do you mean?" asked David.

"Well, Sister Sarah came in this past Monday and asked if anyone had turned in a necklace. She described it very well. That's why I know it belongs to her. I asked her why she was asking about a piece of jewelry, since we're never supposed to wear jewelry. She said her grandmother had given it to her at the last visiting day, and she could hardly refuse it, but that she was going to give it back to her mother on the next visiting day. Her grandmother would never know. She was wearing it to keep it safe, and it somehow fell off, that's what she said. I didn't have the necklace at that point, and I was going to call her in the next few days to tell her about it. I just hadn't gotten around to it. She said it belonged to her. That's why I'm surprised that you're asking about it."

David answered, "Actually, Mother, it doesn't belong to her at all. It belonged to Sister Patricia and it's been missing since she was killed."

Mother Alphonse stood quietly.

"It didn't belong to Sarah? You mean she lied to me?"

"Yes, she did."

David looked at me. Linda and I just stood there, as the implications came to all three of us. Sarah had the necklace. She had taken it, most likely stolen it from Patricia, which meant that she was probably on the roof with her that night and was the person who pushed her off.

"Mother Alphonse, can you call Sister Sarah into your office right now?" David asked.

"Yes, I think I'd better do that." Mother Alphonse walked out to her office where one of the nuns was typing.

"Can you find out where Sister Sarah is right now and tell her to come to my office? Yes, she's a senior, so she probably is in class. I think you have all the class schedules. Thank you."

Mother Alphonse asked us to sit down in her uncomfortable wing-back chairs while we waited.

Alphonse was uncharacteristically chatty. "I just don't understand why Sister Sarah said the necklace belonged to her when you say it was Sister Patricia's."

Linda tried to explain. "Mother, you know that Patricia and I were together—a couple."

Mother Alphonse got a strange look on her face. It seemed like she was trying hard not to be judgmental, but maybe I was wrong.

"Yes, I know."

"I gave her the necklace. It belonged to my grandmother and it's worth a lot—I don't know how much. I told my parents I was going to do that, and they were okay with it. I told Patricia not to tell anyone about it and to hide it. That's why she wore it under her habit all the time. I don't think she ever took it off. After she died, and all her belongings were returned to her parents, I asked them if they had received the necklace. They didn't know what I was talking about. They never got it. So that's why we came to you today, hoping you might know something about it. We're lucky we did."

Mother Alphonse listened carefully, and I could almost see the moment when she realized what the whole situation meant.

The secretary appeared at the door with Sister Sarah.

Mother Alphonse stood up. "Come in, Sister. I have that necklace that you were looking for."

Sarah's eyes lit up as she walked into the room. Then she saw the three of us and stopped. It only took a second for her to realize what was happening. She looked down at the floor.

"Sister," said David. "I think we need to talk."

"Okay."

"I think you know why we want to talk with you. I want to tell you your rights before you say anything."

David told her about how she had the right to a lawyer and that what she said could be used against her in court.

"Do you understand?"

He turned to Mother Alphonse. "Can I take Sister Sarah into one of the parlors to speak with her privately?"

"Yes, of course."

David and Sarah left the room together and walked into the adjoining parlor.

"Please sit down. I have some questions for you. I'm recording your answers."

He took out his small tape recorder and pressed record.

"Yes, but this is ridiculous. I didn't have anything to do with Patricia's death. Are you going to arrest me or something?"

"Why were you asking about Sister Patricia's necklace and claiming it belonged to you?"

Sarah looked angry. "She told me that nobody knew about it. I asked her and she said nobody knew that she had it. She lied to me."

"And then what happened?"

"Okay, I was up on the roof with her. She wanted to go up there and watch the meteor shower. It got better as it got later and she wanted to see it. So I went up there with her. That's all. I came back down because I was tired and she wanted to stay and watch it longer. That's what happened. I don't know what happened after I left. She must have fallen off the roof. I felt terrible when I heard about it the next morning."

"Why did you have her necklace?"

"She gave it to me."

David said, "Why did you lock the door to the roof when you came down? Patricia wouldn't have been able to get down later. You knew that."

Sarah sat quietly. She didn't have an answer for that. She was beginning to realize that she was caught in a web of lies.

"What did you do?" David asked like it was just a normal question.

Sarah was quiet for a minute, which seemed like an eternity. Then she started to talk.

"I asked Patricia if she wanted to go up on the roof to see the meteor shower. She said sure. I was so sick of how the two of them, Patricia and Linda, were always together and I didn't even have a chance. I loved Linda, too. But she was always with her. And the two of them were going to leave and live together and I would never see her again."

"After I got back from the science meeting we met in the chapel and snuck out on the roof. I brought two Dr. Peppers and two plastic glasses. I put a couple of sleeping pills in her drink. I emptied four pills in it, and she drank it all. I asked her about the necklace and she took it off and showed it to me. After a few minutes, she felt dizzy, and I told her I saw something on the lawn and helped her up and over to the side. She practically fell over on her own, but I gave her an extra push. That's when I grabbed the necklace from her hand. The clasp must have broken when I pulled it. I guess that's why it fell off in the kitchen. I had tried to fix the clasp, but I guess I didn't do a good enough job. Then I put the cans and the glasses in my pocket, locked the door to the roof, climbed down the steps and went to bed. That's it. That's what happened."

"And then you were especially nice to Linda so she would realize how much you cared about her?"

"Yes, but she didn't respond. She even told me to stay away. Linda broke my heart. I wanted to kill her, too."

"But murdering Sister Patricia didn't break your heart?"
Sarah was quiet.

"No, it didn't," she answered simply. David couldn't believe the heartlessness, the premeditation, and the lack of remorse. She acted like it was a job interview rather than a murder confession.

David brought Sarah back into Mother Alphonse's office and asked if he could use the phone on her desk. She just nodded.

He called the station and asked for a car and two police to make an arrest.

He turned back to Sarah, who was sitting quietly in the chair, looking out the window towards the front lawn and river. We were sitting quietly on the other side of the parlor.

"I have one more question, Sister. Who did you get to break into Kristen's apartment?"

"What? I don't know what you're talking about. What apartment?"

"Okay, we'll talk about that later. Sister Sarah Holtmeyer, I'm placing you under arrest for the murder of Sister Patricia Larson. You have a right to remain silent. Anything you say ..." He listed all her rights again while she stared straight ahead.

Mother Alphonse had been sitting quietly throughout the entire conversation. She got up and walked over to the window. She didn't say a word.

David turned to me. "Could you tell Sister Karin that the police are on their way and to meet them at the front door?"

"Of course." I walked down the hall to her office. She wasn't there so I continued down the hall and out the front door to wait for the police.

The August afternoon was bright and hot. The green leaves were almost like a canopy covering the front lawn, and I could hardly see the Mississippi River down below. I felt sick. It was over, but it felt so useless, a waste of a life, two lives, over nothing but jealousy and hatred.

I waited for what seemed like a long time, and finally saw

a police car slowly turn on the gravel drive, the crunching loud in the humid air. I waved at them and they stopped directly in front of me.

"You can park here. Detective Kelly is inside," I said to the officer who rolled down his window. "I'll take you to him."

I knew one of the officers, Joe Mangiopane. I had met him before.

"How are you? David said he had someone who confessed to that murder."

"Yes, he'll explain everything."

David was waiting right inside the front door with Sarah. Classes had let out and students were milling around the halls. A lot of them were standing in quiet groups, whispering and trying to see what was going on, and who was there with David.

Sarah and the two policemen walked out to the waiting police car. She looked impassive, her face as still as a mask, like she was simply going to class instead of to jail for murder.

Sister Karin came rushing down the hall and we went with her into a parlor, where David explained the situation. She looked bewildered.

"Are you sure?"

"She confessed to the murder," David explained.

"I can't believe that. Sarah seems so caring and loving. And she was so kind to Linda recently. I can't even imagine it. I taught her for years. I just can't believe she's capable of murder. Oh my God."

Sister Karin said she would call Sarah's parents and tell them. She would explain it to everyone in the class after we left.

Linda thanked us both for taking such good care of her. "I guess I can call my parents and tell them not to bother coming down to pick me up. The murder's been solved, so I can stay here and not worry anymore."

Sister Karin said, "Why don't you have them come down anyway and visit this afternoon, if they want. I think you need some family time with them. You've been through a lot lately."

Linda thanked us again and again and we finally got away and headed down the corridor together.

I had one more thing I had to do. Since David and I had come separately, I said, "David, you go ahead. I want to see Sister Inez. I just have to talk to her. I don't understand why she was so passive about this whole investigation. Maybe I'll get some answers—if she's even in her office."

"Go ahead. I'll see you when you get back—and I get home. But don't expect much. I don't think Inez knows anything. She would have said something by now."

"Yeah, I know. It's been so strange. I just want to talk with her—or try."

"See you soon."

"Okay."

CHAPTER 24

I walked down the corridor and up the big staircase to the fourth floor. I stood outside of Inez's office, wondering if I should even bother knocking on the door. My curiosity won out, and I knocked.

"Come in," Inez's cheerful voice answered.

"Hi," I said as I walked around the corner. She was at her desk, correcting papers.

"Oh, hi Kristin, it's good to see you. What are you doing here?"

I figured it was alright to tell her about what had happened. It would be all over the motherhouse in a few hours anyway.

"David just arrested Sister Sarah for the murder of Patricia. I thought you might want to know about that."

Inez looked away from me and out the window. She didn't look at all surprised.

"Well, I'm glad your detective found out who killed Patricia. It really was a terrible thing that happened."

I decided to tell her what I was thinking.

"I was surprised that you didn't want to help us—I mean David—find out who had killed Patricia. You were so interested in discovering who the murderers were in the other cases. It just seemed strange."

I stopped talking because I didn't know what else to say. Inez didn't turn back to me but kept staring out the window.

"Well, I guess I'll go ..." I started to say.

"Sarah and I talked a lot," Inez said quietly. "She confided in me. I knew how she felt about Patricia—how much she hated her, and how much she loved Sister Linda. Sarah felt there was no one who really understood her and that she didn't have any-one to talk to, which was true. She said I was the only one. When you came up here the day Patricia was murdered, I had the most horrible feeling that it was something Sarah had done. But what could I say? I had no evidence, and I wasn't about to make accusations about a person who had confided in me—at least until I had talked to her."

I listened quietly to Inez. "And did you talk to her about it?"

"Yes, I did. About a week later."

"And did she tell you she had killed Patricia?"

"Yes."

"You didn't go to David and tell him? And you knew all along!"

"It's complicated."

"No, it isn't. You knew who had killed Patricia and she told you and you still didn't tell anyone. I can't believe you did that."

"I was going to tell him. I just needed more time."

"And meanwhile Linda was worried about Sarah and what she might do to her, and you didn't even consider that."

"Oh, Sarah would never have done anything."

"She told David that she would have."

"She did?"

"Yes."

"Then I misjudged her. I had no idea she would do that. I'm sorry."

"You know I have to tell David what you've told me—that you knew about all this and didn't tell him."

"Go ahead. There's nothing he can do about it. I'll just deny that I ever told you. You can't prove any of this, you know. It's my word against yours. And I think everyone will believe me rather than you. I'm the president of the college. And you're just a girl who got kicked out after her first year. Sorry, but it's true."

I stood by her desk, not believing what she had just said. I was so disappointed to find out what Inez was really like. Maybe it wasn't so much finding out about Inez. It was that I, yet again, had made a terrible mistake in judging people, and couldn't tell the good from the bad. Was this going to be my life sentence, never knowing who to trust and who to believe? This had happened to me so many times in the past few years. It seemed to be who I was, and I didn't want to be that person. But I didn't know how to change it. It seemed like everyone I trusted and believed had turned out to be untrustworthy and a liar.

I turned and walked out of the office and down the four flights of stairs. I made my decision. I would never see or speak to Inez again.

David was waiting for me in the main corridor, and we walked out into the bright sunlight together and got in our separate cars.

"You didn't have to wait for me."

"Well, I wanted to know what she had to say."

I wasn't ready to talk to David about the conversation yet.

"She apologized for not being herself that morning. She said she had a lot of things on her mind. She sounded a lot more like herself today. I told her you had arrested Sarah and she was very interested in that. I figured it would be okay since the news will be all around the motherhouse in a few hours."

"That's fine, as long as you're satisfied that there wasn't anything weird going on. I hope you both can still be friends."

"Of course," I answered as sincerely as I could pretend. I would tell him later.

David went back to work and I let myself in his quiet apartment and turned the radio on as quickly as I could. It was just too silent inside. Now that Sarah had confessed to the murder,

I would be going home faster than I had anticipated. I walked in the new, beautiful bedroom. David had gone to a lot of trouble to fix it up for me, and it was lovely. I hoped I could at least spend a few nights in it, but I should be getting back to my place. I missed my piano. I hadn't practiced in weeks and I needed to. I spent the rest of the afternoon doing some reading for class and scrounged in the refrigerator for something to snack on. I couldn't get my mind off all that had happened. The necklace, the confession, the lack of remorse from Sarah, finding out about Inez—it all swirled around in my head. Finally I gave up reading and just spent the next few hours petting the two cats until even they got tired of it and got up and moved into the last remaining sunlight where they could have some peace and quiet.

I heard the door click open. I was so thankful David was home. We sat down on the couch and talked. About the arrest. About Sister Sarah and Linda. I was quieter than usual. I watched him as he sat there, wondering if I was wrong about him too. I had been wrong about so many other people. I couldn't start doubting everyone in my life. That was no way to live. I had to trust people, otherwise what was the point of living and having friends.

I wondered how long I was going to stay, but I didn't want to be the first one to bring it up. I did miss my little bit of freedom, being on my own for the first time in my life. I didn't know if I wanted to give that up. Not that it was an option. I would be going back home soon enough.

I had to tell him the truth as soon as possible.

"I have to tell you about Inez. I wasn't completely honest with you earlier this afternoon. I just had to process it before I could say anything. And think about it for a while. I hope you'll forgive me."

"Okay. And you know I'll forgive you, whatever it is. I'm listening."

I told him everything Inez had said.

He frowned as I told him the story.

"She's going to deny everything she told you, but there are ways around that. First, we'll have to decide if we want to charge her."

"Do you think you should just let it go?"

"No, withholding evidence in a murder investigation isn't just a misdemeanor. It's a big deal. I'm going to interview her and see what evidence I can get to charge her with accessory after the fact. She knew who had committed the murder and didn't tell anyone. That's a crime. When we get to the sentencing phase, which is going to be a lot longer for Sarah than Sister Martha got for killing Sister Anastasia, we might be able to make it part of Sarah's plea deal. If Sarah testifies that she told Sister Inez that she killed Sister Patricia and Sister Inez didn't report it, that will be enough evidence to convict Sister Inez, along with your testimony. It won't just be your word against hers. Sister Inez will be looking at some jail time."

David continued, "I can see why you're upset and why you don't want to be friends with her anymore. I wouldn't either. I'm sorry about that. But I need to talk to you about something else."

"Okay." I guessed it was time for me to get back to my apartment. Well, I knew it was coming, and I was ready. I didn't have much to pack.

Alex had jumped up between us, but David took my hands in his.

"I need to ask you about your friend Paul. How serious are you about him?"

"Oh David, we broke up. He got accepted to Yale Law School and is going very soon. He's probably gone already. We didn't even need to say goodbye to each other. He didn't think our relationship was very serious, and I was about to tell him that I didn't love him anyway. He just beat me to it. I was embarrassed to tell you."

"Well, I have a confession to make too. I broke up with Julie a few months ago, but I didn't want to tell you either, especially after you told me you were seeing someone else. She drove me crazy. All she talked about was getting married and how soon we could do that, and I just wasn't in love with her. I liked her and told her that I wanted to be friends, but it didn't stop her from making these elaborate plans for the future. I broke it off a few months ago. We're still friends. I saw her and her family last weekend. They're wonderful people. I didn't know how to tell you. It didn't seem like it would make any difference because you had found someone else anyway."

He took my hands. "You're the one I love. And I've loved you for years. I'd like for us to get back together, you know, like we were a year ago. Going out together again. And I want you to stay here. Permanently. We can move your piano to this front room. There's plenty of room for it. I don't want to bring up marriage again, because I know how you feel about that, but I've really missed you a lot, and I want us to be together again. What do you think?"

What did I think? I was ready for more, and I hated myself for not knowing what I wanted. I didn't want to get married yet, but I wanted David to be all mine. I didn't care how. For as long as it was possible.

"I think that would be wonderful. You're the one I love. It took me too long to realize that." I said simply. "And I really feel bad that I wasn't completely honest with you. I won't ever let that happen again."

"I should have told you the truth about Julie. I was just too embarrassed to admit that I wasn't seeing anyone, especially since you seemed so happy and content with your new friend. I won't ever lie like that again. I want you to trust me completely."

"And I want you to feel the same about me. Trust me completely. I'll try to be better at earning it."

"And so will I." We sat petting the cats for a few minutes.

"I have to ask you one more thing," he said quietly. He held my hands tightly, but Alex kept pushing his head into our hands to get more petting. Not exactly the most romantic setting.

"I don't know how to put this any other way. I don't really want to wait any longer if you know what I mean. Do you feel strongly that it's a sin to have sex before marriage?"

I had thought about it a lot. The Church was wrong about so many things, and I had to be my own guide through life. I couldn't depend on them anymore.

"Is that an invitation?"

"It's been an invitation for a long time. You know that. I just figured you would always say no."

"Well, I would have, but I've learned a lot these past few months, and I wouldn't say no anymore. But maybe not on the waterbed ..."

David laughed. "I think that can be arranged. Why do you think I fixed up that second bedroom?"

He picked up Alex carefully and put him on the other side of the couch. "Sorry, Alex, but this is more important."

He hugged and kissed me. A lot. Then he poured a glass of wine for us and took my hands and we sat together. I was so happy that we were back together. Who knew what the future would bring? Alex found his way to the cat bed across the room. JC was somewhere else in the apartment, probably dreaming of tuna.

Solving the murder was the last thing on my mind, but as I put my head on David's shoulder with our arms around each other, I hoped I was right about him. I hoped he was the one I could trust completely. I felt sure that he was. I thought about love. Love had come into my life and changed it for the better, but love had been the cause of Patricia's death. Love and jealousy. They were both there in every relationship. I had felt such intense jealousy at the thought of losing David to someone else, but I hoped I could control that. At least I thought I could. I held David's hand tightly, but I couldn't stop thinking about all that had happened that very long day.

"What are you thinking about?" he asked.

I gave him a long kiss and finally answered, "Oh, just murder."

ABOUT THE AUTHOR

SUSAN MATTERN was born and raised in St. Louis, Missouri, and attended Catholic schools. Even though she swore she'd never become a nun, the church reforms in the early sixties convinced her of a great future for the church and she joined the convent. After six years the dream was over, and she left the stifling rules, moved to California, got married, and she and her husband had two children: a boy and a girl.

Susan was still Catholic, until the day her daughter was attacked and almost killed by a mountain lion in a county park, and she began to question her belief in God.

Susan is a classical pianist who has performed and taught her whole life, and only in the last ten years turned to her other love, writing.

Her first book, "Out of the Lion's Den," is about her daughter's attack, recovery, and the well-publicized lawsuit against the county of Orange. It won the *Writer's Digest* Grand Prize two years ago.

She also wrote "Poverty, Chastity and Disobedience," about her years in a Catholic convent.

This latest book, "Who Nun It?" is her first work of fiction, but draws heavily on those convent years, minus the murders.

She is also the president of the Songhai group, supporting an agricultural initiative in Africa that has over fifty projects in seventeen African countries.

You can hear her piano music and some original music on Soundcloud and find her on Instagram as @Mattern.Susan.

ACKNOWLEDGMENTS

I would like to thank my family first. My husband, Donald Small, for his infinite patience with all my writing.

My daughter Laura, who has faithfully read all my many drafts and given me such wonderful encouragement.

My daughter-in-law Heather, who has also been a great inspiration.

My son David, who came up with the name for my novel.

I'd like to thank my neighbor, Oliver Grant, who died suddenly two years ago. He was Police Chief of the Anaheim police department, and I went to him one day and said, "I know a lot about the convent, but nothing about the police. Will you help me?" And he read through all the stories, corrected my many mistakes and gave me an insight into the workings of the police.

I want to thank all the people who encouraged me in my writing, Roselyn Teukolsky, who has just published her first book, *A Reluctant Spy*, and Marcia Sargent, author of *Wing Wife*.

I'd like to thank the editorial staff at *Writer's Digest*—Amy Jones in particular—for the award two years ago, boosting my confidence and enabling me to continue writing.

All of my extended family and book club of many years, especially my niece, Patrice Bryan, who helped edit my manuscript with her English editing skills.

AFTERWORD

Fact or Fiction

Who Nun It? is a work of fiction. But a great deal of it is based on fact. I was a sister in the order of the School Sisters of Notre Dame from 1966 to 1972 and experienced many of the things I wrote about in the books.

I did not experience any murders. That part is all fiction.

But the idea for the book came to me one sleepless night a few years ago when I remembered a night long ago in the convent. I had been talking to S. Inez (actually, the character who Sister Inez was based on). It was past midnight—the year was 1968—and we were in her office in the motherhouse talking about English and vocations and heard the doorbell ringing four stories down at the front entrance.

She dragged me downstairs with her to investigate. After making sure who it was—we could see the lights of the police car in front—we opened the door to the police. They wanted to know if we were missing any life-size statues. We were surprised at the question, but they explained that they had found a garage close by that was completely filled with life-sized statues of religious figures.

We said no, we weren't missing any, and they told us to call if we noticed any were gone. The detective gave us his card and told us he was sorry for interrupting us so late at night. After they drove off, we laughed hysterically at the thought that someone had stolen large statues, enough to fill a garage.

We never heard any more about it but spent the next few days on the lookout every time we passed a statue in the corridors. They were all still there.

But the setting of the motherhouse late at night, the frightening basement, and the police, was enough to make me start thinking about other reasons the police might be called to the motherhouse late at night. Murder was a great reason.

The basement of the motherhouse was scary. Sister Miriam, her real name, did warn us repeatedly about men lurking in the huge basement, especially at night. The basement of the motherhouse seemed like the ancient catacombs of Rome, which I had only read about in books. Long narrow passageways, dim lighting, cold wet walls; it was just the kind of setting for finding a dead body.

I read an article about a medieval chalice discovered in a small parish church in England a few years ago that was appraised at between eight to ten million pounds. No one had any idea of its worth. It had sat there unnoticed for centuries. So that was fact that became fiction for the story. it was easy incorporating that into the plot.

Many of the sisters in the book were based on real people who I met in the convent. Pam was and is one of my best friends. I met her one of the first weeks of high school and we're still friends after all these years. I'm still friends with Louise, and there is a Facebook group with many of the sisters who were in my class.

The rules and regulations of the convent were all fact, not fiction. Many of them were made centuries ago and had no reason for existence. We as postulants, or first year students, were only allowed to speak to the people in our class. We couldn't speak to the other students in the college, even if they were in our classes, supposedly to build our small community, but it cut off an important source of knowledge and friendship with other sisters in the congregation.

Sisters Joan and Maribeth were real people. I became friends with them even though I would have gotten kicked out because of my friendship with them. I talked to them all the time in the music department. They were both wonderful people. Maribeth was not a murderer, although I lost track of her after I left the convent. Sorry, Maribeth, for making you the murderer in my novel. Joan died in a plane crash on her honeymoon in Tahiti a few years after we left. I still remember her kindness and friendship.

We were not allowed to go in rowboats, which was a strange rule. We also couldn't play zithers, and I laughed one afternoon after finding a zither in the convent attic where I was stationed for two years. I wondered who had gotten in trouble for that terrible indiscretion. There were many other rules that made no sense at all.

The second story about Sister Anastasia and the Silent Night manuscript has some fact to it also. There was a sister in our infirmary who really was the great-granddaughter of Franz Gruber, the man who composed the music to Silent Night over a century before. I met with her a few times and attended her funeral in the motherhouse. There was no original manuscript, however. If there had been, it would have been worth a lot of money, which I made as the basis for the story.

The third story about Sister Patricia and Sister Linda, fictional characters, and their relationship was not that unusual in the convent. We were warned repeatedly about "particular friendships," which was simply a code name for lesbian relationships. I knew and continue to know a few people who were lesbians, which was a difficult relationship to have at that time in the convent, as well as in secular society in the sixties. But the Catholic church was particularly harsh on sexual sins, and always has been. Up until recently, even the act of intercourse in marriage was supposed to be done only with procreation in mind, and nothing else. And since sisters took vows of poverty, obedience, and chastity, the church expected sisters to abstain from anything sexual in nature.

There were ways to access the roof, although we weren't supposed to, because it was dangerous. But I went up the spiral staircase to the bell tower many times in the four years. One time was on Christmas Eve, and I felt and watched the snow fall with a girl from California who had never seen snow before. On the night of the moon landing, I went up with another friend, since the TV was turned off a 9:00 p.m. We were so angry that we couldn't watch the most historic event of the century that we went up on the roof and watched the moon from there. Not the best view, but we figured it was better than nothing.

I did a lot of things that were against the rules—there were so many of them—but never got caught. My friend Pam, on the other hand, was more blatant about disobeying the rules, and since she was Black, was easier to spot in an all-white crowd. She lasted about six years also before she couldn't take it any longer.

She told me many years later why she left.

"Susie, I had a vision."

"What?" I was surprised. Pam didn't seem like the kind who had visions.

"Not that kind of vision. I saw myself sitting in the parlor with a bunch of old white nuns watching Lawrence Welk every Friday and Saturday night, and Susie, it scared me. It scared me a lot. I just had to get out! I called my daddy and told him to come and get me the very next day and that was it!"

That's why Pam left the order.

I have been away from the church for many years now, but I do know what has happened to religious life in the past fifty years. The burst of reform in the 1960's with the Second Vatican Council was a much-needed attempt at modernization, but the church gradually fell back into its old, traditional ways. A lot depended on which Pope was leading the church, and how much he was interested in reforming it. And there were so many cardinals and clergy who clung to the old traditional ways that I was surprised we had any reform.

Those of us who hoped for continued progress, especially for women, were sadly disappointed, and still are. The reality of religious life in the United States is a sad experience, once having in 1965 around 180,000 sisters. Now in 2025, the latest numbers are down to 42,000, a 76% decline over the last sixty years. Even more troubling is that 77% of those remaining nuns are older than seventy. The prediction is that by 2040, there will be no more sisters left in American religious institutions.

There are many reasons, but one is the continued lack of equality for women in the church. Until that is corrected, I don't see much of a future for religious life. Sisters were always second-class citizens in the church and remain so to this day. Society has played its part also. No one wants to be part of an institution that takes away your freedom and your choices with very little given in return. Much of the satisfaction from teaching and nursing, which were important jobs of the sisters in the past, can be done without joining a religious organization. Women can have their own jobs, remain single, and don't have to rely on a man to support them. So much has changed in society that makes religious life even less appealing than it once was.

Women are finally, after centuries, closer to being treated as equals, especially in our country, but it's been a long, difficult fight, and no woman wants to go back to the oppression of centuries ago.

I loved writing these stories and incorporating the facts with the fiction. I hope they have given you an insight into what religious life was like in the 1960's in this country. And I hope you've enjoyed reading them.

BOOK CLUB QUESTIONS

1. Why do you think Kristen wants to stay in the convent? Is it rebellion against her parents, or a determination to finish what she said she was going to do?

2. Is Kristen's judgement about people as bad as she thinks it is? Or do we all make mistakes judging other people's motives?

3. By the end of the book, do you think Kristen should be going out with other people to find out what "love" is, or do you think she's already found it with David?

4. What is your impression, even if you aren't religious, of the Catholic convents in the late 1960's when the story takes place? Do you agree with Kristen's assessment of too many rules or are you more understanding of the church's attempts to stay united.

5. Why did the Catholic church, after the reforms of the 2nd Vatican Council, regress back to its conservative roots so quickly within a 10- year period?

6. Does David love Kristen or is he just fascinated by her inter-
    esting story?

7. Attitudes about homosexuality have changed radically
    since the 1960's. Is there anyone in the group who remem-
    bers what the attitudes were like back then? Was David
    unusual in his forward -looking attitude, especially being a
    policeman?

8. Many nuns left religious orders in the 60's and 70's. There
    are fewer than 42,000 nuns now, compared to 180,000 in
    1965. And most of them are in their seventies. What is your
    opinion on this? Do you think this is a good or bad thing?
    Why?

9. Does the book give you any insight into why so many nuns
    have left?

10. What is the role of religion in today? And is it fulfilling its
    role?

Sibylline
PRESS

Sibylline Press is proud to publish the brilliant work of women authors over 50. We are a woman-owned publishing company and, like our authors, represent women of a certain age.